ILLEGAL

"A wild, rollicking road trip . . . **the most original, off-beat and wholly entertaining thriller of the year so far.** Levine, you see, is a brilliant stylist as well as storyteller. . . . Everything about *Illegal* is satisfying. It's one of those rare thrillers that achieves every level it strives for and hits a bull's-eye with every staccato phrase Levine fires off. **Timely, tumultuous and in a word terrific.**"
—*The Providence Sunday Journal*

"This pedal-to-the-metal thriller wraps a gripping story around a current topic. . . . Colorful characters . . . all the twists . . . **Levine had us at the opening.**"
—*Romantic Times Book Reviews*

"**A riveting read,** filled with action, pathos, and even humor. The portrait of the dangers and predations that Latinos face crossing the border is chilling and rings with authenticity. But the book's best quality is the way Levine invests his characters with believable humanity. A compulsively readable yet character-driven thriller."
—*Booklist*

BY PAUL LEVINE

Illegal

Trial & Error

Kill All the Lawyers

The Deep Blue Alibi

Solomon vs. Lord

9 Scorpions

Flesh & Bones

Fool Me Twice

Slashback

Mortal Sin

False Dawn

Night Vision

To Speak for the Dead

ILLEGAL

A NOVEL OF SUSPENSE

PAUL LEVINE

BANTAM BOOKS
NEW YORK

Illegal is a work of fiction. Names, characters, places, and incidents either are the product of the author's imagination or are used fictitiously. Any resemblance to actual persons, living or dead, events, or locales is entirely coincidental.

2010 Bantam Books Mass Market Edition

Published in the United States by Bantam Books, an imprint of The Random House Publishing Group, a division of Random House, Inc., New York.

BANTAM BOOKS and the rooster colophon are registered trademarks of Random House, Inc.

Originally published in hardcover in the United States by Bantam Books in 2009.

This book contains an excerpt from the forthcoming book *Lassiter* by Paul Levine. This excerpt has been set for this edition only and may not reflect the final content of the forthcoming edition.

ISBN 978-0-553-59105-7
eBook ISBN 978-0-553-90612-7

Cover design: Carlos Beltran

Printed in the United States of America

www.bantamdell.com

9 8 7 6 5 4 3 2 1

*To the woman carrying a rucksack,
clutching her child's hand, and kicking up dust
as she scrambled along a desert trail
near Calexico, California.*

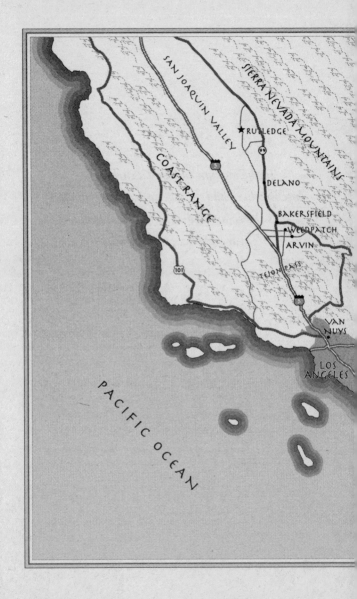

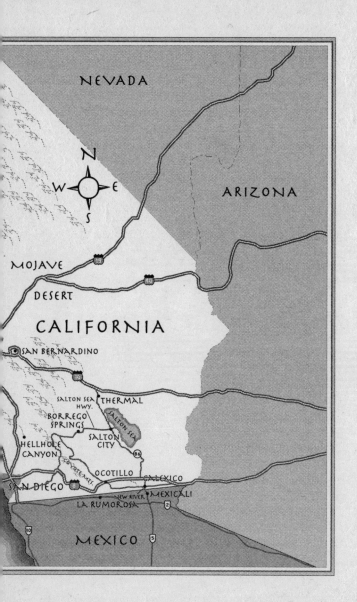

ONE

Judge Rollins drew a handgun from beneath his black robes, pointed the snub-nosed barrel at Jimmy Payne's chest, and said, "Who you pimping for, you low-life shyster?"

Payne gaped at the revolver.

This cannot be happening.

The judge gestured toward the stacks of hundred-dollar bills on his desk. "C'mon, Payne. You're not smart enough to dream this up on your own."

They faced each other in the judge's chambers, a tranquil refuge of leatherbound books and walnut wainscoting. Payne felt his knees wobble. "I swear, Judge. I just represent the defendant. Ramon Carollo."

"Not like you to defend human traffickers. I remember the hell you raised when those wetbacks got barbecued in a trailer truck."

"I like to call them 'undocumented aliens.' "

"Why? They from Mars?"

The judge vaulted out of his high-backed chair. Quick for a big man. Silver hair swept straight back, like feathers on a snow goose. Shoulders as wide as a bookcase.

"Take off your clothes, Payne."

"What?"

"You heard me."

"I swear I'm not wearing a wire. You can pat me down."

"Strip!"

Payne wasn't sure he could. His joints seemed rusted shut.

"Now!"

With jerky motions, Payne kicked off his shoes, unhooked his belt, and dropped his trousers.

"You bring me nine stacks of hundred-dollar bills, fifty to a stack." Judge Rollins motioned toward the open briefcase on his desk and did the math in his head. "Forty-five thousand dollars."

"That's the offer," Payne agreed.

"Odd amount. Like it was supposed to be fifty thousand, but some half-assed bag man skimmed five off the top."

"No, sir." Payne lowered his tie and slipped out of his shirt. "Forty-five is all I've got to spend."

"No sale, shitbird."

"I thought it was worth a shot, Your Honor. But let's just forget the whole thing. I'll put my pants on and—"

"Drop those undershorts, too." The judge waved the gun like a king with a scepter.

Payne pulled down his red-and-white boxers with the Los Angeles Clippers logo. He preferred them to the Lakers purple-and-gold shorts, not for the colors, but because he favored underdogs.

"Now turn around and spread your cheeks."

"No way, Judge."

"Do it!"

At thirty-seven, Payne was in good shape. Flat stomach, decent chest, a sinewy runner's body. He spun around and bent over. "Like I said, Your Honor, no wire."

Judge Rollins gazed off. "I don't know whether to shoot you or arrest you."

Jimmy straightened and turned around. "Just let me go, Judge. There's a lot of good I can do out there."

"Out where? You're Jimmy Payne. Royal Payne. You cut corners. You represent undesirables. You piss people off."

"Honestly, Judge. I'm gonna change my life."

"People don't change, Payne. They just get old and die. Sometimes, they don't even get old."

Payne stepped sideways toward a set of shelves decorated with framed vanity photos. Judge Rollins with Mayor Villaraigosa, Senator Boxer, some local bigwigs, and a pretty young woman in a pink sash, the Rose Bowl queen, maybe. Alongside the photos, the scales of justice. Bronze. Heavy. Tilted heavily to one side. One more step and Payne could grab the scales by the blindfolded lady and take a swing at the judge.

"Freeze, sleazebag." Rollins pulled back the hammer of the .38. As the *click* echoed in his brain, Payne thought of his son, Adam. Ten years old. Loved baseball. Cheeseburgers. Surfing. A boy needs his father.

Just how the hell did I get into this?

TWO

One hour before he stood, naked and terrified, in the chambers of the Honorable Walter Rollins, Jimmy Payne stood, clothed and angry, glaring at a wooden pin some sixty feet away.

The five-pin.

Payne hated the five-pin nearly as much as he hated Cullen Quinn, his ex-wife's fiancé. And there the damn thing stood—the pin, not Quinn—smack in the middle of the lane, taunting him. For most bowlers, the five was the easiest spare, but for Payne, the ten-pin—that loner at the right edge of the lane—was the gimmee. The trick, he knew, was not being afraid of dropping into the gutter.

Payne's second ball whooshed past the five and *thwomp*ed harmlessly into the pit, leaving the pin standing.

Damn. Even Barack Obama could have made that spare.

So could Payne's son. He thought about taking Adam bowling this weekend. His eleventh birthday was coming up, and the boy already threw a decent little hook.

Payne checked the counter behind the ball rack. The stranger still stood there, watching him. He had shown up around the third frame, sipping coffee from a Styrofoam cup. Blue shirt, striped tie thickly knotted, cheap tan suit that needed pressing. Hair that might have been blond once, now turned the yellowish brown of a nicotine stain. A gum chewer, with jaw muscles dancing; a face of angles and planes; a cold stare. A cop? Homicide, maybe.

Not a problem. Payne hadn't killed anyone. He hadn't even represented a murderer in a couple years. Bar brawlers, check bouncers, hookers from the Sepulveda Corridor. He could really use a good murder trial right now. Or a personal injury case with fractures to weight-bearing bones. Even a nasty divorce would do. Lacking any decent cases, bowling alone on a weekday morning provided a break from bill collectors and anger management classes.

Payne hoisted his Hammer Road Hawg from the ball return and settled into his stance. Sensing movement, he glanced over his shoulder. Wrinkled Suit was headed his way. Payne considered challenging the guy to three games at ten bucks a pin.

"Morning, J. Atticus Payne."

Keeping the ball at hip level, Payne turned to face the man. "Jimmy. Jimmy Payne."

"Your Bar card says 'J. Atticus.'"

"My parents were hoping I'd grow up to be Gregory Peck."

"Nah. They named you 'James Andrew.' You changed it. Not legally, of course. Just made it up and put it on your driver's license, which also says you're six feet tall, when you're really five-eleven. You make up a lot of shit."

Grinning now, *Gotcha*. Like he was Sherlock Fucking Holmes.

"Some people think Atticus fits," Payne said, thinking of his ex-wife, Sharon.

"What slimeball you gonna walk today, Atticus?"

That was before she started calling him "the respondent." When Sharon divorced him, her bill of particulars included his reputation for sleazy behavior.

"Respondent has engaged in a pattern of professional activity that is a source of embarrassment to Petitioner, a police officer."

If he'd been different, Payne wondered, if he'd made more money and been more respectable, if he'd lunched at the California Club instead of Hooters, would Sharon still be his wife?

Nah, that wasn't the issue.

"You weren't here for me when I needed you, Jimmy."

"Why do you lie so much?" Wrinkled Suit asked.

Payne shrugged. "I'm a lawyer."

"You rolled a baby split in the third frame. The three-ten. Very makeable. But you hit the 'Reset,' erased the score, and bowled again."

"That a crime?"

"What kind of guy cheats when he's bowling alone?"

"Maybe a guy who wants a second chance."

"To do what? Tell a client to flee the jurisdiction?"

"Who the hell are you?"

The man reached into his jacket pocket and flipped open a vinyl wallet with an L.A.P.D. badge and photo I.D.

Payne read aloud. " 'Detective Eugene Rigney. Public Integrity Unit.' Kinda wussy, isn't it? I mean, compared to Robbery Homicide. Or SWAT."

He turned toward the pins and took his four-step approach. A high back swing, a wrist-snapping release, a fluid follow-through. The ball skidded on the oil, dug in, and hooked hard left into the pocket. A big mix, the clatter of rolling logs. The skinny neck of the six-pin kissed the ten, pushing it over like a wobbly drunk.

Strike! Take that, Mr. Public Integrity.

Rigney didn't look impressed. "You gotta do something for me, Payne."

"What?"

"Bribe a judge." The cop looked at his watch. "And you've got one hour to do it."

THREE

Payne plopped his Road Hawg into its zippered bag. "I'm out of here, Rigney. Go bribe the judge yourself."

"Do you have a client named Molly Kraft?" the cop asked.

Payne stopped in mid-zip.

Molly Kraft. Oh, shit.

"Child custody," Payne said. "Her husband molested their daughter."

"You never proved it."

"The husband's lawyer had a better shrink."

"So you told Molly Kraft to take off with her daughter in violation of a court order."

Rigney pulled a little cop notebook from his suit pocket. He read aloud in a monotone that could put a jury to sleep. It was all true. Payne had bought airline tickets for Molly Kraft and her daughter and sent them off to Puerto Vallarta to keep the girl away from her abusive father. Bored by endless sunshine and numbed by rivers of sangria, Molly sneaked back across the border four days ago, and got arrested in San Ysidro.

"She flipped on you, pal," Rigney said.

Shit. Is it any wonder I hate my clients?

"Molly Kraft's gonna testify to the Grand Jury right after lunch. Once she does, I can't stop the indictment."

"And now you can?"

Rigney didn't answer, letting Payne sweat. Smart.

Payne liked people who were good at their jobs. Perjurers. Pickpockets. Pain-in-the-ass cops.

Several seconds passed. There was only one other bowler in the place, way down at lane thirty-two, the falling pins echoing like distant thunder.

"Do you know Judge Walter Rollins?" Rigney said at last.

"Van Nuys Division. Didn't make partner at one of the downtown firms, so they bought him a seat on the bench."

"That's it?"

"Rollins is condescending to lawyers, bullies his staff, and sucks up to the appellate court. He also doesn't like anyone smarter than him. Which means he has very few friends."

Then there was the business with the car. Payne remembered a day when he was stopped at a traffic light on Lankershim near the In-N-Out Burger. He'd looked over—looked down, actually—from his perch in his Lexus SUV, and there was Judge Rollins, glaring up at him from his Mini Cooper. As if thinking:

"Payne, you asswipe. You don't deserve that fine machine with its G.P.S. whispering directions in your ear like a thousand-dollar hooker."

Truth was, Payne leased the Lexus to impress his clients, especially car thieves.

"Rollins is dirty," Rigney said, then told Payne about Operation Court Sweep. A sting operation. Joint task force of L.A.P.D. and the feds, which Payne figured would have cops shooting one another's dicks off.

"I don't have a case in front of Rollins," Payne said, "so if you're looking for someone to set him up—"

"*We've* got the case."

"Forget it. I'm not a snitch."

"Your choice, Payne. But know this: By tonight, either you or Walter Rollins will be behind bars."

FOUR

Jimmy drove west on Ventura Boulevard, speaking to his ex-wife on the cell. "Sharon, do you know a dickwad named Eugene Rigney?"

"Public Integrity," she answered. "Corruption cases."

"That's him. Can I trust him?"

"Rigney's a hard-ass who lies under oath to get convictions. What are you up to?"

"A little this, a little that. Mostly bribery."

"I'm serious, Atticus."

"Me, too. How's Adam doing with his math?"

"Jimmy, don't do that! I asked you a question. How are you mixed up with Rigney?"

"Late for a hearing. Gotta go. I'll pick up Adam early for baseball Saturday."

"Jimmy, dammit!"

He clicked off and slowed at the intersection of Beverly Glen. On the seat next to him was a cheap briefcase containing fifty thousand dollars in cash.

"Strike that, Madame Court Reporter. Forty-five thousand."

At the traffic light at Coldwater Canyon, he'd grabbed one of the stacks of bills and slid it under the floor mat in the backseat. If Judge Rollins would roll over for fifty thousand, why not forty-five?

And don't I deserve something for bringing down a dirty judge?

The sting was a mousetrap intended to snap the necks

of corrupt judges. Offer cash to reduce bail or dismiss the indictment or, slimiest of all, give up the name of an informant so the defendant can have him killed. So any guilt Payne felt at being a snitch was lessened by the knowledge that Judge Walter Rollins, if he fell for it, was willing to be an accessory to murder.

Our legal system is incompetent and corrupt, Payne thought. A time-wasting, money-sucking three-ring circus of lazy judges, brain-dead juries, and officious clerks in courthouses where there's not enough parking or decent places to eat lunch.

"Why'd you have to make it a human trafficking case?" Payne had asked Rigney.

"What difference does it make?"

"I repped those Mexicans in the tractor-trailer case."

"I know all about it. You got held in contempt. Ethics charges. Anger management. The whole nine yards."

"So would it make sense that I'd represent a guy who doesn't give a shit if the migrants live or die?"

Rigney shrugged. "What do you care? Another case, another peso."

Jeez, how depressing.

If the legal system were a frozen pond, Payne walked too far on ice too thin. Wearing combat boots and stomping his feet. In the tractor-trailer case, the ice broke. Traffickers brought three dozen Mexicans through a tunnel from Tijuana to Otay Mesa in San Diego County. As soon as the migrants popped out of the ground like bleary-eyed gophers, armed *vaquetóns*—street thugs working for the coyotes—jammed the new arrivals into a trailer truck. The Mexicans were headed for a slaughterhouse in Arizona, where they had been promised jobs pulling intestines out of dead cows and ripping their hides off with pliers. Where the migrants came from, this was considered cushy work.

The driver, an American who would be paid $6,000

for the run, stopped in El Centro in the California desert to visit his girlfriend in her air-conditioned trailer, conveniently stocked with ice-cold beer and a queen-size bed. Afraid that the migrants would scatter if he let them out, he kept them locked in the back. The sun, perched high in the August sky, blazed orange as a branding iron. The metal truck became a convection oven. No one heard the migrants' screams or their prayers to the Virgin of Guadalupe.

Tongues swelled. Arms flailed. Limbs locked in spasms. The stricken watched long-departed relatives float by in the darkness. As the hours passed, bowels exploded like mortar shells. Mouths frothed, eyes bulged, brains melted. Eleven people died.

The government promised permanent residency to the survivors if they would testify against the coyotes and the driver. Trial was had, convictions obtained, miscreants jailed. By then, pale new faces manned the desks of the Immigration and Customs Enforcement Office. Tough regulations were enacted, lest any *campesinos* from Chihuahua were working for Osama bin Laden on the sly. Even though the survivors had kept their end of the bargain, a tailored suit from Washington yanked their papers and scheduled them for deportation.

"Government fraud, deception, and outright lies!" Payne told the press. "Mafia hit men get better treatment."

Payne subpoenaed a dozen skinny-tied government types. Not just I.C.E. officials. Mayors. State senators. Governors' aides. Demanded to know who cut their grass, washed their cars, changed their kids' diapers. Proved the hypocrisy of the entire system, or so he thought.

"Mr. Payne, you will refrain from this line of questioning."

"Why, Judge? Because a Honduran woman cleans your toilets?"

"That's enough, Mr. Payne!"

But it wasn't. Payne turned to the table of government lawyers, cleared his throat, and belted out a passable rendition of Tom Russell's "Who's Gonna Build Your Wall?"

Who's gonna cook your Mexican food,
When your Mexican maid is gone?

The judge banged his gavel and shouted,"You're in contempt, buster!"

Forty-eight hours in a holding cell. And a $5,000 fine.

On the brighter side, Payne won the case. Unwilling to risk any more toxic publicity, I.C.E. reversed its decision. Payne's clients got permanent residency.

Now, driving along Ventura Boulevard to the courthouse, Payne planned the rest of his day. Hit the gym, grab some lunch, pick up Adam for a game of pitch-and-catch. But first, there was a judge to bribe.

The day was already steaming. The sidewalk cafés, with their forlorn potted palms, were deserted, except for the Coffee Beans, Starbucks, and Peet's, where wannabe screenwriters pounded at their laptops, dreams of Oscar statuettes, A-list parties, and Malibu mansions warping their brains.

It was a short drive to Van Nuys, Payne's favorite venue for justice to be miscarried. The Lexus spoke then, the pleasant but distant female voice instructing him to *"Turn right in two hundred yards. Van Nuys Boulevard."* She didn't bother to thank him for the five grand under her floor mat.

Payne followed instructions and headed for the courthouse, thinking this wasn't so bad. He was a decent enough liar. He'd get out of the heat, do his civic duty, and pocket five grand. What could go wrong?

FIVE

"You think I'm stupid?" Judge Rollins aimed the gun a few inches north of Payne's shrinking testicles. "Your wife's a cop."

"Ex-wife."

"I remember. She shot you."

"An accident," Payne said. "She was aiming at my client."

"That how you got the scar on your leg?" Gesturing toward a ridge of purple tissue on Payne's bare thigh.

"No." Payne reflexively touched the spot. Beneath his fingertips, fastened to his femur, was a metal plate and five locking screws. "Got the scars in a crash on the P.C.H."

"Jesus, Payne. Bad luck sticks to you like flies on shit." A fuzzy thought came to the judge, and he squinted like a sailor peering through the fog. "What I don't get, is why you think I'd tank a case."

"Not tank it, Your Honor. Just give me the identity of the C.I."

"That's even worse!" The judge was reddening, his tone growing angry. "I give up a confidential informant, your client will have him killed."

I messed it all up, Payne thought. Career. Marriage. Life.

I can't even bribe a crooked judge.

Payne's hands trembled, his fingers jerking like piano keys. He made a vow.

If I get out of this, I really will change.

"Your Honor. I gotta tell you the truth about what I'm doing here."

Judge Rollins waved the gun toward the stacks of hundred-dollar bills. "The money speaks for itself."

"That's the thing, Judge. Ramon Carollo—"

"Is scum. And so's Pedro Martinez. Fuck 'em both."

"Who?"

"Pedro Martinez, for Christ's sake. The C.I. I signed the warrants. I oughta know."

Payne wasn't sure he heard correctly. "You just gave me the informant's name."

"You paid for it, didn't you?" The judge lifted his robes and slipped the .38 back into its shoulder holster. He swept the stacks of currency into a desk drawer like a croupier cleaning up chips. "Sorry I scared you. But with the Grand Jury running wild, I take precautions."

Payne moved robotically. One leg, and then the other, into his boxers. He had trouble believing what had just happened. He was going home, and the judge was going to jail.

"Martinez has a house on the beach in Rosarito, just south of the border," the judge said. "Plus a condo in La Jolla. He shouldn't be hard for your people to find."

My people, Payne thought, will be busting down your door and putting you in handcuffs. He finished dressing in silence and made for the door.

"Take care of yourself, Payne," the judge called after him. "And next time, make it the full fifty thousand."

SIX

An hour after fleeing the courthouse, Payne's hands were still shaking. Either that, or a 5.0 trembler had rocked the Chimney Sweep, a windowless tavern squeezed between a Lebanese restaurant and a discount dentist in a Sherman Oaks strip mall. Payne wrapped a hand around the leaded base of his glass, trying to steady it, but the Jack Daniel's swirled between the ice cubes like molten lava through porous rocks.

"Good work, Payne," Rigney had told him on the phone, minutes earlier.

A pimp high-fiving a hooker, Payne thought, cheerlessly.

"I knew you'd make a great bag man." Rigney's laugh jangled like steel handcuffs.

Bag man.

In Payne's mind, other names floated to the surface, like corpses afer a shipwreck.

Snitch.

Rat.

Shyster.

If word got out, no client would ever trust him. And word *always* got out. Gossip was the coin of the realm in the kingdom of justice.

He drained the sour-mash whiskey, slipped a small vinyl folder from inside his coat pocket, and removed a business card,

J. ATTICUS PAYNE, ESQUIRE

Rigney had nailed it. Not even the name was real.

Payne bummed a pack of matches from the bartender, set the card on fire, watched it disintegrate, ashes drifting into a bowl of peanuts. No ashtrays. You had to cross into Mexico to smoke legally these days. He lit a second card, stared into the orange flames. Why not burn them all?

The only other patron at the bar was a TV writer who had been unemployed since they canceled *Gilligan's Island.* Camped on his stool as if he had a long-term lease, the guy's faded T-shirt read: *"Say It Loud. Say It Plowed."*

Payne hoisted his glass, saluted the fellow, and took a long pull. The liquid gold delivered warmth without solace. He struck another match. Immolated another card, inhaled the acrid smoke, let the flame burn until it singed his fingertips.

Two hundred miles southeast of the tavern where Payne planned to drink the day far into the night, just outside a cantina in Mexicali, Mexico, a wiry twelve-year-old boy named Agustino Perez stood with his mother as city traffic clattered past. The boy had caramel skin and hair so black and thick that women on the street grabbed it by the handful and cooed like quail. Tino's eyes, though, were a startling green. A teacher once said he reminded her of *verde y negro,* a local dessert of mint ice cream topped with chocolate sauce. Boys at school started calling him *"verde y negro"* with a lip-smacking nastiness. It took a flurry of fists and a couple bloody noses to convince the boys that he was not a sweet confection.

Marisol, the boy's mother, was sometimes mistaken for his older sister. The same smile, the same hair with the sheen of black velvet. But the boy did not inherit his light, bright eyes from her. Set above wide cheekbones, her eyes were the color of hot tar.

Glancing from side to side as if someone might be spying on them, Marisol handed her son a business card. He ran a finger across the embossed lettering and read aloud, *"J. Atticus Payne, Esquire. Van Nuys, California."*

"That is Los Angeles. Mr. Payne is a very important man. One of the biggest lawyers in the city."

"So?"

"Put the card in your shoe, Tino."

The shoes were new—Reeboks—purchased that morning for the crossing.

"Why, *Mami?*"

"If anything bad happens and I am not there, go see Mr. Payne. Tell him that you are a friend of Fernando Rodriguez."

"But I am not his friend. I don't even like the *cabrón.*"

His mother raised an eyebrow, her way of demanding: *"Do as I say."* The stern look would carry more weight, Tino thought, if she weren't the prettiest woman in Caborca.

He was used to men complimenting his mother on her adorable son. He knew it was their way to get close to her, smiling wicked smiles, panting like overheated dogs.

"Fernando Rodriguez sits on a stool at La Faena, drinking tequila and bragging about things he has never done," Tino said.

"And what were you doing at La Faena, little boy?"

"¡*Mami!*"

Why did she have to baby him? Maybe that's how it is when you're an only child, and you have no father to toughen you up, often at the end of a leather strap.

Tino decided not to tell his mother that the barman at La Faena was teaching him to mix drinks, and that blindfolded he could already identify several tequilas, both reposados and añejos. They were going to try some *blancos* next week, but then, Tino's life changed in an instant. What his mother called *"nuestro problema."*

Our problem.

Even though he caused the problem. It all happened yesterday, as quick as the chisel that drew the blood. Then, last night, they packed everything they could carry and ran for the bus, traveling north from Caborca to Mexicali.

As for Fernando Rodriguez, he was a *campesino* with bad teeth who returned from *El Norte* driving a shiny blue Dodge Ram with spinning wheel covers. Rodriguez claimed he bought the truck, almost new, in Arizona, after working a year in a dog-food processing plant. Tino was sure the *cabrón* stole the Dodge, along with the ostrich-skin cowboy boots he liked to park on a table at the cantina.

Rodriguez boasted of one other thing that happened to be true. He did not die when he was crammed into the back of a sixteen-wheeler with thirty-five other *mojados* who crossed the border two summers earlier.

Tino could remember every detail, as Rodriguez told the story nearly every evening. The truck had stopped somewhere in the California desert, baking in the sun. The people tried to claw their way out of the locked metal doors, leaving patches of scorched skin and trails of blood. Rodriguez swore that he saw a woman's hair burst into flame. No one at the cantina believed that, but one thing was certain: Eleven Mexicans died inside that truck.

Still, Tino could not understand why Rodriguez would be acquainted with one of the most important lawyers in Los Angeles, or why he'd returned to Mexico, passing out the business cards of such an *abogado brillante*.

"When we get inside," his mother told him now, "if the coyote asks why we must cross over tonight, say nothing."

"Ay, *Mami*. I know what to do."

"I will do the talking. You will be quiet."

He let out a long sigh, like air from a balloon. No use arguing with his mother. No way to make her understand that he was the man of the house. Now he wondered if his actions back home—criminal, yet honorable—were somehow intended to prove his manhood to his mother.

Marisol turned toward the street. An army jeep snaked through traffic, a soldier manning a .50 caliber machine gun. The drug wars, which were only stories on television in Caborca, were very real here. Yesterday, a local police station had been attacked with grenades and rocket launchers. When they had arrived after midnight, the army was sealing off the bus station.

Now Marisol placed an arm around her son's shoulders. "Let's go, Tino. Let's get out of this godforsaken country."

SEVEN

Marisol had never met the coyote, but she recognized him immediately.

Shiny, tight black pants, tucked into pointy boots. Wraparound reflecting sunglasses and black felt *Tejano* hat, he looked like a low-life gambler at a cockfight. His black shirt with pearl-colored buttons was open halfway to his waist, and a heavy gold crucifix dangled in front of his hairy chest. His face was pitted with acne scars shaped like tiny fishhooks.

The man called himself *"El Tigre,"* although this tiger had a paunch pouring over his turquoise belt buckle. At the moment, he was using his fingers to dig into a platter of deep-fried anchovies.

When he saw Marisol and Tino approach, El Tigre wiped his mouth with the back of a hand. The other hand was wrapped around a bottle of Tecate. Nodding, he said, "Do you have the money?"

"We have two thousand, three hundred dollars cash," she answered, taking a seat. "All my savings."

He took a swig of the beer. "Not enough. It is three thousand dollars each. And no discount for the little one."

Tino bristled and started to speak, but his mother kicked him under the table.

"We will pay you the rest when we cross over and can borrow the money from my aunt," she said.

El Tigre's mouth creased into a smile, displaying an

array of gold-lined teeth that had taken on a greenish hue, as if covered with algae. "Your aunt? Why does everyone have an aunt in *El Norte*? I bet she's a rich woman with a mansion in Phoenix."

"A nice house in Torrance, California. My uncle owns a gasoline station there."

Marisol was weaving her story out of threads plucked from the air. True, she had an aunt, a miserly woman who had married an American and refused to return to Mexico, even for her sister's funeral. The last Marisol knew, her aunt lived in Torrance, where she managed a trailer park. But that was ten years ago, and Marisol had no idea where the old crow lived now.

Marisol did not like to lie. Her father taught her the value of honesty and hard work, and she tried to live up to his standards. As a young girl in Hermosillo, how proud she had been of him. In his crisp, clean jumpsuit with the Ford Motor Company logo, he looked . . . well, like an *Americano*. Proud, too, when he told her how he had refused an Anglo supervisor's request to falsify inspection records on Lincoln Continentals.

"I told him I'll rot in hell before I lie to the company!" her father thundered.

Soon after that, the supervisor arranged for Edgardo Perez to be fired. Her father, Marisol knew, was a courageous and honorable man. And, ultimately, a tragic one.

"Sometimes, Papi, it is all right to lie."

"I promise I will pay you," she told the fat and sweaty coyote. "I swear on my father's grave." Neglecting to mention that her nonbelieving father never attended church and the only time Edgardo visited Mexico City, he spat curses in front of Catedral Metropolitana. On the other hand, Marisol's mother attended Mass every morning. It made for interesting discussions over dinner. Marisol's beliefs fell somewhere between the two. She knew her Bible but was not blind to the failings of the Church. She sensed a spirit greater than her own and prayed it would protect Tino and her. Especially now.

"I do not give credit," El Tigre said. "But maybe we can work something out."

He placed a plump hand on Marisol's bare arm. She wore a short-sleeve white peasant blouse with two buttons undone. The pig was studying the rise and fall of her breasts. Nothing new. Marisol was used to men pawing her on job sites. She had learned to accept this fact of life. Only when the abuse became intolerable—a hand slipped down her pants—did she retaliate. Her father had taught her how to throw a punch with a turn of the hips and a straight, quick arm. In her experience at construction sites, a balpeen hammer worked even better.

"Why the rush to leave Mexico?" El Tigre asked.

"Family matters." Keeping it vague.

"I cross tonight and come back tomorrow. Why not stay here a few days, and we can get to know each other better."

"We go when we want!" Tino piped up.

El Tigre scowled. "You go when I say."

"Maybe we cross by ourselves," Tino shot back.

"Tino, quiet," his mother ordered.

"*Mami*, I could build a raft, and we could float up the New River."

El Tigre burped a beer-and-anchovy laugh. "The river is full of shit, and so are you, *chico*."

Marisol winced but did not reply. There were times to kick a man in the kneecap and times to appeal to a slightly higher region. She softened her look and let her eyes water. "Your charges are so high."

El Tigre launched into a defense of his prices. He had expenses. Lookouts and guides and vehicles and drivers. Stash houses on both sides of the border. Bribes to the *judicales* and the *federales*. Protection money to the *mafia de los coyotes* because he was a freelancer. Then there were the risks.

"*¡Pinche rinche por todas partes!*"

Fucking cops everywhere.

Marisol did not appreciate the profanity in front of her son, but for now she must try to get along with this foul and repulsive man.

"If you get caught, they just send you back," El Tigre said. "But for me, it's prison. Or I get shot by bandits. Or vigilantes. The Minutemen. Patriot Patrol. All those *gabachos* with guns. And now, the U.S. Army. The Border Patrol knows what they're doing. But the soldiers! Scared kids who think we're all drug runners."

"Instead of the humanitarians you are," Marisol said, evenly.

He did not catch the sarcasm, rambling on, boasting of his knowledge of the Border Patrol's motion detectors and TV cameras, infrared binoculars, and drone aircraft. How *La Migra* had beefed up patrols. Ford Expeditions, like always. But now on horseback, too, with Indian trackers from Arizona. *Vaqueros y indios.* Cowboys and Indians. Just like in the movies.

"If the wind is right, the Indians can smell your burlap sacks a mile away," he claimed. "You need someone who knows what they're doing. I don't lose people in the mountains or leave them to die in the desert."

Marisol leaned over the table, exposing even more décolletage, showing the line where the darker sunburned skin gave way to the softness of her crème de cacao complexion. She put a wistful note in her voice. "But if you are going tonight, and have room for two more, I promise to pay you later."

El Tigre wiped beads of sweat from his forehead, then drained the rest of his beer. He seemed to be weighing the options, using his limited brains and his even more limited morals.

"I won't disappoint you," she said, spicing her words like chiles in hot sauce.

He took a pen out of a shirt pocket and scribbled an address on a paper napkin. "The stash house. We leave at midnight. Bring the money you have. We will work out the rest."

He smiled a gold-capped grin, the contented look of a wolf contemplating a lamb.

EIGHT

Sleep. Dammit. Sleep!

Maybe it was the oysters, Payne thought.

From the Chimney Sweep, Payne had moved to the Oyster House, a neighborhood saloon in Studio City.

Dinner alone.

Sitting at the bar. A dozen oysters, a spicy cioppino stew, two Sam Adams drafts, and the complimentary peach schnapps the regulars receive.

Payne would have liked to have shared dinner with a woman. But who?

Maybe Carol, a former client who loved shopping at Saks on Wilshire, but skipping the inconvenience of paying. Was she out of jail yet?

Or Polly, a kosher caterer in Brentwood who specialized in festive circumcision brunches. Her business, Prelude to a Bris, was booming.

Or that woman who owned the cat condo in Rancho Cucamonga. Hair in a tabby-colored shag, big hoop earrings. Jeez, what was her name? Well, if he couldn't remember, it must not have gone that well. And now that he thought about it, hadn't Cat Lady had a funky smell?

What about Sharon?

Her scent was warm and sweet. A fresh peach from the tree. And they always had great sex, though it tapered off after she'd shot him. Not that he wasn't willing, once the anesthesia wore off.

Sharon had been aiming her nine millimeter at Lester Koenigsberg when she winged Payne. Unhappy with Payne's handling of his divorce case, Koenigsberg was holding a knife to his lawyer's neck, threatening to slice his jugular. Hardly the reaction Payne expected after disproving Mrs. Koenigsberg's allegations that Lester had a violent temper.

Payne was semi-grateful to Sharon for saving his life. But why a detective in Consumer Frauds even needed a gun was beyond him.

He listened to the paddle fan turn, *clickety-clack*ing.

C'mon, sleep!

He adjusted the pillow under his gimpy knee. Ever since the crash on the P.C.H., the leg wouldn't straighten completely.

Sleep, dammit, sleep!

The bed was just too damn big when you're alone. A cruise ship with one passenger.

The house was a one-story, two-bedroom California bungalow with a small porch devoid of furniture. The faded green stucco could use a fresh coat of paint. The dreary 1950s kitchen smelled of mildew, the low-pitched roof leaking during winter rains. The perfect home for the unhappily divorced man.

Payne flicked on the night-table lamp, made from a bowling pin, and stared straight into Sharon's face. An eight-by-ten glossy, taken on Mammoth Mountain. A ski trip, the background a heaven of powdery snow. Sharon's cheeks pink from the cold, Adam bundled in a parka.

Smiling. Laughing.

Old times. Good times. Short times.

Oak bookshelves lined one wall. Scott Turow and George V. Higgins. Crime stories well told. Payne didn't like those courtroom novels where the lawyers were heroes. Too unrealistic.

No, it wasn't the oysters. Or the lonely bed. Or the choking memories. The day was still with him, and all the days before that. A ton of crap had floated down the stream since the crash and the divorce.

C'mon, think happy thoughts.

Adam playing baseball. The worst part of the divorce was spending nights without his son. At least Sharon was decent about it. He could see Adam practically anytime he wanted.

Payne gave up on sleep, grabbed the TV remote, and turned on Channel 56, home of *Twilight Zone* and *Hawaii Five-O*. Payne loved the classic shows, even though he wasn't born when they first aired.

The TV flickered on, and there was a young James Garner with an even younger Tom Selleck. *The Rockford Files*. Selleck was Lance White, the perfect detective, solving cases without breaking a sweat, pissing off Rockford, who usually got beaten up and tossed into jail, before turning crud into gold. Payne identified with the Rockford character, except his crud always turned into more crud.

At a commercial, Payne flicked to one of the movie channels. *The Big Lebowski* was just coming on, great opening scene, a tumbleweed at the mercy of the wind, blowing from the desert into Los Angeles. The *shit happens* philosophy of life. Who could argue?

He'd seen the movie the first time with Sharon, who didn't share his enthusiasm for a wacky story about a stoned slacker. Sharon was both a good cop and a do-gooding cop, someone who believed the words carved in the granite of the courthouses.

Equal Justice Under Law

Yeah, spend an hour with Judge Rollins, and try singing that tune.

Payne vowed he wouldn't flip to Channel 9. Cullen Quinn's late-night show would be on. He'd be railing about the Mexican border and encouraging the yahoos to shoot all illegals on sight. It wasn't just Quinn's politics that upset Payne. The broad-shouldered, blow-dried bastard was recently engaged to Sharon and had given her a rock so humongous it would make Paris Hilton blush. To Sharon's credit, she seldom wore the engagement ring, explaining that a cop's jewelry shouldn't be worth more than her car.

Payne kept his promise for a full twenty seconds before flipping to the Satan of the Airwaves.

"We're going the way of the Roman Empire." Quinn leaned toward the camera, his silvery blond hair frozen in place. "The Romans opened the gates and the Goths came storming in. With no respect for Roman culture or language or customs, the Goths burned Rome to the ground."

Quinn paused and lifted his chin, as if daring his viewers to take a poke at him. "Did you see those Mexican protesters in the streets? 'Open the borders!' And those weren't the Stars and Stripes they were waving. Those were Mex-i-can flags."

"Mex-i-can" sounding vile, the way you might say *"roach infested."*

"¡La Reconquista!" Quinn boomed in his broadcaster's baritone. "That's what the illegals want. To reconquer *their* land. And we're handing it right back to them. Welfare and schooling, all paid for by *you*, my friends. Their children bring lice and bedbugs into our schools. Our hospitals and prisons overflow with illegals, infected with hepatitis, TB, and chingas."

Chingas, Payne thought. A new one on him.

The big mug seemed to have put on weight. His neck bulged out of his shirt collar. His crooked nose, product of a Golden Gloves fight, actually looked good on him. Made him less of a Ken doll. The son of a Philadelphia butcher, Quinn was a lifelong pal of Sharon's oldest brother, Rory. Both boys had hung out at the Police Athletic League gym, where they would beat each other senseless in the ring. Quinn went on to Villanova and claimed to have fought classmate Howie Long to a draw in club boxing. Long became a collegiate heavyweight champion and, later, a member of the pro football Hall of Fame. Quinn became the mouth that roared on Los Angeles radio and television.

Payne watched as Quinn gestured with a meaty hand.

"And still the wetbacks pour in, thousands every day. Millions on the way. The barbarians are inside our gates, my friends, and our walls are tumbling down. And who's benefiting from this invasion? The big growers like Simeon Rutledge, owner of Rutledge Ranch and Farms. When will Washington crack down on—"

Payne hit the "Mute" button and studied Quinn. With his face tinted orange by makeup, he looked like a scowling pumpkin. He wore a gray Italian suit so finely tailored it disguised the fact that he was beginning to resemble a whale. His designer shirt seemed to be silk, in that trendy off-purple all the rage for the next fifteen minutes or so.

Every night, the same rant. Like being stuck at a dinner party next to a guy complaining about his hemorrhoids.

Just what does Sharon see in this bozo, anyway?

But then, what did she see in me?

Earlier today, Payne told Judge Rollins he was going to change. Of course, a man will say a lot of crazy stuff when he's staring into the barrel of a gun. Had he meant it?

Sure, but just how do I do it?

Payne's eyes grew heavy. With the fog settling in, his mind sorted through a variety of possible weekend plans.

Take the hydrofoil to Catalina.

Bring along Heidi Klum.

Reread the Travis McGee paperback that began: "There are no one hundred percent heroes."

The ringing telephone jarred Payne. He fumbled for the handset.

"Yeah?"

"You stupid shit. You asshole. You total fuck-up."

Payne was fairly certain it wasn't a wrong number. "Judge?"

"I knew you were a sleaze," Walter Rollins said. "But I didn't know you were a rat."

"Judge, I'm sorry, but—"

"Shut up!"

"C'mon, Judge. You're the one who took the bribe."

"I said, shut up! I don't have much time."

Over the phone, Payne heard the judge's doorbell ringing.

"I felt sorry for you, Payne. Everybody did, after that lousy luck you had. But stuff happens. People deal with it."

"I don't want to talk about—"

"Just 'cause your life's shit doesn't mean you have to drag everyone else down the sewer."

Again, the doorbell, the chimes as insistent as machine-gun fire. In the background, Payne heard a man shout, "Police! We have a warrant!"

"Judge, calm down. The state's gonna offer you a deal. You're the first one busted. That puts you in a great position. I'll bet if you resign the bench and cooperate, you could avoid prison—"

"Bullshit. It's over for me."

"The state doesn't want to try the case. They want to work something out."

Payne waited but there was no reply.

"Judge . . . ?"

A thunderclap. The unmistakable sound of a gunshot. Then the soft thud of a body hitting the floor.

NINE

Where is that sack of greasy onions, that sorry excuse for a man who calls himself the Tiger?

Marisol looked out through the broken window, one hand on Tino's shoulder. She would not let the boy out of her sight until they were in the United States. Her worst fear was separation, some horrific event that would pry them apart.

It was after midnight. Of course, El Tigre was late. She supposed it was too much to ask that he display a solid work ethic. Punctuality. Attention to detail. Basic competence. Like Americans.

The thought made her smile. She was beginning to think like her father.

She sat, cross-legged, in an adobe mud house that smelled of raw sewage. The stash house was located in a grim neighborhood of shacks with corrugated metal roofs. Outside, naked children played tag deep into the night. Undernourished dogs rooted in garbage cans, and chickens pecked at the dry ground.

The street was unpaved. The people were unwashed. The cars were skeletons sinking into front yards. The shade trees had long since been chopped into firewood.

Marisol could not wait to say *adios, Méjico.*

Not that she thought the streets of California were lined with rosebushes or paved with bricks of gold. She believed Father Castillo, back home, who warned that the route to the U.S.A. was a trail of thorns through a cemetery without crosses.

But just listen to the others, clucking like roosters. *Campesinos* in straw hats, a Guatemalan family with their woven sacks, a teenage love-struck couple from Ensenada, the girl pregnant. Hopelessly naive in their dreams of the promised land. One woman claimed that everyone in San Diego was a millionaire with a swimming pool, a German car, and a Mexican maid. A middle-aged man smelling of tobacco and sweat boasted that a job waited for him in a fish cannery and that he would own an almost new Chevy Silverado by the end of the summer. A Guatemalan man, his dusty feet in torn huaraches, said that he was headed to the San Joaquin Valley to pick crops. He called it a "Garden of Eden."

Marisol knew that the American Eden can be a garden of bones, that peasants like these often never reach those fertile fields. And those who do? She had heard stories that some growers were kind and decent to the migrants. Others treated them like oxen without the yokes.

She had heard talk of construction jobs in Phoenix, where thousands of homes were being built by rich Americans. But then later, others said the jobs had run as dry as the wells of her village. Who knew for certain?

A cousin from Jaripo had crossed last year. His mother told Marisol he picked grapes for twenty cents a tray. How many grapes in a tray? How long to pick them? She could not even guess.

So yes, there is work. Farms and factories. Restaurants and hotels. Drywall and roofing. Logging and demolition. Fisheries and meat-packing plants. But first, they must arrive safely.

They are the *pollos*. The cooked chickens. Men like El Tigre are the *polleros,* the chicken wranglers.

Marisol again thought of her father and wondered what he would say to her now. He was one of those Mexicans who loved the *idea* of America, insisting that Marisol learn English. Some of her earliest memories were watching *Sesame Street* on American television, after her father salvaged a satellite dish from a trash pile. Edgardo Perez even required her to read the English translations of Mexican authors.

"Papi, doesn't it make more sense to read Carlos Fuentes in Spanish?"

"In Atlanta, they read him in English."

Atlanta being the home of his favorite baseball team, the Braves. He watched on the satellite, cheering for Vinny Castilla, born in Oaxaca. Surely, Edgardo Perez would approve of her going north with Tino. But not like this. Not rushed and unplanned.

When her father worked at the Ford plant in Hermosillo, the company provided a house. Her mother gardened and knitted and cooked. Marisol remembered a childhood filled with fresh flowers, birthday parties, and heart-shaped *ensaimadas,* topped with whipped cream. For a while, at least, it was a life dipped in honey.

After her father was fired, he promised to take the family to *El Norte,* but the closest they got was a village outside Caborca in the state of Sonora. They arrived by bus, for even though Edgardo Perez had built Fords, he did not own one. Just outside the village, in the high desert, a dust devil whirled across the road and blasted the bus windows with a funnel of blinding sand. Welcome to your new life, parched and cruel, the spirits of the desert seemed to say.

Her father tried raising grapes, but there was not enough water. He looked for work. Roofer. Carpenter. Handyman. But the villagers were poor and did their own repairs, if any at all. Even worse, they seemed to resent the Perez family.

"Aristocracia," they called them, with contempt. Thinking the family put on airs along with their freshly washed clothes.

Only in Mexico, Marisol thought, could a fired factory worker with no money in the bank be considered haughty for keeping a clean house and making sure his children finished secondary school.

The roar of an engine stirred her from thoughts of the past. Tino leapt up and looked out the broken window. A red pickup truck with dual rear wheels and a long cargo bed kicked up dust as it slid to a stop in front of the adobe house.

El Tigre wiggled his belly out of the cab, shouting instructions for the *pollos* to hop into the back.

Tino whistled. "A Ford F-350, *Mami.* Brand new. Did *abuelo* make these?"

A note of hopeful pride in his voice, Marisol realizing yet again that her son needed a man in his life.

"I don't think so," she said. "Your grandfather built cars. Lincolns and Fords."

The ten travelers piled into the bed of the shiny red pickup, Marisol thinking, Why not just paint a sign on the doors, *Illegals Here!*

Standing on the running board, El Tigre counted his passengers. "Tonight, you walk in the desert," he proclaimed, like a Mexican Moses. "Tomorrow, you walk in Los Angeles!"

Marisol and Tino sat with their backs pressed against the rear of the metal toolbox that ran the width of the cab. They each wore one backpack. Before they left home, Marisol fought back tears as she told Tino they could only take what they could carry. Not the plates or silverware that had been her grandmother's. Not the kitchen table handmade by her father from mahogany scraps.

Just three changes of clothing each. Tino's baseball glove. Photographs of his *abuela y abuelo,* both gone now. Everything else they left behind.

They each wore jeans and their new Reeboks, purchased in Mexicali along with "travel kits." Tins of sardines and crackers and gallon jugs of water. Band-Aids, blister cream, and sunblock. Everything for the aspiring *pollo* except a green card. Still, Marisol could not shake the feeling that disaster faced them at every bend in the road.

"*And what do you do, Agustino, if anything bad happens and I am not there?*"

"*Call J. Atticus Payne. But don't worry. I will take care of both of us.*"

"*All right, my little* valiente."

"*I am not so little,* Mami."

The truck headed west through a mountain pass on Federal Highway 2, then across a rocky, barren landscape, over bridges that traversed ravines and dry washes, finally curling up a mountain road through narrow canyons, dangerously close to steep cliffs. It was a moonless night—helpful for crossing undetected—the only light the twinkling stars overhead.

"It's okay, *Mami*," Tino said. "Everything will be okay."

Marisol hadn't realized it, but she was squeezing her son's hand. Squeezing so hard, he had to pry her fingers loose.

"Of course it will," she said.

They came to a mountain town called "La Rumorosa"—named for the winds that whistled through the canyons—and stopped outside a small house of sand-colored rocks. A threadbare sofa and two living room chairs, springs sprung, sagged in the front yard, facing a fire of mesquite wood. Three young men lounged on the furniture, one cleaning what looked like a sub-machine gun, the other breaking down a handgun. The third man smoked a joint. He waved in the general direction of the truck but didn't get off the sofa.

El Tigre banged his horn. "Let's go, Rey!"

Rey, the pot smoker, looked to be about twenty years old. Baggy pants, shaved head, his body all cords and wires. A muscle-tee displayed his tattoos: Aztec symbols, Mexican flag, and a green snake that crawled up his neck. His goal in life appeared to be to spend as much time as possible in prison.

Heavy-lidded, Rey jammed a handgun into the front of his pants, lazed his way around the truck, and peered into the bed.

"Who are you?" Tino asked, before Marisol could keep him quiet.

"You ever hear of the Avenue 57 Chicos?" Rey's smile showed yellow teeth and undisguised malice.

"No."

"You will, *chico*."

Great, Marisol thought. A gangbanger. Or, at the very least, someone who wanted to be.

El Tigre hit the horn again. He must like the sound. Then he swung his bulk out of the cab, stood on the running board, and said, "Rey's my nephew. He'll watch for bandits until we cross over. But stay out of his way. He is a terrible shot."

"*¡Chingate, Tío!*"

Rey telling his uncle to have sex with himself. The family must be very proud of the young man, Marisol thought.

El Tigre plopped back into the cab, and his nephew slithered into the passenger seat. With a final toot of the horn, El Tigre gunned the engine. Spitting up dirt, the truck bounced onto the mountain road and into the darkness of the Mexican night.

TEN

Payne called 911 and was immediately cross-examined.

"Yes, I'm sure it was a gunshot."

"No, I'm not at the judge's house."

"No, I'm not armed! Jeez, get the paramedics over there!"

A woman at the other end of the line asked him to hold a moment.

Payne paced in a tight circle. Fully awake now, wound tight, filled with regret. Judge Rollins was corrupt, but he didn't deserve this.

"Is this Mr. James Payne?" asked the woman on the phone.

Oh, shit.

He hadn't given his name.

The woman recited his home address and the fact that he had three unpaid parking tickets and two citations for failing to clear brush from his property.

The L.A.P.D.'s enhanced caller I.D. The city can't fix the potholes, but it can snoop into our living rooms.

Technology would lead the cops straight to his front door. They would ask all those nosy cop questions about his visit to the judge. They probably wouldn't do a Rodney King on his skull, but who wants another Grand Jury looking into his affairs?

Payne clicked off without saying good-bye. He needed time to think, and this wasn't the place. He dressed hurriedly, grabbed the envelope with the five grand he had skimmed, and hopped into his car. Headed west on Oxnard, hung a right on Van Nuys, and parked on Delano, two blocks from his office. Payne was seldom in his office between nine and five, much less in the middle of the night. Still, no use advertising his presence with his Lexus by the door.

The chambers of J. Atticus Payne, Esquire, solo practitioner, occupied a one-story, wood-shingled bungalow built in the 1920s and not updated since. The paint was peeling, the porch sagging, and the siding tearing loose. A California Craftsman gone to seed.

Rent was cheap, and the place was close to the court-house, bail bondsman's office, and the police station. The small backyard had been paved over to provide parking for three cars, even though many of Payne's clients arrived by bus, walking the last few blocks from the Van Nuys Civic Center.

The shelves were lined with law books that Payne never read, the desk cluttered with mail never to be answered. Atop his first-generation fax machine, a single slice of pepperoni pizza looked alarmingly like a chunk of plasterboard with skin cancer. He tossed the envelope with the hundred-dollar bills into a desk drawer and opened a cabinet that was intended for litigation files but contained vodka, bourbon, Scotch, tequila, and coffee liqueur. Payne had not been much of a drinker until the accident. After his surgery, he sought relief from the pain by washing down Vicodin with white Russians.

He contented himself now with some Maker's Mark, neat, in a dirty cup. He kicked some files off an old corduroy sofa and stretched out. He did not know what he would do in the morning, though he vaguely recollected that he had an eight A.M. hearing in Superior Court, just down the street.

Exhaustion kicked in along with the bourbon. His eyes drifted closed, then opened, then descended again like balky garage doors. His last conscious thought was of Adam tossing a ball to him. The boy was rangy, all legs and elbows, with a rubbery arm. He could throw hard. Just like Payne at that age, fast but wild. With that thought, and the timeless echo of a leather ball smacking into the pocket of a finely oiled glove, Jimmy finally cruised into a restless sleep.

ELEVEN

El Tigre pulled the pickup truck off the highway, onto a dirt road west of La Rumorosa. Nothing for miles except dark canyons and sheer cliffs.

Everyone piled out of the truck bed. Two of the *campesinos* from the south began urinating several feet away, the splashing audible. Barnyard animals, Marisol thought, so inconsiderate they cannot walk twenty feet to relieve themselves behind a cactus.

She heard El Tigre screaming into his cell phone.

"¡*Chingalo!* One car? I told you, a van! Asshole! I got ten *pollos.*"

"What's happening?" Mirasol asked Rey, his leaden eyes hidden now behind sunglasses.

"Stupid *gabacho* driver on other side only has one car," Rey said. "We got to make two trips across."

Once again, Marisol tightened her grip on Tino's hand.

After another explosion of Spanish curses, El Tigre clicked off the phone and, for the second time tonight, counted his passengers. Luckily, he had just enough fingers to complete the tabulation. "Five men, five women." He looked toward Tino. "I'm putting you with the men. Are you a good runner?"

"The fastest in Caborca," Tino said.

El Tigre showed his gold-toothed smile. "New plan. Women first."

He explained his strategy as if he were Pancho Villa

at the Battle of Chihuahua. He would take the women through the canyons and across the border to his idiot *gabacho* friend, who had a single car waiting. Then El Tigre would come back and lead the men down the same path. By the time they got across, the driver would have taken the women to a stash house near Calexico and returned to his hiding spot near the border. El Tigre would then take the five men—including Tino—to the same stash house. There would be no charge for El Tigre's extra effort.

"It will all work out." He sounded pleased with his brilliant tactics.

Marisol shook her head. "My son goes with me."

He gave her a poisonous look. "The woman who asks for credit does not make the rules. By the time the second group gets to the border fence, the sun will be up, and we can be spotted. We may need to run."

"I can run as fast as any man here," Marisol said.

"*Chingad.* You will do as I say."

She knew she had embarrassed El Tigre by arguing with him. Backed him into a corner. Now he had to save face. Still, she would not relent.

"My son goes with me."

His face colored. "*¡Chinga to putas!*"

"If my son does not go, neither do I. Please give back our money."

El Tigre's laugh was liquid, a toilet flushing. Then he shouted, "Rey!"

The sleepy-eyed nephew seemed to wake up. He pulled the gun from his waistband and stuck it under Marisol's nose. "Shut up, woman."

Tino leapt at Rey, knocked the gun to the ground, then pummeled him with a flurry of punches. The boy was skinny, but his long arms whirled like propellor blades, and several blows landed, breaking Rey's sunglasses. Off balance, Rey fell awkwardly into an ocotillo shrub, cursing in Spanish and English and maybe some words he just made up.

El Tigre grabbed Tino by the back of his T-shirt, lifted him off his feet, and swung him against the side of the truck.

"Don't touch my son!" Marisol flew at the man, tearing his hand away.

A gunshot echoed off the canyon walls.

Rey stood there, eyes wide, pupils dilated, gun pointing in the air. "We do what my uncle says, or I swear, I will kill someone tonight."

"I'm not afraid of you, *grifo*," Tino said.

"Tino, quiet!" Marisol ordered.

"Listen to your mother, *pendejo*," Rey said. "You die out here, nobody gives a shit. Birds eat your eyeballs for breakfast and your balls for lunch. Out here, you're nothing but a grease spot in the sand."

TWELVE

They had walked two hours, down one canyon, and up another, El Tigre shoving Marisol every time she looked back over her shoulder.

"The little bastard will be fine," he said.

She had long dreamed of leaving Mexico. But not at the barrel of a gun. And not leaving her son behind. She wondered if the separation suited El Tigre's intentions.

She could not run from the stash house until he returned with her son.

"When we get to Calexico," El Tigre had told her, "you can take a bath and change your clothes and I will have your boy there in time for lunch. After dark, there will be a ride to Los Angeles. Between morning and evening, we will have some time together."

Marisol wondered if there might not be something more pleasant to occupy her afternoon. Being bitten by a scorpion perhaps.

"Bring my son to me," she said. "Then we shall see."

He grunted like a pig rooting out a tasty morsel. In the dim light of the stars, she could not make out his expression, but in her imagination, he licked the saliva from his lips.

They followed a rocky trail, the five women and their coyote. In the dark, it was a shadowy landscape of volcanic rocks and sand washes. Scrub oaks and greasewoods. In the distance, outlines of mountains formed the backdrop for the night sky. Marisol realized those mountains were in the United States. Part of the same mountains on this side of the border. The dirt would be the same, the rocks, too. And the people?

We are human beings. We are all of one blood, are we not?

The land leveled out as they neared the border. El Tigre shushed them, for sound carried great distances in the desert night. They were exposed here. Visible to border agents with infrared binoculars.

El Tigre had boasted that he never used the same entrance point twice. Marisol hoped the man knew what he was doing. They were close enough to see the border fence, steel mesh twelve feet high topped by razor wire. No sounds but the crunch of their shoes and the hoot of owls.

Marisol shortened her breaths as she neared the

fence, as if her very exhalations might set off an alarm. El Tigre used wire cutters to make an opening, and within seconds, Marisol stood on the hard-baked earth of *los Estados Unidos*. It felt strangely anticlimactic. Certainly, there was no joy. Not with Tino left behind. But even when he got here, what would her feelings be? What would the future hold? The beginning of some grand adventure, the fulfillment of her father's dream? Or were greater catastrophes ahead?

Lights flashed, and Marisol stiffened. Border Patrol?

But then El Tigre shouted, "Ay! There's the *gabacho* now."

Car headlights. Two more quick flashes. The car hidden in some pinyon trees several hundred yards from the fence. The women ran toward the headlights.

The car was old—very old—but clean. Orange with a white stripe, air scoops on the hood, and an engine growling like a predatory animal. Tino would probably know the name of the car. She did not, but a decal on its long hood had an illustration of a tornado and the word "Duster."

Four women—two *campesinas* from the south, one Guatemalan, and the pregnant girl—squeezed into the backseat. El Tigre motioned Marisol into the front seat, where she was sandwiched between the two men. The driver was a long-haired, bearded young man in a baseball cap. He immediately slid his hand along Marisol's thigh before grabbing the floor-mounted gearshift.

With the headlights off, the man gunned the engine, slipped the gearshift into first gear, and spun up the dirt road, and deeper into California.

They had just pulled onto a paved road when Marisol heard the sirens.

Blue lights flashing, two Ford Expeditions sped after them.

"Shit! Border Patrol!" The driver stomped on the

clutch, shifted gears, and floored the accelerator. The car fishtailed, then straightened, and Marisol was thrown against the seat.

The next few minutes seemed to her to be one high-pitched scream. The actual screams of the four women in the backseat. The wail of the sirens. The shouts in Spanglish from left and right, the driver and El Tigre cursing at each other, arguing where to go.

Marisol saw the arm of the old-fashioned speedometer, as it fluttered between 105 and 110. They would crash. She was sure of it. A tire would explode. They would careen off the road and into a boulder. Her head would fly through the windshield, and Tino would be left alone. She squeezed her eyes shut and chanted a prayer.

"Protégeme de la muerte, y te llevaré una rosa de Castilla, al Santuario de Tepeyac."

"You are winning them!" El Tigre shouted in English. Marisol thinking he meant "losing them," as the two Border Patrol vehicles fell behind.

"Don't matter none," the American driver said. "Bastards will have a chopper over us in a couple minutes."

Barely slowing down, the Duster screeched off the asphalt and onto a gravel road that sloped upward and undulated through a series of rises and dips. Headlights still out, the car seemed to be a missile, launched into the night sky, headed toward some explosive crash landing.

The driver tugged the wheel hard and skidded off the road, coming to rest between a line of manzanita bushes and a single mesquite tree. In front of them, the outline of a mountain appeared as a menacing tower set against the soft glow of the Milky Way.

"Out! Everyone out!" the driver shouted.

"¿Aquí?" El Tigre asked, confused.

"I'm on parole. Ain't gonna be stopped with a car full of greasers."

"Where are we?" Marisol asked. "Where do we go?"

"The trailhead." The driver pointed to a pile of railroad ties. Nothing but the darkness of the mountain beyond.

"You cannot leave us here." Marisol imagined the horrific night. Lost on a mountain with *un coyote estúpido*, whose only competence was probably as a rapist.

"It don't look like it, but there's a good trail," the driver said. "You go up one side of the mountain, come down the other. You'll cross a creek and reach another trailhead, looks just like this one. I'll be there in the morning and take you to the stash house in Ocotillo."

"Ocotillo?" Marisol said, fear creeping up her spine. "But we are going to Calexico."

"Too much heat to go that far. Ocotillo's closer."

"But my son. He will not know where I am."

"Tough shit," the driver snapped. He gestured toward the women in the backseat. "Git out! *¡Vaya! ¡Vaya!*"

Marisol grabbed El Tigre by an arm. "Take me back! Take me to my son now."

"There is no going back," he said glumly, staring at the looming mountain.

They navigated by the light of the stars. No flashlights allowed. Border agents with rifles patrolled these mountains on horseback, El Tigre claimed. Citizen militias, too. Drunken men with guns. Scurrying on all fours up a steep path, she thought she saw a mountain lion. But maybe she imagined it.

Minutes later, an animal howled in the darkness. Eerie, nearly human screams. A peasant Guatemalan woman crossed herself and chanted prayers. Claimed the animal was a *chupacabra*, the bloodsucking creature of myth.

The endless, unknowable night, Marisol thought, had hardly begun.

THIRTEEN

Waiting in the canyon near the border, Tino watched Rey answer his cell phone. El Tigre calling. Rey listened a few seconds. Stomped in a circle. Shouted, *"¡Chingalo! ¡Chingalo!"*

Listened some more. "What am I supposed to do with them?"

Two more *"chingalos."*

"No time to babysit, Uncle. I got my own delivery to make."

"Where's *mi mami*?" Tino demanded when Rey hung up.

"Sucking a border agent's cock," Rey taunted him. "Now, shut up, *chilito*!"

All my fault, Tino thought for the hundredth time. Blaming himself, for who else could he blame? Because of him, they had to run. He wanted to race through the canyons all the way to the border. Desperate to find his mother. Wanting to feel her arms around him.

Rey wouldn't say what had happened. Just waved his pistol and screamed at Tino and the four men to get in the truck. They sped back to La Rumorosa along the same winding road, sliding through steep turns, Tino scraping his elbows in the cargo bed.

Once back at the stone house, Rey grabbed a submachine gun—a Mac-10 Tino recognized from TV shows—and herded the four men into the house, locking them in a back room.

"But you, *chilito . . .* " He waved the gun barrel toward Tino. "You are coming with us."

Before Tino could answer, Rey swung the gun toward a small tree and fired a burst, nearly cutting the trunk in half. Rey's two friends—the morons he called "Mundo" and "Chuco"—laughed like donkeys. They all rapped knuckles and passed around a bottle of wine. Rey offered Tino a sip, but he shook his head, and all three brayed some more, calling him *"lambiscón."*

"I'm no suck ass," Tino said, and they laughed some more.

After several minutes of shooting the gun and drinking the wine, Rey grabbed Tino's backpack and yanked it open. Three T-shirts, two pairs of jeans, some socks. "Nothing but shit here, *cabrón.*"

Tino remained silent. Unwilling to show his fear, hoping they could not see his knees wobbling like a broken bicycle.

Rey pulled out Tino's prized baseball glove. A Vinny Castilla model. Soft brown leather with an aroma better than fresh-baked bread. He had bought the glove with the money he earned delivering lunch to workers at his mother's job site.

Rey smacked Tino across the face with the glove. Turned to his friends. "Ay! Mama's boy thinks he is a baseball player."

He tossed the glove to Mundo, who tossed it to Chuco. All of them seemed to be around the same age. Nineteen or twenty. Shaved heads. Dirty clothes. Stinky bodies. Scratchy facial hair like grass trying to grow out of sand. Now all three pawed through Tino's belongings, mangy dogs at a garbage can.

After finding nothing of interest other than the baseball glove, Rey ordered Tino to take off his shirt. Tino shook his head, and the two others grabbed him, stripped off the shirt, and pinned his arms behind his back.

Mundo grabbed the chain around Tino's neck. Attached to the end was a clear plastic envelope, and inside, a photo of his mother. "Look, *chilito* still sucks his mother's tit."

More laughs, all around.

Rey disappeared into the house, while Mundo and Chuco pushed Tino to the ground. Mundo ripped Tino's sweatpants down to his knees. Tino squirmed and yelled, fearing they were perverts. He got one arm free and flailed at them. He would die fighting before he would let the filthy *maricóns* soil him.

Chuco pulled the sweatpants completely off, then took a knife to the material that enclosed the drawstring. When the cloth tore open, four twenty-dollar bills, rolled up tight, popped out. Tino had put the money there, just as El Tigre had advised, to keep it safe from thieves. Chuco grunted his pleasure and grabbed the bills. Mundo pinned Tino to the ground, the boy screaming, "Give it back! That's all I have!"

Rey returned, straddled Tino, and placed a plastic bag filled with white powder on his chest. It took Tino a moment to figure out what was going on.

¡*Cocaina!* They were not perverts. They were drug traffickers.

Rey wrapped a long strand of tape around Tino's chest, securing the bag in place. They flipped him and taped two more bags on his back.

And they're making me their mule!

Chuco and Mundo carried Tino, still struggling, onto the cargo bed of the truck, opened the toolbox, removed a false bottom, and placed him inside.

"Me and my *carnales,* we're *Eme,*" Rey said.

Mexican Mafia. Tino didn't believe it for a second. These guys were stupid peasants who sold drugs without kicking up a percentage to *La Eme.*

"You got some work to do for us, *chilito,*" Rey continued. "And if you fuck it up, you're gonna get tagged and bagged." He slammed a piece of plywood into a slot, sealing off Tino.

The plywood groaned above Tino's head, tools clattering into the upper half of the box to cover up the false bottom. Then, the *click* of a padlock. Silence. Tino was as alone as a corpse in a coffin. The only light seeped through tiny airholes drilled in the side of the box.

He felt the fear close tight around his heart, fought against it, could not conquer it. But then he came to a realization that startled him, made him feel the passage from boyhood to manhood in one moment of flaming brilliance, as if from a shooting star. He cared for another person more than for himself. So he was not afraid to die. But he could not stand the thought of his mother's heartache if tonight he vanished from the face of the earth.

FOURTEEN

Jimmy Payne clawed through the cobwebs of sleep and awoke on the sofa in his office. His stomach felt as if he'd eaten the shells along with the oysters the night before. His mouth seemed to be full of burrs.

It was the morning after Judge Rollins committed suicide, but Payne had little time to grieve or examine his own complicity in the death. A smear of the morning sun peeked through a dirt-streaked window.

He was late for court.

Payne got up stiffly, his right leg feeling as if someone had filled it with sand. Ever since his femur was patched together with a metal plate and screws, it took half a day to loosen up the muscles and ligaments. A headache dug in like the infantry on D-Day. Popped three aspirin, swallowed them dry. Grabbed his emergency dark suit and a clean shirt from the top of a bookcase.

Tossing aside a mountain of legal papers and unpaid bills, he dug out the file labeled *People v. Scirotto*. Then J. Atticus Payne, Esquire, headed to court, certain this was going to be a six-aspirin day.

Unshaven and unshowered, his head throbbing and shirttail flapping, Payne limped along a corridor of the Van Nuys Courthouse.

Why are people staring?

Haven't they ever seen a lawyer late to court?

No, that's not it.

Less than twenty-four hours ago, Payne was in this very building, on this very floor, in the chambers of the not-so-Honorable Walter Rollins. Less than twelve hours ago, Rollins put a bullet through his temple, rather than face bribery charges. The news had already spread through the courthouse—a beehive of fluttering wings and wagging tongues—that Payne had set up the judge in a sting operation.

Now it seemed that every lawyer, bailiff, secretary, jail guard, probation officer, and three-time loser was glaring at Payne.

"Fucking rat." The words were spat by a rotund, oafish P.D., a young man who thought he'd been ordained by the gods of justice to spring every robber, rapist, and burglar in Southern California.

"Unbelievable, Payne," said a court clerk, a pretty African-American woman who admonished jurors each day not to speak to lawyers, lest some communicable disease be transmitted.

"Asqueroso," hissed Maria, Judge Kelton's stenographer, a woman Payne had thought about asking out. Calling him an asshole probably ruled out margaritas after work.

Payne quickened his pace, and nearly ran into the blocky backside of Mel Grossbard.

"Yo, Suds," Payne greeted him. The lawyer earned the nickname after beating a DUI rap for a drunk truck driver who overturned his rig and spilled twelve hundred cases of Budweiser. "What's up, pal?"

"Morning, douche bag."

"Not you, too, Suds."

"You think a judge will ever appoint you to a case? It's over, Payne. You'll never eat matzoh in this town again."

"I'm not Jewish."

"Thank God. We got enough schlemiels without you."

Judge Gordon Kelton had a weak chin, a weedy mustache, and a pasty face with the grayish hue of a towel in a cheap motel. He wore rimless glasses perched on a nose as pink and pitted as a strawberry. Thin shreds of dishwater brown hair were raked up and over, but failed to cover his egg-shaped skull. To Payne, he resembled Heinrich Himmler, though without the sense of humor.

Payne had never had much luck in Judge Kelton's courtroom, but today was a no-brainer. A quickie guilty plea in the case of *People v. Scirotto*. Three years in the can plus three years probation for a botched 7-Eleven holdup.

Maybe if Payne hadn't been hung over, he would have heard the hoofbeats and sensed the ambush coming round the bend.

"The court rejects the plea," Judge Kelton said, matter-of-factly.

"What?"

" 'What, Your Honor,' " the judge corrected.

What the fuck, Your Honor, Payne thought.

"Your Honor," he said, politely, "both the State and defense have agreed to the plea after full consideration of—"

"The State withdraws its offer," said Richard Zinn. The fuzzy-cheeked prosecutor lived in Kelton's courtroom, sucked at Kelton's teat, and depended on Kelton's recommendation for a juicy job downtown.

"What the hell, Rich?"

"Address your remarks to the bench, Counselor." The judge eyed Payne as if he'd just tasted curdled milk. "And kindly refrain from profanity."

"Your Honor. Why you busting my chops?"

"Trial is set for next Monday at eleven A.M."

"Judge. Your Honor. Sir . . ." Payne stopped just short of *Your Holiness*. "A trial would be a waste of judicial resources."

"What's wrong, Mr. Payne? Too busy entrapping judges to try a case?"

Payne's headache pounded in his ears. "Respectfully, that's bullshit, Your Honor."

The judge removed his spectacles, blew on them, and wiped the lenses on his black robe. "Tell me something, Mr. Payne. Did you suffer brain damage in that crash on the P.C.H.?"

Payne felt a ball of fire rising in his chest. His cheeks reddened. "What I suffered is none of your damn business."

"They should have disbarred you for that fiasco in the trailer-truck case." The judge pointed a bony finger at Payne. "The justice system requires dignity and respect."

"Only when it's earned." The fireball scorched Payne's throat.

"Now, I know you've had personal problems . . ."

"You don't know shit, you old tea bag. You may not be as crooked as Walter Rollins, but you're twice as stupid."

Bang! The judge's gavel echoed. "You're in contempt of court."

"Contempt doesn't begin to describe my feelings," Payne shot back. "How about *disgust*? Throw in some revulsion and a pinch of nausea, too."

"Bailiff, escort Mr. Payne to a holding cell. Twenty-four hours, and then we'll hear his apology."

"Gonna take longer than that." Payne felt his ears begin to melt.

"Make it forty-eight hours. Bailiff!"

Orvis Cosgrove, the uniformed bailiff, was a retired

airport parking lot attendant with painful bunions. He was nearing seventy and enjoyed napping during trials. He used both hands to lever himself out of his chair, his knees crackling like twigs in a fire. Orvis adjusted the crotch of his trousers, then guided Payne by the elbow through a rear door of the courtroom.

When they were in a windowless corridor leading to the holding cells, Payne said, "Orvis, I'm not going back there."

"You gonna escape, Jimmy?"

"Yeah."

"You gonna punch me?"

"Do I have to?"

"Nah. I'll just say you ran and I couldn't catch you."

"Works for me, Orvis."

"Say, Jimmy, everybody knows Rollins was so dirty he could lose weight by taking a shower. But you broke the code. A defense lawyer can't be a snitch."

"I'm hoping it blows over."

The bailiff's laugh sounded like a man choking on a chicken bone. "Sorry, Jimmy, but you best be thinking of another line of work."

Five minutes later, Payne was driving south on the 101. His seething anger had turned inward. If self-loathing were an Olympic sport, he'd give himself the gold medal. Yep, he'd changed his life all right. He'd plunged straight to the bottom.

Traffic was light by L.A. standards. In twenty-five minutes, he'd exited the freeway at Broadway, crossed Cesar Chavez Avenue, and hung a right on Ord, where he slowed to avoid a homeless man pushing a supermarket cart filled, incongruously, with empty soda bottles and a flat-screen TV.

By the time Payne reached Main and Alameda, he

was certain the day could not get any worse. But as usual, he was completely mistaken.

FIFTEEN

It was morning. An orange glow draped the distant peaks like a silk scarf on a woman's shoulders. Blood trickled down Marisol's leg. Barely slowing, she pinched the spot and pried out the thorn of a prickly pear. The path to the U.S.A., it seemed, was indeed a trail of thorns. For hours, she had climbed canyons and descended into ravines. She was in *los Estados Unidos,* but it still looked and felt like *Méjico.*

Six of them—five women and the reptile who called himself "El Tigre"—had spent the night scrambling up slopes, hand over hand, then sliding painfully down rocky paths on the seat of their pants. The trail was overgrown with spiny cactus and hanging vines. The air smelled of sage one moment and skunk the next. A coyote, the four-legged variety, whooped in the distance, and another answered with a series of mournful wails.

Marisol's legs ached, and a blister had formed on her right heel. She heard one of the *campesinas* sobbing. Farther back, the two Guatemalan women had run out of water. An hour earlier, Marisol let them sip from a gallon jug she carried. But how long must the water last? Hours or days?

She recited prayers to keep from losing hope. Remembered the words from Exodus. "I have been a stranger in a strange land." She thought of her father, the nonbeliever, who would laugh at anyone who expected God to provide manna from heaven or water from a rock.

That boulder, the one shaped like a camel. Didn't we pass it before?

They should have reached the trailhead by now. The American driver should have picked them up and taken them to the stash house in Ocotillo. Did El Tigre have any idea where they were? Huffing and puffing uphill, he carried his big belly like a wheelbarrow filled with bricks. Downhill, he stumbled and tripped, setting off little avalanches of rocks.

Moving gingerly along a rocky ledge, high above a dry wash, Marisol tried to concentrate on every step. But her mind was elsewhere.

Where is Agustino? Where is my boy?

Able to contain herself no longer, she shouted at El Tigre, "We are lost!"

"Shut up, woman!" He slashed a hand toward the pair falling behind. "*¡Chucas!* Hurry up! Keep together. We are almost there."

"You don't know where we are," Marisol countered. "You have put everyone in danger."

El Tigre scowled. "Do you know what they call a woman crossing the border by herself? *La chingorda.* The fucked one!" He reached down and grabbed his groin, shaking his sack the way a gambler might jiggle a pair of dice. "Do you know what I have for you here, princess?"

"A vile disease?"

In the fiery glow of the rising sun, his face flared with anger. If ever a man looked like the devil incarnate,

Marisol thought, it was this total waste of human protoplasm.

"You are not special, *chica*. To me, you are no better than those Guatemalan cows shitting in the bushes."

He continued along the ledge, muttering curses.

What a fool, Marisol thought.

But what of me? How could I have placed our lives in the hands of such a man?

Perhaps it would be better if the Border Patrol captured her. She would be sent back. Tino was still in Mexico.

Or was he?

She could not know for certain. All she knew was that she must survive. It is what a mother does for her child.

She thought of her own parents, remembering the hard times in the village near Caborca when her father no longer wore the crisp jumpsuit of the Ford Motor Company. When she was twelve—Tino's age now—Marisol would run to her father's job site the moment school was over. She carried buckets of nails, climbed scaffolds, learned to hammer straight and paint without making a mess.

There came a time that Edgardo Perez could no longer find work. Each day, he brought a book to a small cantina. There he consumed ample quantities of Octavio Paz's writing and Tijuana Morena's beer. Her father loved debating politics with his neighbors who—uncharitably—called him a *comunista*.

"Make up your minds," Edgardo Perez told them. "*Aristocracia* or *comunista*? I cannot be both!"

With money as scarce as desert rain, Marisol's mother took a job in a small fireworks factory, rolling sheets of cardboard into tubes, packing the casings with gunpowder, inserting fuses. Day after day, for eight years, until a horrific fire and explosion killed her. There was not enough left of her to bury. Grief settled over Marisol like a shroud of ashes. Despair filled her, heavy as oil in a drum.

At first, Edgardo blamed the government for his wife's death. Hadn't inspectors taken bribes and ignored safety violations? Next, he blamed Catholicism— "world's greatest superstition"—for hadn't his wife gone to Mass almost every day for forty years? But most of all, he blamed himself. If he had not lost the job in the Ford plant, his wife never would have needed to work. She would be home now, tending her flowers.

Edgardo halted his daily reading but continued his hourly drinking. Six months after his wife's funeral, he stumbled into the path of a car on a darkened street, and Marisol was alone. Shortly after that, she met Gustavo, who would become the father of her son. But he left town as quickly as a wind through the canyon.

Men, she thought. So unreliable.

El hombre promete, promete, y promete. ¡Hasta que te la mete!

The man promises, promises, and promises. Until he gets it in!

Now Marisol watched the morning sun slowly turn the rocks into the color of melted butter. Surely, they should have reached the trailhead by now. They were lost. Would the driver wait for them at the trailhead? Would he even show up?

Suddenly, a throttling noise overhead.

Helicopter! Shining silver, a dagger in the sunlight. Border Patrol!

She dived off the path into a patch of buffalo grass, snakes be damned. The others scattered. The *whopetta-whopetta* grew louder.

She abandoned any thought of surrender. She would run. As long as she was free, she could look for Tino.

And she swore on the spirits of her mother and father that she would find him.

SIXTEEN

Payne had big news for Sharon. He just didn't know how to tell her. Surreptitiously, he watched her attack a double-dipped roast beef sandwich, pausing only to gobble her fries. He always admired his ex-wife for eating like a cop and looking like a volleyball player.

And she was both.

Sharon had a business degree from U.C.L.A., where she'd also played varsity volleyball. After college, she competed in triathlons and learned kickboxing. Payne long suspected she could whip his ass.

The first time he saw her—a dozen years ago—Sharon was digging the ball off the top of the sand at Will Rogers Beach in Santa Monica. Five foot ten barefoot. Bikini briefs and halter top. Long, tanned, muscular legs. Lips with a natural pucker, as if she never stopped whistling.

Payne remembered sucking in his gut, straightening his posture, and watching her until the sun sizzled into the ocean. A two-on-two tournament, all former college varsity players, some on the professional tour. Payne never took his eyes off her. Reddish-brown hair tied in a ponytail, a sprinkle of freckles, an exuberant laugh when she high-fived her partner. Sharon specialized in defense. Blocking, digging, passing, and setting for her partner, who got all the glory for spiking the bejeesus out of the ball while Sharon swallowed mouthfuls of sand.

It said something about her character, he thought. Never seeking the spotlight, always content to be a team player. They started dating, and Payne discovered Sharon was smart, warm, caring, giving, and funny. To this day, he wondered how he had tricked such a terrific woman into loving him.

Sharon sat at a scarred wooden table at Phillipe, a hundred-year-old dive a block from Union Station. The place served up juicy sandwiches, free parking, and, for old times' sake, ten-cent coffee. Paper plates, sawdust floors, and neon beer signs.

No more bikinis. Sharon wore a glen plaid business suit with a shoulder holster underneath. Sensible black pumps. Her legs still had their definition but not much of a tan. She sat with a young woman prosecutor from the D.A.'s office who picked at a boring green salad.

Payne watched Sharon submerge her French dip sandwich into its juice, then take a bite that would not be called "dainty." The sight never failed to arouse him. Back in his single days, Payne concluded that female carnivores were more ferocious in bed, even if they burped occasionally.

Now he sneaked up on her in mid-chew. "Sharon, we gotta talk."

"Atticus!" She swallowed a chunk of beef and wiped her mouth with a napkin. "What are you doing here?"

He glanced around the crowded restaurant. "Can we go outside a second?"

She popped a fry into her mouth, excused herself, and followed him out the door and onto the sidewalk.

"You look great, Sharon." Warming up, trying to figure where to begin. "How's what's-his-name, the Mouth of the Southland?"

"Cullen's fine. Railing about illegals and Simeon Rutledge, but that's nothing new. He's still waiting to hear about a job with Fox."

"I hope they assign him to Mozambique."

"So, why are you here?"

He just blurted it out. "I'm gonna change my life."

"Too little, too late. And too unbelievable."

"I mean it this time. Going someplace where I can get a fresh start."

She studied him a second as a sixteen-wheeler drove by, grinding its gears. "Are you asking me to go along? To hit the road, get a fresh start with you?"

Her questions hung there like a colorful piñata, so he took a whack with his best swing. "It's occurred to me. Change is good, right? And you're stuck in a rut at the Department. So, why not go for some excitement?"

"First, because I love my work. Second, I'm engaged to Cullen."

"Funny, you didn't say you *love* Cullen."

"Stop it, Jimmy."

"Okay. Okay. I just thought that you and me and Adam—"

"Dammit! You need to get some help, Jimmy. Face the facts."

They were both quiet a moment. Then her face softened. "I'm sorry. You must be hurting. I heard about Judge Rollins."

"Yeah. It stinks."

She gave him a look both tender and compassionate, a queen tossing alms to a beggar. "But Jimmy, it's not like you to run away."

"Leaving first thing tomorrow."

She pursed her already puckered lips, giving the optical illusion that she wanted to be kissed. But as Payne knew, she was processing information. After a moment, she said, "Is there anything I can do to help you?"

"Maybe let Adam sleep over tonight."

A shudder went through her body, as if an icy wind had chilled her. "Not this again, Jimmy. Please."

"I'm not gonna kidnap him or anything. I'll take him to school tomorrow and—"

She slapped him. Hard. An open palm against the face, a *crack* as if she'd smacked the volleyball. He staggered a step backward.

"Hey, Detective Payne," a man called out. "Careful, or I'll bust you for assault." Two other men hooted and honked like migrating geese.

The wise guy was Detective Eugene Rigney. A pair of plainclothes buddies with him, heading for the restaurant.

Payne didn't think about what he did next. He just did it. Leapt at Rigney, wrapped both hands around his neck, knocked him back into the restaurant window, the glass shuddering.

Payne heard himself screaming "bastard" and "suckered me" and "nothing left."

"I got nothing left!"

Heard Sharon, too, shouting at him to stop.

Saw the startled look in Rigney's eyes, his hands clawing at Payne's fingers.

Felt sparks flash down his spine, one of the other cops slugging him in the back of the neck. Then a punch to the kidneys that loosened Payne's grip and dropped him to the pavement. Then the hard-shoed kicks. His back. His gut. Inches from his nuts. Cops were great kickers.

He curled into a ball, protecting the family jewels with one hand, his patched leg with the other.

"Stop it!" Sharon shouted, pulling the men off him.

Rigney was coughing and squawking, his voice hoarse. "You fucking loser. If your ex wasn't a cop, I'd toast your ass right here."

"We oughta arrest him," one of his buddies said. "Assaulting an officer."

Sharon got between the men and Payne, who was on all fours, struggling to get to one knee. "Go eat lunch, guys," she told them. "No harm, no foul."

"No harm?" Payne said. "I think I have internal injuries."

"Shut up, Atticus."

Rigney spat on the sidewalk, muttered several multisyllable words that all seemed to have "mother" in them, then led his pals inside.

Sharon crouched down and cradled Payne's head in her palms. Her hands felt cool to the touch on his blazing cheeks. He thought he might cry.

Jeez, what's wrong with me?

When she spoke, her voice was as sweet as a lover's lament. "Jimmy, I want you to get some help."

"I'll be fine once I piss some blood."

"Not what I'm talking about. You know what I mean."

"What?"

She pulled his face to her chest, his chin resting between her breasts. He could stay here a while. Like forever.

"Oh, Jimmy. Baby . . ."

Oh, man. How long since she called him that, her voice soft as a feather? How long since her eyes shone like silk, the color of honey?

"Jimmy. Listen to me. You can't see Adam tonight."

"No?"

"Not tonight. Not tomorrow. Not ever."

Pain, hot as lava, boiled through his body. He felt his

chest tighten, his stomach knot. He wanted to scream at Sharon to stop.

I don't want to hear this!

"Adam's dead," she breathed into his ear. "He's been dead over a year. A Saturday morning on the P.C.H. You were driving the car."

Payne's head throbbed. Boulders careened down a mountain slope, crashed into one another, shook the ground.

Still cupping his face, she wouldn't let him look away, even as his eyes moistened. "Why torture yourself this way? Why torture me?"

A boulder landed on top of him, crushing his skull, grinding him into dust.

Tears tracked down her face. "Our little boy is gone, Jimmy. It doesn't mean we should forget him. But we can't pretend he's still here. Do you understand?"

A tremble ran through his body.

"Jimmy! Answer me!" Her voice sharpening, a finger poked in his eye.

"I understand."

"Do you? Because it's not enough just to say it."

What is enough?

Nothing he could think of.

He'd visited therapists, studied the motel artwork on their walls, listened to their New Age music, all flutes and zithers. Answered their questions as they tiptoed around the stages of grief. Denial. Anger. Bargaining. Blah-blah-blah.

"Do you have suicidal ideations?"

"I have homicidal ideations."

"You want to kill the other driver? The illegal alien."

"Didn't matter he was illegal. He was drunk. And he ran."

Another shrink touted the "healing placidity of Zen." Oddly, the guy had nervous, fluttering hands with nicotine-stained fingernails. He told Jimmy a parable about a man being chased by a tiger. The man leaps off a cliff and grabs a vine. Looking down, he sees another tiger, waiting to devour him. Terrified, the man notices a wild strawberry growing out of the cliff. He swings on the vine and plucks the strawberry from its bush.

"*Oh, how sweet it tasted!*" *the shrink burbled.*

"*I see the tigers,*" Payne said. "*But where's my fucking strawberry?*"

Now Sharon gently ran a hand through his hair. When she spoke, her voice was strained, a dam holding back a flood. "You have to accept our losing Adam. You have to move on, Jimmy. If you don't, you won't make it. You'll die."

SEVENTEEN

Payne drives a vintage Pontiac Firebird, gold as the setting sun. Just like Jim Rockford in the old TV series.

Growling at 60 on a straight stretch of the Pacific Coast Highway, north of the Palisades. Gray, misty morning, onshore breeze ripping at the sand, two fun boards lashed to the roof rack.

Adam says something about the waves looking small and mushy, and if it's not a good day, maybe they can leave early and play catch at the park. Payne saying, fine with him, the water looking cold as steel.

Nearing Malibu, Payne's eyes flick toward the beach, appraising the waves, watching gray terns scavenging the shorebreak.

The blink of an eye, a flash of red to his right, the mere notion of a color, nothing more.

A pickup truck runs the red light at Topanga Canyon, slashes at them from the passenger side. Never braking, just plowing into the Firebird.

Payne instinctively reaches across Adam's chest to press him into his seat. Even belted, Adam is thrown sideways, his head whipping left and right, a rag doll, the crack and snap of vertebrae lost in the explosion of steel and glass. The Firebird catapults across the highway and smashes into a concrete barrier.

Adam doesn't cry out. Just a whoosh of air from his lungs, a gurgling from his throat.

Payne blinks to clear his eyes, hot rivulets of blood streaming from his scalp. He's pinned between his son and the driver's door, which itself is jammed against the concrete barrier. Then the pain. It hits Payne so hard he cannot isolate it, cannot tell torso from limb, but he is reasonably certain his right leg is twisted into an unnatural position. He cannot see his son, though he feels the dead weight of him.

"Adam. Adam, can you hear me?"

A man's voice from outside the driver's-side window. "Lo siento mucho."

"My son," Payne says. "Can you see him? Is he okay?"

The man leans through the open window. Leathery skin as creased as an old belt. The rank odor of tobacco and beer overladen with a fishy smell.

"El chico. El chico. ¡Dios me perdone!"

Suddenly, he is gone, his smell lingering. Footsteps,

the man running along the pavement, the sound fading. Payne hears ocean swells, but when his eyes close, his mind pictures not the surf, but waves of blood pounding a black sand beach.

EIGHTEEN

Lying facedown under a palm tree, Tino's chest was on fire. Moments earlier, Rey and his two idiot friends had ripped off the duct tape, removed the bags of cocaine, and dumped him.

Tino touched his chest, ran a finger around his back. Red and blistered, the tape shredding his skin. He felt dehydrated, disoriented, hungry. It seemed to be midday, the sun high in the sky. City noises. Traffic. Horns.

Where am I? Where is my mother? What is this place?

He got to his feet, blinked against the glare. Used hypodermic needles were scattered on the ground. The sound of splashing water. A large pond, a lake really, with a shooting fountain. He scrambled to its edge, drank from the water, which tasted of rust and algae. On a nearby path, two black women in nurses' uniforms stared at him, eyes alarmed, as if they'd just seen a mouse in the cupboard.

He tied the drawstring of his torn sweatpants and got to his feet. Not far away, towering skyscrapers gleamed in the sunlight. The tallest buildings he had ever seen. He must be in the United States, but where?

He wanted to get moving. What if Rey and the other two came back? What if *La Eme* was looking for him? Or the Border Patrol?

Stiff and aching, he walked along a path that ran past a row of palm trees. A filthy, bearded man in ragged clothes lay snoring alongside a metal shopping cart filled with junk. The man smelled of piss and vomit. Hands folded together on his chest like Tino's *abuelo* in the funeral home. Between the man's knobby fingers, an open bag of potato chips. Tino carefully pried the bag from the man's filthy hand. A grunt, a snort, and the man opened runny eyes that seemed to look in different directions.

"Fucking little greaser!" The man reached for a broom handle under his cart and swung wildly.

Tino ran.

Wherever he was, it was a scarier place than La Rumorosa with those *narcotraficantes*. Running along a path, he saw a boathouse at the edge of the lake. A park, he realized. A park in the middle of a city. He came to an intersection of two busy streets and read the signs. Alvarado. Wilshire.

He chose Wilshire. Ran past a sign for Westlake Avenue, another for Bonnie Brae. Kept running. Past big buildings and parking lots. Burlington. Union. Loma. Feeling stronger with each block flying by. Believing if he ran far enough and fast enough, he could find his mother. Knowing the foolishness of the thought almost before it was formed.

He heard a noise overhead and looked up. A helicopter with police markings. So low and so loud he was certain it had come for him. The Border Patrol? Or the F.B.I.? *They knew about the cocaine.* He saw the markings on the helicopter: *L.A.F.D.*

Los Angeles Fire Department.
Los Angeles!

The helicopter veered toward a huge building, hovered, then descended to its roof. A sign in front of the building: *Good Samaritan Hospital.*

Tino remembered his mother reading him the story of the Good Samaritan from a Bible with pictures. Robbers attack a man walking along a road. They beat him and take his clothes and money. No one will stop and help the man. Someone from the Samaritan tribe comes along. He bandages the man's wounds, takes him to an inn, feeds him, and gives him money. And Jesus says that's how you get to live forever.

A really nice story. Except the stuff from the Bible never happens in real life. In real life, if you're lying by the road, bleeding, someone comes along and steals your shoes.

My Reeboks!

Tino untied his laces, pulled off his right shoe, removed the insole. There was the crumpled card his mother had given him. "J. Atticus Payne, Esquire." A very important man. One of the biggest lawyers in Los Angeles.

"If anything bad happens and I am not there, go see Mr. Payne."

Tino studied the address. Delano Street. He had no idea how to get there. No money. No papers. But his mother had taught him to be brave.

"You're my little valiente."

He looked left. Looked right. Then he started walking.

Cars went by, but few people were on the sidewalk. When he spotted an Anglo woman, he asked in English where he could find a bus station, but she stepped off the curb to avoid him.

Two hours passed. The sleepless night began to take

its toll. Fatigue crawled up his legs. Hunger gnawed at his gut.

A police car rolled past. The cop eyed him, suspiciously. Tino fought the urge to run. The police car kept going.

He stopped in front of a small, neat house and watched as a man with hands stained the color of carne asada fertilized a flower bed. The bed was filled with plants taller than Tino. Stems topped by purple and orange flowers shaped like birds' beaks.

"Flor ave del paraíso," the gardener told him.

Birds of paradise.

Beautiful. Tino had seen them once before, surrounding the house of a rich family in Caborca.

The gardener wiped his forehead with a handkerchief and offered cold water from a cooler. When Tino told him he was hungry but had no money, out came a chicken tortilla wrapped in foil. And then another. The gardener was from Loreto in Baja. He had been here seven years without papers, and that made Tino feel better. He showed the man the card of Mr. J. Atticus Payne, Esquire.

"Van Nuys. I can tell you how to get there," the gardener said, proudly. "The subway station is within walking distance for a strong boy."

"I didn't know there was a subway here."

"Most *gabachos* do not know, either."

The gardener gave him directions to the Wilshire-Vermont station, with instructions to ride to Universal City. There, he would take a bus to Van Nuys. The gardener could not tell him exactly which bus to take, but a smart boy can figure it out. Then he gave Tino money. Winking, he said there are no toll collectors on the subway, so save a dollar twenty-five and buy a Coca-Cola. Use the rest for the bus.

Tino thanked the man and headed toward the subway station. Soon, he thought, he would be speaking to one of the most important lawyers in all of Los Angeles. A good man who had helped the poor *mojados* cooked in that trailer truck. As he walked, Tino grew more confident. J. Atticus Payne, he concluded, must truly be a Good Samaritan.

NINETEEN

Payne imagined swinging Adam's baseball bat.

Smashing Manuel Garcia over the head. Crushing bone to splinters, tissue to mush. Luxuriating in each *crack* and *squish*. Reveling in the blood, feeling no more guilt than a kid stomping a grasshopper.

But could he really do it? Thinking about killing was one thing. Watching the life seep out of a man was another. That was the debate raging inside him.

Payne had left Sharon at the restaurant, her face pale with worry. She had buckled him into the front seat of his Lexus, as if he were a child, giving him a little peck on the cheek. A charity kiss, to be sure.

His body aching from his run-in with the protect-and-serve crowd, Payne headed west on Wilshire. He had a notion about stopping at the La Brea Tar Pits. He used to take Adam to the museum there. All boys love dinosaurs and fossils. Adam would spend hours drawing pictures of the mammoths and saber-toothed tigers, whose remains have been preserved in the tar.

A few minutes into the drive, Payne saw a Home Depot, and by instinct, swung into the parking lot. Two dozen Hispanic men in dirty jeans, T-shirts, and ball caps squatted on their haunches or sat on the curb, smoking, talking, hoping for an honest day's work. Keenly appraising the shoppers exiting the store with lumber, plywood, paint. Offering their services in an eager Spanglish.

"Buen trabajador."

"Puedo arreglar todo bien rápido."

"¡Barato!"

Not a green card in the bunch, of course. A good deal for the homeowner too scared to clean his own roof gutters, too cheap to pay a licensed contractor.

The odds were great that Manuel Garcia wasn't within five hundred miles of here. But didn't Payne have to look, anyway?

Garcia was the driver of the blazing red Dodge Ram truck. An SRT-10 with the 500 horsepower Viper engine. Not the rusted-out Chevy pickup you'd expect an illegal immigrant to drive. Garcia was a solid citizen . . . of Mexico. Without papers, he'd landed a job on a sardine boat on the Monterey docks. He stayed out of trouble, manned double shifts, and with overtime was paid more than most schoolteachers. He sent money home to his wife and kids. He made a down payment on the Ram truck three weeks before driving to L.A., when the sardine boat went into dry dock for maintenance.

So it was by chance that, on a gray and misty Saturday morning fourteen months earlier, Jimmy and Adam Payne crossed paths with the hardworking and hard-drinking *mojado*. A man who would flee on foot from the crash, leaving behind his new truck and a dying boy.

Eight weeks after Adam's funeral and one day after

the cast came off his leg, Payne drove upstate and waited for the sardine boat to return to port. He stood on the dock, a copy of Garcia's driver's license photo in his pocket. He watched the boat, *Fish Reaper,* enter the harbor, a blizzard of cawing gulls tailing it. Garcia was not aboard. The crew hadn't seen him. The boat's skipper said he'd been a solid crewman, nimble with the nets. Never missed a day's work. Never gave anyone any problems, not even when he put away a case of beer on a Sunday night. A clerk at the cannery said Garcia had not picked up his last paycheck.

Payne drove inland and found Garcia's trailer in the little town of Spreckels.

No one home.

Payne broke the flimsy lock. The place clean, the air stuffy. Clothes folded. Small TV on a table of cinder blocks. Letters from his wife. Payne copied down the address from an envelope. The city of Oaxaca in Mexico.

For the next month, Payne haunted the Parker Center downtown. Each day, he'd drop in, taking the homicide detectives to lunch, following up with tips, rumors, ideas. The police couldn't find Garcia. A friend in Homeland Security got Payne a meeting with the regional director of the Border Patrol. No record of Garcia coming in or going out.

Payne carried Adam's aluminum baseball bat in his car. Each evening, when he should have been sitting home with Sharon, holding her, consoling her, he drove through the barrios of East L.A. One night, in Boyle Heights, he thought he saw Garcia walking out of a 7-Eleven. Payne yanked the car into the parking lot and jumped out, waving the baseball bat. "Remember me, asshole? You killed my son!"

The man froze, eyes blank with fear, as if Payne were insane. When he got close, Payne realized it wasn't Garcia. Didn't even look much like him. By this time, several bare-chested, tattooed young men in baggy pants had streamed out of the store. The gang known as K.A.M. Krazy Ass Mexicans. Payne jumped into his car and burned rubber, gunshots peppering his trunk.

Payne figured Garcia had returned home to avoid arrest. He called local police in Oaxaca. No help.

"I'm going to Mexico," he told Sharon three months after they had buried their son.

"Why?"

"To find Garcia."

"And then what?"

He didn't answer.

She begged him not to go. She needed him. She sobbed, shoulders heaving, even after there were no more tears. Jimmy stayed.

His grief formed its own universe, created its own gravity. Grief parched him, drained him of blood and filled him with dust. Grief encircled him like leather cinches on a madman, squeezing the breath from him. He was of no use to Sharon. Whatever she needed, he was unable to give.

A lapsed Catholic, Sharon sought peace in the stillness of Our Lady of Angels downtown. For hours, she sat alone in the sanctuary, sunlight streaming over her through alabaster mosaic windows. With its fifty-foot-high cross and its sunbaked concrete walls, the church was built to withstand an earthquake, but did little for heartache.

Sharon asked Payne to accompany her to Mass, just to hold her hand, just to feel his presence beside her. To the extent he believed in God at all, Payne preferred the pissed off curmudgeon of the Old Testament. That bearded sadist who delighted in flood and famine, plague and pestilence. Payne told Sharon that if she really believed the Father, Son, and Holy Ghost routine, maybe she should have prayed *before* Adam was killed.

It was just one of many thoughtless comments. Was he trying to salve his own pain by worsening hers? He had no idea.

Sharon seethed with anger. Payne wondered if she blamed him for the accident. She never said so, but the silent accusation hung in the air, enveloping them like a poisonous fog. He wanted to scream out:

"Jesus, Sharon. The bastard ran a red light."

But could Payne have avoided the crash? Was he driving too fast? If only he hadn't looked away—

She'd always told him to slow down, to be more careful. He resented her anger. She resented his resentment. They were divorced six months later.

But now, sitting in his car in the Home Depot lot, his son dead, his marriage over, his career ruined, Payne knew precisely what he had to do. This time there was no one to stop him, and no reason to stay.

He had to go to Mexico. He had to find Manuel Garcia. And he had to kill him.

TWENTY

The huge American woman held a rusty machete, her arm plump as a chicken. "C'mon. Git inside."

She pointed the machete at the five women and motioned toward the door of the wooden cabin.

The *Americana* was the largest woman Marisol had

ever seen. Her skin was the bluish white of milk drained
of its fat. Her stomach spilled out of purple nylon bas-
ketball shorts, and her bleached yellow hair was tied
around rollers, like steel cables looped on spools. She
must be the owner of the *clavo*, the stash house, Marisol
concluded. The house was actually half-a-dozen dilapi-
dated cabins next to railroad tracks outside the desert
town of Ocotillo, a few miles north of the border. A sign
out front read *Sugarloaf Lodge*, but there did not seem
to be any lodgers.

"What you waiting for?" the woman bawled at them.
"Git your brown butts inside now. *¡Vaya! !Vaya!*"

Dutifully, the women climbed the three sagging steps
and, like cattle, shouldered their way through the open
door.

"Not her." El Tigre blocked Marisol's path.

The woman waved her machete. "Don't be messing
with my wets, dickwad."

"Yours?"

"Till Ah get paid, you bet your ass."

El Tigre cursed her in Spanish. She shouted that he
owed her money. He yelled that the money was owed by
the *repartidor*, the labor contractor who would take
these worthless peasants to the farms and factories waiting for them.

They argued for several minutes, El Tigre boasting
that only his brilliance and bravery got them here at all.
They were nearly captured at the border. A Border Patrol helicopter missed seeing them on the mountain, as
he had cleverly placed the group so the sun would block
them from view. Despite great odds, the courageous El
Tigre located the trailhead and waited for the driver of
the Duster to bring them here.

He grabbed Marisol's arm and tried to pull her to
him.

The woman pointed the tip of the machete at El

Tigre's groin. "Ah got no problem chopping your little pecker into *chorizo* and feeding it to my dog."

"*¡Bacalao!*" Calling her the filthiest name a man can call a woman.

The woman barked a laugh that made her fleshy arms quiver. "Listen to the Frito Bandito. Pissy as a skunk."

El Tigre still had a grip on Marisol's arm. "This one owes me money."

"That don't give you the right to lay your hands on her. Ah've known men like you all my life, and Ah've drawn blood from more than a few. All without a goddamn regret."

She jabbed the machete between El Tigre's thighs. He hopped back a step and released his grip. Cursed once more, then stomped off.

Marisol nodded a thank-you to the large woman and climbed the steps to the cabin. Bare wooden floors, no furniture. An open toilet, one sink. Perforated metal screens sealing the windows. She sat on the floor, cross-legged, the fatigue and terror of the night seeping into her bones.

"Don't know if you gals speak American, but doncha worry," the huge woman said. "Wanda's got you covered. Welcome, one and all, to the promised fucking land."

TWENTY-ONE

Tino took the subway to the wrong station, then landed on the wrong bus. The street signs flew by, a blur of meaningless names.

Hollywood Freeway. Lankershim Boulevard. Sherman Way.

But where is Van Nuys and the office of Mr. J. Atticus Payne?

He asked for directions then changed buses, dozing off as an elderly couple next to him chattered in Chinese. Nine hours after heading for the subway station, the bus driver dropped him at a complex of government buildings and told him to walk the rest of the way.

The sun was setting as Tino passed the Van Nuys Courthouse. Close by, a one-story building had a flashing neon sign, *Bail Bonds*. Two young black women in very short skirts and very bright wigs walked out of the building. One wore a green stretchy top with letters as gold as melon seeds, spelling out, *"If You Think My T-Shirt Is Tight . . ."*

She spotted Tino and called, "Hi there, cutie!"

The other one approached and ran a hand over his head. "What I wouldn't give to have your hair."

Next door was another small office building. A sign said, *P. J. Steele, Private Investigations.* The windows were darkened glass, the place mysterious.

Two blocks away, he found Delano Street and a sign stuck into the front yard of a small house with peeling paint. *J. Atticus Payne, Esquire.* It was not what he had pictured. In the bus, he had passed tall silver buildings, thin as blades, rising to the sky. He thought that Mr. Payne must be in one of those buildings, conducting important business.

But this?

He walked onto the front porch, floorboards groaning. The door was locked, the windows dark. A driveway led to the back of the house. What must have been a small yard was now pavement with parking for three cars. Empty.

Now what? It was getting dark. Where would he spend the night?

And where is Mami spending this night?

Then he figured that Mr. Payne would be here in the morning.

And so will I.

Tino went to a small side window with three glass louvers in metal slats. Too small for anyone to crawl through. Except maybe a boy.

The window was cracked open two inches. Tino muscled the glass out of the slats and squeezed through, falling onto a tile floor. He found a light switch and looked around. A messy desk. Books. Files. Empty coffee cups, a paper bag greased with French fries. On the floor, cardboard boxes marked *Storage.*

He had never been in a lawyer's office, but he had seen them on *telenovelas.* Usually, a television lawyer had a fancy haircut, wore an expensive suit, and had sex with his beautiful secretary on a clean desk of polished wood. Here, the desk was dirty, and there would be no room for any fun.

Tino opened several cabinet doors. More papers and files.

Then, a liquor cabinet. Half a dozen bottles. He sampled the bourbon and made a face. Same with a bottle of

Scotch. Found a bottle of Chinaco Blanco tequila. Sipped it. Better than the stuff they served at the cantina at home. He found a coffee cup that was nearly clean and filled it.

Looked around some more. On the desk, a photo of a smiling man and a boy with wheat-colored hair, a little younger than himself. The boy wore a baseball uniform and cap. Baseball glove on his knee. Tino thought of his own baseball glove, taken by those *pendejos*. If he had a father, someone like the smiling man who must be J. Atticus Payne, no one would take his most valuable possession.

Tino sat in the cushioned chair behind the desk and spun in a circle, like the merry-go-round at the Caborca *carnaval*. He took another drink of the tequila. And then one more.

Opened the middle desk drawer. Dried-up pens, coins, stamps, a bottle of vitamins, some empty envelopes.

And one envelope that was full. Plump and weighty in the hand. Unsealed.

Filled with hundred-dollar bills!

Tino's breath caught in his throat. He glanced around as if someone might be watching. He felt guilty, like seeing one of the nuns naked.

But I haven't done anything. Yet.

Hastily, he turned off the lights. There was a small refrigerator on the floor behind the desk. Tino dropped to his knees, opened the door, and counted the money in the glow of the tiny light.

Fifty one-hundred-dollar bills.

His mother had taught him never to steal. But this was an emergency. With all that money, maybe he did not need Mr. Payne. From the looks of this office, the lawyer might not be as big and important as his mother had thought.

Tino thought of television shows he had seen. When someone is missing, you hire a private investigator, like the one down the street. P. J. Steele. He liked the name. Strong. American. A private eye could find his mother, Tino thought, especially if he is paid five thousand dollars.

Tino jammed the envelope with the money inside his underwear. He finished the tequila and suddenly felt very warm. He stretched out on the sofa. Maybe just a little nap and then he would leave. He did not need Mr. J. Atticus Payne and his crappy office. In the morning, Tino would be waiting at the front door of Mr. P. J. Steele, Private Investigator. Together, they would find his mother.

TWENTY-TWO

Seconds matter.

In just one second, a red truck flies through a red light and tilts the universe off its keel.

Now the tipping point was sixty seconds. If Payne had left his house one minute later, he would have been arrested. There would have been no road trip. There would be times, later, when he wondered if that wouldn't have been for the best.

On this night, at home, he put on jeans, running shoes, and an orange-and-black Barry Bonds T-shirt. He wasn't a fan of the San Francisco Giants or their former steroid-pumped slugger. He just liked to piss off people.

He threw a change of clothes into a gym bag and copied maps off the Internet. Driving directions to Oaxaca, the home of Manuel Garcia. Adam's old baseball bat was already in the Lexus, but Payne still needed something from his office. The five thousand he'd skimmed from the bribe money.

He left the house and was just pulling up to the stop sign half a block away when he checked his rear-view mirror. An L.A.P.D. black-and-white was pulling into his driveway. Sixty seconds. The difference between custody and freedom.

Two cops in uniform got out and headed for his front door.

No way they're delivering good news. Publishers Clearinghouse doesn't send patrolmen to give you that five-foot-long, million-dollar check. They were there to arrest him for escaping from the holding cell on his contempt charge. Maybe grand larceny, too. The crimes weren't worthy of a segment on *Dateline,* but who needs the hassle?

Payne hit the gas and headed toward Van Nuys Boulevard. He'd pick up the money and leave town straight from the office. Traffic would be light on the freeways. If all went well, he'd be checking into a motel near the border by dawn.

The neighborhood near the civic center was quiet, the offices dark. A lone clerk sat behind bulletproof glass in the bail bond office, open twenty-four hours. Payne pulled into the driveway of the old bungalow, cutting close to the sign planted in the lawn: *J. Atticus Payne, Esquire.* Soon it would read, *Office for Rent.*

Just as he killed the engine, his cell phone rang. Private Number. He answered with a noncommittal "Yeah?"

"Payne, you fucking asshole."

"That you, Rigney?"

"I saw the inventory from Judge Rollins' house. Forty-five thousand bucks recovered."

"So?"

"It's one thing to cheat at bowling, Payne. But you don't steal from the government."

"You take your salary, don't you?"

"There's an arrest warrant out for you."

"Maybe the judge bought a Rolex between the time I bribed him and he blew his brains out."

"You took the money, dipshit."

"You got any evidence, Detective? Maybe you skimmed the five grand and gave me forty-five."

"Gonna bust you, Payne. And when I do, your ex won't be around to wipe your nose."

Payne was working on a pithy retort when Rigney hung up. Time to get moving. When the cops couldn't find him at home, they would zip over here. He planned to be in and out of his office in two minutes.

He unlocked the back door, stepped into the darkened corridor where a water cooler hummed next to the photocopy machine. He was fumbling for the light switch when he heard a noise. What the hell?

"Who's there!"

A squeak. Sneakers on tile.

"I got a gun!" Payne shouted with the authority of a practiced liar.

He kept the lights off. He knew the configuration of the office. The intruder wouldn't. In the darkness, Payne navigated the short corridor. He ran his hand along the wall, passing over the door to the rest room, feeling the rounded edge of the five-gallon water jug atop the cooler, then stopping at the beveled corner of the book-shelf. Needing a diversion, he grabbed a volume of the *Pacific Reporter,* appellate court opinions that could cure insomnia. He aimed toward the opposite wall, where his diploma was framed under glass.

Southwestern School of Law, that bastion of learning on Wilshire.

Cum non laude.

He threw the book, shattering the glass frame of the diploma with a surprisingly loud crash.

A second later, a figure dashed across the room.

Headed for a small window, the port of entry.

Payne had the angle. Ran for the window, ignoring the pain in his bad leg. Dived and grabbed a sneakered foot, just as the bastard tried to climb out.

Pulled him back by a skinny ankle. The guy yelped and crashed to the floor. Payne jammed his throat with a forearm. Noodle neck. Dragged him across the office, hit the light switch, and looked straight into the eyes of . . . a boy!

Caramel complexion, a mop of shiny dark hair falling into green eyes with long girlish lashes. A cute kid. Angelic even.

"Get your fuckin' hands off me, *cabrón*!"

Okay, not *that* angelic.

"Watch your mouth, kid. What the hell are you doing?"

"Looking for *mi mami.*"

"She's not here. Now, what do you say I call the cops and let them haul you off?"

Even as he said it, Payne knew he couldn't call the police. They'd want to give the kid a medal and lock up his own contemptuous, larcenous self.

"No cops. Please, *Señor* Payne." The kid's tone had changed. Pleading now, in a Mexican accent.

"You know my name."

The kid pulled out the crinkled business card.

"Where'd you get that?"

"*Mami.* She got it from Fernando Rodriguez."

It took Payne a second. "The trailer-truck case?"

The kid nodded.

"I still don't get what you're doing here."

"My mother. I told you."

"Kid, don't bullshit a bullshitter."

"*Es verdad.*" His green eyes welled with tears. "My mother came over and disappeared."

Payne studied the boy. He seemed sincere, his sniffles real enough. Payne's gaze stopped on his desk. Middle drawer open.

"Kid, empty your pockets."

"Whatever you say, *gabacho.*"

"Did you just call me 'tomato soup'?"

"Not gazpacho. *Gabacho.* It means '*gringo.*'"

"All right, punk. Just hand over my money."

Fast as a snake, the kid kicked Payne in the balls. The pain closed Jimmy's eyes, and he sank to one knee. The kid bolted across the office, hoisted himself onto a low bookshelf, and swung both legs through the open window. Payne struggled to his feet but couldn't catch the little bastard. The kid was gone.

Cursing to himself and still wincing with pain, Payne leaned against the wall, sucking in air. A second later, the boy scrambled back through the window.

"What the hell?" Payne said.

"*¡La policia!* You can have your money back."

The kid pulled the wad of bills from his pants, and Payne sneaked a sideways glance out the window. A police car was parked next to his Lexus, which had all four doors open. Two uniforms with flashlights snooping inside. Payne decided not to shout about illegal searches.

"Please don't turn me over. They'll send me back. Please!" The kid reverting to his scared little-boy voice.

Payne stuffed the bills into his pants pockets. "You can quit the acting, punk."

"No, really. I'm scared."

"Great. That makes two of us."

Payne peeked out the window again. The cops were walking toward the back door of the office. One had his right hand on his holstered gun. The other used both hands to carry a battering ram. Either they planned to knock down Payne's door or crush his skull. Or both.

•

TWENTY-THREE

A loud rapping at the door. One of the cops banging away.

"James Payne! You in there?"

Payne quickly did the calculations. Even with his bum leg, he might be able to outrun a couple older cops stuffed with Krispy Kremes. But his glance out the window revealed these two to be of the young linebacker type. Pumped on steroid cocktails with a human growth hormone chaser. In any event, he probably couldn't fit out the window.

"Are you a fast runner?" Payne whispered.

"Like the wind," the kid boasted.

"Crawl out the window. Make some noise and run like hell. They'll chase you."

"They'll *shoot* me."

"No. But if they catch you, they might smack you around."

"Payne! We've got a warrant. Open up or we break down the door!"

"Go, kid. Now!"

The boy seemed to think it over. Then a sly smile dimpled his face. "They're looking for you, *chuco*. Not me. Why should I risk it?"

"I'll give you a hundred bucks."

"Two hundred."

"Jeez, what happened to that crying kid who was here a minute ago?"

"That's it, Payne! We're coming in." A *clang* as the battering ram pounded the old wooden door.

"Two hundred," the kid repeated.

"Okay. Half now. Half when I get out of here and pick you up." Payne peeled off a hundred and gave it to the kid. "Take a left out of the parking lot. Cross the street, duck behind the houses, and come out on the next block. Hang a right and get to Van Nuys Boulevard as fast as you can. I'll pick you up at the corner of Van Nuys and Tiara."

Payne helped the boy hoist himself up to the windowsill. Then the kid tumbled out, shouting, "Hey cop. *¡Chinga tu madre!*"

Foul-mouthed brat.

The boy took off, the cops yelling for him to stop. Payne edged close to the window. The kid could run. But only one cop followed him. The other resumed banging on the door.

Shit.

Payne headed down the corridor and ducked into the rest room, closing the door behind him. He had to pee, but that's not why he was here. When the cop passed the rest room, Payne could duck out of the office and run.

The rear door splintered and flew off its hinges. "Payne! Show yourself."

The office lights switched on. A thud on the bare carpet, the cop dropping the battering ram. Payne heard footsteps come closer. He pictured Officer Muscles with his gun drawn, walking cautiously along the corridor, just a few feet from the rest room.

"Mr. Payne. You okay?"

Good question, Payne thought. The cop had just seen a burglar flee the office. Maybe Mr. Payne was lying in a pool of blood. The cop wanted to rescue him; then he'd arrest him.

"You hurt?"

The voice more distant. Good. The cop must have passed the rest room and turned the corner. He'd be near the desk by now, looking around, moving slowly. Payne opened the door a crack, sneaked his hand toward the wall, and flicked off the light switch. The room went black.

"Hey! Who's there?" The cop yelling, fumbling for his flashlight.

Payne dashed into the corridor, toppling the water cooler behind him. The glass jar shattered, and a flood splashed his ankles as he raced out the back door. He heard the cop shout "Sh-it" as he slipped and fell.

Payne jumped into his Lexus and jammed the key into the ignition. He tore out of the parking lot, rounded a corner, and headed for Van Nuys Boulevard. In less than a minute he was at the corner of Tiara and Van Nuys. But where was the kid?

Probably ran off.

Looking for a pocket to pick.

Good story, though, searching for his mother. With proper schooling, the kid could make a helluva con man. Or even a lawyer.

Then Payne spotted him on the sidewalk. Walking half a step behind a family of four. Blending in, perfectly inconspicuous. Payne pulled to the curb. Before he came to a stop, the kid ran for the car and hopped into the passenger seat. Payne burned rubber pulling out, heading for the anonymity of the 101 freeway.

"My name's Tino, Mr. Payne," the boy said.

"Call me Jimmy."

Tino rapped knuckles with him. "Him-my," he said, "we make a good team."

"Yeah, great."

"Where's my other hundred?"

Payne reached into his pocket and gave the kid his money.

"Thanks, *vato*."

Before Payne could say he wasn't the kid's buddy, his cell phone rang. Sharon's number in the window.

"Rigney just called," she said. "Dammit, Jimmy, you're in big trouble."

"That's why I need you."

"For what?"

"That road trip I was talking about."

"No, Jimmy."

"Leaving tonight, and I need your help."

"No!"

"I'll be at your place in fifteen minutes."

"There are warrants out. Grand larceny. Contempt of court. Fleeing custody. If stupidity were a crime, there'd be another count."

"Fifteen minutes," he repeated. "Front door."

"I'll bust you."

"No, you won't," Payne said, feeling a sense of déjà vu. They'd had a similar conversation before. What was it?

Oh, that.

When she'd told him she was divorcing him. He hadn't believed her then, either.

TWENTY-FOUR

"Road trip."

Sharon hated the phrase. Jimmy had said it before, when he planned to go to Mexico and find Manuel Garcia. Not just *find* him. Kill him.

Hanging up the phone, she decided that the only way to help Jimmy was to protect him from himself. She would do what she had just promised. Arrest her ex-husband and take him downtown.

She knew the source of his problems. Jimmy had never come to grips with Adam's death. He either wallowed in his own pain or pretended their son was still alive. His mood swung from raging anger to mute alienation.

In her grief, Sharon had turned to Catholicism, while he embraced nihilism.

Not giving a hoot about anything or anyone, least of all himself.

Always reckless in the courtroom, after Adam's death he had become unhinged. He'd attacked an insurance company lawyer in a personal injury trial. Called the man a "lying, scumbag whore"—as if that were some startling revelation—and tossed him over the railing into the lap of juror number three. The judge ordered anger management counseling, which Payne said *really* pissed him off.

And now this. Stealing five thousand dollars in sting money. Then fleeing a holding cell in the courthouse and resisting arrest. What would he do, Sharon wondered, when she took him downtown?

She could hear him now.

"That's what I get for marrying an Irish cop."

He'd said it whenever she tried to keep him from crossing the hazy line between vigorous advocacy and downright illegality. Sharon's father, Daniel Lacy, was a Philadelphia cop. So were two of her uncles, three cousins, and both brothers. Born rebellious, Sharon was sixteen when she announced at Christmas dinner that she would never join the "family business," as the Lacys called police work.

She exhibited a wanderlust not commonplace in the Lacy brood. While her folks begged her to stay home and go to St. Joe's, she accepted a volleyball scholarship at U.C.L.A. She played the demanding libero position, which showcased her defensive skills. Diving. Digging. Scraping knees and elbows. She loved the no-frills nature of the job. Appealing, too, for a free spirit, the libero wore a different color jersey than the rest of the team.

She majored in English but transferred into Administration of Justice after one too many L.A. juries acquitted a celebrity who killed his wife. Degree in hand, she was accepted into the Police Academy, and a dozen people named Lacy traveled from Philadelphia for her graduation.

Sharon continued playing beach volleyball, which is where she met Jimmy Payne. He still claimed he was jogging in the gray sand of Will Rogers Beach when he picked up an errant ball and she started flirting with him. As she remembered it, Jimmy was passing out business cards to a crew of paramedics resuscitating a swimmer when he spotted her, then planted himself like a palm tree in the sand. Two hours later, he was still there, sunburned and shaggy-haired, waiting to meet her.

In those days, there were so many things to admire about Jimmy. A sense of justice and total commitment to his clients. Fearlessness in court and tenderness toward her. A selflessness and a rejection of materialism.

Jimmy turned out to be a wonderful husband and loving father. It tore at her to see him filled with anger and vengeance, his heart devoid of love.

Now she regretfully prepared to bust him. But first, she had to deal with her fiancé, who had awakened grouchy when the phone rang.

"When will Payne learn he can't turn to you every time he screws up his life?"

"I don't know, Cullen. I'm not responsible for his actions."

"Sure you are." Quinn ran a brush through his fine head of hair. "You encourage him by always being there. Which is more than the bastard did for you. Deep down, he hopes you'll take him back."

"That's not gonna happen."

"I know that. But does Payne?"

The doorbell rang. Jimmy. Early. Damn.

Her ribbon-trimmed satin chemise was all wrong for making an arrest. But no time to change.

Sharon hung a badge on a cord around her neck and grabbed her handcuffs.

"You're going downstairs in your lingerie?" Cullen asked.

"Jimmy's seen me in less." It felt good to say it, what with all the badgering. Cullen scowled, making Sharon regret her words. The doorbell chimed again. "I'm sorry, Cullen. Just let me get this over with, okay?"

Sharon padded barefoot down the stairs. On the landing, she passed a trophy case filled with her fiancé's boxing trophies. Police Athletic League. College club team. Golden Gloves. Twenty-five years and forty pounds ago.

Through a two-story window in the foyer, she could see the lights of the city. The house was built on a precarious slope in the Hollywood Hills above Sunset Boulevard. On a clear day, you could see the skyscrapers downtown, and once in a while, the steel gray ocean to the west.

When she opened the front door, Jimmy grinned from under his tousle of hair. A dozen years ago, she'd fallen for the same grin, the same hair, the same laughing brown eyes. Now she said, "You're under arrest. You have the right to remain—"

"Wow," Jimmy interrupted. "You look great, Sharon."

Of course he wouldn't remain silent. He never did.

"Pink is really your color," he continued. "Makes your complexion . . . I don't know . . . all peachy."

"Cut the crap, Jimmy."

A dark-haired boy stepped out from behind Payne, checked out her butt, whistled, and said, "Nice *calabaza, chica.*"

"Who's your charming friend?" Sharon asked.

"This is Tino. I caught him burgling my office."

"Perfect. A pair of thieves."

Jimmy and Tino stepped inside and closed the door behind them.

"Me and Himmy, we're partners now. *Verdad, vato?*"

"Absolutely not." Payne kept his eyes on Sharon. "But the kid did me a solid when the cops barged in, so I owe him."

"What scam are you pulling now?"

"I just don't want him shipped back to Mexico."

The boy stared at her with eyes like green felt and lashes so dark and lustrous as to make her envious. She figured he was about twelve or thirteen, but with a cagy, appraising look that made him seem older. A cute, sassy kid on his way to becoming devilishly handsome. With those eyes and his jet-black hair, the boy could be posing for Abercrombie & Fitch in a couple years.

"I thought we could help the kid out," Payne said.

"*We?*"

"Well, you. I thought he could stay with you and Quinn until I get back from Oaxaca."

Mexico! Damn, I knew it.

A year ago, Jimmy's threats to kill Garcia seemed to be just a phase, part of his grieving process. But one morning Sharon found her husband packing a bag. Maps. Night-vision binoculars. Adam's baseball bat. And her spare nine-millimeter Glock he'd plucked from a nightstand.

His eyes hollow and distant, Jimmy told her that he was going to kidnap Garcia and beat him to death. Crush every weight-bearing bone, keeping him alive as long as possible.

Adam's death had shriveled his heart and filled his veins with poison. Now Sharon knew she had no choice. "You're under arrest, Jimmy."

"Aw, c'mon, Sharon."

"Anything you say can and will be used against you in a court of law. You have the right to counsel. If you can't afford counsel—"

"I've got five thousand dollars," Payne said. "Actually, four thousand eight hundred."

"Great. You can sign a confession when Rigney gets here."

"Rigney! Here? How could you turn on me like this?"

"Because you're a criminal and I'm a cop."

Just then, Quinn came down the stairs, wearing a white fleecy bathrobe with a towel around his neck. He looked like he was entering the ring for a fight.

"Need any help, sweetie?"

"Stay out of this, Quinn," Jimmy snapped.

"This is my house, Payne."

"Nice place you got here, *gabacho*," Tino said. "You a drug dealer?"

"Jesus, Mary, and Joseph. Who's that?"

"A kid from Mexico who's looking for his mom," Payne said.

"Cullen, please let me handle this," Sharon said.

"Does he have papers?" Quinn said.

"Only to wipe my *culo*," the kid shot back.

"Careful, Tino," Payne said. "Quinn once fought Mike Tyson. For twelve seconds."

"You wouldn't have had the guts to step in the ring," Quinn said.

"I'd have the brains not to."

"You really fought Iron Mike?" Tino asked.

"Golden Gloves. Hundred ninety-five pound division." Quinn seemed to suck in his gut as he cradled his chin with one hand. "Tyson broke my jaw."

"With one punch," Payne added.

"I could still whip your skinny ass."

"Not if I kicked you in the nuts first."

"All right, you two," Sharon warned.

"I'm hungry," Tino said.

"We don't have tortillas and beans," Quinn said.

"Cullen!" Sharon shot her fiancé a laser-beam look. "Tino, I could make you bacon and eggs."

"Maybe a little tequila to wash it down," the kid suggested.

"I don't think so," she said.

"You can cut it with some vanilla liqueur. It's called a 'dirty condom.'"

"There you have it," Quinn said. "The assault on our morals."

"I learned how to mix drinks at the cantina," Tino boasted.

"Yeah?" Payne said. "What's tequila, blackberry brandy, and rum?"

"*Culo de fuego.* A flaming asshole."

"You're good, kid." Jimmy shot a look at Cullen. "Flaming asshole. Bet you knew that one, didn't you, Quinn?"

TWENTY-FIVE

Tino's appetite was amazing. Five eggs, scrambled. Half-a-dozen slices of bacon. Four slices of toast slathered with butter. And black coffee, no tequila, thank you very much.

Sharon watched the boy gobble his food, deriving nearly as much pleasure as he did. Maternal instincts are forever, she thought.

Cullen had tromped back up the stairs, leaving the three of them alone in the kitchen, all granite counters, marble floors, and shiny steel appliances.

The phone rang. Rigney again. Said he'd been driving north from LAX when a tractor trailer jackknifed on the 405. Now he was working his way on city streets to La Cienega. Running late, he'd be there as soon as he could.

"If Payne tries to escape, you have my permission to shoot him," Rigney said.

"Thanks, but I shot him before with no one's permission."

She hung up and turned back to her guests.

"Why'd you take the five thousand, Jimmy?"

"I was pissed at being used. I wanted to stick it to Rigney."

"Smart. Really smart."

"Just let me go to Mexico. When I come back, with or without Garcia's scalp, I'll turn myself in."

"Your problems are here. Nothing you can do will bring Adam back."

"Maybe there's something I can do that will bring *me* back."

"Not something evil. Not killing Garcia."

"Who's Garcia?" Tino demanded, between gulps of food. "And why do you want to kill him?"

"None of your business," Payne said.

"I am not afraid to kill a man," Tino claimed. "Some *cabrón* hurts my mother, I'll slice his neck like a goat."

"That's the spirit," Payne said.

"Stop it, both of you." Sharon turned to the boy. "Tino, tell me about your mother."

Wordlessly, the boy reached inside his shirt. Hanging from a cord around his neck was a plastic envelope. He handed it to Sharon. It held a photo, apparently taken at some formal event, a wedding or a *quince* party. Tino's mother wore a frilly turquoise dress. She had almond-shaped eyes the color of obsidian rocks in a mountain stream. She was not quite smiling, her full lips betraying no emotion. Her hair, which cascaded over bare shoulders, was as dark and lustrous as a river shimmering under a full moon. Her jawline was carved from granite, a Salma Hayek look.

"Your mother's beautiful," Sharon said. "What's her name?"

"Marisol." Tino's voice wobbled.

He tried to be tough, Sharon thought, but he was still a little boy.

"What's really bad," he said, his eyes watery, "it's all my fault."

"What is?"

"That we had to cross over. That *Mami*'s missing." Tears tracked down his cheeks. "I'm the one who ruined everything."

TWENTY-SIX

Even after blurting out his guilt, Tino still didn't know whether he should tell them what really happened back home.

If he told the lawyer and the lady cop, they might turn him over to *La Migra*. He would be sent home and put in jail. Or worse. Rafael Obeso would kill him.

As he ate, Tino sized up the two Americans. He liked the woman. She could cut it in the street, a real *pachuca*. Strong, like his own mother. He was not yet sure about the lawyer. Unfriendly at first. But he had kept his word. Picked him up when the police were chasing. Handed over the promised money, too.

"Judge people by whether they tell you the truth."

That is what his mother taught him. But could he trust them with *his* truth?

"What do you mean you ruined everything?" the lady cop asked, tenderness in her voice.

"I did something that made a man want to kill me.

He said he would cut out my heart and deliver it to *Mami*. Then hurt her, too."

The cop and the lawyer looked toward each other, as if asking whether they should believe him. Funny thing about grown-ups, Tino thought. They will swallow your lies, but the truth is so much harder for them to take.

After thinking it over, Tino told the lawyer and the pretty cop exactly how it happened. What he had seen and what he had done. And why his mother was forced to grab him and run like hell, all the way to *El Norte*.

Three days earlier, Tino had watched his mother scramble up the scaffolding of the big house under construction on a hill above their village. A petite woman, only a few centimeters taller than him. But strong and with womanly curves. Her long thick hair, dark as the desert night, swished across her shoulders as she climbed the scaffold. Workmen stopped. Whistled. Hooted. Mumbled filthy words.

Pigs.

"It is a curse to be a pretty woman," she had told Tino many times.

Warning him not to be like those men. Smelly and foul-mouthed. Beer-swilling and lazy. Working as slowly and as little as possible. Gambling away their money. Brutalizing their women and ignoring their children.

"Men are a plague."

"Was my father that way?"

Her smile was both sweet and sad. She never criticized the man who fled as soon as her belly swelled. She was not angry with him. With his *mestizaje* blood of Spanish ancestors, Gustavo had bequeathed his bright green eyes to Tino. At the time Tino was conceived, Gustavo was barely more than a boy himself.

"Your father sang '*Bésame Mucho*' in a voice that

made my knees go soft. But he could not hold a job or make a plan past the next weekend." She let out a long sigh. "At least your father bathed. He did not stink."

To Tino, it seemed like his mother deserved more than that.

As she climbed the scaffold the day the trouble started, Xavier, a carpenter with a tattooed neck, squeezed her ass through her jeans. Marisol swatted away the *pendejo*'s hand. Another two rungs, another worker, Jesús, tried to grab her breasts. She dangled there, one hand looped on the rung above. With her other hand, she pulled the air-powered nail gun from her tool belt.

"Jesús," she said to the tit grabber, "do you want me to nail your hands and feet to the framing? Should I crucify you like your namesake?"

"Put one through his *pinga,*" another worker called out, laughing.

"Won't need the gun," Marisol replied. "A half-inch staple will do the job."

The other men coughed and belched and hawked up tobacco. Jesús unleashed a torrent of *puta*s and *coño*s and *cachapera*s as Marisol climbed to the roof.

Tino watched all this with a mixture of fear and pride. His mother could take care of herself, but wasn't he the man of the household? When he delivered lunch to the men, shouldn't he order them to stay away from his mother? Or should he just punch Jesús in his stupid mouth? Before he could decide, Rafael Obeso, in his knee-high leather boots, strode through the mud to the foot of the scaffold.

"Leave her alone," Obeso ordered the men. "She's a better carpenter than any of you turds."

"*Sí, jefe.*"

"*Sí, patrón.*"

The men got back to work, picking up their pace.

Worms, Tino thought. Spineless men. Half-day workers, half-day drinkers. Lacking pride and motivation.

Tino had learned a phrase from his mother. *"Amor propio."* Self-esteem.

He admired American men. The ones he had seen on television. Well dressed and handsome, with good teeth and fast cars. He did not read the Spanish subtitles on the screen in order to learn English. The same with his beloved Los Angeles Dodgers. Although he could listen to Jaime Jarrin broadcast the game in Spanish, he preferred Vin Scully.

"Pull up a chair and stick around a while. We've got some baseball for you."

A relaxed, musical voice, smooth as velvet. Sentences that sounded like songs. Someday, he would like to see the Dodgers play in the place Vin Scully called "Chavez Ravine."

Tino got back to his job, delivering tacos and tortillas and cold drinks to the workers. They were building a new house, three stories tall. A grand home for Rafael Obeso, the richest man in the village.

Marisol had told Tino that the roof would have a satellite dish six meters across, even though much smaller ones were just as good, maybe even better.

"Señor Obeso wears boots too big for his feet," she said. "He is very conscious of show. Such men are stupid, no matter how much money they have."

His mother was right about so much, Tino thought, watching stonemasons build the fountain in the courtyard, complete with pissing cherubs.

Obeso was a short, stout man made taller by his boots. He wore a black-fringed shirt, and a bolo tie with a slide shaped like a bull and made of solid gold. His brushy mustache was streaked with gray. He told people he owned a doll-making factory in Mexico City, but no one believed him. Obeso was a drug smuggler with two bodyguards in camo gear, AK-47s slung over their shoulders.

Tino's job was to run errands and feed the chickens in a pen behind the house. Obeso paid in American money. A dollar here, a dollar there, carelessly crumpled and tossed at the boy. When Obeso traveled with his bodyguards, there was no pay. On Fridays, Tino sneaked into the village cantina and drank two beers.

"When you are old enough," Obeso told him, "I will teach you to slaughter chickens by wringing their necks."

"I am old enough."

Obeso turned to nearby workmen. "The boy's not a *marica* like his father." Calling the father Tino never knew a sissy.

Then, imitating Gustavo, Obeso strummed an air guitar and shook his hips like a girl, his workers laughing so hard that spittle flew.

That night, Tino was already in bed when his mother came home to their two-room adobe house. Even in the dim light, he could see the black, curdled blood on her lip and the swelling under one eye. She went to the spigot and washed her face, telling Tino that she was hit by a two-by-four that had dropped from a frame.

He did not believe her. He asked if Jesús had hit her.

No.

The toothless man? Or that truck driver with the huge belly?

No, no.

It came to him then. Only one man would have the nerve. Rafael Obeso.

"Was it *el jefe*?"

She didn't answer. Then Tino saw that his mother's blouse was torn, and when she turned around to undress, he saw brambles lodged in her long, dark hair. He heard himself sniffle.

"Tino, no," his mother said without turning around. *"No hay tiempo ni espacio para llorar."*

There is neither time nor space to cry.

The next morning, Obeso sent Tino's mother to the quarry to pick out limestone for the stairs. *Jefe* called it "women's work," the choosing of colors and grains in the stone. But Tino's mother, bruised and sleepless, was expected to lift dozens of heavy slabs into the bed of a truck.

There would be no need for her hammers and nail guns, so she left them home. Before Tino headed for the job site, he opened her toolbox and removed a wood chisel, which he taped to a leg under his torn jeans.

He delivered breakfast to the men, as always, then waited until he saw Obeso. Pretending not to notice the man, Tino walked casually behind the house to the chicken pen. He knew the fat man would follow just to criticize him for one thing or another. The bodyguards would stay at the front of the property, watching the road for approaching cars.

Tino dropped a handful of feed toward his feet, where a dozen chickens clucked. Just as he thought, Obeso thundered through the gate.

"Throw the feed and put some muscle into it," he ordered, "or the chickens in back will go hungry."

Purposely, Tino again dropped the seeds in front of the closest of the squawkers.

"¡Jesucristo! You throw like a *maricón."*

Obeso stomped over, his boots sinking into a river of chickenshit. "Give me the bucket."

"One more try," Tino pleaded. He wound up like Esteban Loaiza of the Dodgers and threw a handful of seeds straight into the man's fleshy face. Grains flew into Obeso's eyes and his open mouth. He choked and spat and coughed.

"Sorry, *jefe."*

"*¡Agilipollao!* You stupid fool." Clawing at his eyes.

Tino reached under his pants and peeled the wood chisel from the tape. With one smooth motion, he slashed at Obeso's forehead, cutting a horizontal line from right to left, just above the man's bushy eyebrows. Blood poured into Obeso's eyes, mixing with the chicken feed, stinging and blinding him. He stumbled forward, screaming for his bodyguards, when Tino kicked as hard as he could. Straight in the *cojones*.

A high-pitched squeak came from Obeso, who dropped to his knees, then pitched headfirst, straight into a pile of steaming chickenshit. Tino turned to run and looked back when he heard Obeso call out his name. In a hoarse whisper, the man croaked, "Ay, *chilito*. I will cut your heart out and give it to your whore mother."

Tino sprinted to the quarry and told his mother what had happened. She put a hand to her mouth and bit her lower lip.

"Oh, Tino. Why? Why?"

"The *cabrón* stole your honor."

"No, Tino. No man can take a woman's honor unless she gives it to him."

"Are you angry at me, *Mami*?"

"No. But Rafael Obeso is very dangerous."

"I'm not scared."

But Tino *was* confused. There were things he knew, but other things of which he was unsure.

A good man must not run from trouble. A valiente will protect his mother from a cabrón like Obeso. But what happens when doing the right thing is more dangerous than doing nothing?

In moments like this, Tino wished he had a father. A man to talk to, someone who could answer questions that a woman might not understand.

His mother motioned for Tino to follow her. "There is no time to waste."

They left the slabs at the quarry. Someone else would have to build Obeso's staircase.

It only took minutes to pack their belongings, for they could only take what they could carry. They left their small home, hitched a ride into Caborca, and caught the last bus north. As they left the city, Tino patted his mother's hand and said, "I will never let anyone hurt you again."

The bus climbed the hills out of their valley, passing through the dry scrublands and stands of mesquite, hawks soaring in the updrafts. They hurtled past roadside cantinas and country markets, auto junkyards and *vulcanizadoras,* tire repair shacks, the national business of Mexico. Heading north on Federal Highway 2, Tino fell asleep somewhere between Chijubabi and Rancho San Emeterio.

When he awoke, they were just outside San Luis Rio Colorado, so close to the American border that Tino glimpsed signs for Yuma, Arizona. He looked at his mother through hooded eyes and saw a tear rolling down her face. Not wanting to embarrass her, he did not move. She whispered to herself, and he strained to hear, picking up words that seemed to be part prayer and part promise.

"Soy ciudadana del mundo y de una iglesia sin fronteras."

I am a citizen of the world and a church without borders.

TWENTY-SEVEN

Tino checked their faces. Looking for disapproval, anger, horror.

But the lady cop looked like she was going to cry. And the lawyer smiled warmly at him. "You're a terrific kid.

"*¿Verdad?*"

"You bet. Defending a woman is a high calling. If the woman's your mom, bonus points."

Tino told them the rest. El Tigre the coyote. The plan to reach a stash house in Calexico. The foul-up at the border, his mother making the crossing at gunpoint. Rey and the other two *cabrónes* forcing him to carry cocaine.

The cop and the lawyer were quiet when he finished.

"Holy shit," the lawyer said, finally.

"My God, what you've been through," the lady cop said.

Tino finished his coffee, which had gone cold. "Now I can look for *Mami*."

"By yourself?" the lady cop asked.

"I have two hundred dollars now. Is that enough to hire a private eye?"

"For about forty-five minutes," Payne said.

"But who else would help me?"

Sharon had an idea, but before she could work it over, the phone rang. Detective Rigney. He was at Sunset and La Cienega. He'd be up the hill in ten minutes.

"Atticus, I have a deal for you," Sharon said.

"What?" Payne was wary.

"I'll let you go if you promise to help Tino find his mother."

"Okay!" Tino shouted.

But Jimmy was shaking his head. "I know what you're doing, Sharon."

"No time for your bullshit. Yes or no?"

"No. If you bust me, you figure I'll make bail and skip to Mexico. But you know I won't break a promise to you. If I say I'll help this kid, I'll do it. Bottom line, you're just trying to keep me from going after Garcia."

"Not everything's about you, Jimmy. Tino needs help. Your law practice is shot. You have no plans, except to commit mayhem. Why not do something positive?"

"I wouldn't know where to start."

"Find the stash house in Calexico."

"How? You think they advertise on cable?"

"We can do it, Himmy," the boy said. "We can find Mami."

"Don't bet on it, kid. In fact, don't bet on me."

"You know what I think, Atticus?" Sharon said. "I think you're scared to do something for someone else."

"I'm not scared. It's just less of a burden to screw up my own life."

"Your call. What'll it be? A late-night drive through the desert? Or a cement bunk at the jail?"

"What about Rigney?"

"I'll tell him you escaped again."

"You could get in a real jam, Sharon."

"I've been in a jam since the day I met you. Now get out of here."

"I gotta pee first," Tino said.

Sharon gave the boy directions down the hall to the

guest bath, then hurriedly started emptying the refrigerator. Juice. Peaches. Apples. A box of pretzels from under the cupboard. She put everything in brown grocery bags. "Take this for Tino. You know how hungry boys get."

"He's not going to summer camp." Sounding grumpy.

"Can I count on you to take care of him?" Those maternal instincts again.

"He'll probably steal my car when I stop for gas. That kid is a ton of trouble in a hundred-pound body."

"He likes you. I can tell."

"When I can't find his mother, how's he gonna feel?"

"Where's that old confidence? Where's the fearless J. Atticus Payne?"

"You know damn well where. On a hillside at Forest Lawn."

That kept her quiet a moment.

They heard a car pull into the driveway.

"Shit," Sharon said. "Where'd you park?"

"A driveway up the hill, behind some jacaranda trees."

"Go out the back door. I'll get Tino."

"I'm here," the boy said, popping back into the kitchen.

Jimmy still hadn't moved.

"Go!" She brush-kissed him on the lips.

"What about me, *chica*?"

She kissed the boy on the cheek, then smacked his butt.

The doorbell rang. "Good luck, guys," Sharon said, shooing them out the back door.

As they crossed the yard at double time, hunched over like commandos, Tino whispered to Jimmy, "You play your cards right, Himmy, that *chica caliente* will be in your bed soon."

"Too late for that, kid. Sharon's moved on."

"Donde fuego hubo, ascuas quedan."

"Where there was fire . . . " Jimmy couldn't translate the rest.

"Embers remain," Tino helped out.

"I don't know, kid."

"I do, Himmy. I could feel the heat."

TWENTY-EIGHT

Rattlesnake bites.

Dehydration, exposure, and thirst.

Robbery, rape, and murder.

So many ways to die crossing the border.

Just before dawn, Payne was at the wheel of the Lexus, pondering what could have happened to Tino's mother. He figured she didn't meet a wealthy *gringo*, fall in love, and elope to Las Vegas.

The desert was littered with bones of unknown men, women, and children who traveled with one bag of clothing and one jug of water, envisioning the promised land. An achingly sad Freddy Fender song came to Payne. The one about a place with streets of gold, always just across the borderline.

"You could lose more than you'll ever hope to find."

Payne shot a look over his shoulder. The boy was curled up in the backseat. He had fallen asleep before they reached San Bernardino. He awakened when they stopped for gas near Indio, a desert town where a drunken Sinatra and Ava Gardner once shot out street-lamps from the front seat of Frank's Caddy convertible.

By the time the Lexus exited the 10 and headed due south on old State Route 86, Tino was sacked out again. Listening to the tires sing on the pavement, Payne fought to stay awake. He didn't want to be here, hated the re-sponsibility he had taken on. Sharon had convinced him to do something for someone else. As if that would heal him.

Doesn't she see I've got nothing left to give?

There were aid agencies for undocumented migrants. Churches. Nonprofits. Do-gooders all. Payne could find a place, drop the kid off in the morning, and head to Mexico after Manuel Garcia.

No I can't. I just made a promise to Sharon.

Damn, what is this hold she has on me?

Payne's thoughts turned to Marisol Perez, the dark-haired beauty in the photo the boy kept next to his heart. The woman had placed her life into the hands of a coyote and simply vanished into the night.

What if Payne learned she was dead? How could he tell the boy? Not that the experience would be entirely new to him. He once told a mother her boy was dead. *His* boy, too.

Even if Marisol was safe somewhere, how could he find her? All the kid knew was that the coyote named El Tigre was supposed to take them to a stash house near Calexico. But that could be a farmhouse in a remote canyon. All those dirt trails leading into the desert. All those ravines halfway to nowhere. The enormity of their task seemed overwhelming.

Sure, he would do his best to find Marisol Perez. His good deed. *Then* he would go to Mexico and find Manuel Garcia. His murderous deed.

He turned on the radio to keep himself awake. Green Day was singing "Boulevard of Broken Dreams."

"*I walk a lonely road.*"

Tell me about it, Payne thought.

They had driven all night. Payne was sleepy and his patched right leg was beginning to stiffen. Every hour, it seemed, another reminder of Adam. Or more precisely, the last moments of Adam's life.

He pulled off the highway and onto a looping street outside Salton City, a grandiose name for a sun-grilled, scrub-brush town. He needed to stretch and get some coffee. He found North Marina Drive and headed toward the giant lake. At first glance, the stagnant, salty puddle in the middle of the desert would seem to be one of God's grand mistakes. Instead, it was man's malfeasance, hatched when California bigwigs accidentally diverted the Colorado River nearly a century ago. The town was supposed to become a fancy resort, but now most buildings appeared empty, the wood rotted, the air slick with the stench of dead birds and decaying fish. Real estate signs announced waterfront lots for dirt-cheap prices. Great potential, if you wanted to build on the River Styx.

Payne saw a Hispanic man and a young boy carrying fishing poles along a rocky beach. Were there any fish still alive in this cesspool? Payne pulled the Lexus into a diner across the street from the lake. The orange fireball of the sun was just sizzling out of the water. Payne couldn't help but think of fried eggs. He awakened Tino and asked if he wanted some breakfast.

Tino rubbed his eyes, yawned, and said, "If you're paying, Himmy, I'm eating."

TWENTY-NINE

The cop was staring at them, Payne decided. An Imperial County sheriff's deputy. His black-and-white parked in the diner lot. The cop was eating grits and French toast.

Okay, relax. The cop's staring at us because we're the only other customers.

Payne was beginning to think he didn't make a very good fugitive. He looked guilty just eating breakfast.

Tino drowned his pancakes and bacon in gloppy syrup. Payne stuck with a plain omelette, coffee, and dry toast.

The deputy looked up from his own plate. Young guy. Chunky, with a thick neck, his cheeks and nose sunburned, but pale around the eyes from his sunglasses. The waitress, a tired high school girl wearing no makeup, approached the cop's table. "Harley, you want some more coffee?"

The cop raised his cup and nodded. His gaze drifted back to Payne, who looked down and chewed his toast.

"So, Himmy. Why are you divorced from that *chica caliente*?"

"None of your business."

"You cheat on her?"

"Never."

"Beat her up?"

"Of course not."

"You a *drogadicto* or *alcóholico*?"

"Give me a break, kid."

"So how come she dumped you?"

"How do you know I didn't divorce her?"

Tino's laugh was hearty and unself-conscious. A boy's laugh. Adam's laugh.

"I wasn't there for her when she needed me," Payne heard himself confess.

"Where were you, *vato*?"

"I was there but not really *there*. I didn't open up. Didn't give enough." Payne shot a look at the boy. "You don't understand, do you?"

Tino shrugged.

"Just loving somebody isn't enough. You have to dig deep inside yourself and bare everything, no matter how painful."

"Then you can give enough?"

"Then you can bond, and each person gives to the other. It's simple math. Love equals feelings plus action. You may not know it, but that's what you're doing for your mother."

Tino forked a syrupy chunk of pancakes. "I think I get it, *vato*."

They ate in silence. Then Tino pulled an iPod from his pocket and put on the earbuds.

"Where'd you get that?"

Tino pretended he couldn't hear.

Payne repeated the question, doubling the decibels.

Tino unplugged one earbud. "Borrowed it." His tone saying, "*Don't bother me, man.*"

"Who from?"

"*El boxeador* with the big mouth."

"Quinn? Cullen Quinn lent you his iPod?"

"He didn't say no. 'Course, he was sleeping."

"You sneaked into their bedroom?"

"After I went to the toilet."

"Shit. What else did you take?"

"*Nada*. I swear on Saint Teresa."

The boy slipped the earbud back in, listened a moment, and sang off-key, "Rainy days and Mondays always get me down. *¡Qué caca!*"

"The Carpenters. That'd be Quinn."

Several yards away, the deputy patted his mouth with a napkin, stood, and hitched up his belt, loaded down with a gun, ammo, radio, flashlight, and other doodads.

The deputy sidled over to their table. His name tag read, "*H. Dixon.*" "Morning, folks."

"Good morning, Deputy Dixon," Payne said, cheerfully. Just like picking a jury, using the man's name. A sign of friendliness.

"You're not from around here, are you?"

"Hope that's not a crime." Smiling as he said it.

"Nope. We love tourists." The cop paused a beat. "Medium rare."

Payne figured he should laugh, so he did.

"What's with your T-shirt?" The cop nodded his sunburned face toward the steroid-pumped skull of Barry Bonds.

"My José Canseco shirt was dirty."

"You're kind of a wise guy, aren't you?"

"As long as that's not a crime, either."

The cop turned to Tino, who'd kept his head down, forking pancakes into his mouth. "What's your name, son?"

Tino kept eating.

"C'mon now, *chico*. You know your name, doncha?"

Tino pulled out the earbuds. "Harry Potter."

"He's such a joker." Payne kicked the kid under the table.

Dixon kept his eyes on Tino. "Well, you have a good day, Harry." He put on his hat and nodded to Payne. "You drive real careful now, sir. We've lost tourists in some hellish accidents lately."

Payne watched the deputy walk out the front door.

Heading toward his cruiser, the cop stopped alongside the Lexus. Then he walked a full 360 degrees around the vehicle, as if sizing it up on a dealer's lot. Or maybe memorizing the license plate.

Payne was quickly losing his appetite. "Finish your pancakes, kiddo. We gotta get going."

THIRTY

The Lexus was purring at 75 on an empty stretch of road, and Payne could not get Deputy Dixon out of his mind. Was life so boring that the desert cop had to hassle every stranger who came through town? Or did his gut tell him that the Anglo guy in the fuck-you T-shirt and the Hispanic kid with a smart mouth made odd traveling companions?

Payne tried not to think about it as they blasted past saguaro cactus and mesquite trees and creosote bushes in the vast stretches of parched land. He swerved to avoid a raccoon waddling across the road. Turned on the radio. On a distant, scratchy station, Los Lobos were singing "The Road to Gila Bend."

Payne checked the rearview mirror. Shit. A police car, maybe half a mile back. Was it Dixon? He eased his foot off the gas.

Los Lobos turned to full-bore static, and Payne hit the dial. In a second, he heard a familiar baritone voice.

"*Every wetback holds a dagger pointed at the heart of America. I no longer live in California. I live in Mexifornia.*"

"That's the guy who lent you his iPod," Payne told Tino.

"What a *cabrón*," the boy said.

"*This isn't a melting pot,*" Cullen Quinn bellowed. "*It's a cracked pot overflowing with illegals.*"

"That *idiota* talking about me?"

"*If the federal government can't stop the illegals, what about us?*" Quinn ranted. "*The citizenry. What about the good folks who've formed well-armed militias under the Second Amendment? If a burglar breaks into your home, you can shoot him. How about aliens sneaking into our country? Should we start selling hunting licenses?*"

"I don't think he got enough sleep last night," Payne said.

"*And you know who's to blame?*" Quinn said, picking up steam. "*Everyone who hires these lowlifes and freeloaders. Right here in California, we have the biggest employer of illegals in the country. I've called him out before, and I'll do it again.*"

Simeon Rutledge, Payne knew. Quinn's favorite target.

"*It's fat cat Simeon Rutledge in the San Joaquin Valley. Rutledge Ranch and Farms, a quarter million acres of prime valley land. He hires thousands of illegals every year. What terrorists lurk among them? What diseases do they bring with them? Rutledge doesn't care, living in his mansion, thumbing his nose at the law.*"

"Quinn needs new material. He's been beating this drum forever."

Payne glanced again at his rearview mirror. The cop was still there, keeping the same distance.

"*Rutledge lures the wetbacks with promises of greenbacks. But you folks are the ones who pay when the*" *illegals land in our hospitals and jails. And you foot the bill for their hordes of children in our public schools."*

"What an asshole," Tino said. "A real *asqueroso.*"

"We need to crack down on the employers as well as the illegals," Quinn continued. *"Are you listening, Simeon Rutledge? I've challenged you to debate a dozen times, but all I hear from your lawyers is that you're too busy. 'Mr. Rutledge is a working man.' Yeah? Well, I've got another term for it. 'Racketeer.' Why don't the feds bust you? Because you've bought off every politician from Sacramento to Washington. If I'm lying, sue me, Mr. Rutledge. Go on. Get your high-priced lawyers to sue me, you greedy S.O.B."*

Jimmy turned off the radio, looked back. The police car had picked up speed. It closed the distance, its blue bubble light flashing.

THIRTY-ONE

"I won't sue you, Quinn. But I sure as hell might kill you," Simeon Rutledge said.

One hundred seventy-five miles north of the Burbank studio where Cullen Quinn was shouting into a microphone and three hundred miles from where Payne was driving, Rutledge straddled a sawhorse, sharpening the blade of a ranch implement called an "emasculator." As he listened to an old portable radio perched on the railing of a horse stall, his lips stretched into a slash as angry as a knife wound. "I'll strangle you with my bare hands."

"Did I just hear you threaten Cullen Quinn's life?" Charles Whitehurst asked.

"You gonna testify against me, White*bread*?" Rutledge laughed, hawked up some phlegm, and spit into a pile of straw.

"As you well know, Simeon, the attorney-client privilege precludes me from ever testifying—"

"Screw the privilege. If you ever turned on me, Charlie, you'd be singing soprano the rest of your life." Rutledge gestured with the two-bladed emasculator, ordinarily used to de-nut stallions, not shysters. "If a man called my granddad the names Quinn calls me, Granddad would have killed him without a second thought."

"Ezekiel Rutledge's ways don't work anymore, Simeon."

"Don't be too sure."

"Jesus, Simeon. When are you going to stop trying to prove you're as tough as your grandfather?"

Rutledge flashed his lawyer a look that stung like a bullwhip. "Ain't too many men I let talk to me like that."

"I thought that's what you paid me for."

Rutledge laughed, the sound of a boar crashing through a tangle of brush. "My granddaddy never would have hired you, Whitehurst. Wouldn't have understood your ways."

A proud and defiant man, Ezekiel Rutledge had lost his Mississippi cotton plantation to the banks and the boll weevils before heading west to make his fortune in the 1930s. He had the foresight to hire Mexicans for his farmwork. Field hands who complained about working conditions were likely to be flogged or sent back home, sometimes sprawled over the back of a horse. Simeon

Rutledge could still remember his grandfather explaining the economics of cotton farming.

"We used to own our slaves. Now we just rent them."

No, you didn't amass a quarter million acres of prime farmland by being a gentleman or a limousine liberal. You blew up dams, poisoned neighbors' wells, horsewhipped union organizers, and occasionally shot government agents as trespassers.

Then came Jeremiah Rutledge, Simeon's father, who nearly lost the farm. Jeremiah spent money on whores and booze and dice, and drove a sapphire blue Caddy convertible as if the devil were riding shotgun. Marriage and middle age slowed him from a gallop to a canter, and he eventually cleaned up. Remembering his own father's lessons, Jeremiah pushed competing farmers into foreclosure, paid off politicians, and diverted rivers without regard for the law, his neighbors, or the Ten Commandments.

"I'm not trying to turn back the clock." Rutledge doused the blades of the emasculator with disinfectant. "I'd just like to find a way to shut Quinn up."

"You've got bigger problems, Simeon."

"If it's the migrants, we've dealt with that for years."

"Not like this," Whitehurst insisted. "This time it's different."

The two men were just outside the gelding stall in the main barn of Rutledge Ranch and Farms. Whitehurst had been Simeon Rutledge's lawyer for three decades and had gotten him out of numerous scrapes, from breaches of contract to paternity raps. But in recent years, as Whitehurst moved up in society circles, Rutledge felt his legal advice had gotten prettified and sissified. As if he no longer wanted mud on the Persian carpets of his fancy law office. Lately, Rutledge had been wishing his lawyer had the *cojones* of his stallion.

Whitehurst had the trim physique of an aging squash player. Back in the Transamerica Building in San Francisco, his office walls proudly displayed parchment from Stanford and Harvard. When Whitehurst had walked into the barn today, he shot discreet glances downward. Checking his English brogues. You never knew when a wad of horseshit might get stuck in the threading of the hand-cut calfskin.

In his dusty cowboy boots, Rutledge harbored no such fears. His appearance was far less refined. Rutledge thought he could pass for a longshoreman. Or a guy who slopped boiling tar on roofs. Or, with his short, bristly gray hair, a retired Marine Corps drill instructor. Wide shoulders, a thick chest that strained against the buttons of a dirty denim work shirt. His skin was the texture of tree bark and sun-baked the color of tea. Hands thickened with calluses. Knuckles like walnut shells from wrestling steers and shoveling shit and punching out big-mouthed bastards in bars from Fresno to the Mexican border.

Whitehurst had dropped in by helicopter, and Rutledge would end up paying for the charter service as well as $800 per hour for his lawyer's gloomy tidings. The call setting up the meeting had been cryptic. They couldn't speak on the phone. One way to jack up the bill, Rutledge knew, was to predict an apocalyptic event of biblical proportions, which could be avoided only by the skills of your London-tailored savior.

Rutledge was barely curious about what ill winds brought Whitehurst to the ranch. He was too old and too rich and too ornery to give a double damn about whatever his lawyer was toting in his green alligator briefcase. If the I.R.S. or D.H.C. or I.C.E. or any other bureaucratic bull slingers were after him, well, let them take their best shot. As for Whitehurst and all his drama, let him cool his heels. Preferably in horseshit.

Rutledge was not clueless as to the goings-on in Washington. He read the newspapers and even watched that twitchy woman Katie Couric on TV once in a while. The failed immigration legislation the year before had brought the weasels out of their holes, screaming hate at illegals. The Department of Homeland Security was under pressure to do something—anything—to close what was essentially an open border with Mexico. Not good news for the man who employed thousands of migrants in the Central Valley, some for just a few weeks during harvest season, some full-time.

Rutledge had seen these waves of nativism come and go. His father had hired Mexicans legally under the *braceros* program. Even now, Simeon Rutledge employed some documented aliens as guest workers, but the numbers were limited by law, and the paperwork took forever. He didn't see any difference between a Mexican with papers and one without. He paid decent wages and provided the best working conditions he could and still make a profit. He admired the courage of the men and women who risked death to come north and look for honest work. He couldn't understand why Europeans who braved an Atlantic crossing in search of a better life should be held in higher regard than Mexicans who crossed the desert last week, pursuing the same dream.

Big mouths like Quinn and the fear-mongering politicians didn't understand crap. Farmers always faced ruin. The weather was either too hot or too cold. Too much rain or too little. Not enough workers when you needed them, and too many when there was nothing to do. Market prices tumbled without warning. Just now, almond prices were in the crapper, thanks to all those Hollywood health nuts buying acreage and planting trees.

Sure, the government was a threat, but nothing compared to a flooded field or a February frost. So, just because his lawyer showed up with a brow as furrowed as a lettuce field, Rutledge wasn't going to alter the day's schedule, which included castrating a stallion who'd been raising hell in the east pasture.

"So what should I do about Quinn, Counselor? Sue him, shoot him, or debate the damn fool on the radio?" Rutledge scratched at his bushy mustache with a knuckle. The whiskers hid a divot in his upper lip, a re-minder of a bar fight and a broken beer bottle forty years earlier.

"Things the way they are, I'd prefer you kept a low profile, Simeon."

"And just how are things?"

"There's a team in the Justice Department working full time on the investigation," Whitehurst said. "It's called 'Operation New River.' But it might as well be called 'Operation Rutledge.' The feds have targeted you for—"

The barn door opened, and both men were blinded an instant by the blazing sunlight.

"Hold on, Whitebread." All Rutledge could see was the silhouette of a huge horse. A frothy-tailed, rambunc-tious white stallion who'd been terrorizing the mares. It was time to settle him down.

"I'm gonna de-nut White Lightning," Rutledge said, brandishing the shiny steel emasculator. "Then you can tell me why I should crap my pants over some bureau-crats with fat briefcases and skinny ties."

THIRTY-TWO

Payne pulled the Lexus to the berm, and the Imperial County sheriff's cruiser pulled up behind him.

"It's the dude from the diner," Payne said, looking into his side mirror.

"We ain't done nothing wrong," Tino said.

"Maybe so, but let me do the talking."

Payne watched as Deputy Dixon spoke into his radio, then stepped out of the cruiser. He walked slowly toward them, a purposeful, heavyset young man in reflective sunglasses.

Payne zipped the window down and sang out, cheerfully, "Hey, there, Officer. We meet again."

For a moment, no one spoke as an open-bed truck trundled north, a dozen Hispanic men in work clothes huddled in the back. A cyclone of dust swirled across the highway, oily fumes in its wake. Watching the truck pass, Dixon said, "Temporary work permits. Otherwise, the beaners would be hiding under tarps."

Beaners, Payne thought. Not a good sign.

"Where exactly you folks headed?" the deputy asked.

"Just a little vacation," Payne said. "Thought we'd look around Imperial."

"Little bitty town, not much to see unless you like sand dunes."

"Love sand dunes," Payne avowed. "*Lawrence of Arabia* is one of my favorite movies."

"Uh-huh." The deputy peeled a stick of gum and

popped it into his mouth. He turned to Tino and said, "Want a stick, Harry Potter?"

Tino shook his head.

"Please step out of the vehicle. Both of you."

They got out of the air-conditioned metal box. A wave of desert heat rolled over them. Sand blew across the highway.

"Gonna ask you again, kid," the cop said. "What's your name? *Tu nombre?*"

"Tino," the boy said, just as Payne said, "Adam."

The deputy cocked his head. "Which is it, Adam or Tino?"

"Adam Tino Payne," Payne said. "He likes his middle name better."

"Sure he does." The cop flicked his gum wrapper toward a staghorn cactus. "Got some I.D. for Master Adam Tino Payne?"

"I don't need no stinking I.D.," Tino spat out, with an overcooked Mexican accent.

"Can it, kid." Payne turned to the deputy. "My name's James Payne. I'm a lawyer. Like I said, this is my son, Adam. School's out, so we're touring the desert."

The cop took off his sunglasses and gave Tino a long, hard look. "Boy doesn't favor you, does he?"

Beads of sweat tracked down Payne's forehead and stung the corners of his eyes. "If it's any of your business, his mother's Hispanic. My wife. Juanita."

"Okay, husband of Juanita. What's going on here?"

"Like I said, vacation. Father and son bonding. Maybe head over to Phoenix, watch the Diamondbacks play." Winging it now.

"Not buying what you're selling. Now, what are you and your little *mestizo* up to?"

"You asking because my son has brown skin? This some kind of racial profiling?"

"More like pedophile profiling."

"What!"

"We got a problem with guys coming down to the border, buying Mexican kids for lustful purposes."

Lustful purposes?

It was such a ludicrous phrase that Payne laughed.

"What about it, *chico*?" the deputy asked. "This guy try anything funny with you?"

"What you think, I'm some sort of *mayate*? Anybody try that with me, I chop off his *aguacates*."

Using the word for avocados. It occurred to Payne that the Spanish language had an abundance of synonyms for testicles.

"Just asking if the guy tried," Dixon said.

"No, man. He's my *vato*."

"Your bud? So, he's not your father?"

Tino clammed up, and the cop turned to Payne. "You got some I.D., Mr. Payne?"

"It's in the car."

The deputy followed Payne, who opened the passenger door, then clicked open the glove compartment. A blue-steel, short-barreled revolver fell to the floor with a *thud*.

"What the hell!" Payne said.

The deputy grabbed Payne by the shoulder and spun him around. "You got a concealed firearms permit?"

"That's not mine! I don't know how it got there."

"Hands on top of the car, and spread your legs."

Payne did as he was told, and Dixon patted him down, dealing out a painful smack on the scrotum.

"Hands behind your back."

Payne followed orders meekly, and the deputy cuffed him.

Dixon picked up the revolver, sniffed the barrel, rotated the cylinder. "I'm gonna call this in, Payne. You stay right where you are."

When the deputy was out of earshot, Payne said, "Where'd you get the gun, you little shitbird?"

"That *cabrón*'s underwear drawer."

"Quinn? You stole Cullen Quinn's gun!"

"I thought we might need some firepower, *vato*." Tino gave Payne a sheepish look. "Sorry, Himmy."

Dixon strode back to the Lexus, moving quicker now. "There's a warrant out for your arrest, Mr. Payne. Grand Larceny."

"I gotta pee," Tino said, moving toward the berm.

"I'll level with you," Payne told Dixon. "I'm not the boy's father."

"No shit."

"We're looking for his mother."

"Uh-huh."

"God's honest truth. She came over the border with a coyote and disappeared."

"That's a shame."

"C'mon, Deputy. It's a missing persons case. Your job, right?"

"My job's taking you in and turning the boy over to I.C.E. They got something called 'Return to Sender.' A one-way ticket back to Mexico." Pronouncing it *meh-ee-ko* and grinning.

"Have a heart. The boy has no father. His mother is missing."

"I got all that. But why are *you* looking for her?"

"Because I'm trying to change my life."

"You just did. You're under arrest, Payne. You have the right to remain stupid. Any shit you say can be used against you in a court of law. If you cannot afford a shyster, the state will provide one."

"I should warn you I'm very close to Governor Schwarzenegger."

In truth, the closest Payne ever got was sitting in the third row of *Terminator 2*.

"Didn't vote for him. Now take a seat in the back of my cruiser."

Boom!

Startled, Dixon wheeled around.

"Jesus!" Payne yelled.

Tino stood in front of the police car, 12-gauge shotgun in hand. He'd sneaked into the police car and grabbed the gun from its rack. Now the front right tire of the car was shredded, aflame, and reeking of burnt rubber. Tino racked the shotgun and swung it toward the deputy.

"Hands up, *gabacho*."

"Mr. Payne, tell the boy to put down the gun."

"Tino, chill out," Payne ordered.

"He takes you in, Himmy, they'll send me back."

"Better than prison," Dixon said. "They'll whack your skinny ass like a piñata."

"I'm a juvie," Tino said. "A shrink will give me some pills."

"Tino," Payne pleaded. "Trust me. You're doing this all wrong."

"*Mami* needs me. I got no time to fuck around." Tino motioned toward the deputy with the barrel of the shotgun. "Drop your gunbelt."

"Nope. Not gonna do it."

Tino swung the barrel into the open window of the police car and fired. The blast shattered the radio, reducing it to a smoking mass of melting plastic and metal. He pumped the shotgun again and whirled it back toward the deputy.

No one moved. Tino's narrow shoulders were pinched tight, his face slick with sweat. The gun barrel unsteady in his hands.

Payne pictured a horrific accident, the cop's head blown off. "Tino, you're scaring the shit out of me. Please put that gun down."

The boy ignored him and kept his eyes on Dixon. "The gunbelt, señor. I have killed many men for less."

"No you haven't, Tino," Payne said.

"Okay, let's do it your way, *chico*." Dixon lowered his heavy belt to the sandy soil and kicked it away.

Tino's shoulders relaxed.

It took only a second. The cop dropped to the ground, tucked, and rolled into a gulley behind a creosote bush at the edge of the road. Still moving, he snatched a small pistol from an ankle holster, got to one knee, and aimed at Tino through the leafy plant.

The boy ducked behind the cruiser, then turkey-peeked over the hood.

The cop fired, the shot shattering a side window.

Tino lifted the shotgun over the hood and aimed toward the bush.

"Tino. No!" Payne yelled.

The boy ducked as a second pistol shot echoed over the hood of the car.

Payne circled the Lexus and belly-crawled off the road. It would have been easier if his hands weren't cuffed, but he managed to wriggle, face-first, into the gulley. Twenty feet away, the deputy was obscured behind creosote bushes and a jumping cholla cactus.

"Throw down the shotgun, kid!" Dixon hollered.

"No way!" Tino was still crouched behind the cruiser.

"I don't want to shoot you."

Payne struggled to his feet and waited. If the cop fired again, his ears would ring for a few seconds. He would never hear Payne tearing through the bushes.

"Kid, you listening to me? I don't care if you're still wearing diapers, I'll put a hole in you." Dixon fired over the top of his cruiser.

Payne raced through the creosote bushes. Took a breath. Inhaled the scent of coal tar. Planted a foot just in front of the cholla and leapt. If his bum leg didn't hold, he would be impaled by hundreds of deadly spines.

He barely cleared the cactus. Dixon never looked up, and Payne's shoulder caught him squarely in the back, flattening him. Dixon's breath exploded with a *whoosh*, and his pistol slid across the sand. He was facedown, eating dirt, as Payne slid off him.

"Mo-ther-fuck-er," the deputy snarled, leaking blood from a split lip.

Tino jogged over, shotgun still pointed at Dixon. "Way to go, Himmy."

"You two assholes are both cooked."

"Handcuff key," the little gangster ordered.

The cop tossed him the key. Tino held the shotgun in one hand, unlocked Payne's cuffs with the other.

Adrenaline pumping, heart racing, Payne scanned the road. A trailer truck roared past, heading north, the driver oblivious.

Now what?

Payne knew all about the fight-or-flight response. They had just fought. Now it was time to flee. But to where? All he could see was prison. Beatings, boredom, starchy food.

"Himmy, we got to get going."

"Right."

Payne ordered Dixon back into his cruiser and cuffed him to his steering wheel. The deputy unleashed a string of curses.

Tino was already back in the Lexus. Payne got in, sat there a moment, both hands resting on the steering wheel.

"Himmy, go!"

Payne gunned it, burning rubber, heading south on State Route 86. Then Tino, a kid full of surprises, did something Payne never expected. He burst into tears.

The gun-toting, tough-talking, maybe-motherless boy finally looked and acted his age. Payne slung an arm around him.

"It's okay, slugger. Let it out."

The boy spoke between sobs. "You'll still help me find my mother, *vato*?"

"I made a promise, didn't I?"

"People break promises all the time."

It came to Payne then. The boy's desperation. The kid had said he'd do anything to find his mother. And he'd just proved it.

"Listen to me, Tino. You're a great kid. No matter what happens, I won't leave you, and I won't let you down. You got that?"

Tino sniffled and nodded. "Back there, you were a real *valiente*."

"Only if a *valiente* can be scared shitless."

"He can, if he still acts with *valor*."

The boy stopped crying. Payne tousled his hair and gave the Lexus more gas. He smiled and said, "Hey kid. You my *vato*?"

Tino wiped away a tear, and they rapped knuckles.

Now what? The question still hung there. They were heading south, but soon—maybe within minutes—some trucker or another cop would stop and set the deputy free. Every uniform in Imperial County would be looking for them. The deputy had Payne's name, his license plate, and the whole episode would be recorded on the cruiser's video camera. Hell, they'd all probably end up on some cable program: *America's Dumbest Criminals*.

What were their options? If they turned back north, they'd never get as far as San Berdoo. If they headed west, there'd be an A.P.B. for them in San Diego. East, they'd be stopped before they got to the Arizona border. But there was one other choice. A place they'd be safe. A place where Payne could think. Could plan. Could retrace Marisol's steps.

Payne floored the accelerator.

"Where we going, Himmy?"

"Mexico," Payne said.

THIRTY-THREE

"Damn it, Simeon. This is serious," Charles Whitehurst said.

"Yeah. You told me. There's a list. I'm a target." Rutledge wanted to get on with castrating his stallion. But his doomsaying lawyer wouldn't let up.

"You're on the *top* of the list, Simeon. The first raid will be here." He made a circular motion, as if the feds would storm the barn at any moment.

Rutledge spit toward a bale of straw. "We've had Immigration poking around for years. Just P.R. stunts."

"Not this time. A multiagency task force. Homeland Security. F.B.I. I.C.E."

"What about all those subsidiaries you set up? Field hands work for them, not for me."

Whitehurst shook his head. "Corporate dodges don't work anymore."

The lawyer's voice was tense and high-pitched. Not like the unflappable old mouthpiece. It gave Rutledge pause, and now he pictured jeeps and helicopters and swarms of agents in Kevlar vests, kicking in doors, flaunting their automatic weapons. Bees buzzing around a hive. All to appease the yahoos and their prejudices.

"How do you know all this?" he asked.

"That's not important. Just trust me. The suits at Justice checked out every big employer in the West. Meatpacking plants. Hotel chains. Fisheries. They saw your name and said, *'Bingo! Simeon Rutledge.'* You're it. And they'll milk it for all it's worth. You're facing millions in fines. Serious prison time. Forfeiture of your property. They're making you the test case."

"How the hell do you know all this?" Rutledge repeated.

Whitehurst looked around the barn as if the Attorney General might be hiding behind an Appaloosa in a neighboring stall. "We had a young lawyer, a junior associate, leave the firm last year to get trial experience. He's with the U.S. Attorney in San Francisco, and we've maintained a good relationship. Do I have to say any more?"

Whitehurst had bought himself a spy, Rutledge thought. In the high-rise world of the justice system, you didn't have to shovel shit to get your hands dirty.

"When's it coming down?" Rutledge asked.

"Soon. Tomorrow. Next week. A few weeks, at most."

Rutledge ran a hand over his buzz cut. The information sounded legit. "You got some legal advice for me?"

"Get rid of your illegals. All of them. Now."

Rutledge coughed a wet, gravelly laugh, the sound of stones washing down a sluice. "Then who'll pick my artichokes? You?"

"It's time to clean up, Simeon. And not just the farms. You gotta close that pleasure palace up in Hot Springs."

"The Gentleman's Club? Bullshit! My granddad built

that for his friends in Sacramento. Hell, they oughta designate the place a historic monument."

"Why don't you just hire lobbyists like everyone else?"

"What do you think whores are? Granddad used to say you could buy anything with bourbon and pussy."

"Like I've been saying, Simeon, times change."

"Well, I don't. As for the migrants, even George Dumb-ass Bush knew we couldn't run the country without 'em. It shouldn't be a crime to hire able-bodied men and women just because they don't have some papers. Unless John Q. Public wants to pay ten bucks for a head of lettuce, we gotta have these people."

"Not a time for political speeches."

"Maybe it is. They arrest me, I'll have a platform."

"And if you're imprisoned?"

"I'm counting on you to keep that from happening, Charlie."

"You can't buy your way out of this one. Jesus, Simeon, sometimes I wish you'd fire me."

"Say the word, and I'll hire a smart Jew lawyer who's still hungry. So are we done? I'm not getting rid of my *mojados* or my *putas*."

"If you don't take precautions, Simeon," Whitehurst said, "I shudder to think of the consequences."

"While you're shuddering, I'm gonna do some work." Rutledge turned his attention to a young Hispanic man leading a huge white horse into the gelding stall. Alongside, an older man with cabled forearms gripped the horse's halter. The horse whinnied and stomped the floor like a spoiled child, its tail sweeping back and forth like a geisha's fan.

"You know why I castrate fine-looking beasts like White Lightning?" Rutledge asked.

Whitehurst sighed. "So you'll be the only stallion left on the ranch."

"Gelding mellows him out so he can pasture with the mares without humping 'em and dumping 'em."

The older Mexican man stroked the horse's flank and whispered in his ear. The stallion seemed to relax.

"Jorge, I ain't got all day," Rutledge said. "You done singing love songs to that big bastard?"

"*Relámpago Blanco* knows in his heart what you're going to do to him, *jefe*," Jorge answered.

Rutledge moved around the horse, examining it the way a pilot checks an aircraft before taking off. He ran his hands over the horse's sheath and leg, then peered into its eyes. This was a strong and handsome animal, and Rutledge felt something akin to love for him.

Jorge filled two large syringes, one with a tranquilizer, the other with an anesthetic to be injected into the testes. Rutledge would perform the tricky surgery himself. His father had shown him how, just as his father before him. Maybe Whitehurst didn't understand how traditions were passed from fathers to sons in the natural order of the universe. Land. Horses. Crops. Migrants. Whores.

Jorge handled the injections. It took the anesthetic only two minutes to work. While he waited, Rutledge thought about his lawyer's advice. Whitehurst was looking out for him. The savvy old lawyer didn't want him indicted, even though he could make a ton of money with a big show trial, the mother's milk of those silk-suited shysters.

Rutledge watched his lawyer peer over the top of the stall from the outside. Just like a hired mouthpiece. A spectator, enjoying the action from a safe distance.

"It's not just the feds I'm worried about," Whitehurst said. "Legal Services lawyers are making noise about suing you under RICO."

Rutledge picked up a scalpel. He patted the horse's flank, and leaned underneath. He pinched the scrotum, got no reaction, then made a quick incision. "I thought RICO was intended to bust the Mafia and whatnot."

"Smart poverty lawyers use it to go after substandard housing conditions."

As Jorge stroked the horse's muzzle, Rutledge peeled back the walls of the scrotum and pulled out the baseball-size testes. "They think I'm abusing my workers?"

Whitehurst didn't answer. He seemed fascinated as Rutledge tossed the testes into a bucket, where they landed with a *plop-plop*.

"Jorge, how long you work for me?"

"Thirty-two years, *jefe*. I started one week after I crossed over."

"Ever feel abused?"

"Only by mosquitoes during *irrigación*."

Rutledge moved swiftly, attaching the jaws of the emasculator to the spermatic cord. "How are your kids? Camilo, Dulce, Nieve, and one more boy. What's his name?"

Jorge stifled a laugh. "You know his name, *jefe*. It's Simeon."

"Hear that, Whitebread?" Rutledge tightened the emasculator and snapped the handles shut. The device hung from the underside of the horse like a giant, vise-gripped pair of pliers. In three minutes, the tissues of the spermatic cord would be crushed. The horse whinnied and wriggled its hindquarters but didn't seem to be in pain.

"My abused worker names his son after me." Rutledge came up from under the horse. "Young Simeon's a pharmacist in Sacramento. Owns his own shop, competes with the chains and still makes money."

"*El jefe* paid my boy's way through school," Jorge said, his voice filled with reverence. "Paid for the girls, too. Dulce and Nieve both went to Cal Davis. Dulce's a teacher. Nieve's in graduate school learning wine-making."

"I want the first bottle from her vineyard," Rutledge said.

"It will be called 'Zinfandel Simeon.' "

"Named after me or her brother?" Simeon teased.

"After you, *jefe*. Her brother drives her crazy."

Rutledge smiled. His best employees felt like family. He had no one else. He ducked back under the horse, released the emasculator jaws, and checked for bleeding. A few drops, nothing more. "Lots of antibacterial solution," he instructed Jorge. "Check him every couple of hours."

"I'll sleep right here," Jorge said, pointing at a pile of straw.

"No need. White Lightning's not exactly Barbaro."

"Is not a problem, *jefe*. If the horse is in pain, I should be here."

Rutledge threw an arm around Jorge and squeezed his shoulder. "That's my man."

Embarrassed, Jorge broke free and gave a slight bow. "Pardon me, El Patron, but I was listening before, about how some lawyers want to do you harm."

"Nothing to worry about, my friend."

Jorge cupped one of Rutledge's hands in both of his own and lowered his head, as if in the presence of royalty. "I only want to say, that if you ever need me for anything, no matter what, I will do it."

Rutledge smiled playfully at him. "What if I ask you to cut off someone's balls?"

"It would be done, *jefe*. And without painkillers."

THIRTY-FOUR

Wanda, the enormous Americana with the machete, was yelling. "Wake up! Wake up! There's work."

Marisol lifted her head from the dusty wood floor. The cabin at the Sugarloaf Lodge smelled of mice droppings and unwashed bodies. Nearly thirty immigrants were crammed into the one room. The other four women from her group, and perhaps two dozen more from earlier crossings. Men, women, children.

Marisol saw Wanda leaning down, veined breasts tumbling out of her sleeveless shirt like a pair of soccer balls. "C'mon, honey. Ah'm gonna send you out before the Frito Bandito wakes up, horny as a toad."

The Frito Bandito.

That's what Wanda called El Tigre. Wanda owned the Sugarloaf Lodge and housed the migrants until vans arrived to take them north.

"My son," Marisol protested. "I told you—I must wait for him."

"Problem is, the Frito Bandito ain't brought no kid across yet. And as long as you're here, the Bandito's gonna sniff around here, waiting for me to turn my back."

"But my Agustino . . ."

"Ah'll make damn sure the Bandito puts him in the next load."

"You can do that?"

"Me and my machete, damn right. Now, you want to

earn some cash? My driver will take you to the plant and bring you back tonight. By the morning, you'll be eating burritos with your boy."

Marisol wanted to believe it was true. She felt she could trust the woman. Hadn't Wanda already protected her from El Tigre?

"This plant," Marisol said. "What exactly is it?"

"It's a job," Wanda said with a shrug of her mountainous shoulders. "But it ain't exactly a weekend in Palm Springs."

Marisol rode in a van with four stone-faced men, Hondurans and Guatemalans. The driver was an old Mexican farmhand who said they would all be paid twelve dollars an hour. Almost one hundred dollars a day! And Tino would be here in the morning.

If the job is good, perhaps we can find a place to live. Stay a while, save money, then move deeper into California. The farther from the border, the better.

"Twelve dollars an hour is a lot," she said.

"You will earn every nickel," the driver said grimly. "And you will curse the day God created the cow."

Within minutes, they passed a body of water. Black and befouled. Back home, Father Castillo had preached about the fiery pits of hell, but even his imagination could not have stirred up this sight. Islands of manure floated in an ocean of urine, the foulest place she had ever seen. Her stomach clenched at the sulfurous mixture of rotting eggs, diseased flesh, and steaming excrement.

The van neared an enormous gray building with no windows. Outside, endless feed lots, thousands of cattle squeezed so close together, they seemed like one gigantic brown beast, its skin undulating in the morning sun.

Once inside the plant, the migrants were herded into

an office where a middle-aged woman at a desk ordered them to sign documents. Marisol doubted the others could read English. The documents seemed to say that the workers understood the risks of the work and would not seek compensation for any injuries.

A man wearing goggles and a white jumpsuit rushed into the office, shouting he needed half-a-dozen "beaners" for the conveyor line. The man, an Anglo with a reddened, chilled face, cursed the stinking Mexicans who didn't show up for work.

A fucked-up night shift, he complained. The line had shut down for an hour after a man lost a hand in the meat augur. The woman at the desk made a joke about "finger food." The red-faced man's voice was unnaturally loud, as if he might be hard of hearing. One of the stun guns wouldn't fire, and animals were backed up at the kill line. A gut-cooker shorted out, and they ended the shift eight hundred kills short. "Get every beaner you got on the production line," he ordered, looking toward Marisol for the first time. "I need one sticker and one knuckle dropper, preferably sober. Two kidney pullers. Don't matter if they're drunk or on meth. Maybe even better if they are."

The man hurried out, and the woman at the desk sent Marisol to the women's locker room to change. Moments later, the conveyor line foreman, a Chicano named Carlos, chunky with a broom-bristle mustache, strutted into the locker room as Marisol stood in her panties and blouse. She modestly turned her back to him but could feel his eyes on her. He watched silently as she stepped into a jumpsuit, then put on a chain-mail apron, armored gloves, and knee-high rubber boots. She wondered what her job would be and if this man with dried blood under his fingernails would be training her.

Carlos told her to hurry up and get her cute *culo* moving. His only other advice was not to drink any water, because it would be three hours before her first pee break.

"Do you want some tina?" he asked.

"Tina?"

"Crystal meth. To get you through the shift."

She shook her head.

"First day it's free. If you're still here tomorrow, I have the best prices in the plant."

"No, thank you."

He stared at her in the blatant way of Hispanic men, the way a bulldog admires a lamb chop. "Did you come north with a man?"

Another shake of the head.

His look straddled the bridge between sympathy and delight. "Do you know what they call a woman who crosses the border alone?"

The very same thing El Tigre had asked her. Did all these *pendejos* belong to the same club of prehistoric men?

"*La chingorda,*" the foreman said. "The fucked one."

"I can take care of myself."

"You're going to need a friend, *chica*. Now, follow me to the kill floor."

The kill floor.

Whatever she had to do, she told herself, she could handle. She followed Carlos through a heavy metal door and was hit by three sensations at once. The noise, the cold, and the squishing of her boots through puddles of blood. Large men wielded power saws that chunked through the spines of the cows, cutting them in half. Conveyor belts whined and meat grinders whirred at such a high pitch it hurt her ears. The cold was worse than any winter she had experienced.

Hispanic men carried sides of beef on their backs and hoisted the carcasses onto hooks. Other men hacked at the corpses like serial killers, indifferent to their victims.

Men in clean jumpsuits and goggles watched from metal catwalks that crisscrossed the plant twenty feet above the floor.

Carlos led her to a table next to a conveyor belt. Two short, sturdy women with impassive Indian features stood, flanking her, not looking up from their work. Carlos grabbed a chunk of bloody meat from the passing belt, tossed it onto the table and with three swift slices trimmed the fat. In one motion, he tossed the meat back onto the moving belt and hurled the scraps onto a second, higher conveyor. That was the extent of his instruction.

He leaned close and whispered in her ear, "I could have put you on the gut table. Ten hours pulling out intestines by hand." He smiled and scratched his bristly mustache with a blood-sticky fingernail. "But you're too pretty for that job."

He wished her *buena suerte* by grabbing each of her buttocks, then walked away.

Three hours later, Marisol was no longer cold. Sweat ran down her neck and trickled between her breasts under the chain-mail apron. Her right forearm ached and her fingers cramped into a curled position. She tried using her left hand for cutting, but her movements were unsure. She either cut away too much meat or too little. Twice, she sliced into the armored glove of her right hand. Once, the knife flew out of her hand, barely missing the woman to her left.

In her life, she had never imagined such a place.

Again, she thought of Father Castillo. She wanted to tell the priest that hell was not an inferno of sulphuric fires and suffocating heat. Hell was an icy, metallic cold. Hell was the whine of saws chewing through flesh and the stench of torn intestines spilling across countertops.

Marisol had hammered ten-penny nails through two-by-fours for hours. She had spread tar on roofs in the blistering August sun. She had cut sheet metal with hand tools. But no physical labor ever compared with this.

Drained of energy, her jumpsuit splattered with blood, her goggles steamed, Marisol felt her knees buckle. Close to fainting, she braced herself on the table. The woman to her left pointed to the clock and told her to take a break.

Back inside the locker room, Marisol took off her hard hat, apron, and gloves. She washed her hands and blood-speckled face. She saw two women taking paper-wrapped empanadas from their lockers. Marisol could smell the pork. If she spent a full day on the kill floor, she thought, she might never eat again. Certainly not meat.

She hurt everywhere, from a dull ache between her shoulder blades to a tingling sensation down her arms. How would she make it through the day? She pulled off her bloody boots, lay down on a bench, and closed her eyes.

As she drifted off, she thought of Tino. Dreamed of walking with him along a clean stream where the water splashed over rocks with the sound of chiming bells.

Marisol awakened with the sensation that she was falling.

Her feet hit the floor, and she was moving. Being pulled by the hair. Carlos screaming at her: "Break is ten minutes, not thirty!"

Calling her a stupid Mexican bitch. Dragging her across the tile into the shower room. Marisol yelling for help, other women sitting on benches, eating lunch, not making a move.

Carlos banged open a door to a toilet stall, pulled her

inside, slammed the door behind them. His eyes wild and bloodshot. The eyes of a *drogadicto*.

He spoke so rapidly in Spanglish she could barely understand him. He seemed to be comparing her unfavorably to his wife, who had given him four sons and a daughter, cooked like an angel, and had an ass that smelled like roses. Whereas Marisol was a stuck-up *mamey* who should be begging to swallow his *mermelada de miembrillo*. Then he struck the side of her head with an open palm. She staggered backward and her ears rang.

"I should fire you right now."

"Fine. Do it."

"But I'll fuck you first."

"You'll have to kill me and fuck a corpse."

He slapped her again, this time across the face, blurring her eyes. He jammed his hands into her armpits, picked her up, and slammed her against the side of the stall. Once, twice, three times, her head banged the wall. She felt herself go limp.

He ripped the front of her jumpsuit open, breaking the zipper and trapping her arms in the sleeves. Slid his hand into her panties, tore through her thick pubic hair and jammed a finger inside her. She struggled, but he was too strong. He leaned close and stuck a slobbering tongue into her ear. An hour earlier, she had watched cow tongues sailing by on a conveyor, and now she thought she would puke.

He inserted a second finger into her, twisted deeper. She stiffened with pain.

"Dry as an anthill," he complained. "But a pretty mouth."

He tried kissing her. He smelled like chilled blood and decaying flesh.

She swung her head back and forth, but he used his free hand to grip her jaw. In a second his tongue was in her mouth, licking her teeth. More pressure on her jaw muscles, and her mouth popped open, his tongue darting inside. He was saying something and drooling into her mouth at the same time. She gagged.

Then bit down as hard as she could.

Carlos screamed and spit blood.

Marisol spit, too. The tip of the man's tongue flew out of her mouth.

He reached for her throat, but she ducked and clawed at his face. Found his eye socket. Dug two fingers in deep as they would go—another scream—tore downward, tried to rip out the eye. The eye stayed, but the lid opened like a zipper. Blood spurted, and Carlos howled like a wounded boar.

Marisol wanted to slip around him, escape the stall. Carlos sunk to his knees, moaning, his bulk blocking her path. She tried to climb over him to the top of the door. He grabbed her ankle and pinned it.

Struggling to his feet, Carlos wrapped both arms around her legs, immobilizing her lower body. He whipped from side to side, cursing in Spanish, calling her the whore of all eternity, showering both of them with his blood, crushing her against the metal wall of the stall. Bolts of pain shot up her spine and into the base of her skull. She fought to stay conscious, knowing that if she passed out, she would never wake up.

Still in his grip, she wrapped one arm around his neck, squarely across his Adam's apple. Pulled back as hard as she could. Carlos gasped, choked, sprayed more blood. His eyes bulged like a toxic fish. He heaved forward and back, desperate to shake her off. She summoned the last of her strength to pull her arm even tighter around his neck. A gurgle bubbled from his throat like a breath exhaled under water.

His wishbone snapped with a *cra-ack,* and his slivered tongue shot out, a bloody dart between his lips.

She slid off him just as he pitched forward, his forehead banging into the tile wall. He sank to the floor, his skull bouncing off the toilet tank and into the water, which quickly turned a foamy pink.

Marisol stood there, panting and trembling. She could pull his head from the toilet, where he seemed to be drowning, or she could run.

She opened the stall door and ran.

She expected security guards to grab her. Hadn't the noise attracted attention? But the only people in the locker room were three women on their breaks. If they heard the commotion, they did not care to investigate or sound an alarm.

Marisol stripped out of the jumpsuit, now covered with human as well as bovine blood. She climbed into her jeans, tugged on her blouse, slipped into her sneakers, and ran. She passed through the front office, the woman at the desk looking up, saying something, but Marisol was out the door before the words reached her.

Her mind was a blur. A highway ran along the slaughterhouse property. But to where?

I have nowhere to go.

Horrified, she looked at her hands. Bloody and shaking uncontrollably. If *La Migra* caught her, she would be deported. Or worse, sent to prison. If she walked along the highway, the police would stop her.

A van was just pulling out of the parking lot. Six migrants in the back, the driver staring at her. The old Mexican from this morning, the man who brought her here from the stash house. He stopped and waved her to come closer.

Hesitantly, she moved toward the van. The driver opened the window. She could not decipher his look. Anger? Fear? Compassion? Or merely the acknowledgment that the expected had indeed occurred?

In the distance, she heard a police siren.

"Get in, child," the driver said. "There is no time to waste."

THIRTY-FIVE

Ninety minutes after leaving Sheriff Deputy Dixon handcuffed to his steering wheel, Jimmy and Tino drove into Mexico under a gray and sickly sky.

Nothing to it. Payne waved his passport under the nose of a border agent and Tino just waved. Easier getting into Mexico, Payne thought, than it would be returning to the States.

He had a simple plan. Trace Marisol's steps. To do that, he had to find El Tigre, the coyote who took her across. Then, to get back across, Payne needed new I.D. and a car that wasn't posted on the computer screens of every cop from San Diego to Yuma.

Yep. Simple.

The starting point was the cantina where Tino and Marisol met El Tigre. Tino seemed confident he could find the place. Payne wondered, but so far the little guy was proving capable. He seemed to be a skillful burglar, and he excelled at what the law called "resisting arrest with violence."

They drove past the New River, a filthy stream bubbling with foam and rank, brown water. Payne guided the Lexus down Imperial Avenue into the urban sprawl of Mexicali. The A/C was working overtime, but he still sweated heavily. The thermometer on a bank building read 41 degrees. Centigrade. The digital readout on the Lexus dashboard was 106.

They entered a neighborhood where every business seemed to be a bar, a pharmacy, a strip club, or a shop selling purses and pottery to sunburned Yankees in shorts and sandals. Squat, dark women in long dresses strolled the sidewalks, arms outstretched, displaying fake gold chains, chanting "Bargain. Ten dollar."

Payne tuned the radio to a local station. A routine news day in the capital city of the state of Baja. A meth lab had blown up, killing some neighbors. Drug traffickers had assassinated a police chief. And a tunnel had collapsed, killing three people trying to sneak underground to Calexico.

Before long, Payne was lost. They were on a street of storefront dental clinics and doctors whose signs boasted of cheap *cirugia plástica*. They found their way back to a neighborhood of tourist-trap bars. After cruising the same block three times, Tino shouted, "There! That's where we met the *cabrón*."

Payne found a place to park, and they walked through swinging saloon doors and into a cantina that looked like a set of a 1950s Western with Randolph Scott and John Wayne. Paddle fans stirred the air but did little to cool it. Wooden wagon wheels were nailed to the walls. On the speakers, Gene Autry was singing, "Back in the Saddle Again."

Sitting at tables were a few sweating, shorts-and-sneakered Americans. Looking for cheap thrills or cheap Xanax. Still too early and too hot for much of a crowd. Several men who appeared to be locals sat at the bar. Tino scanned the room, then shook his head. El Tigre was not here.

The bartender, a bilingual *Tejano* in a Texas A&M

T-shirt, took their order. A Pacifico for Payne, Pepsi for Tino. The beer and soda both arrived in bottles, both lukewarm.

No, the bartender said. He'd never heard of El Tigre. Sure, plenty of coyotes stopped in there. Drug smugglers, too. They think it's easier to spot Mexican undercover cops in a place like this.

Tino described El Tigre. The bartender laughed. "A fat Mexican man with gold teeth and a crucifix. That narrows it down."

The boy's face showed disappointment.

"Sorry," the bartender said. "No way to keep track of all the hustlers around here. Even if you knew his real name, it wouldn't mean nothing." He looked around, leaned closer to Payne. "But anything else you need, just ask. I got connections."

"I need to sell a car."

"I got a guy for you. A *mestizo* called 'Stingray.' What do you have?"

"Lexus SUV. Leased. I don't have the title."

"Stingray don't care. He's just gonna sell it to some *pachuco*. What do you want for it?"

"Another car."

The bartender nodded as if the request was no more unusual than asking for lime with your Corona. He took down Payne's cell number on a paper napkin and said Stingray would call him within an hour. A few seats down the bar, two middle-aged Mexican men in Western shirts and cowboy boots seemed to take an interest in the conversation.

"What's with those guys?" Payne asked.

"Local *vaquetóns*. Street guys. Petty thieves. Drivers for coyotes. Anything that pays." He lowered his voice to a whisper. "You need anything else?"

"Papers. Documents to get us back into the States."

The bartender gave them a *no-problema* shrug. "I got

a *Chino* with a print shop. Green cards, driver's licenses, whatever you want. Excellent work." He rubbed a thumb against an index finger. "*Pero mucho dinero.* And this *Chino* don't take no American Express."

"Got it covered." Payne still had forty-eight hundred bucks and change.

The bartender wrote the address of the print shop on another napkin and slid it toward Payne.

One of the two *vaquetóns,* a man about forty, smelling of tobacco and beer, came up behind Payne and said, "I know three *pendejos* who call themselves 'El Tigre.' "

"Three?" Payne asked. "How's that possible?"

The man shrugged. "I know two other men who call themselves 'El León.' The Lion. Around here, everyone wants to appear tough, even when they are full of shit."

"So who are the three tigers?"

"One lives near Bataques and runs cockfights. He is perhaps seventy years old."

"Not the man," Tino said.

"Another informs for the *judicales.* A little rodent of a man."

Tino shook his head.

"And there is an El Tigre who owes me money for driving a truck across the desert and getting arrested by *La Migra.* A *pollero* who wears a crucifix but will surely rot in hell."

"That's him!" Tino cried.

"His cousin owns a cantina on the other side of the city. If you tell him you have cash and need a *pollero,* he will set up a meeting."

"What cantina?" the boy asked.

"Five hundred dollars." Looking at Payne now.

"Don't pay him," the bartender advised. "He's hustling you."

The man shrugged. "Your decision."

Payne didn't know if he was being hustled. But they'd come this far, and this was their only lead. He opened his wallet and peeled off five hundred-dollar bills.

"Try a bar called 'El Disco,' " the man told him. "A block from the bullring that's shaped like a flying saucer."

"Let's go, Tino," Payne said.

"One more thing," the man called after them. "El Tigre carries a stiletto in his left boot."

THIRTY-SIX

With Tino navigating, Payne tried following directions to a bar called "El Disco" but was lost within minutes. They cruised around a residential neighborhood of bungalows painted in bright blues, greens, and yellows. Every block seemed to have several one-story houses with naked rebar sticking straight up through the outside walls, awaiting the money to complete a second floor. Sagging bags of cement and piles of sand looked as if they'd been there for years. Ancient cars were propped on cinder blocks in side yards, bright shirts hanging limp on clotheslines.

"What's with all the Virgin Mary statues in the front yards?" Payne asked.

"Only a *gabacho* from Beverly Hills would ask such a stupid question."

"I'm a *gabacho* from Van Nuys."

"A long time ago, some religious dude saw the Virgin Mary walking on a hill."

"The Virgin of Guadalupe?"

"*Exactamente.*"

"So why paint her on the hubcaps of an '83 Plymouth?"

"Just drive, *vato*. Look for the bullring shaped like a flying saucer."

Music poured from open windows. Dogs roamed the streets and chickens squawked in fenced-in yards. Kids pranced under a spraying garden hose. The digital thermometer on the dashboard inched up a notch to 107.

They passed an elementary school, mothers walking home with their children in the protective shade of umbrellas, like ducks under their mother's wings.

They could not find the bullring or the bar called "El Disco." There were taco stands and dance clubs, a Ley supermarket, and a Cinépolis movie theater. It was beginning to look as if Payne had been conned out of five hundred bucks. But just past a complex of government buildings, there it was, a bullfighting arena shaped like a flying saucer.

"Over there," Tino said, pointing toward a lighted sign barely visible in the midday glare. El Disco.

They parked the car and walked into the dark, cool cantina, patrons on bar stools hunched over bottles of Tecate, turning in unison to appraise the newcomers. Shaved heads. Wife-beater tees. Tattoos from wrists to skulls. In L.A., they would be gangbangers. Here? Payne was fairly certain he hadn't stumbled into a meeting of the Rotarians or Elks.

"Tino, I don't like the feel of this place."

"Be cool, Himmy."

Tino bounced up to the bar, chattered in Spanish to

the bartender, pointed at Payne, talked some more, then bounced back.

"What?" Payne asked.

"I told him you were an American with thirty thousand dollars in cash."

"Great. We're gonna get mugged."

"I said you wanted to get a bunch of whores across the border."

"So now I'm a rich pimp?"

"He said for two hundred dollars he would call a man named 'El Tigre' who can help us."

"Wow. Good work." He gave two hundred-dollar bills to Tino, who turned the money over to the bartender, then listened as the man gave directions in Spanish.

Returning to Payne's side, Tino said, "We're supposed to go to a bowling alley named 'Bola.' El Tigre will meet us there in two hours."

"Okay, let's go."

One of the wife-beatered, shaved heads slid off his bar stool and moved toward them. Thick-necked, with short, heavily muscled arms and steroid-pimpled shoulders, he walked on his toes, as if trying to look taller.

"*Cuánto?*" the man growled at Payne.

"How much for what?"

"*El muchacho*. How much for the boy?"

"He's not for sale, but I'm thinking about giving him away."

"He looks like a *quebracho*." Using one of the seemingly endless Spanish words for homosexual.

"Yeah, well you look like a side of beef that got all the wrong hormones."

The man took another step toward Payne. He was only five-eight or so, his nose just inches from Payne's chest. "Maybe I just take the *quebracho* from you."

The guy's breath smelled like pork rinds soaked in

beer. He was waiting for Payne to push him or hit him so he could retaliate with some kung fu bullshit.

Buying time, Payne said, "You know the difference between a Mexican heterosexual and homosexual?"

"*¿Qué?*"

"Two beers."

The bodybuilder jammed a finger into Payne's chest. "That's stupid."

"Cesar Chavez loved that joke. He told it to Jerry Brown, and they had a good laugh."

"*¡No me jodas!* Get the fuck out. The boy stays with me."

Payne swung his head down as fast as he could, butting Pork Breath on the bridge of his nose. The man's septum cracked, and blood spurted onto Payne's shirt. The guy's hands flew to his face, and he sputtered curses in Spanish. A volcano of *chingalo*s and *baboso*s plus some words Payne had never heard.

Tino raced out the door ahead of Payne, but only by a step.

THIRTY-SEVEN

Jimmy and Tino drove through a neighborhood of small shops with brightly painted murals on the stucco walls, depicting Mexico's long history. The Spanish killing Indians. American cavalry killing Mexican soldiers. Mexicans killing one another. It was not a happy history. One mural, labeled "La Frontera," portrayed U.S. Border Patrol agents machine-gunning migrants as they swam across the Rio Grande. Okay, so the artist took some liberties.

The print shop was on the way to Bola, so it made sense to stop there before the meeting with El Tigre. A printer of Chinese descent, a man in his sixties with a bemused smile, said it would cost Payne $1,500 for an Illinois driver's license. Easier to forge than a California license, and harder to check out by a highway patrolman or sheriff's deputy. He would throw in a matching passport for free.

Payne got to choose a new name. California cops would be looking for a James Payne of Van Nuys. Jimmy chose "Alexander Hamilton" of Evanston. He liked sharing the name of a man killed in a duel.

Papers for Tino weren't so simple. Border agents would examine them much more closely. A temporary work permit didn't suit a twelve-year-old. And a green card was out of the question because the border station had scanners that could pick up a phony. The printer had a selection of legitimate visas, some stolen, some lost. His equipment could alter names and photos. He suggested using a visa intended for a transfer student, a Mexican boy attending Temple Emanuel Academy Day School in Beverly Hills.

"Shalom," Payne said.

"Twenty-two hundred dollars," the printer announced happily.

Payne exhaled a whistle. He'd be nearly broke again.

"Guaranteed to work," the printer chuckled, eyes twinkling, "or your money back when you get out of prison."

He snapped digital photos of both of them and said the documents would be ready by eleven that night. Moments later, Payne's cell phone rang. The man who called himself "Stingray," asking about the Lexus Payne wanted to trade.

Stingray claimed to have several cars that wouldn't set off alarms going through the border checkpoints. Payne said they were headed to a bowling alley named "Bola." Why not meet there?

Jimmy and Tino found Bola without getting lost. They were an hour early for the meeting with El Tigre and right on time for Stingray.

The place was ninety percent bar and ten percent bowling alley. Just two warped lanes that looked as if they'd suffered water damage when the Colorado River flooded a hundred years ago. Four men bowled on one lane, waving fistfuls of pesos over their heads, shouting insults at one another as they bet on each frame. Their balls rattled down the lane like cars with bad shocks, clattering into faded yellow pins that showed nicks and hairline fractures from stem to stern.

And then there were the pin-boys.

Payne had never seen a bowling alley with real, live boys working the pit, hand-dropping pins into the setter and rolling the ball down a wooden track that looked like a split-log sluice at an old gold mine.

There were no molded plastic chairs, no video score-boards, no rock music, no pulsating strobes for "rock 'n bowl." There was a single rack of house balls and a cardboard box of smelly shoes of indeterminate size.

Stingray wasn't hard to find. He sat at the bar wearing a T-shirt emblazoned with a red Corvette Stingray. He was a stocky man in his forties with a thick nose, coppery skin, and black hair pulled back into a ponytail. Cradling a chilled Negra Modelo, he said, "I got a couple things in my inventory you might like. A three-year-old Mini Cooper, very clean."

"My Lexus is worth two Mini Coopers," Payne replied.

Stingray shrugged. "Maybe the Mini's not for you, anyway. A real pussy car. You want wheels with machismo, eh?"

"Something that'll blend in but can outrun a cop if we have to."

Stingray grinned. He'd lost a front tooth and never found it. "How about something with a Cobra V-8 on a big block, 428 cubic inches, throws out 335 horse-power?"

"Holy shit. What is it?"

"Mustang convertible, 1969. Acapulco blue."

"That'll be inconspicuous."

"A real classic. Original paint job."

"What about the engine? That original, too?"

"Reconditioned in the nineties. Goes like hell. I had it up to 135 before it started to shimmy. But watch the steering. It pulls right."

"That's all you've got?"

"Special orders take a week."

Payne was beaten. "Bring the Mustang around."

"What license plate you want? I got most of the states, plus Puerto Rico. New Mexico's nice. 'Land of Enchantment.' "

"It should match my new driver's license. Make it Illinois."

" 'Land of Lincoln.' You got it."

Stingray asked for the keys to the Lexus, saying he'd bring the Mustang back within an hour. He promised to transfer their belongings, including the metal baseball bat in the backseat. They would meet later in the alley behind the bowling alley.

It had scam written all over it, Payne thought. But he shot a look at Tino, who nodded his approval. The kid was supposed to know the territory. Payne tossed the keys to someone he knew virtually nothing about. Not even his real name. All Payne knew was the man's occupation: car thief.

"What do we do while we wait for El Tigre?" Tino asked.

Not knowing whether Stingray would return with the Mustang or the police, or even if he would return at all, Payne sighed and said, "We bowl."

THIRTY-EIGHT

Payne checked out Bola's rack of balls, all cratered moonscapes. He chose a black sixteen-pounder, whose brand name had worn off over time. Trying not to inhale, he picked up a couple of mismatched bowling shoes that nearly fit. Tino grabbed an orange eleven-pound ball, and decided to bowl in his socks.

The lane was impossible, the ball hooking on the dry spots and skidding on the oil. Ignoring the scoring, Payne worked with Tino on his form. No one had ever taught the boy the four-step approach or the proper follow-through. But he was a natural. Within a few minutes, he was starting to look smooth, even if the ball hopscotched over the warped boards on the way to the pins.

As he bowled, Payne planned what he would say to

El Tigre. It shouldn't be difficult, right? All he needed was a scrap of information.

Where did you take Marisol Perez, you bastard?

If Marisol was okay, there would be nothing to hide.

In the adjacent lane, a man who'd been winning his bets called over to Payne. "Ey, *gringo*. You want to bowl against me? Twenty dollars a frame."

An image of the Paul Newman movie *The Hustler* flashed through Payne's mind. Local thugs breaking his thumbs after he took their money.

"Sure," Payne said. "Let's roll."

"Himmy. Not such a good idea." Tino shook his head hard, as if trying to get water out of his ears.

The man, in a T-shirt advertising a local strip club, belly protruding over his jeans, carried his ball to their lane. Payne rolled first. If it had been a tee shot in golf, it would have hooked into the woods. The ball lunged toward the left gutter, hitting only the seven pin. The pin-boy rolled Payne's ball back, and this time he released underhanded and hard, rolling it straight for the pocket. Pins clattered, but the six skipped around the ten, leaving it standing.

"Nine pins," his opponent said. He took a strange three-step approach, threw off the wrong foot, and sent a bouncing ball on the Brooklyn side of the headpin. After a decent mix, the two-seven baby split was left standing . . . until the pin-boy swept out a leg and knocked them both over.

"Strike!" the man yelled. "Twenty bucks."

Payne shook his head at the brazenness of the scam and forked over a twenty. He picked up his ball for the second frame. As he settled into his stance, the ball resting comfortably just above his right hip, Tino called to him. "Himmy!"

Payne turned and saw a large man with a fleshy, pockmarked face. He wore wraparound sunglasses, and his jeans were held up by a belt with a huge buckle engraved with a tiger. Expensive cowboy boots. Soft leather—ostrich, maybe. His unbuttoned shirt revealed a chest gone to flab and a heavy gold crucifix. On his head, a thick mass of black hair was lacquered into place with shiny brilliantine.

The man gaped, his eyes darting from Tino to Payne and back again. He was expecting to meet a rich American who wanted to bring whores across the border. Instead, here was the boy he had left behind on his last crossing.

"You?" he asked, his befuddlement turning to anger. "The bastard son of a worthless whore! My nephew gives you a free ride to the U.S.A. and you come back to Mexico? You are one stupid *chilito*."

"Where's my mother!" Tino shouted.

"*Chinga tu madre!*"

"No. Fuck you!"

"Your whore mother owes me money."

"Don't talk to the boy like that." Payne still cradled the sixteen-pound ball.

El Tigre slid his sunglasses down his nose and peered at Payne. "What's your deal, *gabacho*?"

"I'm helping Tino find his mother. The two got separated when you botched the crossing."

"Lies! *¡Pinche puto pendejo baboso!*"

From having been cursed at by cops, clients, and bondsmen, Payne thought he'd just been called a fucking stupid faggot asshole. "Just tell us where she is," he demanded.

"Where I took her is *como se dice, un secreto profesional.*"

"A trade secret?" Tino sneered.

"What's your trade, kidnapping women?" Payne taunted the man.

"*¡Vete a la chingada!*" El Tigre reached down and

drew a knife from inside his left boot. Flicked his wrist, and a silver blade shot out. Held it in his left hand. A southpaw.

Quick movements for a big man, Payne noted, figuring he might need that information in a matter of seconds. Payne wished he still had Quinn's gun. Or a crowbar.

El Tigre pointed the knife at Payne's chest. "Stay out of my business, *pendejo,* or you will go back to the States without your liver."

"Just tell me where you left Marisol. Then I'll get out of your life."

El Tigre stepped closer, waved the knife under Payne's nose. "I swear I fuck you up."

"I'm already fucked up."

"Don't let him scare you, Himmy!"

"He doesn't," Payne lied.

"When I am done with the *gabacho,*" El Tigre said, looking at Tino, "I will take care of you."

"*¡Chingalo!*" Tino shot back.

Just as El Tigre started to say something to Tino, Payne flipped the bowling ball underhanded. It plopped heavily on the soft leather toes of El Tigre's left boot. He yelped and hopped sideways but . . . *shit!* . . . did not drop the knife.

Payne took a step toward the man. Then ducked, El Tigre on one foot, sweeping the air with a roundhouse swipe of the knife.

Payne came up from under, dug a short left into the man's gut, catching some ribs, missing the solar plexus.

El Tigre winced, staggered back a step, but kept the knife chest high.

Payne stood stone still, waited for the man to lunge with the knife. Didn't have to wait long. El Tigre stabbed the air, Payne batted the arm away by blocking an elbow, then throwing a straight left at the chin.

The punch was off, grazing El Tigre's cheek and sliding into his oily hair. But the second half of Payne's combination was just perfect. A right hook straight into the man's solar plexus.

A *whoosh* of air. El Tigre bent over to catch his breath.

"Hit him again, Himmy!" Tino urged, fists raised as if shadow-boxing.

Payne locked both hands and brought them up, straight under the man's chin. Solid contact, knuckles on jaw. A *crunch,* and a yelp of pain, and El Tigre spit out a gold tooth. Payne grabbed him, two hands on a wrist, twisted the arm behind the man's back, kicked a leg out, and propelled him facedown onto the floor.

He straddled El Tigre's back, grabbed the heavy gold chain, and tightened it into a garotte. The chain bit into the man's neck, drawing blood. El Tigre bucked like a rodeo horse, but Payne held on as the man turned blue.

"*¡Dónde!*" Payne yelled. "Where's Marisol Perez?"

The man threw an elbow backward, missing Payne's head.

Payne tightened the chain. "Did you hurt her? Did you!"

"*¡Chingate!*" The curse bubbling out of El Tigre's throat.

"Where is she!"

"Make him tell!" Tino yelled when they got no answer.

Grabbing a handful of slick hair, Payne rammed El Tigre's face into the filthy wooden floor. Still gripping the chain with his other hand, Payne lifted the man's head, slammed it again. Blood spurted from El Tigre's nose. One more time, Payne smashed him into a floorboard, leaving behind a gold-capped tooth impaled in the wood.

"What'd you do to her!" Payne yelled.

Tears squeezed from the man's eyes. Blood pooled on the floor.

"Where is she! Where's Marisol Perez?"

El Tigre tried to talk, and Payne loosened the chain.

It took a few seconds of sputtering and spittle. "*No sé*. Not my business. I just drop off the *pollos*. Someone else cooks them."

"Where'd you drop her?"

The big man coughed up a spray of misting blood. "At Wanda La Ballena's."

"Wanda the Whale?" Tino said.

"Big *gabacha. Enormes chichis.*"

"What's her real name?" Payne said.

"*No sé.*"

"Where's her stash house?"

"Some cabins outside a desert town north of the border."

"What town?"

El Tigre rambled in Spanish, Payne picking up most of it. A few miles west of Plaster City. A little turd of a town. Ocotillo. Sugarloaf Lodge. A dung heap next to the railroad tracks.

Payne heard a shout in Spanish from behind the bar. The bartender pointing a gun and yelling something Payne couldn't understand, though he was fairly sure it wasn't an invitation to happy hour.

Payne slid off El Tigre. "C'mon, Tino!"

The bartender, gun in hand, hustled toward them. They were cut off from the front door.

"This way." Payne pointed down the lane. They sprinted along the gutter, toward the pins, Payne in his borrowed bowling shoes, Tino in his socks. Jimmy dived at the last moment, sliding straight at the headpin, covering his head with his hands. The clattering was so loud that Payne thought the bartender had fired his gun, but it was just the pins, smashing into one another. He left a seven pin standing, but Tino came behind him and cleared it out.

"¡Semipleno!" the pin-boy declared from his perch, awarding a spare.

"Where's the back door?" Payne yelled.

The pin-boy pointed into the darkness behind the lanes.

Jimmy and Tino ran that way. When they reached the alley, Stingray was sitting at the wheel of an old blue Mustang convertible that could use a paint job. The engine was throbbing, a full-throated roar of rolling thunder, Stingray giving it gas, showing off.

Payne threw open the door and yanked Stingray out. Tino hopped over the passenger door, and Payne banged his bad knee on the steering wheel sliding in. He threw the gearshift into first, popped the clutch, and floored the accelerator. The Mustang fishtailed and belched a cloud of oily smoke.

Payne could barely hear his own voice over the racket as he yelled to Tino, "Which way is north, kiddo?"

THIRTY-NINE

What a shithole, Eugene Rigney thought.

One hundred four degrees, shirt sticking like flypaper to the Chrysler's seat back, a blazing wind that seared your throat. Rigney had vowed to follow Jimmy Payne to hell and back. Now the detective thought he'd made it halfway.

Rigney had grown up near Hermosa Beach, surfed as a kid, and thought of California as an endless expanse of ocean. Foggy mornings and chilly waves. God, how he loved to walk barefoot through the shore-break, foamy as a margarita.

And Christ, how I hate the desert.

Endless miles of dirt, baked hard as concrete. Thorny plants that could rip your eyes out. Minutes earlier, the New River had announced its presence with the sulferous aroma of floating turds. Flowing north from Mexico, sizzling in the heat, the brown snake of a river was a steaming current of raw sewage and industrial runoff. Rocky shallows were decorated with shredded Styrofoam coolers, rusted bicycles, and tree limbs bleached the color of skeletons.

A deflated Zodiac was stuck on the rocks. The mode of transport for some illegals, risking hepatitis, flesh-eating bacteria, even polio, the poor bastards. Rigney shot a look at a nearby tract of land. Concrete-block stucco houses, a few trailers. How the hell could people live here?

He watched a dead animal float by, either a dog or a coyote, its limbs stiffened. Earlier, he'd run over an animal on Route 86. The damn thing *crunch*ed under his tires. Armadillo, maybe?

Wishing he could run over Jimmy Payne, hear the music of his bones breaking. But at the moment, Rigney knew he was the one up to his ass in armadillos.

Internal Affairs was investigating. He had failed to follow procedures and couldn't prove he gave Payne $50,000 instead of the $45,000 they recovered. His commander had never signed off on using Payne as the bag man. Judge Rollins's suicide had compromised the investigation and inspired the *Los Angeles Times* to crow about the L.A.P.D.'s "illegal entrapment" and "lethal harassment" of public officials. The preliminary I.A. report called Rigney a "reckless cowboy" and his superior suggested he should retain counsel for a disciplinary hearing.

Shit, I could end up working security at Trader Joe's, collecting shopping carts in the parking lot.

He wanted to kill J. Atticus Payne, Esquire. But only after inflicting a world of pain on the shyster. Now, just outside the shitkicker town of Calexico, Rigney was on his trail. An Imperial County sheriff's deputy had arrested Payne, then let him escape. What's with this Payne-as-Houdini shit? First he gets away from his ex-wife, and now an armed cop? Not that Rigney believed Sharon Payne's story. The woman still had a soft spot for that loser scumbag.

Maybe I can blame her for this whole goat fuck. Tell Internal Affairs she vouched for her ex as the bag man.

Not that it was true. But desperate times call for shitty measures.

He drove past a yellow sign with the silhouettes of a man, a woman, and a little girl running. *"CAUTION"* printed across the top. Warning motorists to avoid turning wetbacks into roadkill on the melting asphalt. Bullet holes peppered the sign, a welcome-to-California from the local yokels.

Ten minutes later, Rigney was sitting in front of Deputy Howard Dixon's desk in a trailer adjacent to a bone-dry drainage ditch. The trailer was a sorry excuse for a sheriff's substation, situated within sight of the Mexican border as part of the futile attempt to keep mules—the human variety—from carrying drugs north. Rigney could barely hear the deputy over the whine of a window air conditioner that dripped rusty water but did nothing to cool the place. He was dying for a beer.

Next to a poster was the taxidermied head of a wild boar. Damn thing stank. Wide-eyed, as if surprised to be decorating a cop shop, the boar stared into the face of Governor Schwarzenegger, whose photo hung on the trailer's opposite wall, a measly six feet away.

"I thought Payne might give me trouble," the deputy was saying, "but not the little beaner. I guess I lost track of him."

On a video monitor, they watched the tape from the cruiser's camera. There was Payne, handcuffed and blabbering a mile a minute to the deputy, the Mexican boy ducking out of the picture.

"The kid said he had to pee," the deputy explained.

Violating Traffic Stops 101, Rigney thought. Letting one of the subjects out of your sight.

"The kid has this innocent look," the deputy continued. "Speaks good English. Neatly groomed. If he'd been the typical beaner, I'd have been more careful. You think that's prejudiced, Detective?"

No, but it's fucking stupid, you sunburned hick.

"Don't sweat it," Rigney said. "Could happen to anyone."

On the monitor, the image jumped and so did Payne. Rigney squinted at the screen. The first shotgun blast had blown out a front tire. The second blast knocked out the picture for a moment. When the grainy image returned, Dixon was giving up his gun.

"Why didn't you shoot Payne when you had the chance?" Rigney asked.

"He wasn't armed."

"Neither was that five hundred pounds of bacon on your wall, but you blasted him." Gesturing toward the boar.

"I wasn't in fear of great bodily harm from Mr. Payne," the deputy said, as if practicing for the sergeant's exam.

"You have any idea what Payne was doing in this godforsaken place?"

"Said he was looking for the kid's mother. She disappeared or something."

"Bullshit. Royal Payne doesn't do diddly-squat for anyone else unless there's an angle."

The deputy's phone rang. He picked it up, said "Yup" a couple times, hung up. "Five hours ago, cameras picked up Payne's Lexus crossing the border into Mexico at the Mexicali station. That'd be about thirty minutes before our bulletins went out."

"Great. Just great." Sweating a river, seething with anger.

"Not to worry, Detective. He'll come back, sooner or later. When he does, we'll grab him."

"You're pretty confident for a guy who lost his gun to a half-pint wetback."

"I want Payne as much as you do. The way I see it, Payne's the cricket, and I'm the spider."

"Actually, Payne is more like a cockroach," Rigney said. "Just when you have the bastard cornered, you learn he can fly."

FORTY

Sitting cross-legged in the shade of a corrugated metal sheet propped on wooden posts, Marisol traced letters in the dust.

"T-I-N-O"

Again and again. Leaving a trail of *Tino*s as she yearned for her missing son.

My boy, my boy. I am so sorry I left you behind.

The driver who brought her here—the old Mexican from the Sugarloaf—called the place "Hellhole Canyon." A farmhouse, a chicken pen, a fenced yard smelling of animal droppings and creosote. An American man with a rifle paced in the sun, guarding the migrants, though the surrounding mountains and canyons seemed sentinels enough. Chickens pecked the ground near the man's feet. He kicked a skinny hen that looked diseased. Sent it squawking, frayed wings flapping.

Marisol tried to focus on her surroundings. Knew she must survive yet another day. She counted eighteen other migrants sitting or crouching or lying in the shade.

Waiting. They had been waiting for hours.

"Don't be thinking I'm gonna feed you." A rifle slung over a bony shoulder, the *Americano* guarding them had the emaciated look of a drug user. "I ain't no KFC, even if I got chickens coming out my ass."

He was shirtless and wore filthy jeans, with a red bandanna around his neck. A bandolier filled with bullets crisscrossed his bare chest like suspenders. His scratchy little goat's beard was spotted with specks of dribbled food. He had several tattoos, but the one on his forehead drew the most attention. A crudely drawn, blue-green swastika. Marisol avoided looking into the man's eyes, which seemed to float in their sockets.

"Ain't my fault you're starving," the man continued. "Vans are late."

He stomped through the chicken droppings, chewing on a green apple, surveying the migrants. "You people eat roadkill, doncha? Hushed puppies. Asphalt armadillo. Pavement possum."

He cackled at his own stupid joke, drool trickling down one corner of his mouth.

It had been several hours since the old driver had rescued her from the slaughterhouse. As he drove, she tearfully told him about the attack in the locker room and how she had fought off the foreman, perhaps even killing him. Alarmed, the driver called Wanda, repeated the story, then listened a moment before hanging up.

"*La jefa* says it is too dangerous for you to come back," he told Marisol.

He had driven along a lake, through a desert, across dry washes, and into the mountains. He turned onto a dirt road and stopped at the old chicken farm, virtually surrounded by steep mountain walls. Vans were supposed to be there to take a group of migrants to farms upstate.

"Watch out for the *encargado*," the driver had warned her, before driving off. "A *drogadicto* who thinks he is a Nazi. Probably insane. Just wait for the van and stay away from him."

With that, Marisol was left in the shade among defecating chickens and snoring migrants, the corrugated roof hot as a griddle.

She heard a scream. A woman yelling, "No! No! No!"

Marisol squinted into the sunlight. The woman's husband, a Mexican of perhaps forty, stood with his back against a tree, his hands up by his ears, holding onto a squirming, squawking chicken. Thirty feet away, the Nazi aimed his rifle at the man.

No, that's not it!

The Nazi was trying to shoot the chicken off the man's head. A surreal sight, a scene from a nightmare, a hallucination.

"Hold still, Pancho!" the Nazi yelled. "Christ! Hold that bird still before it shits on your head!"

Trembles shook the man's body. The chicken flapped its wings and screeched.

The man's wife wailed in Spanish, invoking the names of the Father, the Son, and the Holy Ghost.

"Stand up straight, goddammit!" the Nazi ordered.

The man's knees buckled.

"I can shoot the freckle off a rabbit's nose at fifty feet. But you gotta hold still, Pancho."

The man squeezed his eyes shut.

The sound of the gunshot echoed off the canyon walls. The man fell to the ground, screaming, his face covered with blood.

"You ain't hit, Pancho! If you was hit, you wouldn't be yelling."

The decapitated chicken flopped on the ground, spurting gore.

"Who's next? Who wants to be in the circus?"

The driver was right, Marisol thought. *This man is insane.*

"C'mon now! Deadeye Dickie Chitwood is just warming up."

The migrants studied the tops of their boots, sneakers, and huaraches.

"You! Come on down!" Pointing at a man next to Marisol. Mid-twenties. Honduran, she thought, coppery complexion with Indian features. The man didn't resist, didn't say a word. Just walked to the blood-spattered tree and stood there. Like he'd taken orders all his life.

"My man!" the Nazi shouted. "See!" He gestured to the silent migrants under the corrugated sheet metal. "No fear. This greaser's gonna make a lot of money climbing peach trees for Mr. Rutledge."

The Nazi took an apple from the back pocket of his jeans, placed it on the Honduran's head. The apple fell to the ground.

"Pick that up, goddammit! You let it drop again, I'll dig you a third eye."

The man put the apple back on his head. This time, it stayed in place, even as the man's legs swayed.

The Nazi moved back to a mark he had made in the dirt, then sighted the rifle. "Gotta adjust for wind and curvature of the earth." Another cackle of laughter. He was still laughing when he pulled the trigger.

An explosion blew apart the man's forehead, and he sank to the ground as if his knees were made of butter.

"Oh, shit!" the Nazi said. "Gonna be one wet short for Mr. Rutledge."

Her stomach clenching, Marisol turned away.

One more day, Tino, she promised herself.

I will live one more day, and I will see you before I die.

FORTY-ONE

In Mexicali, heading north toward the border, the souped-up Mustang passed rows of whitewashed wooden crosses, printed with block-lettered names. Honoring the *pollos* who died trying to reach *El Norte*.

Tino watched the crosses fly by, reading the names in the headlights.

Serafin Rivera Lopez.

Pedro Morranchel Quintero.

Graciela Gonzalez.

Several crosses simply said, *No Identificado.*

Tino felt his gut tighten. He knew where his mother had been left. A stash house called "Sugarloaf Lodge." But was she still there? She could have been taken someplace. To another state, even. What if he searched the rest of his life and never found her? What if she was *no identificado*?

It was nearly midnight, but the road north was crowded. *Campesinos* from the countryside pushed carts filled with fruits and vegetables. Along the berm, women sold travel gear. Backpacks, plastic jugs of water, cans of tuna and sardines. *Pollos* buying last-minute supplies before venturing north.

They passed a small stucco building painted red. *Grupo Beta*. A government agency that tried to discourage border crossings. Letters two feet high were painted across the front of the building. *La Búsqueda de un Sueño Americano Puede Ser Tu Peor Pesadilla*—The search for the American dream could be your worst nightmare.

Too late for that warning, Tino thought.

They traveled in silence a few moments before the boy blurted out, "Who's Adam?"

"What?" The question seemed to stun Payne. "Why do you ask?"

"This morning, on the highway, when the cop asked my name, you said 'Adam.' "

Payne let out a long train whistle of a sigh. "My son. He was killed in a car accident. Fourteen months ago. Drunk driver."

"Garcia? The Mexican?"

Payne shot him a look. "How'd you know that?"

"Back in the pretty lady's kitchen. You said you were going to Mexico to kill a man named Garcia."

"Jesus. What else did you hear?"

"Everything you said. Why do grown-ups think kids aren't listening? Where's Garcia now?"

"The best I can figure, back in Oaxaca. Fled the scene of the accident. Left the country."

"No papers, right?"

"Right."

Tino tried to process the information. "What about those Mexicans who got fried in the trailer truck?"

"What about them?"

"You helped them."

"I helped the survivors stay in the country."

"Before or after your accident?"

"Before. Why?"

Tino took a moment, not sure he should ask. "If it had been the other way around, if Garcia had killed Adam first, would you have still helped the *mojados*?"

"I don't hold it against the entire country that one drunk Mexican ran a red light. But I haven't gone out of my way to help anyone—American, Mexican, or Martian—since Adam died."

"You still would have helped the *mojados*."

"What makes you think so?"

"You're helping me, aren't you?"

Payne shot him a glance. "Sharon made me, kiddo."

"Sure, Himmy. Sure."

Turning back to the road, Payne swerved to give room to three old Mexican men walking along the pavement. They wore long-sleeve shirts buttoned up to the neck and carried canvas sacks. Tino had seen men like this all his life. But now, for some unexplainable reason, now the *Mexicanos* looked foreign to him.

"Himmy, I'm real sorry for you and the pretty lady."

Payne took his hand off the wheel and tousled Tino's mop of hair. "Thanks, kiddo."

"I saw his picture. Adam, I mean."

"Where?"

"In your office. He was wearing a uniform."

"Little League. He liked to catch. Used to wear his shin guards around the house."

"That baseball bat." Tino gestured toward the backseat. "Adam's, right?"

"Right."

"I bet you coached his team, too."

"Yep. You keep this up, the L.A.P.D. will give you a detective's shield." Payne was quiet another moment before saying, "It wasn't all Garcia's fault."

"What do you mean? You said he was drunk and ran a red light."

"I was looking out the window at the ocean. Just before Garcia hit us, I was watching some terns feeding in the shore-break. One second, two seconds, maybe. If I'd been looking straight ahead, maybe I'd have seen Garcia's truck coming. Maybe I could have done something."

The memory crashed over Payne, swept by an incoming tide of bone-chilling cold.

If this, maybe that. A second here, a second there.

If he'd seen the truck . . .

He'd be playing catch with Adam today. He'd still be married to Sharon. He wouldn't have gone nuts and said: *"Screw the rules; I don't care anymore."* He wouldn't be the guy the cops set up to bribe a judge. At this very moment, he wouldn't be sneaking back into the United States with phony papers, in a stolen car.

His entire adult life, what Payne wanted most was to be a good father. His own father had abandoned the family when Jimmy was eleven. Leonard Payne considered himself both a wheeler-dealer and an inventor. That sounded better than traveling salesman and tinkerer. The man simply could not hold a job. What he could hold was a grudge. Deluded and bitter, he filed dozens of lawsuits, claiming to have invented various sports drinks, protein bars, and muscle-building powders. With each invention came a "royal screwing," as he called it, "a corporate corn-holing by the big boys."

Leonard Payne went through periods of manic highs, working on top-secret projects in the garage, followed by bouts of near-suicidal depression.

Once he took off, the man never called, never wrote, never sent money. Payne pictured him selling gym equipment on commission somewhere, still railing against the big boys who won't let a man get ahead.

Payne wondered which was worse for a boy—to know the father who abandoned him or, like Tino, to never have even met him. He tried to stir up a warm memory of Leonard Payne. Remembered his father taking him bowling.

No, that's a lie. We never bowled together.

Leonard bowled and dragged Jimmy along to watch. San Bernardino, Riverside, Moreno Valley, Banning. Anywhere his old man could find suckers to bet. First for beer, then a dollar a pin, then five dollars a pin. It was how Leonard made the rent money. A broad-shouldered man, he threw a sweeping, powerful hook with his custom-made "Black Beauty." The ball would scatter the pins with a thunderous clatter, probably because it weighed sixteen pounds, thirteen ounces, nearly a full pound over the legal limit.

A hustler and a cheater.

"Your head's playing tricks on you, Himmy," Tino said, dragging him back to the present.

"What?"

"The accident. No way it was your fault, man."

"The week after it happened, I was supposed to take Adam on a trip. Just the two of us. Visit every Major League ballpark west of the Mississippi. Had it all planned, down to the last hot dog."

"My mother always says, *Si quieres qué Dios se ría, dile tus planes*. If you want to make God laugh, tell Him your plans."

"Your mother's a smart woman."

Payne heard Tino suck in a breath. "There, Himmy."

Just ahead, sodium vapor lights turned the night air into a misty green fog. Traffic slowed as U.S. border agents guided cars into lanes approaching the station. Vendors in baseball caps hawked sodas, pastries, and souvenirs. A grim midnight carnival.

"Mexico" was painted on the asphalt. If they could run this gauntlet, Payne thought, they would see "U.S." on the far side of the station. He sensed Tino stiffen as they approached the invisible line that separated the two countries. The line that separated the boy from his mother, his past from his future.

They were surrounded now. Cars, in front, on both sides, and behind them.

"We're gonna make it, kiddo."

Tino shot him a look. Wanting to believe but maybe not quite buying it. Which made two of them.

FORTY-TWO

Payne pulled the Mustang into a line of cars at the border station. Six lanes were open, each with twenty or so cars backed up.

"Tino, no matter what happens, don't panic."

"I won't."

"Don't get out of the car unless you're ordered to. Don't run."

"Okay. Okay."

"And no mouthing off to the agents."

"I'm not an *idiota*, Himmy."

A husky agent in a blue uniform tugged the leash of a German shepherd that happily sniffed the fenders and trunks of the cars in front of them. Payne hoped the prior owner of the Mustang hadn't been hauling any loco weed. When they were the third car in line, a cute female agent, her dark hair pulled back in a bun, walked along the row with a clipboard. She checked each car's license plate and punched the numbers into a handheld computer.

Payne gave her a "Good evening, ma'am" as she walked past the top-down Mustang. She returned a tight smile and an official nod. Her name tag read *"Rodriguez,"* the patch on her sleeve, *"U.S. Customs and Border Protection."* Payne kept his eyes on her as she jiggled past. Her uniform pants were a size too small, accentuating her bubble butt. Not quite a Jennifer Lopez model, but still what the Greeks would call "callipygous." She examined the Mustang's Land of Lincoln plate, Payne murmuring a little prayer that the car hadn't been recently used in a bank robbery in Cicero.

The cars inched forward, plumes of black exhaust hovering in the night air. When the Mustang reached the front of the line, a male agent in his fifties sidled up to the driver's door. His name tag read "Lopez," and he looked both tired and bored.

"Evening, Agent Lopez," Payne boomed, with gusto. "Long day, huh?"

"Pulled a double shift 'cause we're short tonight."

Good sign, Payne thought. The guy wouldn't want any hassles.

A helicopter droned overhead, its searchlight raking the ten-foot-high border fence.

"We'll be out of your hair and on our way in no time," Payne promised, putting on what he thought was an open, Midwestern smile. "Just a midnight crossing to the Promised Land."

"Nice wheels."

"Indeed," Payne said, employing a word he never used. But then, this wasn't him. This was some educator from Northwestern University, a guy who restored old cars in his spare time. Payne had prepared an entire persona in the last few minutes.

"V-8 under the hood?"

"Four-twenty-eight," Payne bragged.

"Love that pony on the grille. Never understood why they put it off center, though."

Agent Lopez scrutinized Payne's Illinois driver's license and passport and didn't start screaming for reinforcements. He spent more time with Tino's visa, squinting a bit, then holding a flashlight to it.

Shit.

The agent slipped the visa into his shirt pocket and studied Tino. "You're a student at Temple Emanuel Academy Day School in Beverly Hills?" His tone would have worked for *"You just landed here from Mars?"*

"Sí, señor."

"Exchange program," Payne added.

"I'm talking to the boy now, Mr. Hamilton."

Payne clammed up and Agent Lopez said, "How long you going to school there?"

"I start next month, but they asked me to come early and get myself all orientated."

"Uh-huh."

"Then I'm gonna go to Beverly Hills High. Lil' Romeo went there."

"So did Erik Menendez," the agent said, referring to one of the brothers who shotgunned his parents twenty years earlier. "Let's take a look at your luggage."

"Except for a gym bag and baseball bat, we shipped everything," Payne contributed.

Agent Lopez sighed, as if this was going to be too much trouble for this time of night. He leaned over the side of the convertible, a puzzled look on his face. "Are those bowling shoes you're wearing, Mr. Hamilton?"

"There's a story behind that," Payne said.

"Don't wanna hear it. But tell me, just what's your connection with the boy?"

"I'm associate director of Worldwide Student Exchange."

"Never heard of it."

"We're an ecumenical rainbow coalition headquartered at Northwestern University. We encourage diversity in private schools, and this lucky little fellow was chosen, after vigorous competition, to go to Temple Emanuel for intensive study."

"I love *Americanos*," Tino said. "Especially Jews."

"Let me get this straight," the agent said. "You're a religious do-gooder from Illinois. You drive all the way to Mexico and come back with this boy who you claim to be taking to some Jewish school in Beverly Hills."

"In time for Rosh Hashanah," Payne added, helpfully.

The agent took a moment to think things over. In an adjacent lane, under a sign reading *Secondary Inspections,* agents pulled a Lincoln apart, fender by fender, the border equivalent of a body cavity search.

Agent Lopez snatched a radio from his belt. "I need a P-2 check on a Mr. Alexander Hamilton of Evanston, Illinois."

"P-2 check?" Payne said, puzzled.

"Predators and pedophiles."

"What are you talking about?"

"Registered sex offenders. Ex-cons with records of assaulting children."

Not again, Payne thought. Another guy in uniform who suspected him of being a freak. Through a window of the office kiosk, he saw Rodriguez, the cute female officer, now working at a computer. "I assure you that I'm not—"

"You buy this boy in Mexicali?"

"No! Of course not."

"Tijuana, then."

"Never been to Tijuana."

Rodriguez sashayed out of the office, a feminine swing to her hips. She held a computer printout.

Jesus, what did she find? What if a guy from Illinois named Alex Hamilton was a total perv?

Despite his best efforts to appear relaxed, Payne was holding his breath. Looking guilty. *Feeling* guilty. He shot a look at Tino. The boy had one hand on the door handle. The kid was ready to run, Payne wondering if he'd go north or south.

Rodriguez gave Payne a long look, then turned to Lopez. "Car's clean. Mr. Hamilton has no record in Illinois or in the federal database. Nothing in the P-2 file."

Payne let out a long whistling breath, like a punctured bicycle tire.

"And I know for a fact that Mr. Hamilton is heterosexual."

"How?" the male agent said.

"When I read his plate, he checked out my ass like he wanted to pet it."

"Busted," Payne conceded.

"I'm too tired and too old for this shit," Lopez grumbled. "Mr. Hamilton, take this kid to Beverly Hills. Or Tel Aviv, for all I care."

Payne pushed the clutch to the floor, turned the ignition, and put the Mustang in gear. He tried not to burn rubber as they passed the sign welcoming them to the United States of America.

FORTY-THREE

Shortly after midnight, Sharon sat on a sofa in the Green Room of a Burbank television studio. On a TV monitor, Cullen's face took on the color of the setting sun from an overdose of bronze makeup. Her fiancé was happily hosting his "Close the Border Marathon," but Sharon wasn't paying attention.

Her thoughts were of Jimmy. So many emotions. Worry. Fear. Guilt. Blaming herself for the ton of crap that was about to fall on his head. He was like a dog that dug its way out of the yard. The longer he was gone, the more mischief he would get into.

What was I thinking? Why did I send him where he could do so much harm?

The boy. Tino.

She'd done it because of the boy. She didn't need a shrink to tell her about the subconscious connection between a boy looking for his mother and a mother missing her dead son.

But look what's happened in a mere twenty-four hours.

Gossip had raced through the Parker Center like an August brushfire. A dead judge, stolen sting money, a fleeing bag man. To the delight of the donut-munchers, Detective Rigney was rumored to be chasing J. Atticus Payne from Rancho Cucamonga to Mexicali.

"Hey, didja hear? Royal Payne and some Mexican kid shot up a sheriff's car down in Calexico."

"No shit."

"Then they took off for Mexico."

"And Rigney's in deep shit. Internal Affairs's really busting his chops."

"When he catches up with Payne, there's gonna be one dead shyster."

The rumor mill was churning overtime. Payne was into heroin trafficking. Or human trafficking. Or child slavery. The term "international fugitive" floated around. The F.B.I. and the D.E.A. had formed a task force to go after him. Homeland Security, too. Someone matching Payne's description was spotted in a Tijuana cantina drinking beer with a terror suspect. Another report had Payne catching a flight to Cali, Colombia. Sharon wouldn't be surprised if he turned up on a bin Laden videotape.

Still, she was able to confirm part of the story. The shooting. The fleeing. And Mexico.

Mexico!

Did Jimmy abandon the search for Tino's mother and take off after Manuel Garcia in Oaxaca? Had he lied to her?

Jimmy, what's happened to you? You had such promise.

After Adam's death, Sharon had insisted they attend grief counseling. She remembered their last session. A gentle man in his fifties, the psychologist explained the five stages of coping with loss—denial, anger, bargaining, depression, acceptance—and added one of his own, hope. The more the man talked, the more upset Jimmy became.

"You left out one stage, Doc. Revenge. When a neighbor ran over John Gotti's kid, Gotti had the man killed."

"Is that what you want to do? Emulate a mobster?"

"I need to do what my gut tells me."

"Do you think killing that man brought Gotti peace?"

"No. Because he didn't do it himself. He didn't look into the guy's eyes and see the fear."

"Mr. Payne, may I speak freely?"

"Does that mean you're not charging two hundred bucks today?"

"You are in need of intensive therapy. I fear you are well on the way to self-destruction."

"Then all this bullshit talk isn't gonna help."

Jimmy stormed out, and in that moment, Sharon knew her marriage would not survive. She didn't want it to end, but Jimmy was too obsessed to address his own problems, much less their marriage.

Earlier today, she had tried calling his cell phone. No answer. He'd been listed as a fugitive, armed and dangerous. She pictured him squaring off with a SWAT team, dying in a fusillade of gunfire. Maybe he even wanted it to happen. Suicide by cop.

Sharon still had strong feelings for Jimmy, ranging from anger to empathy to a warmth that defied easy description. Mostly anger. The emotional tie was there, but what did it mean?

She turned her attention back to Cullen on the monitor, his broad shoulders filling the screen. Under the hot lights, perched on a bar stool, he looked like a Sequoia planted in a pot. Still talking, he removed his suit coat and loosened his tie. Still another four hours in the marathon. Like a fighter trained to go the distance, Cullen had phenomenal stamina.

She admired many things about him, including his ability to overcome setbacks. He had run for local office as a Republican and been defeated. He'd been a self-help motivational speaker, but his books and tapes never sold. He'd bought television time for get-rich-in-real-estate infomericals that didn't pan out. Still, Cullen never lost his optimism. Maybe that's what attracted her to him. He could take a punch. Then there was Jimmy.

"I'm gonna change my life."

Jimmy's vow, but something Cullen had actually done. He kept reinventing himself and seemed happy with each reincarnation. Sharon disagreed with his political views, but she respected him for never giving up.

There was another side to him, too. Maybe it didn't come through on television. But he was a compassionate man. He had stepped forward at the worst time in her life and comforted her. When she'd told Jimmy that, he barked his cynical laugh.

"Quinn comforted you like a vulture comforts a rabbit. He swooped down when you were at your weakest."

She shot another glance at the flat-screen monitor. Cullen, his square anchorman's chin tilted toward the camera, was deep into his stock speech about the fall of the Roman Empire.

"Rome opened its gates and let in all those foreigners to do their dirty work. By 100 B.C., the foreigners outnumbered Romans three-to-one, and when the revolt came, the Romans were crushed. Well, folks, we're well on our way to the same fate, the fall of America. California, Texas, Arizona, and New Mexico are all headed toward Hispanic majorities."

Cullen had been lining up guests for months. A congressman from Colorado opposed to open borders. A spokesman for La Raza, a vocal supporter of immigrants' rights. A professor from Pepperdine with charts and graphs about how Caucasians will soon be the minority in thirty-five of the country's largest cities. A couple of desert rats from the Patriot Patrol, pleading for donations for camo gear, binoculars, flashlights, and probably cases of Budweiser. City and county commissioners, mayors, a Catholic priest, a Border Patrol agent, a spokesman for United Farm Workers, reporters from the Los Angeles and San Diego newspapers, even a couple illegals hanging around a Home Depot, looking for work. Bill O'Reilly and Lou Dobbs would appear by satellite.

Executives at Fox—the suits who could give him a network gig—would be watching. Celebrity guests were the key, Cullen had told her. He was most excited about Simeon Rutledge. The multimillionaire farmer rarely gave interviews. But astonishingly, Rutledge had called Cullen personally, just hours earlier.

"I'd like to have my say on that dog-and-pony show of yours," Rutledge said.

"I didn't think you had the balls," Quinn replied.

"Talking into a camera don't take balls. You know what courage is? Crossing deserts and mountains carrying your kids and a jug of water. But you wouldn't know squat about that, would you, candy ass?"

"Anytime you want to step into the ring, Rutledge, I'm there. Eight-ounce gloves. Sixteen-ounce. Headgear or bare head. You name it."

"Forget the gloves. Just give me a pool cue and a broken beer bottle."

Quinn laughed. A hearty rumble like distant thunder. "This is gonna be great TV. We'll go at it toe-to-toe."

"Ain't gonna be a dance," Simeon Rutledge said.

FORTY-FOUR

Just before one A.M., Sharon watched the Marlboro Man strut into the Green Room. An aging cowboy. Scuffed boots, faded jeans, a silver belt buckle. Neatly groomed, but she could almost smell straw and horses.

Rutledge had taken off his cowboy hat, as gentlemen do indoors, revealing a forehead half pale and half sunburned. Tall, and thick through the chest, with a leathery face and a brushy mustache. In his cowboy duds, he reminded Sharon of someone. Who was it?

Ah, right. Give him a lariat, trim that brush into a pencil mustache, and he's Clark Gable in The Misfits.

Jimmy had made her watch the damn movie three times, even though she didn't like it. Jimmy, of course, loved everything about it, from the title to Marilyn Monroe's ass. Give Jimmy a story about the struggle for personal freedom and load it with alienation, loneliness, and grief, and he's there. The only part Sharon liked was Thelma Ritter saying that men were as reliable as jackrabbits.

Sharon told Rutledge to help himself to donuts and the latte machine. He smiled at the word "latte," thanked her kindly, saying "Ma'am," sat down, and drew a small silver flask from a buttoned shirt pocket. Jack Daniel's, she guessed, from the aroma.

The Rutledge family had created a dynasty in the San Joaquin Valley. But not without a firestorm of controversy. Simeon Rutledge had been the target of several law enforcement investigations, she knew. Immigration. Taxes. Pollution. Recently, there'd been rumors about a Grand Jury poking around the Rutledge operation. But that was federal, and she didn't know any details.

There were two other men in the Green Room, both members of the Patriot Patrol, the militia group that guarded the border, though no one asked them to. One man, a pudgeball wearing a *"Send 'Em Back"* T-shirt, slouched on the vinyl sofa, snoring, a ball cap pulled down over his eyes. The other man, a wiry, sunburned critter with Willie Nelson pigtails, squinted at a Superman comic book, moving his lips as he read. Both men wore camo fatigues bloused into combat boots.

"You're Rutledge, ain't you?" Pigtails said. He didn't sound like he wanted an autograph.

"Yep," Rutledge allowed. "And you're one of those dumb-ass crackers got nothing better to do than harass poor people looking for work."

"I'm a patriot."

"Pissant is more like it."

Pigtails made a move as if to get up, seemed to think better of it, and dropped down again.

"C'mon, fellow," Rutledge taunted. "Let's see how tough you are."

"All right, boys. Settle down," Sharon ordered. "I'll arrest anyone causing trouble."

Rutledge shot her an inquisitive look.

"*Detective* Sharon Payne," she said.

Rutledge sized her up in her business suit and pumps. "A detective working security?"

"Actually, I'm . . ."

Just what am I, anyway?

"I'm with Cullen."

Rutledge gave her a sly smile. "Well, Quinn's taste in women can't be faulted, even if he doesn't know diddly about immigration."

"All of you better mind your manners or I'll cuff you right here."

"I don't mean no harm," Pigtails said. "But I got a right to tell Mr. Big Shot that he's taking food out of the mouths of real Americans, giving away all them jobs to the beaners."

"Tell you what, fellow," Rutledge said. "If you want to crawl through the dirt picking artichokes when the thermometer pops a hundred, I got a job for you. But you couldn't do half the work of a *campesina* who's seven months pregnant."

"Them Mexi-cants don't feel the heat the way white people do. Anyhow, I ain't gonna work on my hands and knees, beaners farting in my face."

Rutledge shook his head sadly. No use trying to reason with a mule. "Detective Payne, what do you think?"

"I think there ought to be a civil way for people to discuss their differences."

"I'll drink to that." Rutledge took a hit on his flask, his pale eyes wandering off into the distance. "My old man hired *braceros* back in the sixties. One of their kids is chief of police now. Javier Cardenas. I've known him since we played pitch-and-catch with pomegranates. When I was growing up, my best friends were the wild-ass *pachucos*. The first girl I ever . . . " He paused, as if it might not be chivalrous to continue.

"I wouldn't fuck one of them greasy little tacos," Pigtails said.

"You ought not to talk that way in front of a lady," Rutledge warned.

"That's all right," Sharon said. "I've heard worse."

"I respect the people who work for me. I got Guatemalan women five feet tall who can carry a watermelon in each hand. I got Hondurans who pick peaches so damn gracefully you'd think you were watching a conductor at a symphony. Once, an *Indio* from Chiapas chopped off his toe with a machete. He just tied it off at the knuckle and kept on working. When I found out, I drove him to the hospital myself. I wouldn't trade any one of them for a dozen of these losers, blaming everyone else for their own laziness and stupidity."

Pigtails flushed. "Ain't no wonder white people talk about you the way they do."

"You mean white trash, don't you?"

"Maybe you don't know it, Rutledge, but someone posted a note on our website. Twenty thousand bucks to anyone who'll put a bullet in your big, fat head."

Rutledge slipped the flask back into his shirt pocket. "Only twenty grand? Hell, I'm insulted. But you better tell whoever wants that money to shoot me in the back. 'Cause if I see him first, I'll rip his heart out and feed it to my pigs."

It was going to be a damn long night, Sharon thought.

FORTY-FIVE

Payne wondered if Cullen Quinn dyed his hair. The guy was in his mid-forties, and his hair was still blond. Except tonight, on the cheap TV in the motel room, it had taken on the hue of an Orange Crush. All-American looks, a high-paying job, and engaged to the woman Payne still loved. He hated the guy.

Jimmy and Tino had driven north from the border to El Centro, then west on I-8 through the West Mesa Desert. The only traffic was the occasional trailer truck blasting past them, with illustrations of curvaceous women on the mud flaps. The world a velvet black, except for the stars and the Mustang's headlight beams. The tires sang against the pavement, a hypnotic drone. Tino's head fell to his chest, then popped up.

"*Buenos noches,* Himmy," he said, dozing off for good.

Payne had strained to stay alert. He'd driven all last night and hadn't slept in two days. Fearing he'd run off the road and into a ravine, he took the Coyote Wells exit and pulled into the first motel that didn't look like a haven for meth dealers.

A few hours of sleep, and they could find Wanda the Whale's stash house after sunrise. With luck, Marisol Perez would still be there. If not, she would be en route to a job somewhere, and they could pick up the trail.

Payne's thoughts turned to his ex-wife. Was his obsession with finding Marisol a subconscious attempt to win back Sharon? She was the one who sent him on this mission. Would proving himself a *valiente* also prove he was husband material?

Payne had carried Tino to the motel room, stepping around a fat-tailed scorpion scurrying across the sandy parking lot. The room smelled of disinfectants and cigarettes. A place where they changed the sheets every third day, but the cockroaches stayed forever. He eased Tino into one of the twin beds and covered him with a blanket.

Payne splashed water on his face and examined himself in the mirror. He needed a shave. He needed a haircut. He needed a life.

He plopped down on the second bed and turned on the TV. He'd let the drone of the talking box put him to sleep. He clicked through the channels, declining to buy a zirconium ring or send money to a Southern drawling minister. He hit the remote and there was Paul Newman, a down-and-out lawyer, pleading with a jury. *The Verdict,* a personal favorite.

"So much of the time we're just lost. We say, 'Please God, tell us what is right; tell us what is true.' And there is no justice. The rich win, the poor are powerless."

Payne watched until justice was done and Newman redeemed, but it was just a movie. In real life, the rich win and the poor eat shit. Another click of the remote and he stumbled on Cullen Quinn's all-night immigration marathon. Jeez, the bastard was haunting him like Banquo's ghost. Quinn seemed to be in the middle of a debate with an older, craggy-faced cowboy.

"Wake up and smell the tacos," the cowboy was saying. "We need migrant workers, with or without documents."

"The Big Lie," Quinn shot back. "The myth of the indispensable alien."

"Myth? Ask the farmers in Idaho who's gonna pick their potatoes. Or cut the trees in Arkansas. Or slaughter cattle in Wisconsin. You ever been to a meat-packing plant, because I sure as hell know you never worked in one."

"There are American workers who'd be happy to make those wages and pay their taxes, too."

"Got news for you, Quinn. Even Mexicans with phony papers pay taxes when they rent apartments and buy beer and pickup trucks and TV sets. Their employers send Social Security payments to Washington, but the workers never get the benefits. Hell, we're making money off these people."

"Not when they're sending most of their paychecks to Mexico."

"You got something against poor families eating?"

There was a flinty crust to the old cowboy's voice, like the singe of charcoal on steak.

Payne liked this guy. Standing up to Quinn. The cowboy looked so rugged he made Quinn—even with his boxer's jaw—seem effete.

"President Calderón ships us his peasants and his problems," Quinn said. "He plays us for suckers, and you know it, Mr. Rutledge."

Rutledge.

Of course. Rutledge Ranch and Farms. Quinn's favorite target.

"Those 'peasants' are the lifeblood of the San Joaquin Valley," Rutledge said.

Quinn turned away from his guest and faced the camera. "As regular viewers know, I've proposed sending young offenders from Los Angeles to Mr. Rutledge's beloved valley. We can get the crops picked and break up the gangs at the same time."

"You gonna put the Crips on one bus and the Bloods on another, or mix them up?"

"It can all be worked out," Quinn said.

"You city people don't have a clue. If I didn't have migrant labor, my citrus and stone fruit would rot on the trees. My lettuce and melons and artichokes and berries would turn to mush."

"Is that why you horsewhip your workers, to make them speed up?"

"That's a damn lie. I treat my people like family. Free medical care and cheap housing. Preschool for their kids."

"Still no excuse for breaking the law. No excuse for turning our nation into a province of Mexico."

Rutledge raised his voice. "What are you afraid of, Quinn? That's really the heart of it. Fear. Just like the nativists a hundred years ago when the Irish and Italians and Jews were coming over."

"You're pretty cavalier about the takeover of our country," Quinn said. "Twelve million illegals now, more pouring in every day."

"Then change the law to accept the reality."

"So you're for open borders?"

"All I'm saying, you can't turn this country into a gated community."

Quinn shook his head, a practiced look Payne had seen many times. Soap opera acting, but effective in TV land.

"And what about simple fairness?" Rutledge continued. "What about all those Cubans who get papers when they wash up on Miami Beach? All because the phony politicians want the Cuban vote in Florida."

On the wall above the television set, Payne watched a brown spider climb toward the ceiling. At least it looked brown from the bed. Maybe it was black. A black widow. The desert was full of them.

"Stay tuned, folks," Quinn said. "Next, I've got two heroes from the Patriot Patrol, real Americans who are manning our border, doing the job the federal government doesn't have the guts to do. Then I'll present my own ten-point plan for stopping the takeover of America."

Quinn's theme music came up, some bugles and drums that made it sound like the bastard was going to charge San Juan Hill. The camera lingered on the two men. A young woman wearing a headset helped Rutledge unclip his microphone.

Payne watched Sharon walk onto the set, hand Quinn a bottle of water, then mop his forehead gently with a towel. Quinn beamed and said something to her. Sharon leaned close and whispered something back. But what? Feeling like a peeper, Payne studied their body language. Familiar but not affectionate. She never touched him. He never touched her. Of course, they were on-air. No way they'd start groping. But what did it all mean?

He wondered again what Quinn had said and what Sharon had replied.

He wondered what she was thinking.

He wondered if she still had feelings for him.

And with those thoughts swirling through the nooks and crannies of his brain, he finally dozed off, dreaming he was tied to stakes, spread-eagled, in the desert. A scorching wind sand-blasted him, scraping his skin raw. An army of scorpions wriggled across his chest, a trail of black widow spiders bringing up the rear. A rattlesnake coiled alongside his head, its tongue flicking. Payne tried to scream for help but couldn't. Without warning, a fusillade of venomous stings, the arrows of a thousand archers, locked his muscles into excruciating spasms. A searing flame blocked all vision, and then his world turned silent and black.

FORTY-SIX

At just past ten the next morning, Jimmy and Tino sat in the Mustang at a railroad crossing on Shell Canyon Road outside Ocotillo. A freight train rumbled past, a seemingly endless procession of cattle cars, stuffed with Herefords and Angus and all manner of bovines. Thousands of animals, millions of dollars on the hoof.

Payne glimpsed the Sugarloaf Lodge blinking through the rushing cars. Once the train had passed, he crossed the tracks and parked in the shade of a billboard for Truly Nolen Pest Control. Dead ahead was a rocky range called the Coyote Mountains. Given the circumstances, Payne thought, an apt name.

A dry wind pelted the windshield with sand. The Sugarloaf was Wanda the Whale's stash house, the place El Tigre dropped off Marisol. There could be armed guards and pit bulls and who knows what. Payne was reasonably certain there would be no doorman and concierge.

"What are we waiting for?" Tino asked.

"I need to plan our assault."

"Why don't we just find the Whale and ask her about *Mami*?"

"Not how it's done." As if he knew.

He scanned the property. Six squat cabins with cedar siding and drooping porches, spread out across a few scrubby acres. No swimming pool, no restaurant, and damn little shade from the desert sun. A cow fence of unpainted logs ran along the perimeter. A few feet inside the row of logs was another fence, this one of barbed wire. A scarlet eucalyptus tree bloomed in the yard of the nearest cabin. A sign read: *Office* and *No Vacancy*. Parked under the tree was an Eldorado convertible, vintage late-sixties. The car had once been red, and now was the rusty orange of a Tequila Sunrise.

"Only one car out front," Payne said. "No one around, but the sign says the place is full."

"So?"

"You ever see *Rockford Files*?"

Tino shook his head.

"Classic show. We'll watch it sometime."

Tino scowled. "Don't say stuff you don't mean, Himmy."

"I mean it. Channel 56 still shows reruns. Once we find your mom, if she says it's okay, we can hang out."

"¿Verdad?"

"You bet. For a career criminal, you're not a bad kid." Payne tousled the boy's dark hair.

The boy flashed a smile. "So, what's *Rocket Files* have to do with anything?"

"*Rockford* Files. Jim Rockford's a private eye. This is where he'd walk up to the office and tell the woman behind the counter he's looking for someone named Marisol Perez. The woman says, 'Never heard of her.' But Rockford won't let up. Then a big goon with prison tats comes out of a back room and growls, 'This guy giving you trouble, Agnes?' Rockford makes some smart-ass remark, and the guy picks him up by the neck and throws him halfway to L.A."

"But this Rockford doesn't give up, right?"

"*Exactamente,* kiddo. He gets his nose bloodied but never quits."

"Just like you, Himmy. So what do we do now?"

"We avoid the office. We circle around, check the cabins in back, away from the road."

The boy grinned. "Great plan, Rockford."

They got out of the car, both wearing brand-new Nike Zooms, black high-tops, the Kobe model. Payne didn't like Kobe Bryant, and he didn't like the sneakers they'd just bought in Ocotillo. Still, they beat the bowling shoes he'd worn on the way out of Mexico.

With Payne leading, they hopped over the log fence at the side of the property, then paused at the barbed wire. Three strands, rusty and dangerous. While Payne considered how to avoid leaving a trail of blood, Tino jammed a sneaker on the middle strand and pushed it down. He grabbed a smooth spot on the top wire and pulled it up, gesturing to Payne to duck under. Payne got through, then he did the same for Tino, giving him an admiring look.

"Ay, Himmy. All *Mexicanos* know how to get through barbed wire."

They jogged along the edge of the property, hunched over like commandos, staying as far as possible from the front cabin with the *Office* sign. Somewhere nearby, a dog barked. It sounded like a big, unhappy dog.

The closest cabins appeared empty. They circled the perimeter. Still nothing, until they reached the cabin at the rear of the property. From inside, a scratchy Spanish-language radio station played a ballad.

" 'Cielito Lindo,' " Tino said. "Ranchero music."

As they drew closer, they heard overlapping voices, speaking in Spanish. The morning was already hot, and Payne wondered why no one was on the porch or in the yard. Then he saw the slab of wood, a two-by-four, in a slot, sealing the front door. The windows were covered with perforated metal screens. The residents were locked in.

Bienvenidos a los Estados Unidos.

They climbed the steps to the cabin. Payne lifted the board from its slot and opened the door. Stifling inside. Bare floors and walls. No beds, no chairs, no sofas. An open toilet and a sink toward the rear. But the place was not empty. Maybe three dozen men, women, and children, with backpacks, plastic bags stuffed with clothes, and water jugs. The talking stopped dead, everyone staring at them.

No Marisol Perez.

"¡Hola, amigos!" Payne called out, with as much cheer as he could muster.

A man clicked off the radio. The only sound was a horsefly buzzing and banging against one of the screened windows. Then, a girl of about ten started to cry. The migrants exchanged glances and raised their hands in surrender.

"They think you're *La Migra*," Tino told Payne.

"Tell them I'm a friend. Ask where they're going from here. It might be the same place your mom was sent."

Tino began chattering, and the hands eased down. As several men replied in staccato Spanish, Payne looked toward the migrants. Most avoided his gaze. Men with work-hardened hands and wary eyes. Exhausted women clutching their children.

Dark, broad Indian faces, their ancestry tracing back centuries, to the Aztecs. A man and woman with Asian features. Others seemed to be *mestizos,* the mixed-blood descendants of Europeans and indigenous peoples.

Tino nodded toward two men in wife-beater tees with bandannas low on their foreheads. "Those two *cholos* say they're going to L.A. to get rich selling drugs and robbing *gabachos.*"

"Great. That'll make Cullen Quinn happy."

"The Guatemalans over by the shitter say they're going to some vegetable farms upstate, but they don't know where. Those two guys by the window were promised jobs in a gypsum quarry right down the road."

Payne remembered the signs for Plaster City, which wasn't a city or even a town. Just a quarry and a factory turning gypsum into plaster for drywall.

"So why are they still here? They could practically walk there."

"Jobs never happened. There've been immigration raids. Everything's on hold."

One of the men, thin and wiry in a long-sleeve plaid shirt, dusty jeans, and work boots, said, *"Sin papeles no hay trabajo."*

Without papers, no work.

"Different now. Very bad," the man said, trying out his English.

Tino gestured toward a man in the rear of the cabin. "That *guero* says he's a fisherman. The coyotes promised him a job on a sardine boat. A couple of others, landscaping work; and two of the women, janitors in office buildings in San Diego. But they've been here three days, and no one's shown up to get them."

"Who the fuck are you? The employment agency?"

Payne wheeled at the sound of the gravelly voice. Filling the doorway was a humongous woman in purple L.A. Lakers shorts.

"Are you Wanda?"

"No, dipshit. Ah'm Paris Fucking Hilton."

The woman's thighs ballooned out of her shorts like sausages bursting through their casing. Massive breasts, pale as uncooked biscuits, oozed from the sides of her pink sleeveless cropped tee, the word "Princess" spelled out in sequins. Her stringy, bleached hair was fastened to spongy curlers, though it was doubtful a formal evening was in the works. Her jelly-roll belly, the color of Crisco, spilled over the top of her shorts. She raised her right arm, the flesh quivering like flan on a slippery plate. Her meaty hand gripped a three-foot-long machete.

"Ya'all here to poach my beaners?" A voice like spoons banging tin pots. Hillbillies and hayrides and banjos.

"No, ma'am," he said.

"Last time a low-life poacher came around, Ah fed his pecker to my bull mastiff."

"I'm not a trafficker. I swear."

Waving the machete in Payne's face, she said, "You're not a cop. Ah pay enough of 'em to know." She looked Payne up and down, exhaling a little piggy snort. "You look like a city boy." She pushed the flat end of the machete against his hip and turned him a full 360. "Kind of cute, but you got a skinny butt. So what the fuck you doing on my property?"

"I'm looking for a woman."

"Well, you found one, cutie pie." She jabbed the tip of the machete into Payne's midsection, just south of his navel. "But Ah doubt you got enough sweet meat on your bones to do the job."

"The job?"

"Ah ride cowgirl style."

Payne had no answer, other than a lip-trembling, openmouthed gape.

Wanda the Whale let out a laugh that shook her shoulders and rippled her stomach rolls. "Jesus, Ah haven't seen a look like that since Ah strangled a man between my thighs."

FORTY-SEVEN

Once Wanda the Whale was convinced that Payne didn't intend to kidnap her *pollos,* she put down her machete. When she started talking to Tino, she relaxed even more, calling him the "cutest little burrito west of the Pecos."

She took them to her cabin, the one with the *Office* sign, advising them not to pet the dog. As if anyone would try. Chained to the porch railing was a bull mastiff with watery eyes, drooping jowls, and a chest that resembled an iron breastplate. Payne guessed the dog could have boxed middleweight, about 160 pounds.

Once inside, Wanda opened a small fridge and handed them Cokes that could have been cooler. Like a newly christened ship easing down the slipway, she settled her giant buttocks into a sagging plaid recliner. Pleased to have guests who "spoke American," she spent several minutes talking about herself. Her real name was Wanda Baker from Arkadelphia, Arkansas. At eighteen, she'd been an exotic dancer in a bar near the Pine Bluff Arsenal, an army base where she collected sweaty dollar bills from soldiers who liked their women plump and jiggly. She ran off with a corporal, "a cute little bugger," who went AWOL to marry her.

"The smaller the man, the meaner the drunk," she told them, recounting a maxim of married life.

Her husband had read a magazine article about this big lake down by the Mexican border. The Salton Sea. He figured he could earn a living pulling mullet from the water, so they headed west. His business ended when he caught more truck tires than fish. The marriage ended when he started washing down meth with cactus wine. One night, he came after Wanda with a tire iron. She whisked him off his feet and bear-hugged him until she heard his ribs snap like stalks of celery.

Wanda started up a low-rent whorehouse in the cabins, servicing the dust-covered, phlegm-hacking men who worked at the gypsum quarry just down the road. The "Sugarloaf Spa," she called it, in a triumph of marketing over reality. A small operation, with a few Mexican women, a few runaways from the Midwest. Wanda avoided arrest by providing freebies for local cops and town bigwigs. She'd probably still be "Madame Wanda," but for a judge from Ocotillo who picked up a dose of the clap. Cops shut her down but let her open the stash house in return for monthly bundles of cash.

Now, beached in her recliner, Wanda the Whale tried to cool herself with a handheld Japanese silk fan, as rivulets of sweat tracked down her cleavage. She explained that the *No Vacancy* sign was posted because she never rented any cabins. The Sugarloaf was a way station, providing a night or two of housing for the flood of Mexicans, Guatemalans, Hondurans, and Salvadorans who crossed *La Frontera* without papers.

After a couple good years, things had slowed down. Upstate, strawberries and citrus got hammered in a winter freeze. Farmers with only half a crop needed half the workers. The slowdown in home construction killed jobs for laborers. And the feds had scared off a lot of businesses who needed workers.

"A perfect shitstorm," she informed them. "Getting so a woman can't make a semi-honest living." She shifted her weight in the chair, and the cabin may have tilted a little more out of plumb. "So who's this gal you're looking for?"

"*Mi mami,*" Tino said. "Marisol Perez."

The woman's face brightened. "The pretty one. Ah should have known. She told me she got separated from her boy."

"That's her! Is she here?"

"I can see the resemblance now. You got the same shape face, the same complexion. But those green eyes of yours threw me off."

"Where is she?" Payne said. "Is she okay?"

"Ah never would have sent her to the slaughterhouse, except to get her away from that douche bag El Tigre."

"She's working?"

"Where?" Tino pleaded.

Wanda sighed, her breasts heaving under the cropped tee. "Let me tell you what happened."

Tino's eyes filled with tears as Wanda repeated what her driver had told her. Marisol fighting off a foreman at the plant, hurting him real bad. Hell, maybe even killing him.

"Ah couldn't bring her back here. Cops would be banging on my door. If not them, then the cousins of that asshole foreman. Had my driver take her to a stash house in Hellhole Canyon."

"Is she still there?" Payne asked.

Wanda shrugged. "Hard to tell. Place is run by a tweaker named Dickie Chitwood. Real trailer trash. Rumor is, the place is owned by some rich guy upstate."

"We'll need directions."

"Ain't far, as the crow flies. About three hours if you don't get lost. Or three days if you do."

"We'll find it."

"That's what I'm afraid of."

Payne's look shot her a question.

"Chitwood's partial to a Ruger carbine. Damn good shot for someone stoked on crystal meth. And he don't have a kind heart like me, so you take care."

FORTY-EIGHT

On her second day in Hellhole Canyon, Marisol sat in the shade and watched the Nazi argue with a Hispanic man who wore work boots, jeans, and a T-shirt printed with the name of a raisin company. He was about forty, with a sun-creased face.

"You're one *pollo* short, Chitwood."

Chitwood. The Nazi's name. Marisol pledged to remember that. If the time ever came, she would help bring the man to justice for shooting the Honduran man through the forehead, instead of the apple through the core.

"You can't count, Guillermo." Chitwood scratched at his goat's beard with a filthy fingernail. "Must be them inner-city schools."

"If Zaga don't kill you, Rutledge will."

"Fuck them." Chitwood's rifle was slung over a shoulder. Marisol thought Guillermo was either very brave or did not know that Chitwood was an insane *drogadicto*.

Guillermo dug the toe of one boot into the dirt. Came up with a wet clump. Blood. "You shot one, didn't you?"

"What's the matter, Guillermo? Feeling sorry for your countrymen?"

"My family's lived in California for five generations. My ancestors owned ranches when yours were in debtors' prison."

"You're still a greaser to me."

"*Eres un basurero humano.*" Spitting out the words, calling him a human garbage dump. "I don't like the *pollos* any more than you do, Chitwood. They embarrass me, give my people a bad name. But I do my job and get stoned on my own time. You're a fucking lunatic."

"I don't have to take your shit. I don't work for you."

Chitwood fingered the rifle butt. Marisol felt herself stiffen. She pictured him whipping the gun around, killing Guillermo, then shooting all the migrants, herself included.

"Zaga's in Calexico," Guillermo said. "If I call him, he'll be here in two hours."

"Like I give a shit. Just load your goddamn van and get going."

"Maybe I'll call Mr. Rutledge directly. He'll have your ass."

"Then who'll live out here with no hot water, chickenshit up to their ass? Rutledge can't afford to lose me."

"Rutledge can afford to lose anyone he wants."

Chitwood lifted the rifle and fired a burst into the air. Marisol winced. But Guillermo stood in place, never moving. "I'm taking the *pollos,* you stupid shitkicker. But this isn't over."

Five minutes later, Marisol and the others were herded into the back of a windowless white van. A sign on its side read, *Sweet Valley Raisin Co.* Maybe that was where she would be working. The dark, windowless compartment stank of sweat and dust and urine. Nineteen men, women, and children packed inside, shoulders scrunched against one another, arms across knees.

Packed like animals in a pen, Marisol thought. Like the cattle at the slaughterhouse. As the van pulled out and headed to an unknowable destination, she said yet another prayer, not for herself, but for her son, wherever he might be.

FORTY-NINE

Jimmy and Tino headed east on I-8, then turned north on the 86 at El Centro. Near the lake, they took the Salton Sea Highway west into the desert. By midday, the sun was high, the air blazing hot. Sand blew across the highway and *ping*ed off the Mustang's windshield.

Tino could not stop thinking about what Wanda had told him. So many strange feelings. Pride at how his mother fought back, but shame that he wasn't there to rescue her. His mother, who would do anything for him.

"That *cabrón* at the slaughterhouse," the boy said. "You think he's dead?"

"Wanda didn't seem to know."

"If he isn't, I'll kill him myself."

"Keep your eye on the ball, kid. We're looking for your mom, that's all."

"A *gabacho* wouldn't understand."

"You'd be surprised."

"It's a matter of honor," Tino said.

"Fine. After we find your mom, kill whoever you want. But you're riding with me now, and I set the rules."

"You're not my father!"

Payne clenched his teeth so hard his jaw muscles danced. "No, Tino. I'm not."

They were both silent as the car hurtled past creosote washes and scrub mesquite. Tino tried to figure out what had just happened. Why was Jimmy mad at him? Or was he? No, more like he was hurting.

"I'm sorry, Himmy. You been good to me."

"It's okay."

"We'll do what you say."

"Fine."

Tino was dealing with emotions he couldn't quite fathom. He didn't want to lose his new friend. "Still gonna let me watch *Rocket Files* with you someday?"

"Rockford. Yeah. And if I'm not in jail, I'll take you to a Dodgers game."

"You serious, *vato*?"

Jimmy smiled and punched Tino gently on the shoulder.

An odd feeling overcame the boy. He figured the lawyer must have taken his own son to baseball games. Tino pictured Jimmy clearing a path around their seats, shoving guys to give his son a clean shot at a foul pop-up, the kid reaching up with a new glove that Jimmy had oiled for him. Wasn't that what fathers did?

Tino wanted to picture Jimmy doing the same thing for him. But he wouldn't let himself paint the image. Because if Jimmy never followed through, if he turned out to be the kind of man his mother always seemed to meet, well, it's better not to get your hopes up. But this American seemed different. Sometimes, he showed a warm heart. Sometimes, the courage of a *valiente*. And other times, when he grew quiet and looked away, just like now, Tino knew he was in pain.

Payne glanced at Tino, wondering just what he was thinking. Was he picturing a reunion with his mother? Or did he fear he'd never see her again?

They drove through the Borrego Badlands, past stands of cottonwoods and jumping cholla cactus with spines like fishhooks. There was little traffic, and Payne pushed the Mustang to 80 on the straightaways.

Just past a rocky wash, three mangy coyotes stood at the side of the road, staring at them, not even twitching, as they roared past. The old Mustang's A/C struggled to keep the car cool, then failed. Payne slowed and put the top down. Speeding up again, a hot dry wind blasted them.

They turned South onto Peg Leg Road, and a white van with darkened windows crossed the center line heading straight at them. Payne swerved and laid on the horn, catching a look at the craggy-faced driver, who shot him the bird.

Asshole.

A sign on the van said *Sweet Valley Raisin Co.*

They passed through the hamlet of Borrego Springs, where some joker had erected a street sign showing the intersection of Hollywood and Vine. A blinking traffic light, then onto Montezuma Valley Road, which curled up a mountainside dotted with greasewood. A sign warned of mountain lions. Payne was more concerned about a man named Chitwood who was partial to a Ruger carbine.

"There, *vato*." Tino pointed to an unmarked dirt road, just where Wanda had said it would be. Payne braked and downshifted but still took the turn too fast, the Mustang fishtailing.

"Cool, Himmy."

"Yeah. Way cool."

The dirt road, pocked with holes, continued uphill along the mountain's edge. The air began to cool and carried the hint of moisture. They spotted a bighorn sheep perched on a rocky outcropping as if on guard duty. Water tumbled down a rocky cliff and into a small stream. Along the banks, white flowers with yellow centers looked like fried eggs, gleaming in the sunshine.

They came to another dirt road, this one blocked by a locked gate. Two signs welcomed them: *Private Property* and *Trespassers Will Be Eaten.* Just as Wanda had told them. Payne pulled the Mustang as far off the road as possible without putting it into a ditch. From here, they would walk.

They climbed over the gate and headed up a well-maintained private road, just wide enough for a single car. Or maybe a van. Green ferns lined the road, further evidence they'd left the desert behind. Somewhere in the undergrowth, water burbled over rocks. Above them, two golden hawks glided in the afternoon updrafts.

After about a mile, the dirt road opened into a canyon. Boulders the size of ships lined each side. In front of them was a barn, a ranch house made of stones and logs, and an open-air structure of ten-foot-high wooden poles topped by a corrugated metal roof that provided a rectangle of shade. It looked like a giant carport, but its job was to keep migrants from frying in the sun.

No one there.

"What now, Himmy?"

"Now we look around."

They headed toward the shaded area. A dusty, candy-apple red Harley chopper painted with orange flames sat next to one of the wooden poles. Chickens hunted and pecked at the ground, rooting about for whatever it is chickens hunt and peck for. Security cameras sat atop four metal poles, each about fifteen feet high.

The door to the barn was wide open. Inside were three white panel trucks that looked freshly washed. Not a speck of desert dust.

Payne motioned Tino into the barn for a closer look, a few clucking chickens following them. All three vehicles were Ford cargo vans. No windows on the side panels. The rear windows had been tinted so dark as to resemble black mirrors. You could pack a couple dozen people into the cargo area if they were very good friends.

The barn smelled of straw and chickenshit . . . and fresh paint. A gallon can of black paint sat open on the wooden floor, a set of stencils and a spray gun nearby. Several small brushes soaked in a large glass jar filled with turpentine. The lettering on the panels of each truck appeared fresh.

One truck proudly proclaimed it was owned by Precision Glass Co. of Palm Desert. Another said Valley Plumbing, with an address in Apple Valley. The third was Sand Dunes Electrical, Inc., of Calipatria. Each truck had heavy-duty suspension, useful for throwing off Border Patrol agents looking for low-riding vehicles.

Payne was willing to bet his bowling ball that no glass installers, plumbers, or electricians would ever park their asses in these vehicles. He hurriedly scribbled the company names and license plate numbers.

They headed back into the brilliant sunlight of the yard and neared the poles supporting the sheet metal. A *cra-ack* echoed, a single gunshot splintering a pole and showering Payne with wood chips. He dived toward Tino, knocking him to the ground, shielding the boy with his body.

A second gunshot kicked up dirt near Payne's ear. His mind flashed with only one thought.

Save the boy.

FIFTY

Marisol lost all sense of time. Inside the van, the air grew stale and unbearably hot. She felt queasy, forced herself to picture trees, swaying in a breeze. Remembered the Mexicans trapped in the trailer truck the summer before. If she died here, what would become of Tino?

Fight off the fear.

Across from her, an Indio woman struggled to her knees, chanted something Marisol did not understand,

and keeled over, facedown onto the filthy floor. Her lips frosted with white foam and her body twitched.

Marisol squeezed past two men, lifted the woman's head to help her breathe. Someone banged on the wall separating them from Guillermo, the driver. Someone else shouted in Spanish to stop, a woman is dying, but the van continued on.

A Honduran man tore apart the matting that covered the taillight assembly, then punched through a plastic casing and tore out the light by its cord. The pavement appeared through the hole.

Marisol helped carry the woman to the back. Two men held her face close to the opening, begging her to suck in the fresh air. Her body twitched then stilled, twisted into unnatural angles.

Women screamed. Men prayed. Others averted their faces, as if shamed to see the woman so exposed in death.

Finally, the van lurched to a stop. The driver's door opened and slammed shut. Angry voices outside. The rear doors popped open. The migrants, minus one, stumbled out, soaking up the air, baking with the scent of horses and manure. Marisol blinked against the sunlight. A red barn, a corral, a riding ring. Cornfields in the distance, the stalks taller than any man.

Several men—Chicanos and Anglos—surrounded the group. Jeans and blue T-shirts with the lettering: "*Rutledge Ranch and Farms.*"

Guillermo, the driver, demanded to know who damaged the taillight. The Honduran man stepped forward, said something about the dead Indio woman. Guillermo punched him in the stomach, and the man fell to his knees, gagged, and vomited into the dust, spraying the man's boots.

"Fucking peasant!" Guillermo kicked the man.

Maybe not insane like Chitwood, Marisol thought,

but just as mean. Just like Carlos at the meat plant, vicious and cruel to his own people.

"Stop that shit!" another man ordered. Big. Older, with a brushy silver mustache. Cowboy boots and jeans.

"Sorry, Mr. Rutledge, but I'm tired of these fuckers messing up my trucks."

"I'm tired of them dying." Watching two workers haul the Indio woman away. "Give her a proper burial."

Mr. Rutledge, Marisol thought. Back at the chicken ranch, Guillermo said that Mr. Rutledge might kill Chitwood.

This man must be El Patron. There was a tenderness in his manner. He had put a stop to the beating. He treated the dead woman with respect. Maybe this place would not be so bad.

"You're one *pollo* short," Rutledge said.

"Chitwood offed one."

"Shit. Did you tell Zaga to get over there?"

"Yes, sir. Said he'd take care of it."

Guillermo turned back to the migrants and ordered them in Spanish to stand in a line. He asked questions while Rutledge watched. Have you ever picked grapes? Used a backhoe? Anyone here work with wells, irrigation equipment, agricultural limestone?

The men in the Rutledge Farms shirts wrote numbers on the migrants' arms with marking pens. Assignments to the fields where they were to be sent.

"What sweetness do we have here?" Rutledge asked, when he got to Marisol. Looked at her in that way men do. Smiling eyes. Lying eyes. The tenderness seemed to have blown away with the red dust.

"Maybe indoors work, if she can cook," Guillermo said. "If she can't, we're short in the lettuce fields."

"I'm thinking about the club."

"Maybe a bit too old for that, Mr. Rutledge."

"Guillermo, I bet you a hundred bucks she's not a day over twenty-five."

"I'm thirty-one years old," Marisol said in her best English. "And I'm a carpenter, not a field hand."

Both men laughed, El Patron's eyes wrinkling. "I'm sixty-six and still filled with piss and vinegar, *panocha*."

Using the Spanish word for raw sugar, a slang term for vagina. Yes, she had been wrong about El Patron. At first, he had seemed compassionate. But now this disgusting side. And what was this club that she might be too old for?

Rutledge stared hard at her, his lips tightening. He grabbed her blouse with both hands, tore it open, buttons popping. She wore no bra, and her full breasts tumbled free. She made no effort to cover herself, instead glaring back with hatred.

"Like a couple scoops of toffee ice cream," Rutledge said. "And I do love my ice cream."

FIFTY-ONE

Jimmy pushed Tino flat against the ground, his own chest covering the boy's head.

Save the boy.

The third shot plunked into the pole.

Tino squirmed beneath him. "Stay down!" Payne ordered.

He could feel his own heart beating, unless it was coming from Tino, squashed beneath him.

Two more gunshots splintered wood from the pole, each a bit lower, a bit closer. The shooter seemed to be enjoying target practice.

The shooting stopped. Dust filled the shadowy air. Chickens squawked. From somewhere in the canyon, an owl hooted.

"Who the fuck are you!"

Hands raised, Jimmy got to his knees. "My name's Payne. This is Tino. We don't mean any harm."

"Everybody means harm." The man held a Mini-14 carbine with a curved magazine. "Give me your wallet."

Payne reached in his back pocket and tossed over his wallet. The man thumbed through the currency and took out Payne's business card.

"J. Atticus Payne, Esquire. Whoopty-do." He pocketed the card and tossed back the wallet. "Why you here?"

"I'm looking for the boy's mother. Marisol Perez."

"If she's a beaner, she's gone. This ain't no resort."

The man's eyes danced in different directions. Payne had expected a massive ex-con with a shaved head, arms pumped into tree trunks from hoisting iron. But this was a jumpy little guy with long, greasy hair and bloodshot eyes with enlarged pupils. He wore paint-stained jeans and cowboy boots and no shirt. A long, jagged scar ran across his bony chest. A tattoo, a swastika, was crudely etched on his forehead.

"Are you Chitwood?" Payne asked.

"Fucking-A."

"Wanda told us to come see you."

"The Whale? Fuck her with a fire hose. She got no right sending you up here."

"Wanda said you were a kind soul with a good heart,

and you might help us." Payne hadn't told three lies in one sentence since his last trial.

Thoughts trudged across Chitwood's face like a caravan of elephants. "The fuck you talking about?"

"I have *Mami*'s picture." Tino reached inside his shirt and took the photo from the plastic case hanging from his neck. Fearlessly, he walked toward the gun-toting tweaker, who squinted at the photo.

"The little *pistola* from the slaughterhouse." Chitwood cackled a wet laugh and focused on Tino for the first time. "You favor your mama, boy. Coulda used a teddy bear like you at Perryville."

Tino looked confused. Payne chose not to tell him that Perryville was a prison, and from his scrawny looks, Chitwood might have been passed between inmates like a teddy bear himself.

"So you remember her?" Payne said.

"The Whale sent her over after she messed up some foreman at the plant. I shipped her out today."

"Today!" Tino's green eyes went wide.

"You just missed her, *chico*. Hell, you probably passed each other on the highway."

"Where?" Payne asked. "Where'd you send her?"

"Same place I sent everybody the last two months."

"Tell us!" Tino shouted.

"What's in it for me, you little pecker?"

"The way I see it," Payne said, "you're an important player in the ever-changing tapestry of our nation."

Chitwood snorted. "The fuck's that mean?"

"The warp and woof of the twenty-first century. You're running the new Ellis Island, and doing it with great humanity. So, of course you'll help a boy find his mother."

Chitwood cocked his head and studied Payne as if trying to figure if someone had just tried to sell him a Nigerian gold mine. Then he showed a gap-toothed grin.

"Okay, Payne. I'm warping and woofing. Leave the little beaner here, and I'll ship him out on the next van tomorrow, right to his mama."

"Just tell us where she is, and I'll take him there myself."

Without warning, Chitwood wheeled to his left and fired the carbine, blowing off the head of a chicken scratching the ground fifty feet away. Wanda had been right. For a twitchy guy with jumping eyes and a buzz on, Chitwood was a damn good shot.

"Dinner," Chitwood explained as the headless chicken hopped in a circle, spurting blood, before keeling over. Motioning toward the barn with the muzzle, he said, "Let's the three of us talk a bit. Maybe we can work something out."

Once inside the barn, Chitwood ordered Payne and Tino to sit on a bale of straw while he leaned against a wooden staircase that led to a hayloft. Payne waited to hear how they could "work something out," keeping his eyes on the carbine.

"Nice tat." Payne stared at the man's forehead. "Nazi Low Riders?"

"San Berdoo chapter," Chitwood replied, proudly.

Maybe it was the drugs. Or the loneliness of the place. Whatever the reason, Chitwood started talking about himself and didn't want to stop. He droned on about stealing cattle, selling guns, and smuggling drugs from Mexico, all before he was twenty-one. Then prison, parole, and living off the land in the Patagonia Mountains north of Nogales. For a while, some legitimate work on isolated ranches, where the best-looking females were sheep.

Chitwood boasted that he knew the deserts and mountains better than the vultures and bobcats. That's why the D.E.A. hired him—he hawked up some spit at the thought—as a tracker.

He could "cut signs," as the trackers say, following illegals through rocky country that showed no footprints. A tiny stone turned the wrong side up. A snapped branch. A broken spiderweb or a shred of clothing on the thorns of a cholla cactus. If a man pays attention, it's amazing what his senses can tell him. "If the wind's right, I can smell their shit half a mile away."

"Now, about the boy's mother," Payne said, "where did you—"

"And I can tell Mexican shit from white man's shit. It's all those beans and peppers and gristle."

"My mother!" Tino blurted, unable to take it any longer. "You said you knew where she is."

"Relax, *chico*. You stay here tonight, help with chores while your lawyer friend goes back home. Like I said, I'll send you off to your mama tomorrow."

Chitwood was looking at Tino the way a dieter looks at a chocolate eclair.

"Won't work that way," Payne said. Trying not to show his fear.

"Shut up! I need you gone. Zaga's gonna be pissed enough. I ain't gonna start explaining what some lawyer's doing poking around."

"That your boss? Zaga? Why not let me talk to him?" Payne thinking that someone sane and sober—anyone—would be preferable to dealing with this nut job.

"You ain't got a vote on this."

"I just want to tell him that the boy and I are a team. Where I go, he goes."

Chitwood pointed the carbine at Payne's chest. "Keep talking and my chickens will be pecking out your eyes by suppertime. You're gonna git, and the boy's gonna stay."

Payne took inventory. Wire cutters on a Peg-Board. A hammer, a saw, a coil of rope, assorted tools. All too far away. Chitwood would drop him with a single shot just like one of his chickens. On the floor was the can of black paint and the open jar of turpentine. Out of the corner of his eye, Payne saw Tino following his gaze.

"I gotta pee," Tino said.

His cue, Payne thought. The Tino Perez distraction, just like in Quinn's house and with the deputy on the highway.

"Piss over there, *chico*." Chitwood gestured to a pile of straw thick with horse dung. Nearby, leaning against a post, a long-handled pitchfork.

Tino shot Payne a quick sideways glance before walking toward the straw pile. The two of them were beginning to communicate wordlessly.

As he neared the closest cargo van, Tino stumbled and fell. One foot kicked the paint can, which overturned, splattering black paint onto the driver's door.

"Shit!" Chitwood grabbed a rag and hustled toward the van. "Stupid little fuck!"

Payne sprang to his feet.

Sensing movement, Chitwood wheeled around and swung the carbine toward Payne.

Tino grabbed the glass jar, yelled, "*Pinche puto*," and splashed turpentine into Chitwood's eyes.

Chitwood's scream was high-pitched and shrill. Payne barreled into him, knocking him into the cargo van. They bounced off a side panel, and Payne got both hands on the carbine, wrestling it free. The gun flew across the barn. Howling, Chitwood grabbed the wire cutters and slashed at Payne, who took a step backward and slipped in the wet paint. As he fell, Chitwood came at Payne, wheeling the blade left and right.

Payne was on his rump as Chitwood advanced, changing his grip on the wire cutters, prepared to plunge downward. Then the Nazi Low Rider grunted and looked down in disbelief. Stuck into the top of his dusty cowboy boot and pinning his foot to the paint-slicked wood floor was a pitchfork. Hanging on to the handle, his feet airborne like a pole vaulter, was Tino, who shouted, "I'm nobody's teddy bear, *cabrón!*"

FIFTY-TWO

Racing up the dirt road toward the car, Payne discovered something new about Tino. The kid was fast. A blazer. Fluid, head still. No flying elbows or herky-jerky knees. A born sprinter, he'd be a hell of a base stealer.

Payne ran like a lame horse, his mended leg throbbing. Tino reached the Mustang first and vaulted over the door and into the passenger seat. Payne stutter-stepped into the driver's seat. Seconds later, the Mustang kicked up dirt as they roared out of the canyon.

They had tied Chitwood with a coil of rope to a structural beam in the barn. Tino took the wire cutters, while Payne broke down the carbine and tossed the parts into the woods. He used the pitchfork to puncture the tires of the Harley chopper and all three cargo vans. If Chitwood tried to catch up with them, Payne thought, he was going to do it as a pissed-off pedestrian with a bloody foot.

"You're a dead man, Payne!" Chitwood had called

out, as the pair ran from the barn. *"If I don't getcha, Zaga will, and he don't give a shit about the warf and woop of Ellis Island."*

Payne floored the accelerator, heading up the narrow dirt road toward the Salton Sea Highway.

Less than a minute went by before a car appeared, coming straight at them. Flicking its high beams in the daylight.

A big car.

An SUV, maybe.

Then Payne saw it was a black Cadillac Escalade EXT, the combo SUV and pickup, a gas-guzzling monster.

It could be a local rancher. Or a lost tourist. Or . . . Zaga.

The Escalade's horn bleated. If it could talk, it would be saying, *"Back up, asshole!"* Two horses could have passed each other on the dirt road. Maybe even two Mini Coopers. But not the wide-hipped Escalade and the Mustang.

A hand came out the window and waved at Payne, delivering the same message as the horn. It made sense. It would be a shorter drive for Payne to back up to the stash house than for the Escalade to back up to the paved road. But no way Payne was going toward the stash house. Maybe Chitwood had gotten loose. Maybe he called for help. Maybe he had another firearm.

The Escalade door opened, and the driver stepped out. A bantamweight in a Western shirt with piping. A wide Western belt with a turquoise-and-silver buckle. A weathered face with Hispanic features. His age difficult to determine. Fifty? Sixty? Older?

Tight black pants tucked into fancy cowboy boots made of a green hide that might have been rattlesnake. And on his hip, in a Western holster, a handgun that looked as big as a cannon, way outsize on the trim little man.

A revolver. Maybe .50 caliber. Bigger even than Dirty Harry's .44 Magnum.

The man had a fine head of long hair, somewhere between gray and white, the color of spit. The hair was parted in the middle and fell to his shoulders, Wild Bill Hickok style.

"You fellows lost?" the man called out.

Payne kept his right hand on the gearshift and didn't answer.

The big man's right hand rested on his hip, inches from the gun. "I'm asking you nicely to back up. There's a turnoff not far behind you."

Payne depressed the clutch, slipped the gearshift into first, and revved the engine. The throaty roar had a rattle in it.

The man's hand wrapped around the gun butt. "You deaf? Someone's got to back up, and it's you, fellow."

Like two gunslingers.

"Not asking you again."

Payne leaned out the car window and shouted, "Why don't you kiss my sister's black cat's ass?" Not a great line, but Bo Hopkins said it in *The Wild Bunch*.

The question seemed to startle the little man with the big gun. "There something wrong with your brain, son?"

Payne took a stab at it. "Nope. Something wrong with yours, Zaga?"

The man froze at the mention of the name. Still as a boulder, he seemed to size up the situation. "You a dope fiend? One of Chitwood's asshole friends?"

Yep. Zaga, all right.

" 'Cause I warned that tweaker to get off the meth. If you're supplying him, I'll bury you without a second thought."

"Brace yourself, Tino," Payne whispered.

Payne let out the clutch and put the pedal to the rusty metal. Dirt spun from the rear wheels. The Mustang rocketed forward, right at Zaga, who vaulted to one side, drawing the handgun in a smooth motion.

The Mustang flew by, sheering off the Escalade's side-view mirror.

On its passenger side, the Mustang scraped the road-side boulders with metallic shrieks of dying soldiers.

Payne barely heard the first gunshot.

The second bullet clanged into the Mustang's trunk.

"Get down, Tino! On the floor!"

But the boy was propped on his knees, looking back at the man with the gun.

"Tino!" Payne tried to shove him down into his seat.

"In a second, *vato*."

Two more gunshots sounded.

When they slid around a bend in the road and Zaga was no longer in sight, Tino dropped into his seat.

"Jesus! What the hell's wrong with you, kid? You could have been killed."

"I memorized the *pistolero*'s license plate."

"Oh."

Tino rattled off the numbers and letters.

"Okay," Payne said. "Good. Very good. How'd you think of that?"

"It's what Rockford would have done," Tino said.

FIFTY-THREE

Marisol's lips were crusted together, and her mouth felt as if it were filled with sand.

The sheets were cool and clean but sweat poured from her. She tried to open her eyes, but the lids were heavy as church doors.

Her head throbbed.

Somewhere, a man's voice echoed, the words overlapping.

"You'll get used to it. It's better than picking melons."

She was naked under the sheet. She tried to remember where she was and how she got here.

A drink. She remembered being given a cold Pepsi. Then growing sleepy.

A patchwork of images. A man carrying her over his shoulder. Women's voices. Carpeted rooms. Soft music. Twinkling chandeliers.

The bed felt like a raft in a stormy sea. Her fingernails dug into the mattress to steady herself. In her mind, an eagle's claw gripped a tree limb. But if she were an eagle, she would fly away.

The man was talking again. The voice seemed familiar, but it bounced off the walls. Her eyes clouded over, and she could not put a face to the voice.

"You'll learn to like the club. No field hands. Gentlemen only." He laughed, a throaty growl. "Like me, *panocha*."

Panocha! Now, she remembered those first few moments after the van dumped out the migrants like a truckload of melons.

"I'm sixty-six and still filled with piss and vinegar, panocha."

El Patron. Mr. Rutledge.

Marisol felt his callused hand under the sheet, moving up her thigh.

Her eyes opened just enough to let in a slit of light. She saw his lips tighten, then crease into a smile sharp as a razor. A smile devoid of joy, but born of power and wickedness.

She closed her eyes and thought of the priest blessing her back home.

"Vaya con Dios, mija."

Wherever I am, Marisol thought, it is not with God.

FIFTY-FOUR

Sharon loathed restaurants where the waiter's haircut cost more than hers, but she made an exception for the California Club. It was a century old, a quiet place of quiet money. Travertine archways, dark woods, and wall tapestries. A decorative, thirty-foot-high carved ceiling with a vaguely baroque look, as if you were dining in a sixteenth-century castle. Chandeliers hung from the ceiling by chains heavy enough to moor a cruise ship.

The young waiter in this staid old establishment had soap opera good looks and Superman's black hair, right down to the spit curl. An aspiring actor, no doubt. At the moment, he was politely whispering in her ear that she had a phone call.

Who even knew she was here?

Sharon left Cullen Quinn slurping his gazpacho and headed to a private booth of polished mahogany.

"Didn't want to call you on your cell," Payne said, when she answered. "I tried Philippe's and Langer's Deli. Then I figured Cullen asked you to his club. You were always a slut for sliced tenderloin."

"Jesus, Jimmy. Where are you?"

"I've picked up Marisol's trail."

"Have you lost your mind? There's a manhunt after you."

"At first, I was afraid it was hopeless. The hardest part was figuring out where to start. Turned out, it was Mexicali. Now we're getting close."

"Are you listening? You're wanted from here to the border, you idiot. Is this what you meant about changing your life?"

"Hey, you're the one who told me to help the kid."

"I didn't tell you to shoot at a sheriff's deputy."

"At his car, not at him. And Tino did the shooting, not me."

"If Rigney finds you—"

"He won't."

"Look, I was wrong. I never should have let you leave my house. Now you've got to come in and straighten it out. You've got to surrender."

"I will. After I find Tino's mother. I promise."

"The longer you're out there, the worse it's gonna get."

"C'mon, Sharon. I'm doing something for someone else. And you know what? It feels good. Tino's a terrific kid who's never gotten a break. No father, his mother doing the best she can. Did you know he's a natural athlete? The way he runs, he looks a little like Adam, only faster."

"Oh, Jimmy. Don't." Hearing him say their son's name—so unexpected—knocked the breath out of her.

"We have to be able to talk about Adam," Payne said.

"Now? Why couldn't you talk a year ago? Why'd you go into your cave and shut me out?" Her shock turned to anger.

"I felt the pain more than you did."

"Screw you, Jimmy. You *showed* the pain more. You swam in it. You drank it until you were intoxicated by it. But you didn't *feel* any more than I did. Any more than I *do*!"

"Sorry. That came out wrong."

"Damn right it did."

They each stayed silent, and it occurred to her that Jimmy never said why he was calling. But knowing him, it could only be one thing. "What's the favor you want?"

"I need you to run a license plate for me. A Cadillac Escalade. And get me the corporate info on three businesses."

"Forget it. Turn yourself in, Jimmy."

"You won't be doing it for me. It's for Tino and his mother."

"I know what you're doing, even if you don't."

"I'm helping a kid find his mother. Simple as that."

"You're paying penance. You blame yourself for what happened to Adam."

"Got nothing to do with it."

"Even if you find Tino's mother, then what? You'll

wake up the next morning, and Adam will still be gone. Tino will be out of your life, too."

Payne stayed quiet, and she listened to the static on the line.

"Okay, so maybe it has something to do with Adam," Payne confessed. "Maybe every day I remember watching some damn birds flying over the ocean. Maybe if I'd kept my eyes on the road, I could have braked or swerved. Maybe Adam would be alive."

Another moment of silence.

"Let me finish the job," Payne pleaded. "You know it's the right thing to do. You knew it the minute I walked into your kitchen the other night."

Somewhere across the dining room, a man laughed so heartily it sounded obscene.

"Precision Glass Company," Payne continued, giving her the name painted on one of the vans in Chitwood's barn. "Supposedly in Palm Desert, but I doubt it exists."

"I can't do it!"

"Two more. Valley Plumbing and Sand Dunes Electrical. Probably fictitious, too. Are you writing this down?"

"No, Jimmy."

Payne rattled off the license plate number of Zaga's Escalade, then repeated it a second time.

"No. No. No."

"Don't call my cell," Payne said. "I'm sure Rigney's triangulating my calls." He gave her the number of the pay phone of the Joshua Tree Park 'n Eat, and she slammed the receiver down so hard it sounded like a gunshot.

Jimmy hung up and joined Tino in a red vinyl booth at the breakfast joint near the desert town of Thermal, just north of the Imperial County line. On a fluttering TV set, shelved above the counter, the news came on with stock footage of mountains and cactus. The anchor was a coppery-skinned, wizened old coot with a string tie. A local cable station, Payne figured, since big-city television seemed to recruit their anchors from *America's Next Top Model*.

"She won't help, will she?" Tino said.

"Sure she will, kid." Not letting the boy see his concern.

Sharon at the California Club, Payne thought, unhappily. Dining with that prick fiancé of hers. Quinn's kind of place. Dark woods, old money, and raw power. Since the nineteenth century, the movers and shakers had been moving and shaking there. It's where William Mulholland hatched his plans to steal water from the Owens Valley. A ruthless scheme that bankrupted farmers and ranchers and turned a pristine lake into a parched and poisonous bed of alkali. On the plus side, it inspired the movie *Chinatown*.

While on the phone, Payne noticed the sign taped above the pass-through window to the kitchen. *English Spoken Here.*

One of those little put-downs of aliens, legal and illegal. Back home, Payne's Mexican-American plumber had two bumper stickers on his truck. One proclaimed his love of the Dodgers. The other, *"Broken English Spoken Here."* Not only could the guy fix the shut-off valve on a gravity sump, he had a sense of humor, too.

On the TV, the lead story seemed to be the weather. A hundred five degrees yesterday; a hundred five degrees today, a cooling trend tomorrow, at a hundred four.

The waitress, a tired forty-year-old with a messy bird's-nest of bleached hair and no wedding band, moseyed over to take their order.

"Chicken croquettes," Tino announced. "And a Coke."

"Eggs, ranch style," Payne said.

"Ranch style?" The waitress chewed on her pencil. "You mean, like a Denver omelette?"

"No omelette of any kind. Just eggs, ranch style."

"I'll ask the cook if he can make it."

"Sure he can. It's number three on the menu."

The waitress looked over his shoulder as he pointed to the item. "That's *huevos rancheros,* mister."

"Shhh." He motioned toward the sign. "English spoken here."

"You some sort of wise guy?"

"Just trying to follow the rules."

She walked away, muttering, "City people."

Sharon hadn't moved from the phone booth. She glanced toward Cullen at the table. Two men—a city councilman and a county supervisor—were kibitzing with him. Chuckles all around. Maybe planning their costumes for the Sheherazade Ball. The councilman gave Cullen a politician's whomp on the shoulder, no doubt congratulating him for holding the fort against the swarm of illegals. Sharon hoped the busboys didn't hear, fearing what they might slip into Cullen's drink.

Her fiancé was in his element. Smiling his anchorman smile. Looking damn pleased with himself. Not seeming to wonder about her whereabouts.

She replayed her conversation with Payne. He had sounded excited. Involved. Optimistic. How long had it been since she'd heard that in his voice?

She looked down at the linen napkin she had carried from the table. Now covered with scribbles, the names and numbers Payne had given her.

Damn you, Jimmy Payne!

FIFTY-FIVE

Tino studied Jimmy. "You tell me the truth just now? Pretty lady's gonna help?"

"She's never let me down, kid. Except when she shot me and divorced me."

"But she's a cop. Can't she get in trouble?"

"When you love someone, you take chances for them."

"If she loves you, why she gonna marry that *cabrón* on the TV?"

"It's complicated. Adult stuff."

"You saying she doesn't know she loves you?"

"She knows, Tino. But she fights it."

The pay phone at the end of the counter rang, and Payne raced to answer it.

He reached the phone just as a bighorn sheep came on the TV news. Something about the animal's shrinking habitat.

"Sharon?" Praying it was her.

"Precision Glass. Sand Dunes Electrical. Valley Plumbing," she said flatly. "They all exist."

"Damn. Blows my theory out of the water."

"Just listen a second. On paper, they're legitimate. But none are doing business. And get this: All three were incorporated by the law firm of Whitehurst and Booth in San Francisco."

"So what?"

"They're general counsel for Rutledge Ranch and Farms, Inc. Simeon Rutledge is—"

"I know who he is. But that law firm's got a bunch of big clients, right? Banks. Insurance companies. Maybe other big growers, too."

"Sure they do. But that Cadillac Escalade. It's owned by a man from Kings County named Enrique Zaga."

"That's him. What else can you tell me?"

"Only this," Sharon replied, drawing out the moment. "He's worked for Rutledge Farms since he was a kid. Picker. Foreman. Crew chief. Been head of security the last dozen years."

"Yes! You found Marisol. You're terrific, Sharon." Payne's voice was so loud, the waitress who already hated his guts gave him a dirty look. He caught Tino's eye and shot him the thumbs-up. The boy bounced out of the booth and ran toward him.

"I don't know why I did this," Sharon said, softly.

"Sure you do," Payne said.

"Don't start with me."

Tino interrupted, gesturing wildly toward the TV set. Under the caption *"WANTED"* were two photos lifted from a police car's video. Blurry, but still no mistaking Jimmy and Tino. Beneath the photos, another caption: *"Police Hunt Suspects."*

"Shit," Payne said. "Sharon, we gotta go."

"Where?"

"Where do you think? To Rutledge Ranch and Farms."

"Jimmy, be careful. I've met Simeon Rutledge. He's a rough guy."

"So what?"

"There are stories. A Grand Jury. Indictments coming. It's a pretty big deal."

"Still don't see what that's got to do with Marisol Perez. Or with me."

"Only this: Whenever you hear the name Rutledge, it's always attached to the word 'ruthless.' "

FIFTY-SIX

Payne downshifted as the Mustang climbed toward the peak of the Tejon Pass, a slash in the mountains that separated the Mojave Desert from the San Joaquin Valley. Road signs warned drivers to turn off their A/C, for fear of overheating.

Jimmy and Tino were headed north through the Los Angeles National Forest toward the town of Rutledge in Kings County, home of the far-flung empire of Simeon Rutledge. They had begun the day below sea level in the desert. Now, they ascended to over 4,000 feet, the temperature dropping 35 degrees. Tino began to shiver. He declined Payne's offer to put the top up and sat quietly while the radio filled the car with the throbbing guitars and hoarse voices of the Gipsy Kings playing "Pasajero."

They passed a lake, far below them in a valley, boats stirring up foamy wakes. Tino barely seemed to notice.

"Everything okay, kid?"

"Sure, Himmy."

Payne tried to decipher the boy's serious look. Nothing apparent, but consider the last few days. Back home, Tino had stabbed his mother's abusive and dangerous boss, who then threatened to cut the boy's heart out. He'd run from the cops in Van Nuys and rescued Payne from the sheriff's deputy along the highway. Then the run-in with El Tigre and the horrors of two stash houses. He'd heard how his mother fought off a rapist at the slaughterhouse. Just this morning, he'd escaped a pedophile ex-con and been shot at by a pint-size cowboy.

Not exactly the problems of kids from Bel-Air or Beverly Hills. Missing a goal in soccer practice or losing the debate tournament doesn't measure up.

"What are you thinking about, kid?"

"Back at the chicken ranch, when Chitwood started shooting, why'd you jump on top of me?"

Payne shrugged. "If anyone was gonna take a bullet, I wanted it to be me."

"Because you're a *valiente*."

"It doesn't need a name. It's just what a man does."

"A man does it for his own *hijo*. But you did it for someone who's not your own blood, and that makes you a *valiente*."

"If you say so, kiddo."

Tino squinted into the windstream, then blurted out, "You think *mi mami*'s pretty?"

"From the picture, *muy bonita*. Why?"

"Maybe if Sharon marries that *cabrón* Quinn, and you like *mi mami*, you can marry her."

"You left something out, kid. Your mother would have to like me, too."

"She will," Tino said. "She's never met a man like you."

FIFTY-SEVEN

Jimmy and Tino were twenty miles south of Bakersfield. Payne turned on the radio and picked up a Dodgers game from Shea Stadium, the Mets leading by a run. They heard the *cra-ack* of bat on ball and listened to the melodious Vin Scully describe Rafael Furcal banging a double off the left field wall.

"*¡Sólido conectando!*" Tino chimed in. "Furcal's my favorite."

Payne smiled. Tino loved baseball. That made two of them.

"I gotta pee, Himmy."

"You sure?" Payne remembering the boy's gotta-pee distractions.

" 'Course I'm sure. Can you stop in the next town?"

"As long as you're not gonna rob a bank."

They took the exit at Route 223 and headed east. They passed the freshly painted wooden barracks of Weedpatch Camp. A forlorn settlement of Okies during the Great Depression, the place was made famous in *The Grapes of Wrath*. A banner hung limply in the still air, inviting folks to the upcoming Dust Bowl Festival, promising corn bread, chili, and tri-tip steak.

Close to the restored camp, bare wooden shacks were still occupied by migrants—Hispanics, not Okies—tending nearby onion fields. The shacks weren't as nice as the freshly painted Weedpatch barracks. Payne wondered if anyone noticed the irony.

A roadside sign announced the dusty little town of Arvin, the "Garden in the Sun." They found a sporting goods store with a rest room in the back. While he waited for Tino, Jimmy bought two baseball gloves, a big-webbed, Wilson brown steerhide for himself, and a Mizuno black pigskin youth model for Tino. Then he grabbed two handfuls of Pony League balls.

Payne was already in the driver's seat, engine running, when Tino hopped in and found his new glove waiting. "For me?"

"You look like a shortstop to me. Lots of range."

"Oh, man!" A smile rippled across the boy's face like a cool breeze on a mountain lake. "After those *cabróns* stole my glove, I didn't know when I'd ever get another one."

"Once we find your mom, we'll play some ball, see what you've got." Payne thinking of Kevin Costner in *Field of Dreams* saying, "You wanna have a catch?"

They drove off, Tino running his fingertips over the raised red seams of one of the balls. Then he pounded the ball into the pocket of the glove, over and over. Payne imagined the boy sleeping with the ball and glove.

They passed Bakersfield and Delano, Pixley and Tipton, the temperature soaring as they drove deeper into the valley. With the Mustang's top down and the hot air enveloping them, Payne was reminded of his college job in a pizza shop, manning the ovens.

In nearby fields, cows lazed under shade trees. A few lonely oil wells pumped endlessly to their own rhythm. Neat rows of grapes formed straight lines across finely tended vineyards. Fat, round peaches dangled heavily from tree limbs. Hispanic men in hats and long-sleeve shirts hauled honeydews, big as volleyballs, to waiting wagons.

There were almond trees and melon fields and berry

patches. Lettuce and tomatoes, asparagus and artichokes, all soaking up the sun, crystalline water exploding in great plumes from rotating sprinklers, rainbows dancing in the mist.

Towering silos of grain stood like missiles alongside railroad tracks that paralleled the highway. Warehouses and pallet yards and fertilizer tanks and billboards with the reminder, *Crops Grow Where Water Flows*.

There seemed to be nothing here that wasn't devoted to the soil and its bounty. Could migrants be blamed for believing that America was paved, if not with gold, with tasty treasures ripe for the picking?

The Dodgers game was lost to static, and Payne twirled the old-fashioned radio dial. He found a Spanish-language station and another in Portuguese, then stopped when he heard Los Lobos belting out "Good Morning Aztlán." He remembered how much Sharon loved the up-tempo song and how she once told him to listen carefully to the lyrics. All about not trying to run and hide away. *"Here it comes, here comes another day."*

He was never much for drawing philosophical lessons from music, be it "Margaritaville" or "Ave Maria." But who could argue with that message? He had been running. Ever since Adam died. Running from his grief, hiding under a mountain of pain. Not caring about the next sunrise or the new day.

Helping Tino had energized and focused him. He anticipated the pure joy of the boy's reunion with his mother and his own joy of helping them, asking nothing in return. But then what? Sharon's words came back to him. *"You'll wake up the next morning, and Adam will still be gone. And you know what? Tino will be out of your life, too."*

With that thought tormenting him, Payne saw a billboard along the road. It would have been hard to miss.

Dominating the sign was a three-story-high likeness of Simeon Rutledge, a crooked smile on his craggy, cowboy face. And this greeting: *Rutledge Ranch and Farms, Inc., Welcomes You to Kings County. Drive Carefully.*

FIFTY-EIGHT

Detective Rigney answered the phone in his Parker Center office. Surprised to hear Deputy Sheriff Dixon calling from his piece-of-shit trailer outside Calexico. Rigney could practically smell the ratty boar's head on the wall.

"Just got a call from a waitress at the Park 'n Eat," Dixon told him. "A diner up by Thermal. Technically, that's in Riverside County, out of my jurisdiction, but—"

"Get to the point, Dixon, before global warming fries our asses."

"Payne and the kid were there. Had breakfast this morning. Want to know what they ate?"

"She's sure it's them? She's absolutely sure?" Excitement bubbling up like the oil at the tar pits.

"She I.D.'ed them from a TV report. Said the guy was a real smart-ass."

"That'd be Payne."

"He used the pay phone. Twice. One call out, one call in."

"You gonna subpoena the numbers?"

"Don't need to. My sister-in-law works at the phone company. I'll have everything in an hour."

"Can't wait to see that bastard's face when I bust him." Thinking the A-Form would report that the subject resisted arrest, resulting in his subsequent injuries.

"They left in a hurry," Dixon said. "An old blue Mustang convertible. The waitress couldn't make out the plates, except they were out of state. Car headed north toward an entrance to the I-10."

A physical sensation, Rigney's skin tingling, like the anticipation of sex. "You did great, Dixon. Sorry for busting your chops."

"It's okay. I just want a piece of that shyster."

"You got it, pal. You can have whatever's left when I'm done with him."

FIFTY-NINE

The teenage girl with the black curly hair threw her head back and made a sound somewhere between gargling and drowning.

Her idea of an orgasm, Simeon Rutledge thought. Probably watched too many *telenovelas* on Univision. Taking her doggie style over a bale of straw, he continued thrusting, but his heart wasn't in it. He slapped her butt once, twice, three times. Firm as a honeydew.

She looked back over her shoulder, her tongue darting out and licking her lower lip. "Ride me, *jefe*! Fuck me hard!"

Where was she coming up with this shit? His mind wandered to the broken pump on Irrigation Culvert Number Three.

Jesus, was there anything more pathetic than a lack-luster fuck?

He didn't blame the girl. She moaned and whooped and wailed and chanted, *"¡Dios mio! ¡Dios mio! ¡Dios fucking mio!"*

Put a lid on it, chica. *Nobody's that good. Not even me.*

Not that he wasn't damn proud of his virility. Funny thing about sex, the more you do it, the more you want it. The less you do it, the easier it is to do without.

That *panocha* pie he'd been breaking in at the club had stirred up the juices. *Marisol.* Passive when drugged, she'd turn into a hellcat, he figured, given enough time.

Just now, his member was barely at half-staff, but Ana or Anita or Angelita—he never quite caught her name—was caterwauling like a coyote.

This morning, Rutledge had not planned on a barn-banging. But Beatriz, the girl's mother, an assistant crew chief who'd been working for him for twenty years, brought her around when he'd been checking out the south peach orchard. Elegant Ladies, fat and firm with a pink blush, were at their peak in the summer heat. Rutledge twisted one off a tree and bit into it, the sweet juice streaming down his face. That's when he saw Beatriz's daughter. Canvas shorts and a sweat-stained T-shirt with no bra, boobs undulating as she hip-swayed through the rows of trees.

Do their mothers teach them this shit or is it in their genes?

Maybe it was the intoxicating aroma of the fruit or even the memory of banging the girl's mother back in the Reagan years.

In the same barn.

Over a different bale of straw.

Slam, bam. *Gracias*, ma'am.

Back then, Beatriz had just arrived from Chihuahua and looked as if she'd walked the whole way. But she had the wide hips, the slim waist, and the pendulous breasts that Rutledge favored. Humping *el jefe* got Beatriz out of the melon fields and into the shade. She probably thought the same magic would work for Ana or Anita or Angelita.

"She's only sixteen and a virgin, *jefe*."

"Sure, Bea, and I'm the King of Siam."

But he took the bait. The girl had the same round breasts and oversize nipples as her mother. Same big ass, too. In twenty years, with five kids, she'd have to turn sideways to make it through the doorway of the double-wide.

Now the girl was wriggling her butt and tightening her pussy, trying to get him to come. But his mind was elsewhere and his dick felt as if it had been anesthetized.

His cell phone rang, and he plucked it from his shirt pocket while squeezing the girl's ass with the other hand. Enrique Zaga. Shit. Now what? Did Chitwood kill another *pollo*?

Rutledge slid out of her. She looked back over her shoulder. "*¿Una segunda vuelta, jefe?*"

He hadn't come, but she was offering seconds. With as much passion as a waitress refilling your iced tea.

"Give it a rest, *chica*."

She bounced up and walked naked to a refrigerator by the stalls. Rutledge hoped she knew the difference between lemonade and horse semen. He pulled up his jeans and sank back into the bale of straw.

"What's the problem, Z?"

Zaga apologized for bothering him, then said flat out, "We had some visitors in Hellhole Canyon."

"Chitwood's asshole friends?"

"Worse, Sim." He summarized Chitwood's confrontation with a lawyer from L.A. and a Mexican kid looking for his mother.

"I don't think they'll cause trouble, Sim," Zaga said, "as long as we get the boy back with his mom."

"Fine. What's her name?"

"Marisol Perez."

"Shit."

"What, Sim?"

"She's training at the club."

"So?"

"I'm the one breaking her in, and she ain't exactly a volunteer."

"Jeez, Sim. Still thinking with your dick at your age."

Rutledge silently cursed himself. "You're right, Z. Dammit, you're right."

The men had known each other all their lives. Raced horses at the county fairgrounds. Got drunk together. Banged the same girls. Zaga was his most trusted employee.

Rutledge knew there were plenty of women who took to the indoor work at the Hot Springs Gentleman's Club. Some gave rub-and-tugs. Some sucked and fucked a select group of lobbyists and legislators who drove down from Sacramento. If you sensed a woman was trouble, you could ship her to the Midwest to pick sugar beets. Or throw her in the back of a truck and drop her off in Tijuana. Once in a great while, you'd come across some pain-in-the-ass who wouldn't let it go. Rutledge remembered a Honduran girl, a blow-job artist who worked at the club for six months before deciding she'd been coerced. She'd come after him with a carving knife. Her carcass ended up fertilizing a cornfield.

"Damn stupid of me," Rutledge confessed. "All the willing *panocha* around here, and I gotta rassle me some."

"Aw, shit, Sim. Like your daddy used to say, what's done's done, and what ain't ain't."

Sometimes, Rutledge thought, Zaga admired Jeremiah Rutledge more than he did. Jeremiah had been many things. Philosopher. Philanderer. Poker player. And one vicious S.O.B. when riled or drunk, which was six days out of seven, Sundays being reserved for Church, followed by humping a couple migrant girls. In some ways, Rutledge thought, maybe the peach didn't fall too damn far from the tree.

"Forget about letting the woman see her kid," Rutledge said. "Especially with a lawyer involved. Last thing I need now is some rape charge."

"I hear you, Sim."

"I don't suppose that idiot Chitwood got the lawyer's name."

"Got his card. J. Atticus Payne. Office in Van Nuys."

Rutledge thought a second. "I met a lady cop named Payne down in L.A. She's with that asshole Cullen Quinn."

"Small fucking world."

"Tell Javier to get everything he can on the lawyer."

"I dunno. Javier's been taking that chief-of-police shit real serious lately. Not into personal favors."

"Just tell him it's for me. I need a full background check and risk assessment."

Zaga chuckled over the phone.

"What now, Z?"

" 'Risk assessment.' I was just thinking, if it was your daddy talking to mine, he woulda said, 'Amancio, git your shovel and dig a hole in Levee Five. Ah got some varmint to bury.' "

"Times change." Rutledge echoed his lawyer's words without completely believing them. "Soon as you can, let me know what Javier finds out. And Z . . ."

"Yeah, Sim?"

"You keep your daddy's shovel handy, okay?"

SIXTY

Sharon exited the Parker Center. The 1950's glass shoe box was named after the former police chief best remembered for running a department long on corruption and short on civil liberties. On the other hand, Chief William H. Parker did a fine job making sure the *Dragnet* scripts polished the L.A.P.D.'s image.

Leaving the cop shop on the Los Angeles Street side, Sharon avoided looking at *The Family Group,* an angular bronze sculpture depicting a man, woman, and son. A reminder of her lost life, the artwork as subtle as an arrow to the heart.

A strange thought then. If Jimmy didn't find Tino's mother, if the boy was left without a parent, did her ex think he could keep him like some stray cat? And something else. Did he think that Tino was the key to re-creating the family, to getting back together with her?

She could picture Jimmy saying it.

"He's got nobody but us, Sharon."

To Jimmy, there was still an "us." Something else he hadn't come to grips with.

Sharon had walked a block when she heard, "Detective Payne!"

She turned to find Rigney on her heels, jabbing at her with an index finger. She hated finger jabbers. Rigney wore a regulation wrinkled brown suit with a mismatched tie.

"You hear about your ex?" Rigney's tone as nasty as a rabbit punch. "The feds picked up his Lexus coming from Tijuana with eighty kilos of coke."

"So why don't you go down there and check it out?"

Rigney hawked up a wet laugh. "Why would I do that? We both know it's bullshit."

She stopped at the Temple Street intersection, waiting for the *Don't Walk* to change.

Rigney moved closer and whispered, "Payne dumped the Lexus in Mexico, and it ended up with some *narco-traficante*."

"I wouldn't know."

"Really? How was lunch today?"

Sharon tried to read the look on his face but couldn't get past the smirk.

"California Club, right?" he said. "Your TV star fiancé is a member."

"Wow. You've been playing detective again."

"I got a waiter who puts Quinn at table nineteen, dining with a tall woman with reddish-brown hair. The woman used the private phone booth in the dining room. Want to take a wild guess who called the club from some diner at 12:38 P.M.?"

"I'm impressed, Rigney. Maybe someday you'll pass the sergeant's exam."

"Where's he headed?"

The light changed, and she headed up Temple toward City Hall. "Who?"

"Royal Fucking Payne! You're helping him, and we both know it."

"If you can prove that, take it to Internal Affairs."

"I'll take it to the D.A. I'll throw the going-away party when they ship you to Chowchilla."

"You know what I think, Rigney? I think you're taking a lot of heat because you ran a sting that got a judge killed. The more blame you can shift to Jimmy, the better off you are. And as long as you can't find him, why not pick on me?"

"Bullshit. Payne's dirty and you're protecting him."

The Criminal Court Building loomed ahead.

"Where the hell you going?" he demanded.

"Back off, Rigney."

She moved at a brisk pace. Her legs were longer than Rigney's, and he hustled to keep up.

"You going to court?" he asked.

"No."

"Then, what—"

"I'm going to church, okay? Our Lady of the Angels."

"Why? You catch another priest diddling an altar boy?"

She wheeled and faced him head-on. "My maiden name's Lacy. The Lacys of County Clare. I missed Mass this morning. I've got six brothers who could each beat the shit out of you, and I could, too."

She turned and swept past the Hall of Records, toward the downtown cathedral. She was so angry it took another moment to realize that she had jabbed her own finger at Rigney, denting his polyester tie.

SIXTY-ONE

The welcome sign on the outskirts of town informed travelers that the burg of Rutledge had 17,068 souls and that "healthy soil makes for healthy people." The sign didn't say if the undocumented migrants were as healthy as the 17,068 regular folks.

The town's streets were wide, the sidewalks in good repair. Several businesses flew American flags. On the main drag, prosaically named "Artichoke Avenue," there was a barbershop with a rotating red-and-white pole and, next door, Hilda's Ice Cream Shoppe. Two towheaded boys tore along the street on bicycles, fishing poles lodged on their shoulders. To Payne, it all seemed like a backlot designed by Walt Disney and painted by Norman Rockwell.

The town square had a leafy park with towering white oaks and a bandstand fit for John Philip Sousa. There was a vintage merry-go-round with hand-carved horses, and organ music.

Payne hated merry-go-rounds. As a toddler, he once fell off his rocking horse. After that, all merry-go-round horses looked like monsters with giant teeth. The final scene of *Strangers on a Train* didn't help that phobia one bit.

"They named the town after this dude?" Tino asked.

"After one of his ancestors, but he's poured lots of money into the place."

They drove past the Rutledge Free Library, the Rutledge Town Swimming Pool, and the Rutledge Senior Citizens Center, all with signs in both English and Spanish.

"How much money this guy got?" Tino asked.

"You know who Carlos Slim is?"

"*Claro.* Richest man south of the border."

"Rutledge is to the San Joaquin Valley what Slim is to Mexico."

Tino whistled.

The businesses downtown were mostly wood-framed buildings with awnings shading the sidewalk and front doors propped open. There was one movie theater, the Rialto, with one screen. If you wanted to catch a film in this town, you'd better like *Indiana Jones and the Kingdom of the Crystal Skull.*

One structure stood out. A two-story redbrick building on Peach Street with barred windows and a camera mounted above a heavy metal door. A brass plate read:

Rutledge Ranch and Farms, Inc.
Corporate Headquarters

Jimmy parked the Mustang, reached in his pocket, and gave Tino a twenty-dollar bill. "Go get a hot fudge sundae and wait for me here."

"C'mon, Himmy. We go in together with the baseball bat. It's the *valiente* way."

"Just do what I say, okay?"

Tino pouted but headed toward Hilda's Ice Cream Shoppe. Payne approached the front door and stood there a moment, gathering his thoughts. He planned a straightforward approach. No trial lawyer tricks. No reason not to tell the truth. And no baseball bats. A boy and his mother got separated. We think she's here. Please help us get them together. Who could object to that?

On the sidewalk, a newspaper rack held both the *Rutledge Gazette* and *La Opinión*. The *Gazette* headline fretted over the ongoing drought. Plastered on the Spanish paper's front page was a satellite photo of a hurricane moving toward the Yucatan.

There was a keypad at the front door and a button for visitors to announce themselves. Payne pushed, said his name, and a buzzer welcomed him inside.

"May I help you?" The woman at the reception desk smiled at Payne in a businesslike way. She was in her twenties and wearing a short-sleeve cotton dress splashed with big sunflowers.

"I hope so, ma'am. I surely do." Putting a bit of country into his voice. Not intentionally. It just seemed to come out in this farming town. He told Ms. Sunflowers that he was trying to locate a Rutledge employee whose son was looking for her.

"Could I see some identification?" she asked, pleasantly.

He handed over his driver's license, and she made a notation on a clean white pad.

"Been a while since I was carded," he said. "My first six-pack at Trader Joe's, as I recall."

"I'm sorry, Mr. Payne. But we've had numerous threats against Mr. Rutledge. He's quite outspoken, as you probably know."

"I like what he says. He's a good man." Slathering butter on the toast.

"One moment, please." She picked up her phone, pushed a button, and said, "Louise. I wonder if you could help me up front."

Payne hoped that wasn't code for "Send out the Doberman pinschers."

In a moment, a woman came through an interior door, marched up to Payne, and introduced herself as Louise Antrim. *Mrs.* Louise Antrim, in case Payne had any salacious thoughts. About fifty, trim, in a beige business suit, gray-streaked hair bunned on top of her head. A pair of eyeglasses dangled from her neck on a beaded chain. Her eyes were alert and frosty blue.

Payne repeated his request. Missing mother. Son desperate to find her. He filled in the name, "Marisol Perez."

Mrs. Antrim gave him a sad smile. "I'm sorry, Mr. Payne, but it would be an invasion of privacy for the company to either confirm or deny that Ms. Perez is an employee here."

"But I'm trying to put a family back together."

"Do you have a signed statement from Ms. Perez authorizing our releasing the information?"

"If I had a statement, Ms. Perez wouldn't be missing."

"But if she's missing, how could she be working here?"

"I'll be happy to ask her when you take me to her."

"Do you have any documentation, Mr. Payne? Her Social Security number. A green card."

"Don't think so."

"An H-2 visa. Is she a guest worker?"

"She's undocumented."

"Well then, of course she couldn't be working here."

"Are you shitting—? I'm sorry. Are you kidding me? Your boss practically boasts about hiring undocumented migrants."

"Mr. Rutledge has strong feelings about reforming our immigration laws. But I assure you, as the head of Human Resources, we employ only documented workers."

Sounding like a tape recording.

"Mrs. Antrim, I'm just asking for a little compassion."

"Mr. Payne, as a lawyer, surely you know that we cannot—"

"I didn't say I was a lawyer."

"Didn't you?" Her cheeks colored just a bit, like the blush on a ripe peach. "Well, you seem so lawyerlike."

"Funny. Judges never think so."

"I guess I just assumed you were representing the Perez boy."

"No, you didn't. You *knew* I was coming."

At Hilda's Ice Cream Shoppe, Tino bought five cups of icy drinks. Coffee, tea, root beer. With the cups balanced in a cardboard tray, he hurried back and circled the Rutledge building, looking for a way to get inside.

We're a team, Himmy. You said so yourself.

Tino found nothing but barred windows and locked doors. Behind the building, a tiled patio. Round tables with umbrellas, workers in casual clothes. Smoking, talking, drinking coffee.

He walked purposely toward the rear door, holding the tray in both hands.

The delivery boy.

He used a few words of Spanglish to ask if anyone would get the door for him. *Americanos* always wanted to show they were smart enough to understand anything a stupid Mexican might say.

A young woman, whose face glowed pink in the baking heat, took a drag on her cigarette, squashed it under her open-toed sandal, and gave Tino a big, friendly smile. She punched a code in a keypad and opened the door.

"Gracias, señorita," Tino said, with as much humility as he could muster. He stepped into an air-conditioned corridor and began exploring.

*   *   *

"I don't know what you mean." Mrs. Antrim shifted her weight from one leg to the other. "How would I know you were coming, Mr. Payne?"

"Because that little bastard in the black Escalade called you. Enrique Zaga."

"I'll thank you to watch your tongue. We don't tolerate profanity here."

"What do you tolerate? Kidnapping?"

"Please lower your voice, Mr. Payne."

"And where's Zaga? I want to talk to him."

"Our director of security has nothing to do with this."

"He's a human trafficker! He stashes Mexicans down in Hellhole Canyon. Unless you're grinding them into dog food, you're hiring them. You know it. I know it. I'll bet half the Legislature knows it."

"I'm afraid I'm going to have to ask you to leave now."

Payne watched the receptionist hit another button on her desk phone.

Tino moved briskly down the corridor as if he knew where he was going. Carrying the tray of drinks, he passed several offices with open doors. Men in short-sleeve shirts and women in summer outfits worked at computers. Some doors had little placards. Accounting. Marketing. Purchasing. Transportation. Legal.

Legal, Tino thought. What he needed was an office named "Illegal."

A man with a ponytail and a blond soul patch came around a corner. Tino smiled at him.

Polite delivery boy.

The man seemed as wide as he was tall. Thick neck, thighs bulging through gray pants, a blue sport jacket that bunched tight at his shoulders. He had his eyes on the icy drinks. "Hey, *chico*. Those for Harry and the girls?"

"*Sí*. Harry and the girls."

"Second floor. Room 207."

Tino headed toward a stairwell, the man watching him go.

On the second floor, Tino continued snooping. More doors, more offices. Shipping. Security. Human Resources.

He checked out Human Resources. No one there. Two desks and several file cabinets running the length of the room. He ducked inside and placed the drinks on one of the desks. The file cabinets were labeled with what seemed to be the names of different companies. Rutledge Ranch and Farms. Kings County Excavation. Rutledge Tool Company.

How much does this guy own?

Way more, Tino quickly found out.

Rutledge Trucking. Valley Paving. Rutledge Realty.

Tino opened one of the file drawers. Hundreds of folders. Thousands in total. He could spend a week in here.

He picked several folders at random from a folder labeled: *San Joaquin Irrigation*. Each employee seemed to have a file with name, photo, salary, and comments by supervisors.

More companies. Weedpatch Pest Control. Rutledge Aviation. Hot Springs Gentleman's Club.

Gentleman's Club? Doesn't sound like farming or ranching.

Tino was about to open the Gentleman's Club drawer when he sensed movement behind him. He glanced over his shoulder and saw Soul Patch, his legs spread, his shoulders filling the doorway. "Ain't no Harry working here, *chico*," the man said.

* * *

"If you don't give me access to Marisol Perez," Payne said, "I can get a court order."

Mrs. Antrim let the corners of her mouth curl into a tiny smile. "The courthouse is three blocks from here. I believe Judge Rutledge is in most afternoons."

"*Judge* Rutledge?"

"Simeon's cousin."

"You folks dish out home cooking like two-dollar hash browns."

The interior door opened. A burly man hustled into the reception area without appearing to hurry. An African-American with a shaved head and a thick neck, he wore gray slacks, a white shirt, and a blue blazer. The uniform of a classy security guard. In his thirties, Shaved Head had the look of an ex-linebacker who stayed in shape.

"There a problem here, Mrs. Antrim?" Shaved Head said.

"Not if this gentleman leaves the premises." *Gentleman* with a tone you might use to describe a pus-filled wound.

The interior door opened again, and a ponytailed, soul-patched man dressed identically to Shaved Head tromped out, carrying Tino under one arm. The boy kicking and wriggling.

Shit! How'd he get in here?

"Asswipe! Cocksucker! Dipshit!" Tino practicing English words Jimmy had taught him.

"Put him down," Payne said.

"You don't give the orders here, lawyer," Soul Patch said.

Everybody seemed to know he was a lawyer, Payne thought. Maybe he should open an office in town.

"I'll kill you!" Tino cried out, trying to pry the man's fingers from his waist.

"Let him go, Clyde," Shaved Head ordered.

Soul Patch dropped Tino to the floor.

"*Pendejo!*" Tino had returned to his native tongue.

Shaved Head looked at Payne with an air of placid indifference. "We can do it pretty or we can do it ugly."

"We're leaving," Payne said. "But I gotta ask you two something."

They waited, staring Payne down.

"Is it true that steroids shrink your testicles?"

Soul Patch and Shaved Head were remarkably gentle. They swept Payne up by the arms, carried him through the doorway, and deposited him on the sidewalk without mussing his shirt. He admired their proficiency.

SIXTY-TWO

Exhausted by an endless day that began at Wanda the Whale's stash house in the desert, continued with gunfire in Hellhole Canyon, and concluded in the heart of the San Joaquin Valley, Jimmy and Tino checked into the Rutledge Arms Hotel.

Jimmy ordered from room service. Pork chops for Tino with mashed potatoes, onion rings, applesauce, and a chocolate milk shake. Payne crashed, leaving a burger half-uneaten. He fell asleep watching the news on a Sacramento station, then awoke at three A.M. to find the kid engrossed in porn on the pay channel. Jimmy gave him hell, then watched a few minutes of action between a pizza delivery boy and a bored housewife. He dozed off again just as Tino said, "*Buenos noches,* Himmy."

They slept until nearly noon.

"Where we going?" Tino asked as Jimmy got out of the shower.

"*I'm* going to the police station. You're going to the Rialto to see *Indiana Jones and his Kingdom of Goofy Plots.*"

"No way, José. We're a team."

Payne tried to give the kid a stern look. Tino responded the way a sixth grader treats a substitute teacher who demands quiet. He laughed.

"C'mon, Himmy. You know I'll just show up at the police station, anyway."

Payne had expected an old-fashioned courthouse in the town square, something built of sturdy limestone by the Civil Works Administration in the 1930s. The police station and coroner's office would be a block away in nondescript brick buildings.

Instead, the Municipal Center stood on the edge of town, a series of modern one-story buildings with brown shingle roofs. Courtyards bloomed with roses and rhododendrons. A fountain generated a stream that meandered from the Zoning Department past the City Commission Chambers, toward the Police Department.

Jimmy and Tino crossed a wooden footbridge that arched gracefully over the stream. They followed flagstone steps through a rock garden planted with bonsai trees. It looked like a dandy place for afternoon tea.

They found Police Chief Javier Cardenas sitting on a

redwood bench along the stream, chewing a sandwich. A handsome man in his mid-thirties, he had a cocoa complexion so smooth it appeared he'd just shaved and slapped on cologne. Dark hair fashionably cut. Black trousers and a crisply pressed white shirt with epaulets and a gold badge.

"I hear you two caused a stir over at the Rutledge office yesterday," the chief said, even before Payne introduced himself.

"Not our fault," Payne replied. "They treat strangers like weevils in a cotton field."

"Next time that *cabrón* with the fuzzy lip grabs me, I'll kick him in the *cojones*," Tino said.

"Quiet, Tino," Payne said. "Chief, don't you think it's suspicious they guard the place like it's the Pentagon?"

"Nothing suspicious about it," Cardenas said. "The Patriot Patrol put a price on Simeon's head, so the company beefed up security." Cardenas took a bite of his sandwich. Bacon, lettuce, and tomato on whole wheat. "Now, why don't you tell me what you need, Mr. Payne? It is Mr. J. Atticus Payne of Van Nuys, correct?"

"Ay, he's messing with you, Himmy," Tino said.

"Yeah, I'm Jimmy Payne. And I'm trying to help this boy find his mother." He summarized the story of Marisol becoming separated from her son and as much as he knew of her harrowing crossing and the two stash houses she'd passed through.

"So you want to file a missing persons report?" the chief asked.

"She's not exactly missing. More like she's working for Simeon Rutledge but his people won't let me get to her."

"Working for my *tío* Sim?"

Payne felt as if he'd been sucker-punched. "You're shitting me. Rutledge is your uncle?"

An easy smile. The guy had a politician's set of teeth.

"Not a blood uncle," Cardenas said. "More like my godfather. It's a long story."

Tino nudged Payne in the ribs. "And you *gabachos* say Mexico is all dirty politics."

"Why do I feel like I'm playing a road game?" Payne said to the chief.

"More like you're the Washington Generals and you're playing the Harlem Globetrotters," Cardenas said.

"So how the hell can you investigate Rutledge's business?"

"Didn't know it needed investigating. Did I mention *Tío* Sim bought me my first gun and my first car?"

"What about your badge? He buy that, too?"

Cardenas let out a soft train whistle of a sigh. "You work hard to get under people's skin, don't you, Mr. Payne?"

"Nah. It just comes naturally."

The chief was silent a moment. He seemed to be figuring out what to do with his unwelcome visitors. Then he gestured with his sandwich. "You want a B.L.T., Mr. Payne? And what about you, young man? Donna over in Planning and Zoning made a bunch today."

"No thanks," Payne said.

"Me, neither," Tino said.

It was the first time Payne ever saw the boy turn down food.

"Suit yourselves. But it's mighty good. Rutledge lettuce. Rutledge tomatoes. Bacon from Rutledge hogs. All courtesy of *Tío* Sim."

"All Rutledge, all the time," Payne said. "You're sending a message, right?"

The chief's smile gleamed like the blade of a knife. "If that's what I wanted, I'd lock you up right now on all those outstanding warrants."

That stopped Payne, who took a moment to think it through. Once Rutledge learned about the cluster fuck in Hellhole Canyon, he would have wanted a dossier on J. Atticus Payne, Esquire. Enter Cardenas, who had to do something to earn his bacon, lettuce, and tomatoes.

"You're a one-man crime wave, Mr. Payne. Grand larceny in L.A. County. Resisting arrest and assaulting an officer in Imperial County. Importing drugs from Mexico into San Diego County."

"The drug rap's bogus," Payne said.

"And that cop," Tino said. "*I'm* the one who resisted and assaulted."

"So why aren't you gonna arrest me?" Payne demanded.

"And deal with all that paperwork?" Cardenas said. "Three different jurisdictions fighting over your sorry butt." The chief let his eyes twinkle. "I'd miss the County Fair over in Hanford."

"But if Rutledge told you to do it, you'd throw my sorry butt in jail."

The chief laughed, showing those good teeth. "Mr. Payne, you and Sim are more alike than you realize. You both overlook the fine print of the law. Hell, you overlook the large print. And you both go out of your way to help people."

"No, I don't. And I doubt he does."

"Don't be modest. Sim respects what you're doing for the boy. So do I."

"But you refuse to help."

"What makes you say that? I arranged lunch for you tomorrow with Sim."

"No way."

"He might try to poison you, Himmy," Tino said. "Happens on *telenovelas* all the time."

"Sim said he'll have his people do everything they can

to find the boy's mother. He'll have a report for you by lunchtime tomorrow."

"Great," Payne said, not sure he believed the chief. "Sorry about what I said before."

"Not a problem. There's one more thing Sim said. What was it, now?"

"Yeah?"

"Oh, I remember." The chief's smile turned sly. "He said, 'Javie, ask that persistent little pissant if he likes sheep balls in coyote gravy.' "

SIXTY-THREE

It was dark outside the window when Marisol tried her door again.

Locked from the outside.

Dizzy, she returned to the bed.

They must have put something in her food. An older black woman, a uniformed housekeeper, had delivered a tray. Grilled vegetables, a green salad, and rice pudding. *"They don't want you putting on any weight, honey."*

Now, lying on her back, looking at the mirrored ceiling, Marisol heard voices in the corridor. Laughing men, voices fueled by liquor. Giggling women, teasing talk. Grunts and yells through the wall next to her bed. A man brayed like a goat. A woman fired off words like bullets from a machine gun. "¡Sí! ¡Sí! ¡Sí! No! No! No! Don't stop!"

Marisol wondered if that room was like her own. Dim lights. Mirrors. No telephone. A television that played only filthy movies. A tiny bathroom with a shower and toilet and a dozen hand towels.

She heard a key turn the lock, and the door opened. A heavy-bosomed American woman with teased platinum hair came in, carrying a satchel. The woman's translucent skin was stretched tight over her cheekbones, but her neck crinkled with turkey wattles. She was either forty or sixty, no way to tell. The woman opened the satchel.

"For you, dearie."

Out came lingerie, black as midnight, glittering with sequins. A leather bustier with tie strings. Leopard-spotted bras and panties. A satin slip with garters and stockings. Items she'd never seen except in the movies, the American woman calling them teddies and baby dolls, camisoles and peek-a-boos. Giving her shoes with velvety skin and heels longer than a sixteen-penny nail.

"I do not belong here," Marisol said.

A shrug. "Who does?"

The woman showed her how to apply layers of makeup and hauled out small bottles of lotions and tubes of lubricants. Plus lipstick a whorish red.

When tears filled Marisol's eyes, the woman said, "Honey, I can share a few tricks that'll make it a bit easier for you. Let me show you how to make a John think he's getting a blow job when you're really just jerking him off."

A man appeared in the open doorway. "Helen, get out of here and take that shit with you."

"Yes, sir, Mr. Zaga." The woman gathered up her satchel and left the room.

The man was as old as El Patron. But smaller. Hispanic features. Grayish hair falling nearly to his shoulders, a Western shirt with the sleeves rolled up. Arms corded with thick veins.

Marisol tensed as he approached. If he grabbed her, she would fight.

"Relax, *chica*. I'm here to talk, not fuck. Back home, did you read newspapers?"

It was such an odd question Marisol had no answer.

"You understand English?"

"Yes. I read newspapers. Books, too."

"What's your favorite book?"

"Why do you ask such a thing?"

"Just answer me."

"El Amor en los Tiempos del Colera."

"You read it in English or Spanish?"

"English. My father insisted. Why do you care?"

Appearing unhappy, the man mumbled to himself, "What the hell are we gonna do with you?"

"I do not understand."

"Rutledge has a soft spot for your type. Those damn gypsy eyes."

Marisol felt dazed, the dizziness returning. "And he cares if I read books?"

"He don't care if you can count to ten. But it's my job to protect him from himself. You're not some illiterate *campesina*. We let you go, you could cause the boss some real problems."

"No. I would never—"

"Five, ten years ago, it might have been different. But it's too hot out there. Too many people want the boss's scalp."

"I swear I will not make trouble."

"Damn right you won't."

He turned and left the room, locking the door from the outside.

SIXTY-FOUR

"You like horses?" Simeon Rutledge asked.

"Not the ones that rob me blind at Santa Anita," Payne answered. It was ten o'clock in the morning of his third day in Kings County. Payne had no idea why Rutledge had asked him to come to the ranch, but his own mission was clear.

Why the runaround at your office? What are you hiding? Where the hell is Marisol Perez?

Tino had pleaded to come along. Jimmy told him he wasn't invited, then dropped him off at a video arcade. Tino asked for fifty dollars, Jimmy offered twenty, and they settled on thirty-five.

Now Payne leaned on a fence post of a corral, the dirt as finely groomed as a sand trap at Riviera Country Club. A stable hand tightened the cinch of a saddle on an Appaloosa speckled like a Dalmatian. Rutledge saddled his own horse, a midnight black stallion with angry eyes. He wore weathered chaps and a black felt Stetson with a flat brim.

"We'll ride a bit, then have lunch," Rutledge said.

It didn't sound like a question or even an invitation, so Payne didn't answer.

The midday sun poured down, a ball of orange fire. They mounted up, and Rutledge gestured toward a long building of yellow pine with a steeply pitched roof. "Knocked off my first piece of ass in those stables."

Payne decided not to say *"congratulations."* Instead,

he tried to keep his horse from sidestepping and crushing him against the corral rail.

"Maria something-or-other," Rutledge reminisced. "Grape picker. Hands stained like she worked an old printing press. Went on for a month before my daddy caught us. I was afraid he'd beat me, maybe send the girl back to Mexico. But he hauled out a bottle of Old Grand-dad and told us to do it again. He wanted to watch. Then he had his way with her."

Sick fuck, Payne thought. "Nothing like fathers and sons sharing quality time."

"My point is, we're all a product of our upbringing."

"Why not just cut the bullshit and tell me what's happened to Marisol Perez?"

Rutledge gave him a look as hard as polished oak. "There's a time I would have horsewhipped a man who spoke to me that way."

"All I'm saying, how tough can it be to check who started work the last few days?"

"We're looking into it. Now, let's ride." Rutledge *cluck*ed in the stallion's ear and tugged on the reins to turn the big animal. Payne followed, bouncing in the saddle.

The path took them past two workmen polishing a pickup truck, an ancient short-bed Ford with a gleaming finish the color of freshly washed spinach. Rutledge noticed Payne admiring the truck.

"A 1951 F-100. My daddy's. Do you know why I keep it?"

"Tradition, I guess. Another link to your past."

"You got it, Payne." Nodding with approval. "Your father hand anything down to you?"

"Only a bowling ball he forgot to take with him."

Rutledge grunted, nudged his stallion, and they headed toward the fields at a steady trot. The horses *clop*ped along a path of brick-colored dirt. After a few moments, Rutledge said, "Attorney Payne, I admire what you did in that trailer-truck case."

"Forty-eight hours in an air-conditioned cell. Nothing compared to what the migrants went through."

"Point is, you risked your career for a cause you believed in."

"Wasn't that hot a career."

"Still deserves respect. Damn few men of principle left. Much less men of action."

A realization came to Payne.

He's complimenting himself. Simeon Rutledge considers himself a man of principles and action. But what principles? And what actions?

They came to a barren stretch of black earth. Two dozen workers chopped at dirt clumps with hoes, smoothing out the soil.

"Notice anything about those hoes?" Rutledge asked him.

"Not really."

"The handles are five feet long. Lets the worker stand straight. Used to be, all the growers insisted on *el cortito,* the short-handled hoe. The closer to the dirt, the better the weeding. But the poor sumbitches had to work all hunched over, ten hours at a time. It was inhumane, and everybody knew it. But I couldn't find any long-handled hoes on the market, so we started milling the wood ourselves. I had my workers weed the strawberry fields standing up. Proved to everyone it could be done."

"That's a good deed. A very good deed." Payne meant it. Rutledge was damn complicated. But then, who wasn't?

"I try to make my workers' lives more bearable. Ice water in the coolers, hot water in the showers. I give loans without collateral. I take care of my people."

A feudal lord, looking after his adoring peasants. Nagging thoughts tugged at Payne.

Why's he greasing me?

Why does Simeon Rutledge care what I think of him?

And where the hell is Marisol?

In the distance, a small plane flew low over a field, dropping a billowing cloud of white flaky pesticide. Payne wondered if the migrants, enjoying cold drinking water and hot showers, were downwind.

The horses picked up speed, cantering past fields popping with red and yellow peppers. They approached an apple orchard, the fruit nearing ripeness. To their right was a spillway. Water poured into an irrigation culvert. They neared a concrete-and-steel structure that looked like a dam, rising above the culvert, which disappeared behind an earthen levee twenty-five-feet high. A *chuga-chuga* sound came from unseen machinery. A sign read, *Pump Station Three.*

Near the top of the levee, a bizarre sight. The grille, bumper, and headlights of an old car peeked out of the dirt.

"What the hell is that?" Payne asked.

"A '56 Chevy."

"What's it doing there?"

"A memorial to Hector."

"Hector?"

"Javie's father."

"Cardenas? The chief who calls you his uncle?"

"His old man saved my ass when we got hit by three Pacific storms, back-to-back in '79. Worst flooding in a hundred years. We ran out of sandbags, and the levee was gonna breach. I was damn close to owning a hundred-thousand-acre lake instead of a farm. Then Hector Cardenas came up with the craziest idea. Reinforce the levee with scrapped cars. We called every junkyard from here to San Francisco, got three thousand chassis for scrap metal prices. All the *braceros* pitched in, tough little fuckers, working in mud up to their chests. Townspeople, too, women making coffee and sandwiches. Worked seventy-two hours straight through storms and gale-force winds, but we saved the levee. Saved the farm."

Payne could picture it. Simeon Rutledge standing knee-deep in muck atop the levee, shouting orders. If he couldn't command the rain to stop falling, he would push men and machines to reconfigure the earth where the rain fell.

"But we couldn't celebrate," Rutledge continued, his voice dropping a notch. "One of the cranes toppled over and pinned Hector underwater. Drowned before we could get him out."

"Jeez, that's awful." Payne figuring this was the "long story" Cardenas referred to, the source of Rutledge becoming *Tío* Sim. "So you raised Javier?"

"His mother raised him. I just made their lives a little easier."

The horses followed a straight path that ran in the shadow of the towering levee. Gesturing toward the levee, Rutledge said, "Where do you suppose that water comes from?"

"Wells, I suppose," Payne said. "I saw some back by the vegetable fields."

"Not up here. I dammed a river and diverted the water for the orchards. Now I got state and federal agencies crawling up my ass. Some crap about not getting permits and polluting the water with fertilizers."

"You must have some high-priced legal talent working on it."

"Whitehurst and Booth in San Francisco."

"They're good."

"Good and expensive. Long on bills and short on balls. They want to negotiate fines that'll cost me millions."

"That's what deep-carpet firms do."

"What would you do, Counselor?"

"O.D.D. Obstruct. Delay. Distract." For the next five minutes, Payne gave his theory of pettifoggery. Hang tough, he advised. Outlast the bureaucrats. Only a matter of time until they jump to the private sector or just get so damn tired that they'll dismiss charges or settle for pennies on the dollar. He told Rutledge to file counterclaims. Sue for inverse condemnation, claim the government has destroyed the value of the land. Seize on little mistakes like missed filing periods.

"Always bring a contingent of your workers to court," Payne said. "Let them track mud into the gallery. Hard workers who'll lose their jobs if the government prevails. Put a human face on the billion-dollar corporation."

Rutledge scratched at his brushy mustache with a knuckle but didn't say a word. They entered a fragrant-smelling orchard of peach trees, the horses slowing to a walk. The earth had become a rich, sandy loam. Workers carried totes, plastic boxes slung around their necks, just like peanut vendors at Dodger Stadium. Rutledge greeted a crew chief by name, then allowed as how it was time for lunch.

They started back, the horses picking up their pace. Like human folk, they enjoyed going home.

Rutledge guided his black stallion alongside Payne's horse. "Been thinking about your legal strategy. I could use someone with your brains and balls."

"You're joking."

"You want to make some real money?"

He's not joking, Payne thought. Rutledge's strong suit was not his sense of humor.

"I want you to cocounsel with Whitehurst and Booth," Rutledge continued.

"They hire the brightest lawyers around. I doubt they need my help."

"They do if I say so. Charlie Whitehurst has gone soft."

"And you think I'm a better lawyer?"

"I think you're a tougher lawyer. You got a hard bark. You'll go to jail for your clients."

"Went to jail for some migrants. Doubt I would for you."

"You're proving my point." Rutledge allowed himself a crooked grin. "I don't scare you. You got bigger balls than Whitehurst."

Rutledge slowed the stallion and said, "How about a retainer of two hundred thousand. When you need more, you let me know."

Payne's mouth opened but nothing came out. If the devil had been perched on his shoulder, the offer could not have been more tempting.

"That's a lot of money," Payne said, finally.

"There's just one condition."

Of course there is, Payne thought.

"You gotta stop poking your nose into places where you got no business."

Payne didn't need to be a tough, hard-barked, big-balled lawyer to figure that one out. He'd been offered a bribe. Rutledge wanted his disappearing skills, not his lawyering skills.

"I'm not going to stop looking for Marisol Perez," Payne said.

"Nothing but trouble down that road. A real patch of quicksand."

Rutledge glared at him, waiting for a response.

After a moment, Payne said, "That trouble down the road. That patch of quicksand. Would that be a problem for me? Or for you, Rutledge?"

SIXTY-FIVE

Sitting ramrod straight astride his stallion, Rutledge felt like knocking the wiseass shyster off the Appaloosa and straight onto his skinny ass. "Goddammit, Payne. I offer you two hundred grand and you give me guff?"

Payne leaned on the saddle horn, taking pressure off his bad leg. "That's the thing. The money's way too rich. So I'm asking myself, what are you afraid of? What's the harm to you if I find Marisol Perez?"

"For once in your life, Payne, be smart."

"By dancing with the devil?"

"This devil don't dance. This devil calls the tunes."

"Just so we're clear, Rutledge. If I stop looking for Marisol, you make my life comfortable. What happens if I don't?"

"No need to go there."

"Bullshit. You're threatening me."

"I know your life's crap," Rutledge barked. "You lost your son. You lost your wife to that asshole on TV. You'll probably lose your law license. Maybe you don't believe it, but I feel for you."

"You're right. I don't believe it."

Rutledge's glare turned cold as a frozen lake. "I've taken enough of your shit. What'll it be, yea or nay?"

"Keep your money. I promised a boy I'd find his mother."

Rutledge hadn't expected this. In his experience, most men buckled at sweet pussy or fast money. But this two-bit shyster, prickly as a bale of straw, was saying no, and saying it loud. "You know what you are, Payne? You're a dishonest man with principles. That makes you dangerous. Believe me, I know."

"I'm just trying to do what's right."

Rutledge shook his head, as if saddened to put down a crippled horse. He would make one last offer. If Payne took it, fine. If not, there were a hundred miles of levee where he could bury the son-of-a-bitch.

"I can give you something you want more than a potful of gold," Rutledge said. "Something you want more than anything in the world."

"I seriously doubt it."

"I can give you Manuel Garcia," Rutledge said. "I can give you the drunken bastard who killed your son. And I can do it tonight."

SIXTY-SIX

The mention of Garcia's name sent a bolt of lightning up Payne's spine. "You're fucking with me, right? Mind games."

"If that's what you want to believe." Rutledge kept riding toward the barn, forcing Payne to catch up.

"Where is he?" Payne demanded.

No answer. Just the clop of hooves and the distant putter of a tractor. Payne brought the Appaloosa so close the two men's legs nearly touched. "How the hell did you find Garcia?"

"Not hard to do. Not with my connections."

"Is he here? In the valley?"

Rutledge patted the stallion's neck. "Took a new name, got a job working for a friend of mine down by Corcoran."

"How do I know you're telling the truth?"

"You can pay Garcia a visit after dinner, do what you gotta do. You'll be back in time to catch Leno. But once I tell you where he is, we got a deal. No more of your fussing about that Mexican woman."

Payne had more questions, but Rutledge dug his heels into the stallion, which took off at a gallop. The best Payne's horse could manage was a school-zone canter. By the time Payne reached the corral, Rutledge had hopped off the stallion and turned it over to a stable hand. Payne dismounted and painfully stretched, his bad leg throbbing. He hurried to catch up with Rutledge, who strode up a path lined with orange-and-white impatiens. The path wound up a ridge and curled behind his sprawling country home.

When Payne came abreast of Rutledge, he said, "What makes you think I want to kill Garcia?"

"A year ago, you opened your big mouth to half the homicide detectives in L.A."

Javier Cardenas, Payne thought. The police chief had made some calls. "I didn't mean it. It was all talk."

"Bullcrap. You got yourself a primal urge. It's what I would do if someone murdered my son."

"How do you know? You don't have any children."

The older man shrugged. "Hell, if someone killed Javie, I'd gut the bastard like a hog."

"And you think I'm like you?"

Rutledge's smile was as thin as the brim of his Stetson. "More than you know."

They stopped on a rise behind the farmhouse, a three-story structure with wide porches, green shutters, and Southern plantation white pillars. From this elevation, they looked over thousands of acres, blooming with fruits and vegetables.

"C'mon, Payne. You never even met the Perez woman. She's nothing to you. But the bastard who killed your son? Jesus! He stuck a knife in your heart."

Payne fought off the urge for vengeance. Ever since Adam's death, he had felt it as a searing heat, a torrent of molten steel. He had yearned to do what the law couldn't. Kill the man and settle the score.

"C'mere, Payne. I want to show you something."

Rutledge walked toward three gnarly and shrunken peach trees, Payne trailing. Two feet of sandy loam formed a berm around each trunk, as if someone had lovingly tucked the trees to sleep under a blanket of rich soil.

"Before I was born, my granddaddy planted four hundred Elbertas on this ridge. They're my roots, my family's sweat and tears. No way any of them should still be alive." He ran a callused hand over a tree trunk. "But look here. Three Elbertas, still growing, still bearing fruit. Like the three generations of Rutledge men."

Rutledge reached for a peach—a soft golden orb blushing with red—from the nearest tree. "Watch now. Just a gentle turn of the wrist so the stem doesn't tear out of the socket. The older I get, the more I learn that brute force is seldom the answer to life's problems."

He twisted the peach off its stem and bit into it, juice oozing from his mouth and onto his bristly mustache. He radiated a feral bliss as he polished off the fruit.

"Go ahead, Payne. Take one."

Payne shook his head, thinking of the snake and the forbidden fruit. He didn't quite picture himself as Eve—

but Rutledge as a serpent, no problem with the imagery there.

Rutledge moved a few steps toward an enclosure made of railroad ties. Inside was a pile of manure so ripe it steamed in the midday sun. He tossed several handfuls into a bucket, which he carried to the nearest tree. Crouching on his haunches, he used his bare hands to shape a mound of manure around the tree trunk. Clearly, Payne thought, not a man afraid of getting his hands dirty.

"These trees will outlive me," Rutledge told him. "The way a son is supposed to outlive his father. So the father can pass on what's his. Knowledge. Property. Tradition. A father who's deprived of that, well, he's got a right to seek justice. Hell, he's got a duty to."

"I get your point."

"Last chance, Payne. Are you man enough to do what has to be done?"

Payne's thoughts turned to that misty morning on the Pacific Coast Highway. Pictured Adam, just moments before the crash. Animated, talkative, innocent. Heard the thunderclap as the pickup truck broadsided them, Adam's body crushed against his own. A moment later, the man's head appearing through the driver's window. The tang of liquor on his breath.

Now Payne inhaled the pungent aroma of the manure. He looked at the old trees, listened to the breeze tickle their leaves. He thought of his promises made. To Sharon. To Tino. And to himself.

But every thought returned to Adam and to the endless pain of losing him. His son's baseball bat was in the trunk of the Mustang. If Payne closed his eyes, he could see himself crushing Garcia's skull, could hear the bones splinter, could feel the warm stickiness of his blood.

"Tell me how I can find Garcia," Payne said. "I'll do it tonight and be gone by tomorrow."

SIXTY-SEVEN

Rigney liked his whiskey neat and his women messy.

At the moment, he was sipping Johnnie Walker Red and eyeing a woman with a little too much belly for her outfit, a sleeveless crop-top that stopped a foot short of torn, low-slung jeans. She was bent over the pool table, showing the crack of her ass to three young cops drinking Coronas and bantering with her.

I'd fuck her, but I wouldn't spend the night.

Rigney returned to his Scotch. He was hunched over the bar in a hole-in-the-wall tavern on San Pedro, two blocks from the Parker Center. Considering just how the shitstorm named Royal Payne had so totally fucked up his life.

Rigney had been grilled by Internal Affairs in the hundred-year-old Bradbury Building on South Broadway, and it hadn't gone well. The questions were antagonistic and threatening. The investigators seemed to blame him for Judge Rollins' suicide, Payne's escape, and the layer of smog that blanketed Pasadena.

Officially, he wasn't supposed to be looking for Payne, but he didn't give a shit. He wanted to find the bastard first, crack his head open, make him pay. He'd stopped by Sharon Payne's cubicle earlier today, but she wasn't in. He'd toyed with the idea of bugging her phone or planting a G.P.S. transmitter on her car. But if he was caught, they'd pull his badge and he could share a cell with Anthony Pellicano.

"Hey, Riggs. Don't you owe me a drink?"

A pudgeball named Lou Parell plopped onto the adjacent stool. Homicide. Three years from retirement. If Rigney had to hear about all the marlin the fat bastard planned to catch off Cabo San Lucas, he'd strangle the jerk.

"I don't owe you a drink, Lou. You owe me thirty bucks from poker."

"You sure?"

"At Schulian's house. You don't remember?"

Parell signaled the bartender and pointed to one of the taps. Bud Lite. As if low-cal beer would take off those forty extra pounds he was packing.

"Riggs, you catch Payne yet?"

Rigney drained his glass. "Don't bust my chops, Lou."

"I'm not. Just wondered if you knew you had competition."

"Meaning what?"

"Some badge from East Bumfuck called Homicide asking about the asshole."

Rigney slammed the cocktail glass on the bar. "Who? Who the fuck called?"

"Lemme think." Parell's light beer arrived, yellow as chilled piss. "Spanish name. But he didn't have an accent."

"What'd he say?"

"Asked about Payne hanging around our office last year. You know, when he was planning to go after that wetback who killed his kid."

"You ask the cop why he gave a damn?"

"Why would I?"

"Oh, I don't know. Maybe because you're a detective, and detectives are supposed to be curious about shit that don't smell right."

"I figured he had his reasons."

"Jesus." Rigney signaled for a refill. "Did you tell him we had warrants out on Payne?"

"Yeah. He said he'd keep his eyes open."

"And you don't remember the cop's name or where he's from?"

Parell took a long pull on his beer. "Said he was the chief of police."

"Where, Lou? For Christ's sake, where?"

Parell seemed deep in thought, or as deep as he could go without a tutor. "In the San Joaquin Valley. I remember asking if they have much crime up there. And he said, just some migrants getting drunk and fighting when the peaches are all in and they get paid."

"Jesus, that really narrows it down. They grow peaches for three hundred miles."

If he could find the police chief, Rigney thought, he could find Butch Cassidy and the Mexican Kid. The last time anybody saw them, they were in a diner in the desert town of Thermal. What were they doing upstate? And what hell had Payne raised to get the locals on his case?

"A fish pond!" Parell blurted.

"What?"

"The cop said he was eating lunch outside his office, tossing bacon to the fish."

"Jesus, how do you remember that and not remember where he's from?"

"I don't know. It just stuck in my brain."

Like dogshit to treaded shoes, Rigney thought.

"A man's name," Parell said. "I just remembered. The town is named after some guy."

"Who?"

"I don't remember."

"Hanford?"

"Nope."

"Bakersfield?"

"Nah."

"The name's on the tip of my tongue," Parell said.

"Foam's on the tip of your tongue."

"Rutledge! The guy's the chief of police in Rutledge. You know where that is?"

"I can find it," Rigney said.

SIXTY-EIGHT

"Did you know rats can't vomit?" Charles Whitehurst asked.

"What?" Javier Cardenas wasn't sure he had heard the lawyer correctly.

"If a rat comes across some strange food, it will only take a nibble. That way, if it gets sick, it won't die. If the rat doesn't get sick, next time, it'll eat the whole damn thing."

At the moment, Cardenas was eating his own lunch, his customary B.L.T., as he sat on the redwood bench under a bonsai tree outside the Rutledge Police Department. The phone call from Whitehurst did not improve his appetite.

"Simeon's like that rat," the lawyer continued. "If he poisons a neighbor's well and nothing happens, next time, he'll divert a whole river. Hire a few illegal aliens one day, pretty soon he's running stash houses and whorehouses and paying off half the legislators in Sacramento.

He thinks he's invincible. Then one day, he wolfs down that poison."

Whitehurst's sharp tone shocked Cardenas. The lawyer never would have spoken like that in front of Uncle Sim.

"What the hell are you talking about?" Cardenas demanded.

"A sealed indictment. Racketeering. Bribery. Human trafficking. A hundred seventy-two counts, thick as a phone book. United States of America versus Simeon Rutledge."

"Jesus!" Cardenas tossed his sandwich into the stream. Koi jumped for the bacon, miniature whirlpools stirring in their wake. "What can I do to help?"

"I'm hoping he'll listen to you, Javier."

A realization then. Though the chief had met Whitehurst dozens of times over the years, never had the deep-carpet attorney called him by his first name.

"Simeon respects you and trusts you," Whitehurst continued. "You're the son he never had."

"I'll do anything for Sim. You know that."

"The U.S. Attorney offered a deal. Simeon pleads to one count of racketeering and does a token amount of time at a country club prison. Six to nine months. He pays five million in fines, plus steps down as president of the company. The court will appoint a trustee to oversee the operation."

Cardenas laughed, but it was as bitter as hemlock. "The trustee better have a thick hide, because Uncle Sim will take a bullwhip to him."

"That's pretty much what Simeon said, except he mentioned a shotgun."

"What can I do if he's already rejected the deal?"

"Help me sell him on it."

Cardenas shook his head. "You know Sim. He'll fight to the end. He'll never surrender."

"Then he'll lose what it took three generations to build. The ranch. The farms. All the businesses. Everything forfeited to the government. He'll die in prison. His only wish interred with his bones."

"What wish?"

"For you to take over the business when he's gone."

"Jesus." Cardenas sucked in a breath. "I thought Sim wanted me to be governor or a senator. He never mentioned the business."

"You're the sole heir."

"You're sure?" Cardenas blurted out.

Whitehurst laughed. "I better be. I wrote the will."

For a moment, the only sound was the hum on the line.

"Just to be clear, Javie," Whitehurst continued, "if Simeon Rutledge dies tomorrow, you inherit everything."

Cardenas shook his head, resisting the notion. "And the criminal case, what happens to that?"

"A very astute question," the lawyer praised him. "In the untoward event of Simeon's death, the criminal case dies with him. The government will move on to other cases of notoriety, and you'll take over the company."

Cardenas was aware of a tingling sensation, an electrical impulse sparking up his spine. It was not an unpleasant feeling.

"While it hardly needs to be said," Whitehurst continued, obviously believing it did need to be said, "rest assured that I will always be your trusted advisor, Javie. Just as I have been to Simeon."

Cardenas stayed quiet. He sensed Whitehurst wasn't finished.

"But if Simeon's convicted," the lawyer started again, "there'll be nothing to pass on. The sad fact is, the only way for your uncle Sim to achieve his fondest wish is for him to die."

Javier Cardenas discovered he was holding his breath, his throat dry as sand. He exhaled, a hot wind rustling dried leaves. "Neither of us wants that to happen."

"Of course not," the lawyer assured him.

SIXTY-NINE

"What do you mean you're going out tonight?" Tino asked.

"Something I gotta do, that's all." Jimmy keeping it nonchalant. No way he would tell the boy he was setting out to kill a man.

"So you're leaving me alone in the hotel?"

"You want a babysitter?"

"Not unless she wants to watch the titty channel with me."

They had just finished dinner at a barbecue joint, attracted there by the hickory smoke wafting over downtown Rutledge. Ribs, chicken, tri-tip, baked beans, and sweet potato fries. For a skinny kid, Tino could pack it away. Now they were walking back to the hotel, their conversation interrupted by frequent burps and the occasional fart.

"How long till you're back?" Tino asked.

"It'll be late. You'll be asleep."

"You hooking up with that waitress?"

"What waitress?"

"Ay, Himmy. The one you were hitting on, the one whose hair smelled like carne asada."

"Nope."

"Why the big secret, *vato*? You afraid I won't understand?"

"Exactly."

But that was a lie. Tino would surely understand. He'd expressed the very same emotion a number of times when confronted with someone who would hurt his mother. Tino knew very well the driving force of bloodlust and the bone-deep need for revenge.

SEVENTY

I'm not like Simeon Rutledge.

Sure, we're both members of the human race, but that's where the resemblance ends.

Still, Payne was on his way to kill a man. To snuff out a life with what the law calls "premeditation and malice aforethought."

A nice phrase. "Malice aforethought." He'd surely *aforethoughted* a truckload of malice in the last year.

An hour after sundown, Payne drove past fields of cotton and alfalfa, swarms of gnats committing suicide on his windshield. There had once been a large lake in these parts, fed by the Tule River, but it had long ago been drained by Ezekiel Rutledge's ambition to go from merely rich to incredibly wealthy. Nothing changes. The rich get richer, Payne thought, and the poor still live in Weedpatch Barracks.

He skirted the town of Corcoran with its massive state prison, home to Charles Manson, among several thousand other miscreants. Powerful lights curdled the night sky into a sickly shade of green. Payne couldn't fight off the notion that someone who committed a murder in these parts might himself spend the rest of his days inside those walls.

He fiddled with the radio dial. The strongest signal was an oldies rock station, and he picked up Link Wray's "Rumble" with its slow, tantalizing guitar licks. Another few miles and Payne found the side road Rutledge had described. A dusty, one-lane, unpaved path through tomato and onion fields. Darkened shacks, propped on cinder blocks, abandoned and forlorn. The road grew bumpier and narrower, the fields smaller and less tended. The Sierra Nevadas were silhouetted to the east, the Diablo Range to the west, the stars a countless sprinkling of sugar on a black velvet cake. He spotted the Big Dipper, traced a path upward from the two stars that formed the cup's far end. Found Polaris, the North Star, glowing more fiercely than it ever did in the city.

He looked back to the road just in time to avoid a waddling possum, then swerved again, barely missing a rough-barked sycamore encroaching on the narrow road. Then he saw it. A small aluminum trailer, one end protruding from a thicket of scrub oak trees.

Payne pulled off the road and killed the engine. From somewhere in the darkened fields, birds cried like frightened children, and insects played a hundred different symphonies. Sounds came from inside the trailer, too. Voices with a metallic edge. Judging from the cathode glow on the porthole window, a television set.

Payne got out of the Mustang, Adam's Louisville Slugger in hand. Metal alloy. Only eighteen ounces. It made a metallic *clonk* hitting a baseball. Payne wondered for the thousandth time just what sound would it make crushing a skull.

He took a few swings, as if in the on-deck circle. Two-handed, level and strong. A line drive swing. Then, one-handed. A fine *whoosh* through the warm night air.

Payne crept toward the half-hidden trailer. An Airstream about twenty feet long, a silver sausage. Propane tank leaning against the hitch. Metal poles cockeyed in the ground, propping up a torn, green-striped awning. A muddy Chevy half-ton pickup sat alongside. Someone had taken the trouble to back it into the trees. Faster exit, maybe?

Ten feet from the door, Payne could clearly hear the television. Music and the high-pitched voices of a cartoon. The smell of cooked pork drifted from the trailer's open windows.

Payne thought about Rutledge and his smug assumptions.

"Hell, if someone killed Javier I'd gut the bastard like a hog."

"And you think I'm like you?"

"More than you know."

Payne figured that, under the right circumstances, everyone is capable of killing. No great revelation there. Just the searing awareness that homicide is grafted onto our genes.

Payne's murderous intent came with a promise attached. He had looked Rutledge squarely in his flinty eyes and given an oath along with a bloody handshake. In return for the whereabouts of Manuel Garcia, he would give up the search for Marisol. He would kill tonight and go home tomorrow.

But I lied.

Not for one moment, not for the infinitesimal blink of a faraway star, would he let Tino down. It was easy to choose which promise to break.

To hell with you, Rutledge.

Approaching the trailer, Payne tripped. He caught his balance and realized he'd just trampled Our Lady of Guadalupe, or at least a knee-high statue of her, jammed into the dust just outside the front door. Her eyes were lowered in prayer. Pink blossoms grew at her feet, and her dainty shoulders were covered with a turquoise shroud.

The Virgin won't protect you, Garcia. She's got a higher calling than hit-and-run drivers.

Now, standing on the doorstep of the old trailer, Payne felt exhilarated, a weight lifting from his body like a Zeppelin untethered from its port. Gripping the baseball bat in one hand, he drew his foot back and smashed in the flimsy screen door.

"I'm here, Garcia! Goddammit, I'm here at last!"

SEVENTY-ONE

I lost the bet, Javier Cardenas thought.

He couldn't believe it. Here was Payne, sneaking up to the trailer like some Special Forces wannabe.

Bastard's gonna kill the guy, and it's gonna cost me a Black Ice bow.

Not that Cardenas had paid for the sleek hunting bow, which must have cost six hundred bucks new. He'd seized it as evidence from a hunter who lacked a license. He also confiscated the guy's arrows, broad heads, tree stands, camo gear, and tent. If the hunter'd had an English bulldog, Cardenas would have taken that, too.

Now he sat in his cruiser, under a white alder tree, engine idling, A/C on, iPod plugged in, listening to Salma Hayek whisper *"Quedate Aqui"* from the *Desperado* soundtrack. The cruiser was parked on a small rise near Manuel Garcia's rusted-out trailer. Cardenas had been waiting two hours, convinced Payne wouldn't show up and he'd win Sim's Mossberg shotgun, the combo over-under model with 12- and 20-gauge barrels. That was the bet, the Black Ice bow for the Mossberg shotgun. It seemed like such a sure thing.

"Payne's not a killer, Sim."

"You think you're that good a judge of character?"

"It's what I do."

"And here's what I'm gonna do, Javie. I'm gonna shoot a wild boar with that bow and arrow. The one that used to be yours!"

They had bantered a few minutes. Planning a trip to Hog Haven up in Geyersville. Been going there since Javier was ten years old. Hunting those huge smelly boars with the wide snouts, sharp tusks, and grouchy dispositions.

"Don't shoot till he's ten yards away. Then make it a kill shot."

Simeon had barked those instructions when Cardenas was a boy and repeated them to this day. Instilled confidence and courage.

Back then, Cardenas knew that if he missed a shot, Uncle Sim would be there to rescue him. These days, Cardenas was not so sure. The certainties of childhood had been replaced by the complexities of the adult world.

He endlessly replayed the phone call with Charles Whitehurst. Like polishing a jagged piece of quartz, he kept finding new angles. On the surface, the lawyer appeared concerned for Simeon's welfare. But underneath, Whitehurst feared losing his biggest client. If the government took over the business, he could say adios to all those legal fees.

So Whitehurst's advice—convince Simeon to plead out—was never sincere. Then what was the real purpose of the call? What message was the lawyer sending? It could only be one thing.

That everyone would be better off with Simeon out of the picture.

To drive home the point, Whitehurst had told Cardenas about Simeon's will, to hell with attorney-client privilege. And what about that bone-chilling statement?

"The sad fact is, the only way for your uncle Sim to achieve his fondest wish is for him to die."

How the lawyer must have rehearsed that line, pruning the words of any manifest intent.

Earlier today, when Simeon had called, Cardenas did not mention the conversation with Whitehurst. He hoped Simeon would bring up the indictment, ask for advice, but of course, that did not happen.

Cardenas was lost in a fog of conflicting emotions. Simeon was a surrogate father, no other way to put it.

Now Cardenas watched Payne kick open the trailer's screen door.

Heard shouts.

Wondered if Garcia had a gun.

Thinking it was just as likely that Garcia would kill Payne as the other way around. He wouldn't arrest Garcia for murder. The man would be defending his family and his home against a violent invasion by a man sworn to kill him. But if Payne killed Garcia, different story. Cardenas would arrest Payne for premeditated murder.

Either way, Payne was gone, and Sim would be happy. For now.

Poor Jimmy Payne. *Heads, you lose your freedom. Tails, you lose your head.*

Keeping his eyes on the trailer, Javier Cardenas checked the clip on his 9mm Beretta and waited to see who walked out the door.

SEVENTY-TWO

As he burst through the fallen door, Payne scanned the dimly lit trailer, his heightened senses taking in a stained leopard carpet, the glow of a small television screen, and a short, chunky woman washing dishes at a small sink.

The woman dropped a plate and screamed. A piercing sound, made sharper by the aluminum walls. Something stirred behind her, a lump rising from a quilt on a gaucho bed.

The form of a man. Boxer shorts, bare feet, and a dirty wife-beater tee.

Manuel Garcia.

Shorter than Payne thought. Square head. Round body. A fifty-five gallon drum with arms and thick-fingered hands.

"Hey, asshole!" Payne wailed. "Remember me?" He stepped toward the bed and cocked the bat, yelling a phrase he'd practiced just for this occasion. *"¿Te acuer-das de mi, pendejo?"*

Garcia grunted and dug a small revolver from under a pillow. Turned toward Payne, fumbling with the gun. Fredo in *The Godfather,* hapless under pressure.

Payne's backswing clipped the curved wall. Shit. His timing fouled up, he swung and missed Garcia.

The woman still screaming.

The gun shaking in Garcia's hand. A shot. A cherry bomb exploding in a tin can, the bullet punched a hole in the metal roof.

Payne swung again. Garcia danced a step backward and the bat caught him just above the knee. Garcia howled and fell, the gun flying into the tangle of quilts.

"¡No tenemos dinero!" the woman wailed.

"Don't want your money!" Payne hoisted Garcia back onto the bed, pressed the bat crosswise under his chin, bore down with two hands. "Tell her why I'm here, you piece of shit!"

Garcia choked and sputtered. Confused and terrified.

"You don't remember? You forget that easy!" Payne was enraged, seeing the man up close. The leathery face, the smell of tobacco and sweat. Everything came back.

Payne jammed up against the car door, his leg broken, forehead gashed, eyes filling with blood.

"My son. Can you see him? Is he okay?"

The man leaning through the open window. The frozen look of cold, stark fear.

Garcia's plaintive cry. "El chico. El chico. ¡Dios me perdone!"

Forcing the bat into Garcia's Adam's apple, Payne heard a wet, burbling sound. He could break the cartilage so easily, could crush his trachea, watch him die.

"You don't remember me? You don't remember my boy? Ten years old! You worthless piece of garbage!"

Garcia's eyes registered. His fear taking on meaning.

"That's right! I'm not here to rob you. I'm here to kill you."

Garcia stammered something. Payne eased the pressure just a bit.

"Sorry. Sorry. I never meant to . . ."

"Fuck that. You killed my son. You killed *me*."

Behind him, the woman had dropped to her knees. Crossed herself, ticked off prayers in Spanish at high speed.

Payne grabbed Garcia by the front of his T-shirt. Yanked him to his feet. Drew back the bat, measured the distance to the man's temple, anticipated the delicious crack of metal on bone.

A child coughed.

From the darkness at the rear of the trailer, a girl of about four walked toward them, cradling a tattered stuffed animal in her arms. Bugs Bunny maybe, but with an ear missing. She coughed again, a parched hack.

"Daddy? Why did you fire the gun?" Her voice small and scratchy.

"Lourdes," the woman wailed. *"¡Métete en la cama!"* Ordering her daughter back to bed.

The girl focused on Payne. "Is that man hurting Daddy?" she asked her mother.

"Not here," Garcia begged. "Please. Not here."

Payne let the bat fall to his side. "Fine. Outside. In the trees."

Payne grabbed the handgun from the bed, a .22 revolver, stuck it in his pants, and dragged Garcia out the door. The man didn't head for the trees and he didn't try to run. He just dropped to his knees in front of the Lady of Guadalupe statue, and began mumbling, *"Padre nuestro, que estás en los cielos . . ."*

Payne scanned the dirt road. No cars. If Garcia screamed—and Payne doubted he would—there would be no one to hear.

"Santificado sea tu Nombre . . ."

"Why'd you come back?" Payne snarled.

Garcia stopped praying. Sucking in air, he said, "Your police contacted police in Oaxaca. Instead of sending me back, the *judicales* took my money. When I had nothing more to give, they threatened my family. They would have . . ."

He didn't have to finish. It was safer for Manuel Garcia to sneak into the country where he was wanted for homicide than to stay home. He talked softly in accented but decent English. He knew people working in the cotton fields near Tulare, and he knew how to drive a tractor, so he came across with his family and got a job.

"What's wrong with your daughter?"

"Asthma." He looked skyward. "The dust and pesticides. Very bad after spraying."

Payne felt something drain out of him. "That job of yours. You get medical insurance?"

Still on his knees, Garcia shook his head.

"Asthma's not hard to treat. Medication. Inhalers."

Garcia looked up at him, puzzled.

"What I'm saying, you gotta get your daughter to a doctor."

Garcia stared at the ground. "I still owe the coyote three thousand dollars for the crossing."

Payne took out his wallet. Four hundred-dollar bills, three twenties, a couple tens, a few ones. He thrust the money to Garcia, their hands briefly touching.

Then Payne dropped Garcia's gun on the ground, slung the bat onto his shoulder, and headed back to his car.

SEVENTY-THREE

Javier Cardenas watched the surreal scene alongside the trailer.

Way to go, Jimmy Payne. You plan to kill a man, and instead you pay him.

Cardenas pictured the Mossberg shotgun he'd just won. Could feel the smooth walnut stock, could see the polished silver receiver with the gold inlay.

He would wait until morning to tell Simeon to deliver the gun. It would take a few hours more to determine if Jimmy Payne kept his promise to get the hell out of town.

Cardenas waited until Payne drove off, leaving Garcia kneeling in front of the trailer, staring after him. Probably wondering what the hell just happened.

Cardenas thought he knew.

Some men can kill. Some can't. Simple as that.

Cardenas had seen it in Payne's eyes. Not a softness exactly. But a weakness by another name.

Humanity.

Payne cared for his fellow man. Especially for those in worse shape than himself. How else to explain taking to the road in pursuit of the Mexican boy's mother? Payne could have been killed in Hellhole Canyon. Still, he drove on to Rutledge, a place even more dangerous.

Hey, Uncle Sim. You whiffed. You spent more time with Payne than I did, but you completely misjudged him.

Simeon was getting old. Losing his edge, getting care-
less. That's what Whitehurst had meant with his little
parable about rats who can't vomit. No wonder Simeon
got himself indicted. The investigation posed major
problems for Cardenas, too. The records and bank ac-
counts of Rutledge Ranch and Farms, Inc., were fair
game for a U.S. Attorney. Cardenas knew his name
would crop up in places where no police chief's ought
to be.

If Simeon takes a fall, he'll take me with him.

For years, Cardenas had known about the stash
houses, the human trafficking, the thousands of undocumented workers who'd come through Kings County,
thanks to Rutledge livery. Cardenas also knew about the
Hot Springs Gentleman's Club, a place that had been
off-limits to him as a young man.

*"You stay away from that pussy ranch, Javie. It ain't
for you."*

There were other evils Simeon never talked about and
Cardenas chose to ignore. He knew that Simeon could
be kind and generous one day and ornery and violent
the next. When the old man talked about burying bodies along levees and orchards, it was neither a boast nor
a threat. It was reality.

*So, get the hell out of town, Jimmy Payne, or Simeon
will add your carcass to the compost heap.*

Murder seemed so much easier to get away with than
the vices that left paper trails. Another thought came to
Cardenas as he eased his cruiser out of its hiding spot
and onto the dirt road. The government might offer a
deal to a police chief with an excellent memory for
times, places, and amounts of money. Maybe he could
get immunity for flipping.

*No, I couldn't do that. I could no more testify against
Tío Sim than I could turn the shotgun on him.*

Cardenas clicked his iPod back on, found the *Desperado* soundtrack again, and slowly drove away, listening to Tito & Tarantula wailing "Strange Face of Love."

SEVENTY-FOUR

Just after eight A.M. on a day that simmered with a dry, baking heat, Simeon Rutledge swung his right arm over his head, and with a smooth motion snapped the bullwhip. The *cr-ack* sounded eerily like a gunshot.

Another forward toss, the circus throw of a lion tamer.

Cr-ack.

Standing in his corral with the sun rising over his cornfields, Rutledge kept his arm moving. Three different throws, without stopping. The backward, the overhead, the circus throw.

Cr-ack. Cr-ack. Cr-ack.

The popper at the end of the whip snapping so fast it created a miniature sonic boom.

The solid feel of the whip in his hand calmed him. He breathed in the scent of the soil and the crops, even the sweetness of the manure. This was his land, and he belonged to it, as much as it belonged to him.

The initials "EJR" were engraved into the worn leather handle of the whip, which had been custom-made for Ezekiel Rutledge in the 1920s. In a Tulare bar,

Ezekiel had taken out a man's eye, and good thing, as the man was drawing a Colt .45 at the time. Ezekiel wasn't above snapping the whip at a worker who was "lazing off." Seldom hit one, though. He saved the lashes for the union organizers. "Those goddamn Jews and commies from the city."

Rutledge pictured the whip in Ezekiel's hand, imagined his grandfather listening to the same *cr-ack*, the sound stretching across decades. At moments like this, handling the whip, or riding his stallion along an old trail, or pruning his grandfather's peach trees, Rutledge felt a bone-deep kinship with family, with the land, and with the past itself.

Within minutes, Rutledge's mind cleared. There were decisions to be made. The government would unseal those damn indictments any day now. It would be all over the news. The banks would go batshit. Lines of credit would be pulled, loans called. In a business with an erratic cash flow, that could mean financial death.

Then there was the lesser, but not insignificant problem of that damn Mexican woman. Rutledge had learned from his father that a ship can sink from the tiniest breach in the hull. Like the old nursery rhyme said, "For want of a nail, the shoe was lost." An accountant gets busted for drugs and strikes a deal to testify against his tax-evading employer. A legislator finds God and spills his guts about bribes. Or a woman yells "rape" and brings down an empire.

Jesus, all they had on Al Capone was rinky-dink tax evasion, and he went to Alcatraz.

The Mexican woman would be no problem if not for the pissant lawyer from the City of Fucking Angels. Javier had called and told him Payne chickened out last night. Now what was the shyster going to do?

His grandfather wouldn't have worried about it. Not with all the potential grave sites in fields and levees.

Deep, dark places a body would never be found, not even by a pack of coyotes. But then, his grandfather didn't have to deal with Grand Juries, and prosecutors out to make their bones.

God, what a time that must have been!

SEVENTY-FIVE

A Spanish-speaking gardener was trimming a rosebush when Payne asked where he could find *el jefe*.

In the corral, the man answered.

Batting away a swarm of gnats, Payne headed down an inclined path. A moment later, he heard a horse whinny and a voice barked, "You better be here to say adios!"

Simeon Rutledge, in dusty boots and faded jeans, sat astride a caramel-colored palomino with an ivory mane. The gate was open and Payne walked into the enclosure.

"I couldn't do it." Payne looked up at Rutledge on the palomino. "Garcia, I mean."

"I don't give a shit if you killed Garcia or butt-fucked him. I gave you what you wanted. Now get your ass back to L.A."

Payne noticed a couple stable hands watching them. Two Hispanic men, each with a foot on the bottom rail of the corral fence.

"I made a promise to a boy, and I'm not gonna let him down. Not this time."

Rutledge's laugh was as sharp as barbed wire. "Got a news flash for you, Payne. Every day, kids in Africa starve to death. Women in Tecate are raped and murdered. A little boy riding with his father gets broadsided by a drunk. Grow the fuck up!"

"Not growing up. Not giving up. Just give me Marisol Perez, and I'll go away. Whatever's happened, we'll let it go. No authorities. No investigations."

"You got no idea what's at stake here. Or what I'll do to protect it." Rutledge leaned forward, both hands on the saddle horn. A look crossed his face like quick, scudding clouds covering the sun before a storm. "Don't you get it, Payne? You're the one endangering the woman's life. You fuck with me, her blood's on your hands. Not mine."

Rutledge reached into a holster fitted alongside his saddle.

Payne heard the *cr-ack* before he felt the pain.

The tip of the bullwhip had struck his shoulder like a rattlesnake.

"I could take out your eye before you could blink," Rutledge taunted him.

A second *cr-ack,* and the leather flicked at Payne's neck, drawing blood. The sting of a hundred bees.

The two Hispanic men leaning against the rail didn't move. They could have been watching their boss shoe a horse.

Payne raised an arm and blocked the third throw. But the popper wrapped itself around his forearm like a snake. Rutledge tugged at the reins and turned the horse, yanking Payne off his feet. A nudge in the ribs, and the horse cantered around the perimeter of the corral, dragging Payne through the red dirt. His face scraped the ground, a blowtorch to the skin. He tried to get his feet under him but could not. A knee twisted and buckled. Pain shot through his metal-plated leg, a dagger deep to the bone. He pulled with his trapped arm, tried to rip the whip out of Rutledge's hand, could not get the leverage.

The horse picked up speed, and Payne dug his sneakers into the dirt, trying to slow down. One sneaker came off, then the other. He felt his shoulder pop out of its socket. His right arm was aflame, and he spat blood.

He heard himself scream. Hated the sound, a shameful shriek of pain and fear.

Rutledge gave slack to the whip and wrestled it free from Payne's arm. He slung himself off his horse. Payne writhed on the ground, face pasted with dirt and blood. His stomach heaved. He thought he would puke. He struggled to his knees, just as a shadow moved over him, blocking out the sun. The shadow kicked him. A cowboy boot straight to the gut. Another kick, this one to the side of the head, and his vision blurred.

"Damn you!" Rutledge brayed. "Damn you to hell! A smart man would have taken the money. A real man would have killed Garcia."

Rutledge kicked him again, aiming for his balls, but catching the inner thigh. Payne curled into the fetal position, yet another humiliation. Rutledge towered above him. Face reddened, saliva oozing into his mustache.

"Turns out you're stupid and a coward. Ain't that right, Payne? *Estúpido y cobarde.*"

Payne remembered Tino calling him a *valiente.* But he was neither brave nor cowardly. He was just a flawed man trying to fix one thing in a broken world.

"You just gonna lay there like a whipped dog?"

Payne got to one knee, and collapsed, blood spraying from his blistered lips.

Rutledge spat into the dirt near Payne's head. "My daddy always told me if I was to stomp a man, I should

squash him like a cockroach. Leave nothing but a tobacco stain on the ground."

The heel of a boot appeared above Payne's head. Rutledge grunted as he put all his weight into it. A lightning
bolt shot through Payne's brain. Sparklers burned, and
he saw the capillaries, like twining streams, behind his
eyelids. The pain took a detour, paused like a pedestrian
at a traffic light, then crow-barred him between the eyes.
A second later, he was aware of nothing at all.

SEVENTY-SIX

Kneeling in the moist earth of the brothel's garden, clip-
ping at the rosebushes with pruning shears, Marisol
planned her escape. She had been docile ever since Mr.
Zaga asked whether she could read and speak English.
He would not expect her to run today.

Where would she go? She didn't know. She would
search for Tino, but where? Had he crossed over or was
he still in Mexico? How would she ever find him?

When the enormity of the task made her tremble, she
focused on the first step of the journey. From her bedroom window, she could see that the brothel was an island in a sea of farmland. Almond trees. Cow pastures.
Strawberry fields stretching to the horizon. Everything
owned by *el jefe*. Mr. Rutledge. The man who had come

to her room and taken what he wanted. As if he owned her.

Through a stand of oak trees, she had seen a building perhaps three hundred feet away. One story, made of concrete blocks, with a flat roof. Seemingly abandoned. A small parking lot and a yard full of weeds. A flagpole with no flag. Just beyond the building was a road. If she could make it there, she could flag down a driver. But not those white trucks with the sign *Rutledge Ranch and Farms, Inc.*

She gripped the stem of a brilliant red rose, avoiding the thorns. Snipped with the shears. Soon, she would carry two armloads inside to the parlor. White roses as fluffy as a bride's gown. Pink roses, delicate as a blush. Purples, as dark and rich as wine. All far too beautiful for such a place.

Mr. Zaga had put her on yard and kitchen duty. She sensed that it was temporary, that they had other plans for her. The women working there, the *putas,* whispered about her. Strangely, many of them—Mexicans, Guatemalans, Hondurans—did not seem to mind their despoliation. This morning, in an adjacent bedroom, three women from Chihuahua, dumber than cows, were fixing one another's hair, giggling and babbling. Marisol thought of them as *putas parlanchinas.*

Chatterbox whores.

Giggling, they described their customers' genitals in disgusting terms and boasted about providing extras in return for bigger tips. One of the women slapped her rump, shouting, *"¡Métemela por el culo, vaquero!"*

Demanding it in her back door. How vulgar. How crude.

The other women laughed. They claimed to be sending home enormous sums of money. Marisol could stand it no longer. "Do you tell your families how you make this money?"

"¡Chingate!" the ass-slapper hissed.

"She'd better," another one brayed. "No one else will."

More laughter.

"You are free to leave," Marisol told them. "Why don't you just walk away?"

"To where? The fields?"

"I have no man to protect me," the third one said. "I'd be raped every night."

"Better to be paid for it," the ass-slapper said. "And have good food, too."

"If you don't like it here," the second one said, "go back to whatever shithole you came from."

Marisol would have gone in an instant. But there were different rules for her. These women, the trusted ones, could go into town to shop. They could use the telephone.

Just now, the daytime guard stood on the rear porch watching her. An Asian face. Said to be from Vietnam. Not young and not appearing physically strong, but Marisol had heard whispers that he was a trained killer from a long-ago war, that he enjoyed hurting women with his knife. There were many such rumors here.

The guard kept his eyes on Marisol. Had Mr. Rutledge ordered it? She tried to suppress the memory of his trips to her room but could not. She had struggled at first, then realized he enjoyed it more when she fought back. She had gone limp. Motionless. Silent. Eyes squeezed shut. Imagining she was far away, floating on a cloud, oblivious to his violation of her. Hoping his interest would wane.

Instead, he slapped her across the face and pulled her hair.

"Move your ass, chica!"

His face aflame and the vein in his neck throbbing. If

she had the pruning shears then, she would have snipped that vein like the stem of a rose.

When he was finished, she asked him to let her go. Didn't beg. Just asked, saying she would never cause trouble. But he just pulled up his jeans, cinched his belt, and left her room.

Now she carried the flowers by their thorny stems to the kitchen, avoiding the gaze of the guard. The building was old, maybe a hundred years. To Marisol, it looked like something from England she had seen on television.

Four stories with turrets and towers, painted the same color as the pink blushing roses. To her, the house resembled a steamship, chimneys like smokestacks and wide porches like covered decks. But it was a *burdel,* a den of debauchery. And for her, a prison.

Jacqueline would be in the kitchen preparing the evening meal for *el jefe*'s guests. A black woman from Georgia, Jacqueline had befriended Marisol, giving her ice for her bruises and advice on dealing with her situation.

"Just don't rile Mr. Simeon. You don't wanna get yourself buried in the cellar like some of the girls."

The warning shook her. Marisol had heard about the cellar from the *putas parlanchinas.* Stories of pregnant women who refused abortions. Forced to drink poison, they miscarried. Sometimes, they died. The cellar was said to contain the bones of these women and their unborn babies.

Jacqueline said the cellar scared her. Cobwebs and dirt floors and the spirits of the dead. Yesterday, she asked Marisol to haul up a case of liquor. Marisol tiptoed down the creaking wooden staircase. Even with its shadows and musty corners, the cellar was not as frightening as the cook had said. No ghosts hiding in the dark.

Marisol took her time. Examined the shelves of canned foods, bottles of liquor and wine. Found a door with a rusted iron frame, and vertical bars. Through the bars, nothing but darkness, and air as cool as in a mine shaft. An antique padlock fastened the door to its frame.

Marisol did not ask Jacqueline about the door or where it led. She didn't have to. Two days earlier, Marisol had been carrying a tray of clean glasses to the room called the "library," but really it was a bar. The bartender, a man in his fifties, was talking to a customer, saying that his grandfather had worked for Mr. Rutledge's grandfather.

"In those days, half the Legislature drove down here on weekends. Told their wives they had meetings at the Valley Improvement Society. That's the empty building next door. They'd play billiards and drink whiskey and take bribes to divvy up land and water for the big growers. Then the old tomcats would sneak through a tunnel right into our basement and up the stairs. All of 'em sniffing after pussy!"

The customer laughed, and the bartender joined in. Barely noticing Marisol stacking glasses on the shelves.

Now she planned her escape. The rusted iron door in the basement must lead to the tunnel. The tunnel led to the building next door. The road was just beyond. That would be her route. She prayed that the tunnel would not collapse and bury her with the other corpses, cold and forgotten belowground.

She knew there was a chance the guard would catch her. But she vowed to fight until one of them was dead. With that thought, she tucked the pruning shears into her apron, her fingers caressing the cool steel blade.

SEVENTY-SEVEN

Chief Javier Cardenas felt powerless. An L.A.P.D. detective was roaming his office like a jungle cat.

Just how much does Detective Eugene Rigney know?

Cardenas had never faced anything like this. He could scarcely remember a time he hadn't been taking orders from Uncle Sim. They had an unspoken arrangement. If Cardenas did what he was told, Simeon would boost his career, make his life more comfortable, and protect him.

Neither man had ever used the word "bribe." Not even "gift" or "present." Sometimes, Simeon would say, "I'm sending over a little something for the fridge." Slabs of freshly butchered ribs would arrive on ice, a stack of cold cash bagged separately. Other times, a Rutledge truck would deliver cartons of vegetables, Ben Franklin's quizzical face peering out from beneath the lettuce leaves.

Whenever Cardenas had a problem, Simeon was there to help. Except today. *Hell, Uncle Sim's to blame for the spot I'm in.*

Cardenas put on his friendly smile and leaned back in his ergonomically correct chair. His desk was an asymmetrical glass slab mounted on blocks of blue glass that resembled chunks of glacial ice. Outside, the thermometer on the Rutledge State Bank read 110. Inside the police station, the smooth, silent flow of the A/C kept the temperature a brisk 72.

So why am I sweating?

Maybe because at this moment, a swinging dick from L.A. was inspecting the office as if it were a crime scene.

"Never saw a cop shop like this." Detective Rigney stared at a lionfish darting in and out of a coral house in the chief's aquarium. "Must have cost a fortune."

"Private donations." He chose not to say that the donations all came from Simeon Rutledge. From the high-tech communications gear to the cushy leather chairs and sofas, it was all Uncle Sim's doing.

"Looks like a sports bar," Rigney said, checking out the five LCD monitors on the chief's back wall. It was the only wall not made of glass. The aquarium, six feet wide and twenty feet long, formed the wall with the bullpen. Glass block walls on either side separated the chief's quarters from adjacent offices.

The glass blocks multiplied the images on the other side. Cardenas often wondered if Uncle Sim was sending him a message there. *Things are not always what they seem.* Or, *Someone's always watching.* Or maybe, *People in glass houses shouldn't peer too deeply into other people's lives.*

Not that the place reflected Uncle Sim's taste. He did his business at his grandfather's rolltop desk with its hundred nooks and crannies, a piece of furniture as bulky as a battleship. For the Rutledge Municipal Building, Simeon hired a San Francisco designer, a noodle-necked young man who blew into town in black leather pants and a red silk scarf. By the time he left, Cardenas had an office where he couldn't scratch his nuts without being observed by meter maids crossing the bullpen to grab a demitasse from the gleaming titanium espresso machine.

That, too, hadn't escaped Rigney's notice. "You running a police station or a Starbucks here?" Sarcasm steaming like milk in a latte.

"We find that a pleasant atmosphere helps morale."

Cardenas nearly biting his tongue, thinking he sounded like one of those dweebs in Human Resources.

Rigney scanned the office as if he wanted to take prints off the artwork, starting with the granite sculpture of a horse pulling a plow.

Just what was the detective thinking? Cardenas wondered. The chief knew Rigney was a cop in deep trouble. A blown sting operation. A judge's suicide. Jimmy Payne's escape.

Rigney studied the chief through weary cop eyes. "So I'm still trying to figure out why you called L.A.P.D., asking about Payne."

"I had a report about this lawyer causing a scene over at the Rutledge corporate office. I ran his name, found the outstanding warrants. I called."

"But you ended up talking to Homicide, not Warrants."

"The call was misdirected. Maybe that's why the detective seemed so confused."

"Lou Parell may be fat and lazy, but he's not stupid. He says you never mentioned Payne was up here."

"Your detective is mistaken. Why else would I have called?"

"You tell me, Chief. Driving up here today, I kept asking myself: Why's this small-town cop mixed up with an asshole like Royal Payne?"

"All I know, Mr. Payne became agitated when he couldn't locate a woman he thought was working at Rutledge Farms."

"Where'd he pop up next?"

"He didn't. Hasn't been seen since he left the Rutledge office a couple days ago."

"So you never met him."

"Afraid not." Cardenas met Rigney's gaze. Turning away or blinking would make the lie too obvious. The less said, the better the chance the L.A. cop would leave town.

"Then you just dropped it? Never followed up, even though you knew about those warrants."

"Not my jurisdiction, and it's been busy up here."

"I'll bet."

Cardenas cursed himself for having made the call to the L.A.P.D. He needed Rigney here like a farmer needs a February freeze. But Uncle Sim had ordered him to do it. Charlie Whitehurst was right.

The old man's losing it.

"If Payne's still looking for that woman," the chief said, "he's probably checking out other growers. It's a big valley."

"And filled with a lot of horseshit." Rigney dropped into one of the soft leather chairs. He didn't seem in any hurry. "I pictured your office like something out of a black-and-white movie. Paddle fans, an old sergeant pecking away at a manual typewriter, a holding cell for the town drunk. But the place looks like Mission Control."

"I'm not following you, Detective."

"I'm just wondering, if the Attorney General started poking around in Hell's Little Oven here, what would he find?"

"An efficient police department, I suspect." Cardenas got up and walked to his glass-doored mini-fridge. He took out a pitcher. "Lemonade, Detective? Made from Rutledge lemons."

"No lemonade. No sarsaparilla. No peeing on my leg and calling it champagne."

Cardenas poured two glasses, anyway. "Seems like you're under some stress, Detective."

"No shit."

Another friendly smile. The lies weren't working; the chief decided to change his approach. He remembered some advice Simeon had dished out years ago, when he was still sharp as a cactus.

"Never been a horse that can't be rode. Never been a man who can't be sold."

"We get a lot of city cops who take early retirement and move up here," Cardenas said. "Got a couple working for us, couple more over at the Sheriff's Department. One or two even had some blemishes on their records."

"What the hell are you saying?"

"Just that a man should always be open to new opportunities."

"So I should move here and arrest artichoke poachers?"

"You'd be surprised how easy it is to make money in the Valley." Letting it hang there, like bacon dangling above the koi.

"Just how would I do that?" Rigney didn't jump at the bait, but he didn't swim the other direction, either. "Make easy money, I mean."

"You hungry, Detective? Clara over in Zoning makes the best B.L.T.s you've ever eaten."

Rigney studied him a moment, scowling. Then he answered, "Yeah, I'm hungry. In fact, I'm starving."

SEVENTY-EIGHT

I must be dead, Payne thought.

If I'm not dead, why don't I feel any pain? Why don't I feel anything?

"Are you conscious, Jimmy? Can you hear me?"

Sweet voice. Quiet voice. Sharon's voice.

Yep. I'm dead.

He mustered all his effort to open his eyes. As easy as lifting a ten-ton truck by cranking a hand jack. But there she was, reddish-brown hair, honey-colored eyes looking down at him, filled with compassion and caring, and . . .

"You stupid bastard," Sharon said.

And maybe a tad of anger.

"Himmy, I knew you weren't dead."

Tino looking down at him, black hair falling into his green eyes.

"Hey, kid."

Where the hell am I?

Payne tried sitting up, felt a tugging, found a tube stuck into the back of his hand. An IV bag dangled from a cart. Putting two and two together and being decent at math, he figured he was in a hospital. If that weren't enough proof, the place smelled like laundry bleach.

"I told you not to come here," Sharon reminded him, in case he'd forgotten. "I knew something like this would happen."

"Why is everything always my fault?" he said.

"Oh, I don't know. Maybe because you're reckless and self-destructive."

"Himmy's a good man," Tino said. "I trust him with my life."

"Thanks, kid. As soon as I get feeling back in my right arm, we'll play some catch." Payne's lips felt dry and thick.

"How'd I get here? How'd you get here?"

"You came by ambulance," Sharon said. "I came after the local police chief called me."

"Javier Cardenas?"

"He found my card in your wallet. Asked if I knew who would do this to you."

"And you said . . . ?"

" 'Lots of people.' "

Payne's laugh was a pitiful wheeze. "Cardenas knows who did it. Rutledge must have called him to scrape me off the ground. His way of saying, *'Don't bother filing charges.'* "

"Simeon Rutledge did this?" Sounding suspicious.

"I'll kill the *pendejo*," Tino said.

"Calm down, Ace," Payne cautioned. He gripped the bed railing, struggled again to sit up. The room whirled, and he sank back into the pillows.

Sharon adjusted the IV tube, which had twisted itself around Payne's forearm. He winced, thinking of the bullwhip.

"You're supposed to rest," she said.

"Screw that. There's something I gotta do." He looked toward Tino. "I think I know how to find your mother."

"You mean it?"

"I thought of it when I was getting the shit kicked out of me. Or maybe when I was unconscious. I don't know exactly. But I've got a plan."

The boy's eyes glistened with hope.

Sharon cocked her head, her skeptical look.

"Trust me, Sharon," Payne said. "Marisol's here. Somewhere close. But she's in trouble."

"Atticus, you sound like one of those palm readers. What's going on?"

"I need to get out of here. There's something I gotta do."

"You've got a concussion. You're on painkillers. The doctor wants to keep you overnight for observation."

"I don't want to be observed." Payne glanced toward the window. A pink glow of sunset. The last he remembered, it was breakfast time, and he was getting his ass whomped. As soon as the room stopped spinning, he intended to get out of bed.

"Sharon, I need you to take care of Tino tonight."

"What do you think you're going to do?"

"Gonna need your gun, too."

"Not unless you pry it from my cold, dead, out-of-a-job fingers."

"Listen to me for a second. Rutledge offered me two hundred grand to go away."

"A bribe?" Her accusing look, little vertical lines creasing the middle of her forehead. "Are you sure?"

"I didn't get it in writing, but yeah, I'm sure." He swung both legs out of the bed.

"Dammit, Jimmy!" Sharon blocked him from standing.

"What's your plan, Himmy?" Tino's face taking on the character of a man. Worry weighing on him, the mortgage of adulthood.

"Rutledge didn't offer me money for the hell of it. He knows where your mother is."

"How do we make him tell us?"

"We can't, kiddo. But I can get him to lead me to her."

"¿Cómo?"

"Rutledge is the king of the county. His whole adult life, he's been in control of everything around him. I can knock him off balance. Make him lose that cowboy calm of his."

"What are you talking about?" Sharon asked.

"I'm gonna hit him right in his weak spot."

"Which is what?" she demanded.

"His pride. His sense of tradition passed down from grandfather to father to son."

"That's pretty damn vague, Atticus."

"You ever know a man who loves some old trees so much he thinks of them as his children?"

"No."

"I do," Jimmy said, getting to his feet. "And I know how to hurt him in a way nobody ever has."

SEVENTY-NINE

Fifteen minutes, Marisol thought, neatly folding the white damask tablecloth, squaring the corners.

In fifteen minutes, she would be gone.

She placed the tablecloth in the top drawer of the mahogany sideboard. She had already cleared the dirty dishes and silverware from the dining room. Tonight's guests—all male, all older than forty—had not lingered over their meals. They had headed for the parlor to choose their companions and soon were hidden away in upstairs rooms.

Marisol checked the antique grandfather's clock that ticked loudly in the corner. Nearly midnight. A brass plate affixed to the clock read:

Hot Springs Gentleman's Club. Established 1899.

The Vietnamese guard sat at the bar in the library, just down the corridor. Every twenty minutes, he would pass the dining room on the way to the parlor. Then he would circle back to the kitchen and return to the bar, where he sipped an endless supply of club soda. Every third trip, he stopped in the rest room at the end of the corridor. Like the grandfather's clock, very dependable.

The next time he stopped to relieve himself, Marisol would walk into the kitchen—but not too fast—and retrieve the key from its place in the pantry. She would unlock the door to the cellar, head down the wooden staircase, and with a mallet she had found on top of a wine cask, break the old padlock on the tunnel door. For a weapon, she had the pruning shears.

If all went well, she would not be missed until morning. With luck, she could flag down a trucker on a late-night run. If not, she would walk. She was strong. She could cover twenty miles a day. She would pick fruits and vegetables from the fields. She would travel at night, using the stars for guidance, heading due south. Toward Mexico. Toward her son, she hoped and prayed.

Again, she looked at the ticking clock. The guard's bathroom break was ten minutes away.

Marisol was wearing the required maid's outfit, a ridiculously short black satin dress with velvet choker, white apron, lace fishnet stockings, and garter. The black stiletto heels that completed the look of a lascivious *lavandera* would not do for her escape or crosscountry walk. She had hidden a pair of jeans, a T-shirt, and sneakers in the cellar.

Now, standing on tiptoes, she returned a soup tureen to the top shelf of the sideboard. She looked toward the ceiling and let herself smile ruefully at the frescoes of a blue sky and white clouds. It was the only sky she was permitted to see without the supervision of the guard.

Her work finished in the dining room, she moved briskly down the corridor, a lighted path of Tiffany lamps and polished hardwood. Passing the library, she glimpsed the guard on one of the bar stools. Once in the parlor, she emptied ashtrays and brushed cigar residue from the red velvet upholstery of the overstuffed chairs.

The room had stained-glass windows, but unlike a church, these were illustrated with naked nymphs and frolicking satyrs. A huge fireplace rose at one end of the room, the hearth as tall as a man.

When the ashtrays were clean and the upholstery brushed, Marisol returned to the kitchen. To her relief, her timing was perfect. Just as she reentered the corridor, the guard disappeared into the rest room.

Two minutes later, Marisol padded quietly down the staircase to the cellar. She carried a flashlight she'd found in a utility closet, leaving the cellar lights off, fearing they could be seen beneath the pantry door.

She had taken off the stiletto heels but hadn't yet put on her change of clothing. Now she grabbed the wooden mallet. She would have preferred a steel hammer but recognized the wood as iron bark. Marisol had been swinging hammers and sawing wood since she was five years old, her father teaching her to hit hard and true. The mallet could do the job.

She placed the flashlight on a shelf, aiming the beam at the padlock on the metal, slatted door. Her first swing caught the curved shackle just where it entered the body of the lock. So did the second and the third. The shackle was thin and graceful, as was the antique lock itself, which seemed to have been designed by an artist, rather than an engineer. Another swing, and the lock clattered against the iron door frame, but did not break.

Another blow, and this time, a tiny pin flew out the side of the lock. *Excelente.* Just a tap now, and the lock should break apart.

What's that noise?

Did the stairs just creak?

She froze.

The lights were still out. No one would come down those steps without turning on the lights, would they?

She clicked off the flashlight and blinked against the darkness.

Another sound. Maybe just the groan of the caissons that supported the ground floor. Or was it the squeak of leather boots on wooden stairs? Or nothing at all.

She remained motionless.

There it was again. Louder this time. Was someone coming closer?

She forced herself to remain calm, listened with all her concentration, tried to see into the darkness. Heard her own breathing, as hot and fast as a cornered animal. She waited another thirty seconds. Then thirty seconds more. Nothing.

She swung the mallet again. The lock banged against the door frame, and the latch sprang from its slot.

Marisol pulled the lock free and yanked at the door. Stuck. She grabbed one of the vertical bars and put her weight into it. A squeal of rusty metal, and the door opened a few inches. Just as she pushed her shoulder against the frame, a strong hand grabbed her by the hair and yanked her sideways.

"Where you think you're going, *chica*?" A man's chilling voice. Mr. Zaga.

She reached for the mallet, but Zaga's foot swept her legs out from under her, and she tumbled to the dirt floor. He twisted one of her arms behind her back, pinned her down with a knee digging into her ribs. Leaning close, he whispered in her ear, his breath caressing her neck. "Just like always. Sim makes a mess, and I gotta clean it up."

EIGHTY

Payne peered up at the second-floor windows of Rutledge's sprawling farmhouse.

Dark and quiet.

The only sounds came from the fields, crackling insects, and whirring sprinklers. That would change soon enough. Payne wondered if Rutledge was a sound sleeper.

Payne's plan was both simple and dangerous. Rutledge had no wife and no children. But he had those three old peach trees he treated the way perfumed ladies treat their French poodles.

Payne had parked on a side access road and, lugging a chainsaw, crawled over a fence of painted white logs. Thanks to the wonders of Vicodin, he wasn't in pain. More like numb and light-headed. Very little feeling from the shoulders down, other than a tingling in his fingertips, as if he'd grabbed the wrong end of a sparkler on the Fourth of July.

Something in the air had changed. What was it? A sizzle. Not quite a sound, more like a scent. Overhead, the stars were obscured by thick clouds.

It smells like rain.

Payne used two hands to muscle the machine—a McCulloch Xtreme he'd bought at a twenty-four-hour Wal-Mart—to the base of the nearest peach tree. He should be wearing a helmet, work boots, and cut-resistant pants. Instead, he wore U.C.L.A. shorts, black

Nike Zooms, and a T-shirt with the slogan *"I'm Already Against the Next War."*

Payne tried yanking the cord, but his right hand wouldn't close properly. Awkwardly, he used his left hand. The starter kicked over and the chainsaw coughed and sputtered to life.

He bent over in an awkward crouch. If the chain slipped or bucked, he could slice his thigh. With all the painkillers, would he even feel it? The chain bit into the wood, making a high-pitched whine, like a frightened horse. Chips blasted his bare legs. He shot a look over his shoulder toward Rutledge's house. Still dark.

The tree trunk was less than two feet in diameter, the wood soft, and the task did not take long. He put the saw on idle, yelled "Timber!" and pushed. The tree fell with a *whoosh* of branches and leaves, ripe peaches smushing into the ground. The air smelled of wet earth and sweet fruit, mixed with gasoline fumes.

Still no sign of life from the farmhouse. In the distance, to the southeast, summer lightning backlit the clouds that shrouded the Sierra Nevadas.

Halfway through the second tree, the chain jerked and kicked back. Payne got control just before the saw would have pierced his femoral artery. A moment later, a light came on at a second-floor window.

Hurrying, Payne finished off the tree. The silhouette of a large man emerged onto the balcony.

Simeon Rutledge.

Shouting something Payne couldn't make out over the roar of the chainsaw. Rutledge disappeared from the balcony, and the second tree toppled.

Payne crouched at the base of the third tree just as Rutledge reappeared on the balcony. Gun in his hands. Rifle or shotgun, too dark to tell.

A *blast*. Definitely a shotgun. But the trees were a good two hundred feet from the house. The buckshot ran out of steam before reaching Payne, the pellets pelting the leaves like a soft spring rain.

Another blast, another shower of buckshot, dribbling through branches and rolling harmlessly across the soft earth.

Payne kept at it, the chainsaw chunking through the last tree.

One more gunshot echoed across the yard.

Payne pushed the tree over and clicked off the chainsaw. In the distance, the rumble of thunder. Yep, rain was coming.

Rutledge shouted something. His ears still ringing from the chainsaw, Payne waved at the old man, the way a gardener might acknowledge his boss.

"¡El jefe!" he shouted. "You were wrong! The trees didn't outlive you."

"Dead man!"

Now Payne could hear him.

"You're a dead man, Payne. And she's a dead woman!"

His blood aflame. Rutledge burning for revenge.

Payne dropped the chainsaw and took off at a trot. He would disappear behind a stand of live oak trees and circle back to where Rutledge would never look for him. The front of the house. Enraged that Payne had gotten away, Rutledge would move quickly to fulfill his threat. And, without knowing it, he would lead Payne right to Marisol.

Payne could not be sure about any of these things. All he believed with absolute certainty was that if he did not rescue Marisol, within the hour she would be dead.

EIGHTY-ONE

The pain was a roaring fire, a welding torch applied to ribs and spine.

Marisol did not even try to struggle as Zaga squeezed the breath from her. She was facedown, Zaga on top of her. He shifted position, dug an elbow—sharp as a pickax—into her ribs.

Breath shot from her lungs.

Then a sharp jab in her lower abdomen.

The pruning shears!

In the pocket of her apron. The thumb lever that locked the blades now tore at her flesh through the thin fabric.

If I can get my hand under my body, I can grab the shears.

The cellar was lit only by the narrow beam of her flashlight, aimed above her head. She tried to judge just where Zaga's face would be in the darkness. Pictured herself plunging the curved blades straight through an eye. But his weight kept her pinned to the dirt floor, the shears trapped in place.

Zaga made a sound, a half laugh, half snort, as he ran a hand up the back of Marisol's right leg, tearing at the fishnet stockings.

"So they finally dress you like the *puta* you are."

His hand slid under the short dress and pulled at the elastic of the lacy underpants. "What do you think? One *rapidito* before you leave us?"

"Let me up, and I'll treat you good, Mr. Zaga."

Another snort-laugh. "Oh, you'll treat me good, but you'll do it facedown in the dirt. You and your precious *almeja* you don't share with nobody."

He slid a finger into the crack of her ass.

His phone rang.

Zaga adjusted his weight, reached into a buttoned pocket of his Western shirt, and pulled out his cell phone. He checked the LCD display and answered, "Sim, I was just gonna call you."

Marisol sucked in a breath, drawing in dust along with oxygen. Above her, Zaga was silent, listening. If he stood, she would have a chance to go for the shears.

"He did what? The bastard!" Shouting into the phone.

Another few seconds of silence.

"Sure, I know where she is. I got her right here. Bitch was trying to run."

Why is el jefe *asking about me?*

"Jeez, Sim. Why dirty your hands? I'll take care of her. Then me and Javie can go after Payne."

Another pause. Then, "Okay, okay. I know who's boss. And Sim, I'm sorry about those Elberta trees. I know how you felt about them. Jesus."

Zaga clicked off the phone and slipped it back in his pocket. "The boss got a hair up his ass. He wants to do you himself."

Zaga got to his feet, dusted off his jeans. "No use arguing with the biggest bull in the pasture."

He grabbed Marisol by one arm and slung her to her feet.

As she rose, Marisol grabbed the pruning shears from her apron. Her momentum carried her close to Zaga. She swung the shears in a tight, hard arc. An uppercut he didn't see in the darkness.

The curved blade buried itself in his neck, catching

the cartilage just below his voice box. He gasped and made a choking sound.

Her thumb found the lever, unlocked the mechanism, and the spring-loaded blades flew apart, widening the wound.

A wet, gurgling sound bubbled from inside his throat. He staggered back a step, then wobbled to one side. She yanked out the shears. A hot breath of air whistled from the wound. Misting blood showered her face. She stabbed again, deeper into the soft tissue of his neck. She must have hit an artery. A gusher of blood poured over her.

His body spasmed and his legs buckled as if his spine had just melted. He dropped to his knees, like a parishioner in church. The rest of him followed, collapsing slowly and neatly, straight down, like one of those old hotels demolished by well-placed explosives.

Marisol stood there soaked in his blood, breathing hard, her body trembling. She was about to pick up her change of clothes and head through the tunnel door when the staircase lights blinked on.

"Mr. Zaga. You down there?"

The guard.

"Mr. Z. You okay?"

Barefoot and bloody, Marisol grabbed the flashlight, swung open the iron door and, flailing at cobwebs, plunged into the black hole of the tunnel.

EIGHTY-TWO

Wired and edgy, Sharon believed it would be a sleepless night. She was holed up with a twelve-year-old boy in the hotel room. Jimmy was out there in the dark somewhere, playing lumberjack with some old peach trees.

Trespass.

Malicious mischief.

Destruction of property.

And just maybe, getting a young woman and himself killed.

She hadn't been able to talk him out of it.

Foolish. Reckless. Dangerous. Pure Payne.

Her job tonight was to keep Tino safe. They had talked for hours, the boy chattering about going to a Dodgers game with Jimmy and enrolling in some school Jimmy had picked out, and Jimmy somehow getting them immigration papers, even if he had to fudge the truth a little.

Jimmy. Jimmy. Jimmy.

Tino was the president of the Jimmy Payne Fan Club. Maybe its sole member. The boy worshiped him. But would he still, after tonight? What if Jimmy didn't rescue Marisol? What if his actions led to her death? Sharon couldn't help but think of all the horrible possibilities.

Tino couldn't sleep, either. Together they watched television. Sharon made microwave popcorn. In typical male fashion, the boy asked for the remote, then hop-scotched through the channels. Just like his hero.

Sharon couldn't keep her mind on the programs. Jay Leno's jokes seemed duller than usual. *Sports Center*'s nightly baseball clips all looked the same. Tino clicked through one channel after another, settling on a shopping network that sold diamond rings for thirty-nine dollars.

Tino stared into space, his attention wavering. Sharon could only guess what fears plagued him tonight.

Then he surprised her. Without warning or prelude, he said softly, "Himmy told me what happened. To your son."

"Oh."

"Himmy's really messed up about it."

"I know."

Tino picked up his baseball glove—the one Jimmy bought him—and pounded a ball into the pocket. "Maybe the two of you will get back together. You know, help each other with all that bad stuff."

"Did Jimmy tell you to say that?"

"No way. I just see how he feels about you."

"I'm hoping he'll get over that."

Tino gave her a look. Too serious for a twelve-year-old. "But will you get over him?"

"What do you mean?"

"If you didn't love Himmy, you wouldn't have come up here."

Before she could process that, the door burst open, splintering off its hinges.

Sharon dived for her shoulder holster, slung from the bedpost.

"Freeze!" Rigney in the doorway, aiming his Glock at her.

She obeyed, hands inches from her gun.

Tino jumped out of bed and pivoted like Omar

Vizquel at shortstop, sidearming the ball straight into Rigney's chest. The cop howled and staggered a step backward but didn't drop his gun. "Punk! You little punk greaser."

"*¡Chingate!*"

"No, fuck you, kid."

"Put the gun away, Rigney." Sharon glared at him. "Jimmy's not here."

"No shit. He's out playing Paul Bunyan." He gave her a *gotcha* grin while using his free hand to gingerly touch a rib where the ball had nailed him. Moving toward the bed, he grabbed Sharon's holster from the bedpost.

"What are you doing here?"

"Enforcing the law." He flipped over a badge hanging around his neck. "Duly appointed deputy, named by the chief himself."

Sharon felt like spitting at him. "How much they paying you, Rigney?"

"Take it easy, Detective. I'm saving your ass."

"What about Jimmy? You saving him, too?"

"Your ex is dead meat. But I got nothing to do with that." Rigney turned to Tino. "C'mon, kid. Let's go."

"No fucking way," Tino said.

"Relax. I'm taking you to your mother. The chief's gonna send both of you back to Mexico. With some cash, for all your trouble."

"Is that what Cardenas told you?" Sharon said.

"He's a cop, for Christ's sake. What do you think he's gonna do—kill them?"

"You are so dense, Rigney. Cardenas works for Rutledge."

"So what? Who do you think we work for, the Red Cross? Money buys everything and everyone. Rutledge is no different than the bigwigs in L.A. He just wears cowboy boots instead of Italian suits."

"We're supposed to fight corruption, Rigney."

"Losing battle." He reached into a jacket pocket and tossed a pair of handcuffs to Tino. "Cuff her to the bed frame."

"*Chingate,*" Tino said for the second time.

Rigney grabbed the boy by the scruff of the neck and shoved him toward the bed.

"Go ahead, Tino," Sharon said.

Tino hesitated. Rigney clopped him on the side of the head with an open hand. "Now!"

"Do as he says, Tino," Sharon said.

The boy snapped one cuff around Sharon's right wrist, and the other to the metal frame.

Rigney pulled out a roll of duct tape and tore off a piece. "Someday you'll thank me, Detective." Before she could reply, he covered her mouth with the tape. Then he grabbed Tino by the arm and said, "C'mon kid, smile. You're headed to a family reunion."

EIGHTY-THREE

The bed of a farmer's pickup truck could be filled with a pile of fragrant manure, or sacks of lung-searing pesticides, or a basket of rusty rakes and dirt-clodden hoes. Simeon Rutledge's green Ford, built during the Korean War, smelled of polish and gleamed with wax. Had a moon been peeking through the rain clouds, the truck would have shined in the dark.

Payne lay on his back in the short, stubby cargo bed, Adam's Louisville Slugger at his side. The truck was parked in the circular driveway in front of the farmhouse. If someone drove up—say, Enrique Zaga, hauling Marisol along—Payne would leap over the low side panel and flail away at the man's skull, like Juan Marichal on Johnny Roseboro in Candlestick Park.

The other option was Rutledge driving to wherever Marisol was being held.

Payne heard the front door of the farmhouse bang closed. He fought the urge to peek over the side panel. Rutledge's cowboy boots crunched the gravel, his steps quick. The driver's door opened, and Rutledge's weight settled into the front seat.

The old Ford coughed and cleared its throat. Rutledge put it in gear and spun out of the driveway, spraying gravel.

Payne stayed down, bracing his feet against the back of the cab. He lost his sense of direction after several turns. Asphalt. Unpaved road. Potholes the size of canoes. The painkillers must be wearing off. His temples throbbed. His head was filled with billiard balls, clacking into one another. At the same time, some gremlin with a hammer was engaged in carpentry on his hip bone.

Lightning flashed from the southeast, a summer storm born in Mexico, crashing toward the valley. The heat of the day gave way, the air cool and moist, the smell of rain even stronger now.

The truck bounced along, branches of sycamore and birch trees forming a canopy over the bed. The dirt road gave way to another stretch of pavement.

Thunder rumbled across the sky. Zeus hurling thunderbolts. Angels bowling. God farting. Whatever.

Payne crept onto his knees and peered cautiously through the window into the cab. Rutledge's right hand rested on the spindly gearshift shaped like a question mark. His left elbow stuck out the open window.

A jagged lightning bolt creased the sky and exploded somewhere close by. Payne pictured a mighty oak tree splintered and smoking. Raindrops, fat and cold, pelted him, pinging off the truck bed.

Rutledge's cell phone rang, and Payne strained to hear. Over the noise of the wind and the engine, he couldn't make out what the old man was saying. But a second later, the brakes whinnied like a tired horse, and the truck skidded to a stop.

Rutledge jumped out of the cab, cell pressed to his ear. "That bitch! I don't fucking believe it! Jesus, Mary, and Joseph."

He paced in front of the truck, rain soaking him. The thunder sounded like a mallet banging a kettle drum.

Payne edged to the side panel. Saw Rutledge framed in the headlights. Jeans, boots, a black felt *Tejano* hat with a silver buckle. A Western holster was tied to his right leg. It housed a big-ass revolver, an old Colt .45. The gun called the "Peacemaker." As if Rutledge had just arrived by stagecoach from Deadwood. On his left leg, a scabbard held a foot-long Marine fighting knife.

Raindrops shined in the headlights, silver daggers from the sky.

"Dammit!" Rutledge yelled into the phone. "The little gook was supposed to be watching her."

What the hell's he talking about?

"Payne must know where she is," Rutledge ventured. "That's why he cut down the trees. A diversion so she can run. It's all planned."

News to me, Payne thought, wishing he'd been that smart. Playing those words over in his mind.

"*. . . so she can run. It's all planned.*"

"I can't believe Z's dead," Rutledge said. "Goddammit, I can't believe it."

Enrique Zaga? Oh, Jesus. Had Marisol killed Zaga and run for it?

"Me and Z grew up together. Little fucker was like my brother."

Payne ducked as Rutledge strode back to the truck, hoisted one boot onto the running board, and stared straight across the cargo bed. Water dripped from his hat brim, splashing Payne's face. If Rutledge looked down, he'd spot Payne, flipped on his back like a tortoise.

"Javie, you find her, and quick."

Javie. Javier Cardenas. Rutledge's private police force.

"Bring her to the old pump station. I'm gonna clean up this mess once and for all."

Another lightning bolt hit, close enough to shimmy the truck. The air smelled of ozone.

"Don't get on your high horse with me, Javie. Where's the fire in your guts? Your old man wasn't like that. Hector would have begged me to let him kill them himself."

Rutledge listened a few seconds, then barked, "Don't give me that 'Calm down, Sim' crap. You know what your problem is? You're pussified. Your mother babied you. And I gave you too much. Just do what the fuck I say!"

Rutledge clicked off and sank his butt onto the running board.

Payne curled his fingers around the handle of the aluminum bat, gripping it so tightly the muscles of his forearm knotted. He could do it now. Beat the tar out of Rutledge. Split his skull wide open. But then, how would he find Marisol?

The old pump station?

Where the hell was that?

For a moment, there was only the rain exploding like glass beads off metal. Then a wailing like brass horns, as startling as an orchestra in a desert. Simeon Rutledge was sobbing. Great, wracking sobs that sent tremors through his body and shook the bed of the truck.

EIGHTY-FOUR

The smell of dust and creosote and rotting wood filled the tunnel, the air dank and rancid. Marisol's ribs ached and her skull throbbed. Springy cobwebs stuck to her face, feeling like desiccated fingers of corpses. Fractured beams—ancient railroad ties—sagged under the weight of the earth above her. The splintered plywood roof leaked funnels of dirt.

She scrambled barefoot through the tunnel, hunched over to keep from hitting her head on the drooping beams. Fearing the worst. The tunnel a dead end or an endless maze.

She followed the beam of the flashlight, one hand running along the side of the tunnel, rough and jagged to the touch. From somewhere, water dripped.

She stumbled into a puddle, the *splash* as loud as a whale breaching. The cold water startled her.

Another frightening thought. The guard, knife drawn, could be following her.

She clicked off the flashlight, blinked against the darkness, and listened for footsteps. Only the *drip* she had heard before, but in the confined space, magnified into watery explosions. She turned the beam back on and continued deeper into the tunnel. Without warning, her right knee buckled, and she toppled into a hole, bracing herself with one arm. Pain shot through her wrist, and something sharp pierced her hand, which immediately started to bleed. It felt as if she'd fallen on a railroad spike or a piece of sharpened bamboo.

She scrambled to her feet, tore off a piece of her dress, and made a bandage, stopping the blood flow. Aimed the flashlight into the hole. What was that? A white, bony . . . oh, God . . . rib cage! A human skeleton lodged into the dirt. She had stumbled into a human grave and slashed her hand on a human bone. A woman from the brothel? A customer? Some personal enemy, a long forgotten victim of violence? The horror of a lonely death without prayers.

Who would bless her, Marisol wondered, if she was entombed in this passage to hell?

She played the flashlight across the floor of the tunnel. No other skeletons. No other holes. She picked up the pruning shears, which had fallen from her apron. Then hurried along, bent over, faster now, until she came to an obstruction.

A door! The end of the tunnel.

Old and ornate, with carvings of cherubs. A doorknob of green glass, an antique look.

The door was locked.

Marisol played the flashlight beam around the door frame. Dry-rotted wood. She dug at the frame with the pruning shears. Sawdust dribbled out; the wood crumbled. She freed the lock from its latch and pushed the door open.

A dark room. Cool. A basement. Crates covered by

decades of dust. She wiped off a box, checked the stenciled name: *Valley Improvement Society*. She was in the right place. The building next to the brothel, the place the rich politicians gathered before traveling underground for their pleasure.

A set of stairs. A door open at the top.

She moved cautiously up the stairs, flinching when they groaned under her weight. On the ground floor, an ancient pool table, a long wooden bar with a cracked mirror. More cobwebs, overstuffed furniture draped in dust covers.

A haunted house.

She raced to the front door. The knob turned but the door wouldn't open. She put her shoulder to it. It didn't budge. Shined the light along the door frame.

The door was boarded with wooden planks, nailed from the outside. Pushed again, but the wood held tight. Thick, sturdy nails. No way to force her way out. She fought back tears.

She checked the windows. The glass broken, but two-by-fours crosshatched the openings here, too.

Intended to keep people out, the fortifications trapped her inside.

A noise.

She stood frozen in place.

A car engine.

She moved to one of the windows, peeked out between the boards. A car approached slowly, turning sideways in the driveway. A rack of lights on its roof, a star painted on its side.

¡La policia!

But she had seen policemen at the brothel. Everyone, it seemed, worked for Rutledge.

The driver's door opened. A man in uniform got out and took several steps toward the building. Backlit by the car's headlight beams, he threw off a shadow ten feet tall. "Marisol! Marisol Perez. You in there?"

She stayed quiet.

"You're safe now, señorita," the man called. "I'm the chief of police."

Why should she trust this man? Except for her father, what man could she trust?

"I'm here to help you."

Help me do what?

The policeman stepped back to the car, opened the rear door, and pulled a boy from the backseat. Her breath caught in her throat.

Could it be?

He was the size of her Agustino, but she could not make out the boy's face.

"Lemme make it easy for you." The policeman's tone had gone hard. "We've got your kid. Give a signal you're in there."

"No! *Mami*, hide! Run!"

Tino's voice!

The policeman grabbed Tino's neck. "I don't want to hurt anybody."

Tino flailed, tried to twist free. "I'll kill you, *cabrón*." Sounding as if he was choking.

"Let him go!" Marisol screamed, pounding a fist against a window plank. "Let him go! And take me!"

EIGHTY-FIVE

The old truck wheezed to a stop alongside an earthen levee. Payne heard a *chuga-chuga*. The pump station. Peering up from the cargo bed, he saw the grille of an old Chevy poking out of the dirt, where it had been left after a flood thirty years ago. He had passed this place on his horseback ride.

Rutledge leapt out of the truck cab and trudged up the slope, his boots sinking into the wet clay, the color of cinnamon. The rain had slowed. Lightning blinked to the northwest, the storm past them now.

Payne waited until Rutledge had crested the levee, which stood twenty-five feet above the surrounding fields. Louisville Slugger in hand, Payne climbed out of the cargo bed and scampered on all fours up the levee. He lay on the ground at the top, peering at the pump station straddling the stream. A concrete-and-steel structure resembling a dam, the station channeled water into three separate culverts. Utility poles topped by sodium vapor lights gave the streams an orange, toxic tint.

Payne watched Rutledge at the foot of the levee, yelling into his cell phone.

"Where the fuck are you! Do you have her?" He whisked the *Tejano* from his head and slapped it against his thigh, shaking water from the brim. "Okay, good work, Javie. Now get her the hell over here."

Javier Cardenas again. And he has Marisol.

Payne sized up the situation. One man with a kid's baseball bat against·one man with a gun and knife. That was bad enough. But two men with guns? He had to take out Rutledge before Cardenas got here.

Rutledge walked along the shoreline, crouched on his haunches, and peered toward the sluice pipe, the artery that carried the lifeblood of his empire. Payne calculated the distance between them. Down the side of the levee and across a flat space to the culvert. Ninety feet. Maybe a hundred.

Rutledge's back was turned. Payne figured that the noise of the pumps and the angry flow of the water would mask his footfalls. It better. The fear rose in his chest, and for one paralyzing moment he questioned whether he could do it. Then he thought of Tino and Adam, and all that had been lost, and all that could still be saved.

Payne got to his feet and crab-walked down the muddy slope, cutting a diagonal path across the levee.

Eighty feet away.

Rutledge stared into the water. Was he looking into his past? Three generations of men who lusted for land and water. Men who built wealth and power on the backs of the poor, all the while telling themselves they were pioneers and visionaries and men of the soil.

Seventy feet.

Payne's Nikes squished in the mud, the suction slowing him down.

Sixty feet.

Rutledge rose from his haunches and stretched his neck, working out a kink with the palm of a hand.

Fifty feet.

Payne raised the bat to shoulder height. Tripped on a rock embedded in the muck. Caught himself but lost a step.

Forty feet.

Rutledge cocked his head, as if sensing something.

Thirty feet.

Payne planned his swing. He'd smash Rutledge's skull right above the temple.

Twenty feet.

Rutledge pivoted. "You? You sorry son-of-a-bitch!" He pulled the big revolver from its holster.

Payne drew back the bat.

The gun was waist high, the barrel sweeping toward Payne's chest.

Three more steps. I won't make it.

Payne let the bat fly. Just as Rutledge pulled the trigger, the Louisville Slugger caught the tip of his shoulder. The slug smacked the mud at Payne's feet.

Rutledge grunted and dropped the gun. Payne went low, aimed for Rutledge's knees. Tackled him, shoulders square, a linebacker wrapping up a running back.

The men toppled backward, rolled over each other. A flailing of arms and elbows and knees. Both men struggled to their feet. Rutledge got his hands around Payne's neck. "You stupid shit! You could have been rich."

Payne broke Rutledge's grip and threw a left jab that caught him squarely on the nose. A *snap* of cartilage and a fountain of blood.

Rutledge roared. More in anger than pain. He came at Payne. They collided head-on and tumbled into the culvert, the sluice pipe dousing them from overhead. Waist deep, the water slowed their movements. Scrambling to get their footing, they each clawed their way to shore like prehistoric amphibians. Payne slipped and Rutledge got to dry land first. Diving face-first into the mud, Rutledge reached for the gun, which slipped from his wet fingers. Payne leapt onto Rutledge's back and squeezed his right arm around the man's neck. Gripping his right wrist with his left hand, Payne pulled upward, catching Rutledge in a choke hold. Rutledge spat mud, grunted, snorted an unintelligible curse, and jackknifed an elbow backward, burning Payne's right ear.

Rutledge was strong and slippery, all long muscles and hard bones and wiry gristle a dog couldn't chew. Swallowing his own blood, he lurched to his knees, dipped a shoulder, and tossed Payne off his back. Payne clambered to his feet just as Rutledge came at him. Payne shifted his weight to one leg, swiveled a hip, and used Rutledge's momentum to toss him to the ground, the gun out of reach.

Payne saw the bat on the wet ground. Scooped it up. Turned, thinking Rutledge would still be going for the gun, several yards away. Instead, the man was just an arm's length away, drawing the foot-long knife from the scabbard on his leg. Payne sidestepped a forward thrust. But a downward slash sliced him from the tip of the left shoulder halfway to the elbow. The cut long but shallow.

The movement left Rutledge off balance. Before the pain from the wound even reached Payne's brain, he latched both hands around Rutledge's wrist. Payne twisted the arm outward, Rutledge yelping with pain.

The knife fell to the wet clay.

Payne, bleeding from his left arm, threw a straight right into Rutledge's already shattered nose. Rutledge staggered backward, blood pouring from his nostrils and soaking his brushy mustache. But still, he didn't fall. He wobbled side-to-side, arms down, eyes unfocused. Payne picked up the knife and tightened his grip.

Lightning blinked in the distant sky. In Payne's mind, a flare burst with dazzling images of startling clarity. Adam, so young. Sharon, stoic in her loss. Tino, filled with life and promise. Marisol, what horrors had she known, and what dread must she feel now?

Payne sized up just where he would bury the blade. The gut? The chest? Maybe the neck. Let him drown in his own blood. He would kill the man for Adam and Tino and Sharon and Marisol. And for himself.

He would plunge the knife to its hilt, tearing tissue and ripping organs from their moorings. He would hear the steam explode from pierced lungs. He would yank out the blade, time and again, to the satisfying *squish* of flesh sucking at steel. He would strike a hundred times, baptizing himself in the bastard's blood.

Holding the knife in an underhand grip, Payne advanced a step. Rutledge's eyes seemed to clear, to focus on the blade.

Let him taste the fear and hear his own last breath.

A gunshot echoed off the concrete walls of the pump station.

"Freeze, Payne!"

Cardenas stood atop the levee, aiming his 9mm Glock at Payne's head, Marisol and Tino a few steps to one side.

It had all come crashing down, Payne thought, the weight of his actions pounding at him. He had tried to save Marisol but succeeded only in delivering her—and Tino and himself—to wet and lonely graves.

EIGHTY-SIX

"Toss the knife down," Cardenas ordered. "Then step away."

Fighting off dizziness, his arm bleeding, Payne obeyed. In his mind, he saw the last seconds of his life ticking away, his body buried in a levee alongside an old Chevy. Strangely calm, he accepted his own death in a way he had never accepted Adam's.

"About goddamn time you got here, Javie." Rutledge spat blood, then wiped his mouth with the back of his sleeve.

"Now, there's a thank you, *Tío* Sim."

"Don't be so damn prickly." Rutledge picked up the .45 and slid it into his holster. "Payne don't have the guts. If he couldn't do the *pollo* who killed his boy, he sure as hell couldn't do me."

"Give me back the knife," Payne said, "and we'll see."

"You had your chance. Just like with your own boy. You blew it then and you blew it now."

Payne felt a molten wave of heat flow through his chest. He could bull-rush Rutledge, knock him down, go for the gun. Then what? Get shot by Cardenas. That wouldn't help Tino or his mother.

The chief motioned with his gun. "Move on down, both of you."

Marisol and Tino angled across the levee like skiers carving their way down a slope.

"You okay, kiddo?" Payne asked, pressing his right hand against the wound on his left arm.

"I'm good, Himmy. I got *mi mami*."

Payne looked toward Marisol. All this time, he felt he knew her, but he was setting eyes on her for the first time. Soaking wet. Hair tangled. Face bruised. Still a beautiful woman, with a stubborn jaw carved from stone.

"Marisol, you've got a great son. You're gonna be really proud of him."

As if the boy would grow up. As if she'd be around to see him.

"Tino has told me all about you, Mr. Payne. You are a wonderful man." A strong woman with a tender voice. "Bless you."

Something passed between them. The mother who feared for her son and the man who had watched his own son die.

"Tino's a real *valiente*," Payne continued.

"Very fucking touching." Rutledge tore strips of cloth from his shirt and jammed them up his nostrils. "Take care of those two, Javie." His voice was hollow as a foghorn. "I'll handle Payne myself."

Cardenas scratched a knuckle against his chin, as if checking to see if he had shaved. "I've done a lot of shit, Sim. But I never killed anyone. Much less a woman and a boy."

"About time you got your hands dirty."

"Not this way."

"Don't fuck with me, Javie. You want to see that *puta* on the witness stand?"

Tino's hands balled into fists. "Don't talk that way about *mi mami*!"

"Hush, Tino," Marisol ordered.

"So what are you saying, Sim?" Cardenas asked. "We kill three people to keep you out of prison?"

"You're goddamn right we do."

"Problem is, you're gonna do time, anyway." Cardenas swung his 9mm toward Rutledge. "Keep your hands where I can see them, Sim."

"What the fuck?"

Stunned, Payne tried to figure out what was going on. The police chief defying the man he called *"mi tío."* It made no sense.

Rutledge kept his right hand perched just above the walnut grip of his holstered revolver. The men were staring each other down, two cowboys itching for a shootout. But what was the fight about?

Marisol looked at Payne, her dark eyes alert, as if asking what to do. The Marine knife lay in the mud. Adam's baseball bat nearby. But there were two men with guns. Payne chose to wait it out.

"Javie, I got plans for you," Rutledge said. "Always did, ever since you were a baby."

"I've got my own plans."

"What the hell's that mean?"

"I know about the indictments and the plea you turned down. About your will, too."

"Whitehurst?" The realization seemed to nail Rutledge to the ground with a railroad spike. "That shyster. The going gets tough, and that damn lawyer turns yellow. Hell, you both do."

"Your time has passed, Sim."

"Not while I'm still standing, you little pecker. So you'd better put a bullet in my heart or lay your gun down."

EIGHTY-SEVEN

Rutledge didn't want to kill Javie, though he knew he could.

Just look at him. Stiff as a scarecrow. A death grip on his gun.

Rutledge would prefer to talk Javie down. Hell, he liked the boy. Always had. "Jesus, Javie. Haven't I treated you like my own son?"

That brought a rueful smile. "In school, the kids thought so. Told me I *was* your son."

"Bullshit. Not that I didn't wish it was true."

"I remember coming into *Mami*'s bedroom in the morning and finding you there."

"Only after your daddy died." Watching the barrel of the Glock.

Are your hands shaking, Javie?

"At the very end, in the hospital, she told me you'd been taking her to the barn long before that. Even before I was born. *'Me montó como un caballo.'* Her exact words. 'He mounted me like a horse.' "

"The woman was on morphine, for Christ's sake."

"She didn't want to fuck you, but you let her know *Papi* wouldn't have a job otherwise."

"Not the way it happened." Rutledge thinking Javie would get off the first shot.

But you'll miss. Most gunshots do.

Keeping his eyes on Rutledge, Cardenas said, "Hey, Payne. Did *mi tío* ever tell you about his first fuck?"

"Yeah. Some girl in the barn with hands stained from picking grapes."

"He tell you her name?"

"Maria something. He couldn't remember her last name."

"Sure he could. My mother, Sim! You fucked my mother when she was just a kid."

Goddamn Maria, Rutledge thought.

Quiet all those years, then she opens up like she's confessing to Jesus.

"She couldn't turn down the boss's son, could she?" Cardenas taunted him. "Then you turned her over to your father. You're poison, Sim. A degenerate. You and your father and your grandfather. A family of sick, twisted bastards."

"Fuck you, Javie."

"Yeah. Fuck me for selling out. Fuck me for being a coward." Cardenas exhaled a long, sad breath and his eyes went dark, embers turning to ash. He looked toward the sluice pipe.

"My mother told me something else in the hospital," the chief said. "She told me what happened the night of the flood."

"She wasn't here. She can't know."

"*Mami* harangued Zaga about it for years. It took a lot of tequila to loosen his tongue."

"Jesus on the cross! Your father drowned in the flood. I saw it happen." Rutledge thinking he would have no choice.

I'm gonna have to kill you, Javie.

"Why not just admit it, Sim? After all this time, say it once before you die. Say it, goddammit!"

Rutledge kept his right hand poised above the big revolver. He hacked up a viscous wad of bloody snot and spat into the mud. The memories came flowing back, like hot lava down a steep slope.

"Not tonight, Javie," he whispered. "Not fucking tonight."

EIGHTY-EIGHT

A December wind drives the cold rain in great sweeping arcs across the valley. Three hell-raising Pacific storms, back-to-back, have pummeled the state for the past week.

Wearing a poncho and fishing boots, Simeon Rutledge, in his forties, stands knee-deep in mud. The rain falls hard and fast, like buckshot piercing the skin. Atop the earthen levee, he gauges the depth of the stream and the strength of the soil holding it back. A single fissure and one hundred thousand acres will flood. Crops lost, equipment destroyed, loans called. Three generations of sweating and bleeding, of clawing and scratching. All undone by Mother Fucking Nature in one week of gales and floods.

"Faster! Drop the damn chassis!" Shouting at the crane operator, guiding a Plymouth Duster along the ridge of the levee. "No style points, Luis! Just drop the damn thing!"

Thank God for Hector Cardenas. It was his idea to use junked cars to shore up the levee. One chassis worth two hundred sandbags.

Rutledge watches Cardenas and Zaga run their crews, shoveling mud around the rusted-out cars, both men on their feet for days, taking breaks only to piss, snort cocaine, and sip whiskey. Good men, both of them. Brothers in arms.

Cardenas is half-buried in muck, his arms braced

*against the hood of a Mercury Marquis that has flipped
onto its side halfway down the levee. Two of his men,
grunting and cursing, muscle the car upright. One man
slips in the mud, screams something unintelligible, and
lets go. The Mercury slides down the slope into the
water, spins in a circle, catches the current, and sails
downstream.*

*Rutledge watches it, cursing. Fuck! The damn car
will crash into Pump Station Two, fouling the pipes,
maybe even cracking the concrete caissons.* "Christ,
Hector! Watch what your men are doing."

*Cardenas peers toward his boss. In the rain and fog
and diesel fumes, Rutledge can't make out the Mexican's
face. Cardenas trudges through the mud toward him.*

"What now, Hector? Got no time for your shit."

*Cardenas reaches under his slicker and pulls a pint
bottle of cheap blended whiskey from a back pocket. He
takes his time draining it, then hurls the empty bottle at
Rutledge. It sails into the darkness.*

"Goddammit, Hector! Get your brown ass back to
work."

*Cardenas charges him. Rubber boots glopping in the
mud, it seems to take forever for the short, stocky Mexican to close the distance. Rutledge crouches, sidesteps,
and clotheslines Cardenas, catching him under the chin,
knocking his feet out from under him. A quick kick to
the backside flattens Cardenas, facedown in the mud.*

*Spitting a wad of clotted earth, Cardenas gets to his
feet.* "You fuck my wife, bastard cocksucker."

"Got no time for this, Hector! Not tonight. Not fucking tonight."

*Cardenas comes at him again, taking Rutledge to the
ground. They roll down the slope to the water's edge.
Rutledge gains leverage, gets his hands around Cardenas's neck, and squeezes hard enough to crack walnuts.*

Cardenas tries to pry his hands off, but Rutledge is bigger, stronger, and meaner.

Zaga splashes toward them. "Hey, Sim. How 'bout letting up now?"

"Shut up, Z!"

Rutledge twists Cardenas's head to one side, forces the Mexican's mouth and nose underwater. Cardenas chokes, and inhales the slime. His limbs spasm. The other workers look away. Rutledge does not let go until Cardenas stops twitching.

"I told him, not tonight," Rutledge says to Zaga. "Not fucking tonight!" He turns to the rest of the crew. "Get the fuck back to work!"

EIGHTY-NINE

Payne watched each man's body language. Cardenas stood stiffly, locked into a two-handed grip. Rutledge appeared relaxed, his limbs loose, even with his right hand hovering above the holstered .45.

"When you get down to it, Javie, your old man was weak." Rutledge pinched a nostril and blew out a clot of blood, soiling his mustache. "If he'd come to me first thing and told me to stay the hell away from your mother, I'd have respected that. But he just let it go on. Then, with everything I own on the table, he melts down."

"So you killed him? A man who gave you everything. Even his wife."

"You're goddamn right I killed him! And now that I think about it, you're sure as hell Hector's son and not mine. A gelding's got more balls than either one of you."

Cardenas's jaw muscles danced and his eyes narrowed.

Now Payne was certain. The chief was going to shoot the old bastard. But there would be three witnesses.

Just what will Cardenas do to us?

Again, Payne glanced toward the ground. Still one knife, one baseball bat. And two men with guns.

NINETY

"At long last," Cardenas said, "the real Simeon Rutledge. Rapist and murderer."

"Ain't asking your forgiveness," Rutledge said.

"Ain't giving it."

One of these men was about to die, Marisol knew. The policeman's eyes burned with hatred. But Rutledge seemed defiant, his right hand motionless, his fingers spread, close enough to draw his gun in a split second.

The policeman held his own *pistola* in both hands. But were his arms trembling? Marisol had the horrible thought that the old man—even with a gun pointed at him—was the one in control. She doubted that the young policeman had ever killed a man. But with Rutledge, there were no doubts. He would neither hesitate before killing nor be remorseful after.

"Do what you got to do, Javie," Rutledge challenged.

Marisol wrapped her arm around Agustino. She had left Mexico, had come all this way, wanting only one thing, to save her son from harm. She looked toward Payne. Agustino had told her all about the man. He had turned down money—a fortune—to bring Agustino back to her. So decent and courageous. She had never known such a man. Now she sought some gesture from him, some instruction. *What can we do to save ourselves?*

Without taking his eyes off Rutledge, Cardenas spoke to Marisol in a formal policeman's voice. "Ms. Perez, do you recognize Mr. Simeon Rutledge?"

"Yes."

"Is he the man who raped you?"

"Yes, that's the pig."

Tino spit in Rutledge's direction. "I'll kill you, old man."

"No, you won't," his mother said.

"I will!" The boy squirmed out of her embrace. "He hurt you, *Mami.*"

"Quiet, now!" She grabbed his arm.

"Payne, how about you?" the chief asked. "Is Simeon Rutledge the man who horsewhipped you?"

"You know he is," Payne answered without hesitation.

"Unhook your gunbelt, Sim, and drop it to the ground," Cardenas ordered.

Rutledge coughed and a pink bubble of blood formed on his lips. "Why not try taking it away from me?"

"You resisting arrest, Sim?"

"That's what you want, isn't it? Shoot me down right

where your daddy sucked his lungs full of mud. Poetic fucking justice."

"Last warning."

"You been holding that sissy gun a long time, Javie. Your arms ain't getting tired, are they?"

Cardenas moved the barrel a bit lower. "Right in the belly, Sim. Gonna watch your guts spill out."

"I remember your first wild hog. What'd it take? Three shots? Four?"

"Drop the gunbelt, Sim."

"Thought you already gave your last warning."

Marisol tightened her grip on Tino. She did not want him to see this, but did not know how to prevent it.

Rutledge's fingers flexed and seemed to move even closer to his gun. "You'll get off one shot, for sure. But when you miss, I'll blow a hole right through your chest."

"Shoot him!" Tino yelled at Cardenas.

Cardenas's eyes flicked toward the boy.

Instantly, Rutledge drew the .45. Cardenas fired and missed.

Rutledge slapped back the hammer.

Tino tore away from his mother and scooped up the knife. "I'll kill you, *cabrón*!"

Marisol reached for him, but he dodged her.

Rutledge swung the gun toward the boy just as Marisol stepped between them. She felt a thunderbolt strike her chest, felt her feet fly from the ground, and by the time she landed flat on her back, felt nothing at all.

NINETY-ONE

The day baked with desert heat, the Santa Ana winds pushing the smog out to sea. The San Miguel Cementerio, leaves rustling on its spindly pear trees, was a patch of green in the parched foothills of the San Gabriel Mountains a few miles from Pasadena.

Next to the open grave, three people were squeezed so close together as to seem to have one body. His hair trimmed and brushed back, Tino stood rigidly, a stoic little man in a crisp new suit. He clutched a bouquet of white lilies so tightly that the stems might snap. On one side, Sharon gripped the boy's shoulder. On the other side, Payne, his left arm bandaged, wrapped his right arm around Tino's waist.

A somber altar boy from Saint Phillipe the Apostle swung a silver thurible over the grave, smoke wisping upward before disappearing into the breeze. The air smelled of incense, freshly cut grass, and moist earth. An elderly priest, a Mexican-American man in his sixties with a kindly face and a soft voice, prayed aloud. Payne tried to listen but heard only fragments.

"God's merciful love."

"Communion of saints."

"Consolation to the living."

Payne did not feel consoled. He felt guilty. Again.

He had moved as quickly as he could. When Tino grabbed the knife, Payne snatched the bat from the ground. Then everything happened at once. Rutledge wheeled the gun toward Tino just as Payne swung the bat, and Marisol moved into the line of fire. Rutledge pulled the trigger a split second before the bat crushed his temple with an explosion of bone and blood. The .45 slug caught Marisol just above the sternum. The half-dozen gunshots Cardenas fired into Rutledge's body were unnecessary, except for the chief's own needs.

Now Payne looked down at Tino, whose lips trembled, but whose eyes remained dry.

"It's okay to cry," Payne whispered.

The little *valiente* shook his head.

"Don't hold it in like I did."

All the while knowing that tears could never wash away the anger or the pain. Thinking that Tino needed someone who understood, someone whose heart had been seared by the same branding iron, Payne squeezed the boy even harder.

The priest sprinkled holy water and asked the angels to carry Marisol to paradise. Tino stepped forward and fluttered the lilies into the grave, where they landed like white birds, fanning out across the mahogany coffin.

With a gentle hand on the boy's shoulder, the priest said, "Agustino, would you recite the *Oraciónes por las almas*?"

"No," the boy replied.

The priest's eyes widened.

"In English. My mother would have wanted English."

The priest nodded, and Tino spoke in a clear voice, *"Oh God, who hast commanded us to honor our father and our mother . . ."*

"It's my fault," Payne whispered to Sharon.

She shook her head. "You climbed out of that hole and did something for someone else."

"In Thy mercy have pity on the soul of my mother, and forgive her her trespasses."

"I failed him."

"You saved him. And yourself."

"*Let me see her again in the joy of everlasting brightness.*"

Sharon leaned closer. "Forgive yourself, Jimmy. For everything."

NINETY-TWO

Just after sunset, in the kitchen of his Van Nuys bungalow, Jimmy Payne contemplated the blur of the last several days. Washing down painkillers with sour-mash whiskey, he tried to divine the complex equations of the universe.

A mother dead, a boy alive.

A soulless man, facedown in the dirt.

What is the meaning of all this, and . . .

Where do I go from here?

Payne had read the front page story in the *Los Angeles Times*. The body of multimillionaire grower Simeon Rutledge had been found alongside an irrigation culvert in Kings County. He had been beaten, shot multiple times, and his skull fractured by blunt trauma. The brutal murder shocked the close-knit community. Local police chief Javier Cardenas said the investigation was focused on the Patriot Patrol, an anti-immigration vigilante group that had placed a bounty on Rutledge's head. The chief broke down in tears at his press conference as he vowed to bring the killers to justice. No mention that Cardenas was the sole beneficiary of Rutledge's estate.

Another tumbler of Jack Daniel's made the story go down easier.

Earlier today, the deputy director of the local immigration office had called, asking for Detective Sharon Payne. He had reviewed her affidavit regarding a boy named Tino Perez from Caborca, Mexico. Rafael Obeso, a well-known Mexican drug smuggler, had threatened to cut the boy's heart out. So, too, a vicious coyote who called himself El Tigre vowed to kill the boy on sight. No need to fill out a Form I-590, the deputy director said. Tino Perez would be granted refugee status by administrative order.

An hour later, Quinn called to express his condolences about Marisol and ask how Payne's arm was healing. Such a decent gesture, it caught Payne off guard. Quinn apologized for missing the funeral, explaining he had to catch a flight to New York. It's okay, Payne said. Sharon had already told him about Quinn's new job, the talk show on Fox. Payne congratulated him, and meant it. *Really* meant it, because Sharon wasn't going east with Quinn.

Then, just minutes ago, as Payne poured another Jack Daniel's, Rigney knocked on the front door. He had a new look. A sleek Armani suit of a gray fabric that shimmered like a wet shark. Gold nugget cuff links poked out of the sleeves of his silk shirt like shiny wrist bones. His hair seemed to be a new color, not unlike the yellowish orange of the one-ball in billiards.

"You look like shit," Rigney said. Studying the bruises, cuts, and scrapes on Payne's face.

Payne figured it out, even before Rigney told him. With Enrique Zaga dead, Rutledge Ranch and Farms needed a new head of security. Rigney had already proved his worth to Cardenas. The payoff was a job at triple his detective's salary.

"Got some good news for you, too," Rigney said. "That five grand we thought you skimmed from the bribe money. It was in the evidence room all along."

"C'mon. I took the money. You know I took the money."

Rigney lowered his voice. "You took it. I put it back."

"Why?"

"A word of advice, Payne. Don't look a gift horse up the ass."

"Doesn't make sense. Why'd you do it?"

" 'Cause Cardenas told me to. It's his money now, and he's spreading it around. Just bought four new Hummers for the Imperial County Sheriff. He's so happy he's dropping all charges against you."

Payne was flummoxed. "Why's Cardenas looking out for me?"

"He admires you. The way you risked everything for the Mexican kid."

Payne shrugged. "I had nothing to risk."

"Not the way he sees it."

Once Rigney left, Payne returned to the pleasant task of becoming reacquainted with Mr. Jack Daniel's. Just as they were getting to be *buenos amigos,* Payne heard footsteps in the corridor. A moment later, Sharon appeared in the kitchen.

"Tino asleep?" he asked, pouring her a drink over ice.

"Just dozed off."

She joined Payne on a bar stool at the counter. "You call Harvard-Westlake today?" she asked. Referring to the ritzy private school in Studio City.

"Seventh grade awaits. As do massive tuition bills."

"We'll split the costs."

"Yeah. But I was hoping . . ."

"What?"

"That maybe you'd move in. For Tino's sake, I mean."

"Slow down, Jimmy. I was engaged until twenty-four hours ago."

"Okay. Okay." Payne sipped the whiskey, let it warm his throat. "No hurry."

Sharon swirled her glass, the ice cubes clinking against one another. "Just before he fell asleep, Tino asked me to tell you good night."

Payne smiled. "He does that every night. '*Buenos noches,* Himmy.' "

"Not what he said."

"In English, then."

"Nope."

"I don't get it."

"He said, 'Say good night to *mi papi.*' "

"Oh, man." Payne had not been prepared for the sheer weight of those words. The mixture of joy and obligation they conveyed. "I hope I'm up to this."

"You'll be a great father. I've seen your work, remember?" She gently placed her fingertips on his forehead, scraped raw in the fight with Rutledge.

"I know," Payne said. "I look like shit."

"The wounds will heal." She leaned close and kissed his bruised cheek. "You won't even have a scar."

ACKNOWLEDGMENTS

I received assistance and advice from many friends, including Randall Anderson, James O. Born, Angel Castillo, Jr., Carmen Finestra, Carol Fitzgerald, Edward Shohat, Maria Shohat, and Patricia Smiley.

Special thanks to Alan R. Asdoorian and Lora Asdoorian of Island Farms in Kingsburg, California. Give me enough time, and I'll learn to pick those peaches without tearing out the stems. Thanks, too, to the good people at www.OneDogAtATime.org.

As always, I am indebted to my agent, Albert Zuckerman, my editor, Kate Miciak, and my publicist, Sharon Propson.

If you enjoy the novels of Paul Levine,
get ready to welcome back an old friend.

Please read on for a preview of

L A S S I T E R

Paul Levine's newest novel, featuring tough-as-nails,
dry-as-a-martini attorney Jake Lassiter.

Coming in hardcover from
Bantam Books in Fall 2011

PROLOGUE

I presented my Florida Bar card at the security window and eased onto a metal bench that would likely throw my back out if the wait lasted more than a few minutes.

It did.

I stood, stretched, and studied the frescoes covering the cracks in the plaster walls. Island scenes of towering palms along a placid sea. Laughing mothers and hopscotching children in splashy Caribbean colors. The paintings made the place even more dreary, the inmates' lives even more hopeless.

Finally, a female guard brought my client from her cell. With her face scrubbed of makeup and her dark hair in a ponytail, Amy Larkin looked more like a college cheerleader than a woman charged with first-degree murder.

"I didn't kill him, Jake," she blurted out. "Honest, I didn't."

"Hold that thought."

I settled into a straight-back chair, and we faced each other across a table with cigarette scars from the days lawyers smoked in the visitors' room, just to cover the smells.

"Where were you last night?" I asked.

"Nowhere near Ziegler's."

An alibi? Attending mass with a hundred witnesses would do just fine.

"I was with a man," Amy said.

Not as good as church, but better than the scene of the crime.

"Who's the lucky guy?"

"Can't tell you."

"Why the hell not?"

"It's too dangerous."

I gave her my big, dumb guy look. It's not much of a stretch. "What's that mean?"

"If he testified, his life would be in danger."

"What about *your* life?"

She fingered the opening of her jailhouse smock, flimsy as crepe paper. "He wants to help, but I won't let him."

"That's my decision, not yours. Give me his name."

"I can't."

My lower back was throbbing again. Too many blind side hits had knocked a lumbar vertebra off-kilter.

"I'm thinking your alibi is bullshit."

"You have to trust me, Jake."

"The hell I do."

I get my hands dirty for my clients. I fight prosecutors in court and occasionally in the alley behind the Reasonable Doubt tavern. I stand up to judges who threaten me with contempt and to Bar Association bigwigs who would love to pull my ticket. But I won't tote my briefcase across the street for a client who deceives me.

"Lie to your priest or your lover. But if you lie to me, I can't help you."

"I'm not! I wasn't at Ziegler's. I didn't shoot anyone."

I looked for the averted gaze, the tightened lips, the nervous twitch. Nothing.

"I'm innocent, Jake. Dammit, isn't that enough?"

"Innocence is irrelevant! All that matters is evidence. So give me your alibi, or the jury will give you life."

She took a moment to think it over before saying, "I'm sorry, Jake. You'll have to win without an alibi."

I pushed my chair away from the table and got to my feet. "Enjoy your stay, Amy. It's gonna be a long one."

A BREW AND BURGER GUY

Eight days earlier . . .

When the hot brunette in the tight black skirt waltzed into the courtroom, I was cross-examining a stubborn cop who wouldn't agree to "good morning."

"Isn't it true my client passed the field sobriety test?" I asked him.

"No, sir. He couldn't walk a straight line."

"Just how wide is that line, Officer?"

The cop shrugged, bunching the muscles of his neck. "Never measured it."

"Why not?"

He smirked at me. "It's imaginary."

"Really?" Pretending to be surprised. "And how long's that imaginary line of yours? Six feet? A mile? What?"

"I guess you could say it's infinite."

The brunette shimmied into a front-row seat, tugged the hem of her skirt, then fixed me with a look as friendly as an indictment.

"So, my client stepped off an imaginary line, which has an infinite length and an indefinite width. An invisible line. Is that your testimony?"

"Not at all. I can see the line."

"You can see imaginary lines." I paused. "So you're delusional?"

The cop's eyes flicked toward the prosecutor. *Help.* But he didn't get any.

"Officer . . . ?" I prompted him.

"I'm trained and experienced. I've arrested hundreds of drunk drivers in the last—"

"I'm sure you have," I interrupted. "Now, what other imaginary objects do you see?"

"None I can think of."

"No unicorns?"

"No, sir," he said, through gritted teeth.

"Leprechauns, then?"

"No."

"Not even a *chupacabra* crawling out of the Everglades?"

"Objection!" Harold Flagler III, the young pup of a prosecutor, belatedly hopped to his feet.

"Grounds?" Judge Philbrick asked.

"Mr. Lassiter is badgering the witness."

"It's my *job* to badger the witness," I fired back.

"Judge Philbrick," Flagler whined.

"I get *paid* to badger the witness."

"Your Honor, please admonish—"

"C'mon, Flagler. Didn't they teach you trial tactics at Yale?"

"Mr. Lassiter!" Judge Philbrick wagged a bony finger at me. "Address your remarks to the court, not opposing counsel."

"I apologize, Your Honor." Sounding so sincere I nearly believed myself.

I swung around, as if pondering my next question. In truth, I wanted a good look at the woman in the gallery. Slender with military school posture, an angular jaw line, and a somber expression. Tucked into her pencil skirt was a silk blouse, red as blood, with those big, puffy sleeves, as if she might be hiding an ace of hearts, or maybe a derringer. Chin tilted up, she stared me down.

I gave her a quick, crinkly grin and looked for any

hint of interest. No inviting eyes or playful smile. *Nada.* Maybe if I wowed her in closing argument, she'd lighten up and slip me her phone number.

Occasionally, I get a groupie or two. Women attracted to a big lug with a craggy profile, a broken nose, and hair the color of saw grass after a drought. Two hundred and thirty-five pounds of ex-linebacker crammed into an off-the-rack, wrinkled brown suit. A brew and burger guy in a Chardonnay and pâté world. I wrapped up my cross-exam while sneaking peeks at our visitor. She pulled something out of her purse. I walked toward the rail and saw it was a photo, but I couldn't make out any details.

Flagler stood, fondled his Phi Beta Kappa key, and announced the great state of Florida rested its case.

My turn. No way would I let the presumably innocent Pepito Dominguez testify. He was a twenty-year-old smart ass with a diamond earring and a barbed-wire tattoo circling his neck. With no witnesses, I rested, too.

The bailiff tucked the jurors into their windowless room where they could surf for porn on their PDAs, and the judge turned to me. "Mr. Lassiter, Ah assume you got some legal mumbo jumbo for the record." His Honor came from a family of gentleman farmers in Homestead by way of Kentucky, and his voice rippled with bourbon and branch water.

"Motion to exclude the Breathalyzer test," I began, going through the motions of making my motions.

"Grounds?"

"No evidence the operator was properly trained, the equipment properly maintained, and the test properly administered."

Boilerplate stuff. No chance.

"Denied." *De-nahd.*

"Motion to exclude my client's statements to the arresting officer."

"Denied."

I checked the gallery. Mystery Woman was still there, eyes drilling me.

Who the hell are you?

I had multiple concussions on the football field. Still, I thought I remembered all my disgruntled ex-clients and infuriated ex-girlfriends. Maybe she was a Florida Bar investigator, building a case against me for yet another insult to the dignity of the court. Or maybe just one of those women with blood lust. You see them at boxing matches and bullfights and murder trials. Not usually a rinky-dink DUI.

At the next break I intended to plop down beside her. If she didn't serve me with a subpoena, I might ask her out for a drink.

"Motion for directed verdict. Do you want to hear argument, Judge?"

"About as much as Ah want to hit Dixie Highway during rush hour."

"For the record, I'd like to state my grounds."

"You can pour syrup on a turd, but that don't make it a pancake. Got any more motions you want denied, Mr. Lassiter?"

"I'm plumb out," I said, adopting a Southern accent of my own. Judge Philbrick peered at me over his spectacles, wondering if I was mocking him.

At the prosecution table, Flagler gave me his Ivy League snicker. If I wanted, I could dangle him out the window by his ankles. But then, I was picking up penalties for late hits while he was singing tenor with the Whiffenpoofs. Okay, so I'm not Yale Law Review, but I'm proud of my diploma. University of Miami. Night division. Top half of the bottom third of my class.

"You two want to talk a minute before Ah bring the jury in for closing?" Judge Philbrick picked up a cellphone and wheeled around in his chair to give us some privacy.

Flagler sidled up to me and said, "Perhaps it is a propitious time to discuss a deal."

"If my client wanted to plead guilty, he wouldn't need me."

"We could recess, have a latte downstairs, and work it out."

"I don't drink latte, with or without a hint of nutmeg."

"If I win, I'm asking for jail time."

"Ooh, scary."

Shaking his head, Flagler returned to the prosecution table and picked up his neatly printed note cards. The jurors filed back in, and Judge Philbrick ordered them to listen carefully to closing argument, but to rely on their own memories, not those of the lying shysters. Actually, he said "learned counsel," but everybody knew what he meant.

I glanced toward the gallery. Yep, the woman was still there in the front row. I gave her a neighborly nod. She took it and gave nothing back.

Flagler bowed obsequiously to the judge and thanked the jury for leaving their fascinating jobs and coming to the courthouse in the service of justice.

Or a reasonable facsimile thereof.

After twenty minutes, he sat down and I stood up. "How did my client blow a point-six when stopped by the police officer but only a point-zero-nine at the station?"

Judging from their blank looks, math was not the jury's favorite subject.

"I'll tell you how," I continued. "There's *no* way! At point-six, my client's breath could have ignited charcoal in a hibachi."

Fearing he'd belch beer into the cop's face, my too-damn-clever client had squirted enough Listerine into his mouth to disinfect a knife wound. The mouthwash vaulted the kid's *mouth* alcohol off the charts, while the *blood* alcohol test accurately pinned the number at a notch above the lawful limit.

Often times, complete dickwads are undeservedly lucky, while the good get crapped on by life's endless shit storm. So it was with Pepito Dominguez, who inadvertently, but fortuitously, screwed up the alcohol tests.

"If the tests don't fit, you must acquit!" I boomed.

Rest in peace, Johnnie Cochran.

After some more double-talk and sleight of hand, I thanked the good citizens for not falling asleep and sat down. The judge recited his instructions, and the bailiff returned the jurors to their little dungeon.

I spun through the swinging gate and plopped down next to Mystery Woman. Up close, she had full lips and a flawless complexion, without the hint of foundation, blush, or war paint. Her eyes were green with a touch of a golden sunset, her dark hair pulled straight back and held by a squiggly elastic band. Late twenties or early thirties.

"Hey there." I gave her a lopsided grin that has been known to charm a number of barmaids.

"Hello, Mr. Lassiter." No smile. No warmth. No nothing.

"Have we met before?"

"My name is Amy Larkin."

She waited a moment, as if the name might provoke a reaction. It didn't.

"So what brings you to the courthouse, Amy Larkin?"

"You do, Mr. Lassiter. I need to ask you some questions."

Something in the way she said "questions" convinced me we weren't going to be chatting over Happy Hour.

"Fire away," I said.

She handed me the photo she had been holding. A small cocktail table in front of a stage. Pole dancer in the background. Front and center, two young woman in string bikinis were draped over a thick-necked guy with shaggy hair over his ears and a bushy mustache the color of beach sand. The Sundance Kid with a shit-eating grin. Young. Cocky. Stupid.

I should know. The guy was me.

Embarrassing to look at now. I was a glassy-eyed drunk in a Dolphins jersey. Number 58. Not even traveling incognito. A red scab ran horizontally across the bridge of my nose. If you make enough helmet-first tackles, your face mask will take divots out of your flesh.

"Long time ago. Birthday party my teammates threw for me," I said. "Where'd you get the picture?"

She ignored my question and shot back her own. "Do you know the girls?"

One of them, a big-boned blonde, had her arms locked around my neck, her enhanced breasts squashed against my chest. The other one was younger. Slender. Auburn hair. Girl-next-door looks. She was kissing my cheek.

"The one with coconut boobs was a stripper. Sonia something-or-other. She hung around with one of my teammates. I don't know the younger one's name."

"Krista."

I flipped the photo over. On the back, someone had scrawled "The Whore of Babylon."

"Okay. The girl's name is Krista. We're in a picture together. So what?"

She gave me a look hard enough to leave bruises. "She was my sister."

"Was?"

"She's gone."

"Gone meaning dead?"

"Disappeared and presumed dead."

Except for the two of us, the courtroom was empty now and silent as a mausoleum.

"I'm sorry. I'm very sorry to hear that." She studied me through hard, cold eyes. "But what's all this have to do with me?"

"I think you know, Mr. Lassiter."

"No, I don't. So why not stop dancing around and just tell me?"

"You seem agitated, Mr. Lassiter. Why is that?"

"Because you're playing me and you're not very good at it. Where'd you learn your interrogation technique, *Law & Order*?"

"Why would I need to interrogate you? Have you committed a crime?"

I stood up. "Cut the crap. If you're not going to tell me what's going on—"

"It's quite simple, Mr. Lassiter." Her eyes locked on mine, daring me to leave. "You're the last person who saw Krista alive."